Devil's ESCAPE

THE DEVIL'S DEMONS BOOK ONE

rachel callahan

Devil's Escape: The Devil's Demons Book One by Rachel Callahan

Published by Rachel Callahan https://sites.google.com/view/rachelcallahanauthor

Cover by DoElle Designs

Editing by Cassie at Inked Imagination Author Services

Editing by Dee's Notes Editing & Proofreading Services

ISBN: 978-1-7776969-9-3 (ebook)

ISBN: 978-1-7782689-5-3 (paperback)

Introduction

Devil's escape is a dark contemporary why choose romance about reclaiming oneself, toppling an unjust power structure, finding the people who love us for who we are, and shifting into a villain era. There will be a lot of character development for our heroine as she escapes an abusive relationship and finds her path.

*Domestic abuse (physical and emotional) from partner she is trying to leave.

*Flashback of abuse by parents.

*Mention of drug and alcohol use.

*Drugging and abduction.

*Violence.

Contents

CHAPTER ONE

GIANA

NOW

I SQUEEZED MY EYES shut, willing my heartbeat to calm its frantic pace as light flashed against my closed eyelids, the sunlight streaming past the towering buildings. My breaths came in short, shallow pants as my fingernails dug into my knee, begging my body to cooperate and not let me break down in the back of a cab.

The driver slammed on his brakes, screaming at the back of another car in the middle of bumper-to-bumper traffic. My body jerked against the seatbelt at the abrupt motion. Cars were cutting each other off left, right, and center, their horns blaring as people desperately attempted to make their way out of the city for the weekend. Most of them were probably heading out to The Hamptons, the playground of the wealthy New

Yorker, where they'd spend the next couple of days drunk on rosé before speeding back to the office on Monday morning.

I knew that because that was my life—well, *was* my life ... until now. The frivolity and mindless partying were a way to numb myself from reality, to make myself believe I could live this life. The rose-colored wine acted like glasses of the same shade, calming me before my inevitable slaughter. Because that was how it felt every day I was stuck in that life, another piece of my soul was chipped away, plummeting me further into the numbness. If I didn't leave now, there would be nothing left. I'd be an empty shell of a person, retreating so far into myself there'd be no turning back.

New York was supposed to be my escape, my shot at another life, at leaving behind my past that still clung to me. But instead, it turned into my prison. The walls of the penthouse condo felt restrictive like bars on a cell, except my jailer was glued to my side all hours of the day. The only reprieve I had was a few hours at work. Other than that, he followed me around like a dark shadow, haunting my every waking moment while also lurking in my dreams, which were more like my nightmares. The same one played on repeat, leaving me in a cold sweat every night. I fought against the weighted press of sleep only to wake up to the same monster nestled into my side.

"We may be a few minutes late, Miss," the cab driver said, breaking through my innermost thoughts and shattering the cold press of fear that had settled over my skin, pebbling it into goosebumps despite the sweltering heat pressing in on me. The summer sun beat down on me through the windows of the car, drawing my gaze outside.

"That's fine, as long as we get there." The airport felt like a safety net because it was large enough to get lost in. If I didn't make this flight, I would catch the next, just as long as I got there unscathed. The security and cameras alone would ensure my safety. But if he caught me—I refused to think of the consequences of that, who he would hurt or what else he could take from me, telling myself everything would be fine.

"If you say so," he scoffed, shaking his head while he pressed on the horn again, a string of curses leaving his lips aimed at the black sedan that cut us off. My gaze swiveled around the cab, surveying the cars, and making sure none of them were familiar. When none of them were, I reminded myself to relax and take a deep breath. The last thing I needed was for the driver to get suspicious and call the cops or something. No, that would be bad, *really* bad.

Pulling my purse onto my lap, I dug into its depths, searching for my phone in the mess of papers. I didn't let my mind linger too long on those papers. They were my ticket to a new life, to freedom. My fingers grasped the plastic case and I pulled it out, letting myself celebrate the small win as I opened my contacts and scrolled the listings.

My hand shook as I brought the phone to my ear and the ring sounded through the speaker. My foot bounced against the cab floor, anxiety rushing through me as I waited for her to answer.

"Gi, is everything alright? You're supposed to be at the airport right now," my best friend, Sophia, said, not bothering to waste time on pleasantries. I sighed a breath of relief, taking comfort in having someone with me right now, even if it was only over the phone. It would've been too suspicious for her to come with me. Too easy to track me, since she would have to come back. *Her life is here in New York,* I reminded myself, fighting back the urge to beg her to leave with me. I knew she would. If I told her the full terrible story of the past few years, she would leave to keep me safe.

I loved her to pieces, but I couldn't do that to her. I couldn't even let her know where I was going because he could get that from her; he could manipulate anyone into telling him anything he wanted to know. He didn't even need to lift a finger, that's what his men were for. All he needed to do was press a single button on a phone and he would have you in the palm of his hand.

"I'm alright, Soph, just traffic," I whispered, hitching my voice low so the driver couldn't hear through the thin pane of glass that separated us. The horn blared a moment later punctuating my words.

"Fuck, Gi, that's not good. I knew you should have left earlier," Soph groaned, her pacing audible, even through the phone.

"I know, but if I had, it would've raised too many red flags, you know that," I explained, leaning back in the seat, attempting to ease the tension in my shoulders as we continued our steady pace through the crowded, rush-hour streets. The plan was to book a flight for around the same time that I normally flew out on the jet to The Hamptons, so by the time he noticed that I wasn't there, I would already be safely through the airport and on another flight out of the country.

"I know you're right. I just worry." She sighed, flopping down on her leather couch if my ears heard correctly. "Are you sure you can't tell me where you're going?"

"You know I can't, Soph. Not until it's safe." I winced at the lie as soon as it left my lips, knowing it would never be safe, not for me at least. Moving here, I'd hoped his grip would loosen in the midst of this large city, that he would find someone else. But no, his claws only dug deeper into my flesh, his fear ratcheting up in the expanse of the concrete jungle, worried I might slip off without him ... which had been my plan all along. It had been six years since we came to the city, since I began planning my escape. But this was my last straw.

I'd always walked on eggshells to avoid him following through on his threats and someone innocent suffering because of his wrath. But when he'd raised his hand to strike me, I knew I had to go, because if he was willing to go that far, I knew there'd be a next time, and he wouldn't hesitate again. I couldn't let that happen, and I couldn't risk him killing the next guy who unknowingly got too close... I had to do this now. I was barely treading water as it was. Another moment longer and I'd sink into the dark depths of the wide-open sea, swallowed whole by this life, by him.

"You promise to let me know as soon as I can see you?" Her question came out more like a plea, as though she could sense the lie behind my words but didn't want to admit it for my sake. Because after last week—No, I couldn't let my mind wander there, otherwise, tears would flood my eyes and desperate sobs would rack my chest. Even now, my breaths came in quick, shallow pants after I'd finally calmed them, the beginning signs of hyperventilation setting in.

"I promise," I said, the lie tasting foul on my tongue as bile rose in my throat. But I swallowed it, needing to pull on the mask one last time to force those emotions down that threatened to bubble up. One last lie and then I'd be *free*.

The word sounded foreign even in the recesses of my mind. It was something I'd dreamed of for years, my entire life really, but never truly let myself believe would happen. I'd pretended and clung to the idea without having to truly commit, to have to risk losing that tiny sliver of hope that shimmered in the distance any time I closed my eyes.

"You better," she warned, sighing a breath of exasperation. I could almost see her lying back on her couch, her arm poised over her eyes, manifesting her strength to deal with the situation like she'd done so many times before. "I could always ask my dad—"

"No," I cut her off before she could finish her sentence. Sophia's estranged father was the senator of New York, which was one of the only reasons my *fiancé* hadn't threatened her as leverage against me. But I couldn't let her put herself or her family at risk, because while it made him wary, I was sure that he wouldn't hesitate to kill either of them if they interfered.

"We're pulling up," the cab driver shouted, slamming open the plastic divider and grumbling something under his breath about cell phones. I huffed out a breath of relief, some of the tension in my chest easing at the excuse to end the conversation. I couldn't put her in any more danger than she already was.

"I have to go, Soph. Lie low for the next few weeks," I pleaded, cupping the phone close to my lips so the driver couldn't hear.

"Don't worry about me. You run through that airport and get on that plane safely." Her pacing picked up again, betraying her nerves. I wished I could do the same right now. My knee bounced, with my foot tapping an anxious rhythm on the cab floor once more. *Soon*, I told myself as the car pulled up at the departures terminal.

"I will. Love you, girl," I said one last time, pulling my bag into my lap. Another thing that had annoyed the driver as he'd insisted I put them in the trunk. No way was I wasting time to pull my bag from the trunk while he groaned about it weighing a ton just to get a bigger tip. I was already going to give him a hefty sum in the hopes that it would buy his silence long enough for me to board my flight.

"Love you too, babe. Have a safe flight," she said with a hitch in her voice. My throat bobbed as I disconnected the call, in an attempt to keep the tears that pricked at my eyes from falling. I stuffed the phone in my bag, grateful for the distraction as the driver pulled to a stop.

"Here, thanks a lot," I blurted, shoving a wad of cash at him. I swung the bag over my shoulder as I rushed out the door.

"Oh, shit, thanks, Miss. Hope you catch your flight," he called after me, the shuffling of bills audible along with his words as I closed the door behind me. I dashed to the entrance, weaving through the droves of passengers taking their time as they meandered through the hall. Their eyes were glued to the screen, searching for their gate as they mindlessly trod along, not bothering to look where they were going.

I already knew where I was going, having mapped out this route countless times in preparation for this moment. Thankfully my flight didn't leave for another two hours, giving me plenty of time to make it to my gate. I wouldn't feel secure until

I made it past security. Only a few passengers were ahead of me as they tossed their suitcases onto the conveyor belt. I weaved my way through the queue, and by the time I made it to the front, the last few passengers got their boarding passes and shuffled off to the security check.

"Next," the lady drawled in a bored tone, her manicured red nails tapping impatiently on the desk. "Olivia Rothchild," she murmured, reading out the fake name I'd made up for the forged passport. Lifting it, she checked the picture against my face and undoubtedly the security features. My stomach churned with anxiety, my face paling, but I pushed it down, willing my face not to let any of that show. I couldn't get this far just to mess up at the counter.

To my relief, she continued on, typing away at her computer as she checked me in. "What's your destination?" she asked, her tone betraying her fatigue as it most likely was nearing the end of her shift. With only two hours before departure, most of the passengers would have already made it through to the gate.

"Vancouver, British Columbia," I answered, and she nodded, ensuring I was about to get on the right flight before she printed off the boarding pass.

"Anything to check?" I shook my head in response. His family owned a house in The Hamptons and we kept some summer clothes and toiletries there. So the only bag I took with me was a carry-on that wouldn't need to be checked. I didn't have time to collect luggage, let alone pack it in the first place. That would have raised his suspicions before I even left.

Vancouver was only the first stop for me, I had to keep moving and a direct flight would be too easy to catch me. I'd considered flying to Toronto, but it was too close. He could have men there in a matter of hours if he found out too soon. No, the other side of Canada would be my first stop.

"Go to security gate C," she instructed, shoving my passport back at me, the boarding pass tucked inside. My lips parted, about to say thank you, but she cut me off with a curt, "Next."

I fumbled around for my phone and turned it off as I moved to the side, not wanting to endure the wrath of the impatient airport lady. I'd need to dispose of it when I landed. With the number of cameras here at the airport, it would look suspicious if I threw it in the trash. Perhaps I could leave it under my seat and pretend I'd dropped it if anyone decided to be a good Samaritan today. But first, I needed to get through security.

I could get whatever I needed when I landed or when I arrived in the next city. I couldn't risk being caught, because if he found me, I had nothing else for him to take, and no one else's safety to threaten or hold over my head. Which was why Sophia had to stay here and not give him any reason to be reckless and go after her. I had no doubt in my mind he'd make me suffer this time, maybe even kill me if I was lucky. At least then I would escape his clutches for good.

I strode over to the security gate the clerk directed me toward, my steps confident and sure despite the emotions raging inside me. Nausea bubbled up in my stomach and I urged it away, needing to do this first, then I could hurl my guts out once I was past this point. He was driving up to The Hamptons later with a few business associates and stopping for dinner on the way. That made today the perfect day for this as normally he would be here with me, holding my hand each step of the way.

The picture-perfect supportive partner, when in reality it was his own insecurities that made him clench my hand so hard the bones rubbed together.

"Passport and boarding pass," the airport security demanded, jolting me from my thoughts. I gave him a polite smile, handing over my documents. My anxiety eased a fraction at how close I was. He couldn't do anything, not here, not with all the guards, police, and cameras. They would be on him as quickly as I could scream.

My lips trembled as I attempted to hold my smile while the guard scanned the boarding pass. But it must've looked more like a grimace judging by the look he gave me. My chest tightened as cold tendrils of fear skittered up my spine, my anxiety spiking until he handed the paperwork back and my bag went through the scanner. A guard on the other side of the metal detectors waved me through. Following her direction, I moved through the barrier, my fingernails digging into the soft flesh of my palms as I attempted to keep myself calm. This was it; my freedom was mere steps away. I passed through and a wave of relief washed over me when she nodded, gesturing to my baggage already waiting for me on the other side of the scanner.

I made it, I actually made it. A sob racked my chest as I collected my carry-on, and I forced myself to take a deep breath to keep the tears at bay. This might've been the first step, but it was the most important. He couldn't do anything to me, not here. Now I just needed to focus on staying ahead of him. As soon as I landed in Vancouver, I'd be getting on a cruise to Alaska. I couldn't take another plane right away. That would be the obvious choice and way too easy to track.

I turned to exit the security area, the tension in my chest easing with each footstep toward the bustling concourse, filled with shops and restaurants. Excited travelers spoke animatedly about their upcoming trips as they picked through the duty-free shop, the normalcy helping to ease away the anxiety. Just a few more steps until I could join them, immerse myself in the real world, and finally breathe again. The weight of this world, of him, eased inch by inch.

"Miss?" That one word cut through me like a knife, the male voice echoing in my ear like the final toll of a bell signaling my execution. The warm comforting relief that had rushed over me just seconds before was replaced with the cold press of fear stiffening my muscles. I turned to see who spoke, and a uniformed man closed in beside me. Fuckity fuck, fuck. Had I forgotten something maybe?

"Yes, sir, how can I help you?" I asked in the sweetest, most innocent voice I could muster. Was there an issue with the passport? No, I was assured this was authentic, that the paper trail was already in place. Everything should look legit. Besides, they would've said something before, they wouldn't have risked me getting past security, right?

"I need you to come with me," he instructed, his hands flexing at his side. The movement drew my gaze lower, and I caught sight of exactly what he was readying to grab … the Glock holstered at his hip. What the hell? This couldn't be possible, this had to be a nightmare. I was so close I could taste the clean, ocean air already. I glanced back at the shop, the travelers milling about, completely oblivious to the woman just feet from them, the woman whose freedom was about to be snatched away from her, just when it was finally within arm's reach.

Another armed guard stepped before me, his wide chest blocking off my view of the airport beyond. The flicker of hope I'd desperately clung to for so long had begun to burn anew. But this towering man blocked out even the overhead halogen lights, casting a dark shadow on me and extinguishing any chance I had at escaping.

"Of course," I murmured, my head drooping slightly as they moved behind me and guided me to the metal door with the word Security emblazoned across the front. My hands shook as panic set in, the tremors running all the way to my feet. My small heels clicked against the hard floors more than necessary as I fought to control my stride. If I was about to have my last hope at a normal life taken away from me, I would walk toward my inevitable doom with dignity, with my head held high. I wouldn't let him take that from me, not like he'd taken everything else.

The guards swiped a card to allow us to pass, the door hinges squeaking as it swung inward. They began to close the door behind us as they ushered me into the narrow hallway with numbered doors lining each side. I glanced back just as the door shut, darkness pressing in on me, the muted lights of the hall barely able to illuminate the way. I blinked against the sudden change as they pushed me along, no longer worrying about optics now that I was behind this closed door with no one about to speak out or record their manhandling. An involuntary whimper escaped my lips as they roughly grabbed my arms, panic sending my heartbeat into a rapid thumping. My mouth dried as I felt my pulse in my tongue, and I sucked in a dry breath, the inhale scratching against my throat.

One of the guards let out a chuckle, apparently taking pleasure in my panic attack. *Who knows if these men even work for the airport?* I really wouldn't be surprised if they worked for *him*, even if I didn't recognize them.

The hallway seemed to go on forever, my mind fogging over as my stomach churned, attempting to block out my reality, becoming numb to what was about to happen. It took more effort than normal, especially since I'd just tasted freedom. It was still so close, yet so far now, like a distant memory.

"Get in," the first guard ordered, pushing me to a door. I numbly realized we'd stopped, unsure how long we'd been standing there before I noticed. I anticipated what the guards were about to do seconds before he pushed me once more, barely getting my hands up in time to stop myself from colliding with the steel door. Their chuckles echoed in the silent hallway, and I darted a wary glance, the lingering shreds of hope decimated by the fact that no one else stood in the hall, no one to stop them, no one to save me.

But I should have been used to that. This world is so singularly focused, not many would lift a finger to help someone else. They'd rather record it to put online, profiting off the views it generated as it went viral. Countless people had seen me drowning, had seen the life flickering out from my eyes, dimming more and more each year and they never bothered to help. Even people that called me their friend feigned ignorance to my suffering.

"Useless," the guard grumbled, reaching for the door handle and pushing it open, stealing those precious seconds from me. I swore to myself I wouldn't forget these two as I stumbled forward, just catching myself before I was splayed on the hard linoleum floor. I'd repay their cruelty tenfold if I ever met them again.

The click of the door startled me from the dark thoughts swirling through my mind, bringing me back to reality. The bright lights shone overhead, such a cruel joke that this room where my world was about to crash and burn would be this bright. It was like the fates were laughing at my broken, bruised body as they landed blow after blow, stomping me into the earth for daring to dream. No, my world was one of nightmares.

I squeezed my eyes shut, opening and closing them as I tried to fight off the wave of dizziness that settled over me when my eyes locked on a pair of freshly polished, dark-brown Italian loafers. Adrenaline rushed through my veins at that sight, giving me the strength to fight off the near faint my body almost fell into, and I stumbled back.

The cool press of the metal door seeped into my bones as my back collided with it, wishing I could dematerialize and sink through it back to the hallway. Give me the asshole guards over this man any day.

"I bet you didn't expect to see me here, did you?" He chuckled darkly, sending a shiver of fear up my spine. That laugh promised pain. "You really thought you could escape me?"

He closed in on me, caging me against the door, his crisp, Italian, custom-tailored suit brushing up against me. I flattened myself against the hard surface, but it was no use, he took up the few inches afforded to him, his presence suffocating me. I focused on his white shirt and the red tie he always paired it with, refusing to meet his eyes. My mind hoped that if I didn't look at him then he might not be real. I could still trick myself into thinking that I had some chance at escape.

He slipped a finger beneath my chin, much to my chagrin, tilting my face up to meet his. My eyes followed reluctantly, unable to put this off any longer. His jaw ticked in anger as he held himself back, the leash barely containing the monster inside, the one I'd seen let loose too many times to count. Thankfully not on me, not yet, but I knew it was only a matter of time. The real possibility of it being this time felt more like reality with every heartbeat. He could barely control his anger, and he had been close, far too close to taking it out on me last week. Which was one of the main reasons that pushed me to take this step today.

His mahogany-brown eyes sparkled with triumph as I met them, and I could almost see the beast caged just beneath them, rattling at its cage, begging to be set free. His black hair was perfectly styled, like always, not a strand out of place. He was attractive, that was for sure, that was what drew me to him in the first place. But his outside didn't reflect the person he was on the inside. He was cold, controlling, and emotionally abusive to list a few of his faults.

"Tommaso, please," I begged, knowing it wouldn't do any good, but I still had to try.

"Please what, mi amore?" he whispered, the caress of his warm breath teasing my skin. Goosebumps rose along my skin as I suppressed the shudder that begged to run over my body. A mixture of desire and revulsion swirled in my gut, my response sickening me even more. I hated that my body still responded to him despite everything he'd done, everything he would do to me.

"Please, let me go," I pleaded, my voice shaking, betraying the fear coursing through my body. I internally scolded myself for how weak I sounded, for what he made me become. I wasn't this woman, the one to beg for her freedom, but this was my only shot, no matter how slim it may be.

"You know that will never happen. You're mine, now and forever. I'll never let you go," he vowed, anger darkening his confession, his lips mere inches from mine. I inhaled sharply, my hatred growing for him even more as his lips lowered on mine. I wished I could push him away, I wished I could bolt from this room and hop on that plane like I'd hoped.

Not a second later, his hand fisted in my hair, pulling it as he devoured me, and my lips parted under the force. Pain radiated from my scalp as he continued to crush his lips to mine, and I pulled in desperate, ragged breaths through my nose, screaming into his mouth from the ache.

He pulled back, yanking on my head to force me to look up at him. I winced and an unbidden gasp of agony escaped before I could reel it in. His eyes lit up at the noise, loving the power he had over me, the control. I should've known I wouldn't be able to get away, not like this. I should've driven to another state, another city, and left from there, because of course he would have people at the airport here in New York. I'd let my desperation cloud my judgment, and now I might never get the chance to try again.

"This was your last straw, Giana. I've given you so much. I let you put off the wedding to focus on school, on your career, but enough is enough." His voice was distraught and full of pain. A spark of outrage flickered inside me, at the sheer audacity. But this was his game. He made it sound like he was the victim, like I'd gone into this relationship willingly.

He clutched me to his chest, and I stood there limply, letting him embrace me as his hand finally released my hair, sliding down to wrap around my shoulders. I choked back the sob of relief that shook my chest, not wanting to give him the satisfaction. But he must've felt it against him since his grip on me tightened, apparently mistaking it as a reaction to his touch.

"You've forced my hand, mi amore. No more threats to keep you in line. I have no choice." He cradled my head against his chest, as though he was attempting to comfort me when *he* was the monster I needed to be protected from. *He* was the one causing me this pain. "We're going home, for good."

I sucked in a startled breath, not having expected those words. Home—I'm not sure such a place could ever exist for me. And that place certainly would never be my home.

This was worse, so much worse than I could've imagined. Our hometown held too many memories, too much heartache that I'd tried to repress, that I'd tried to bury beneath all the trauma. Tommaso and his family owned the small town in Connecticut that we came from. If I thought he was powerful here in the huge city, he would be unstoppable there. They paid off everyone and took what they wanted. And with his father back in the picture, my future grew bleaker and bleaker with each passing second.

A shiver ran over me and he soothed a hand over my back, rubbing the exposed skin there, mistakenly interpreting the tremor as relief rather than the fear that slithered up my spine. But I only had myself to blame, and I'd be reminded of that time and time again if we went back. I chose this to save them. They'd never know though, they'd always view me as a monster, on the same level as my husband-to-be it seemed. If I thought there was no one to save me here in New York, there wouldn't be a single soul that would lift a finger to help me there.

And the few that would've, I was sure they'd rather see me six-feet-under than ever come to my aid again.

CHAPTER TWO

GIANA

NOW

*W*ELL, AT LEAST SOMETHING *went according to plan today. No one was hurt and I'm on a plane, just not to Vancouver.* I stared out the window longingly, wishing today had gone how it was supposed to. I should have been sitting in coach on a commercial flight to Vancouver. Instead, I was sitting on a private jet, heading to the worst place imaginable. Rather than strangers next to me and the back of a headrest obstructing my view, I had guards and a monster ahead of me.

So I kept my gaze trained out the window, retreating into my mind. In my imagination, I had made it. I was on a flight to the West Coast, anxiety and excitement mixing in my gut at the next step. I had made it to a drugstore to dye my dirty-blonde hair to black before hopping on the cruise ship to Alaska, my fake passport being the key to a new life.

Clouds obscured my view, and the houses, offices, and people below us faded into nothing, bringing me back to my reality. There was no one that could save me now, no one that would save me, not after everything I'd done. I thought I was helping them, and I knew what the cost was when I did it, but somehow it had always been too hard to swallow. They stuck in the back of my mind, before I slept, before my dreams turned to nightmares. I imagined what could have been, if I'd been honest, if I hadn't been too afraid.

My chest tightened with dread, and my hand itched to rub there, to soothe the ache, but I wouldn't give him the satisfaction. He preyed on signs of weakness, soaking it in as though he needed it to live. I refused to give him any more power.

The shutter over the window slapped closed, jolting me from my thoughts. I blinked to adjust my vision, only now realizing how blurred it had gotten as I retreated into myself, the only safe place I knew ... at least until I closed my eyes. I was left staring at the back of Tommaso's hand as he waited for me to draw my gaze back to him. I couldn't help but stare a moment longer, lingering in the dark thoughts that crossed my mind. The action was a metaphor for what he did to me, trapped me away, cut off the light, along with the hope of a life beyond his world.

"Look at me," he growled, the tone menacing but borderline desperate. My lips twitched, reveling in my small act of defiance. But I knew my seconds were numbered. I either had to give him my attention or he'd make me, and I couldn't allow him that win.

I turned to him slowly, needing the small act of resistance to keep myself present. His smooth jaw ticked with anger but he swallowed it back, not wanting to make a scene in front of his guards. If we were alone though ...

"Yes?" I asked, in a singsong voice. I knew I was pushing my luck, but I couldn't help it. Anger mixed with fear burned in my veins, as though I was starting to wake up for the first time in years.

"I think you owe me an apology, mi amore," he sneered, the term of endearment a mocking joke on his tongue. He didn't love me, despite telling me often enough and calling me his love. He had no more room in his heart to fit anyone else, not with how much he loved himself. "Do you have any idea how worried I was about you?"

I choked down my laugh, knowing that would be pushing it too far. He would tolerate my small acts of rebellion, but to outwardly go against him to his face? No, he wouldn't let that stand.

"Worried? It seems you knew exactly where I was, darling," I said, mocking a concerned tone. "How did you know?" I asked, pitching my voice low enough for only him to hear.

My lips pursed at the look of satisfaction that crossed his face as he smirked triumphantly. I didn't want to indulge him, but I had to know where I went wrong. How to fix it, if and when I tried again.

"Give us some room," he instructed his guards, and the three men, including the two that had manhandled me in the airport, moved to the back of the plane, out of earshot. They chuckled to themselves, giving me a dark look as they passed, reveling in the scolding they knew I was about to receive. I vowed silently in that moment, before I got free, I would take them down, some way, somehow ...

I swallowed thickly at the distance. Even though I knew they couldn't help me, having them close gave me the illusion of safety. His guards would never lift a finger against him, many had watched time and time again without saying a word as Tommaso berated me. Not that I blamed them. If they'd stepped in to combat the verbal abuse, it would've cost them their lives. His guards usually gave me sympathetic looks, not that I wanted their pity, but at least it showed that they had a shred of humanity left in their dark souls.

"So you want to know how I found you?" Tommaso asked, standing from his seat to hover over me. The soft fabric of his suit swished as he moved past me, his hand trailing over my exposed knee in a teasing caress. I shuddered in a mix of lust and revulsion, hating that he could still make me feel both after everything he'd done.

My stomach churned, and I swallowed the bile rising in my throat. Pushing down the hem of my floral skirt, I turned my glare on him. He smirked at the look, taking pleasure in the fact that he knew how to get under my skin. His gaze roved over the flush spreading along my chest, and I worked to draw in a long, steady breath.

"It's honestly hilarious that you thought I wouldn't find you, mi amore." He chuckled, shaking his head as he leaned against my seat. I knew why he stood exactly when he did it. He needed that power, that reassurance he was in control, that he had won. "You think I don't have a hand in every shady business in the city? I knew the moment you went to get your fake papers. I put an alert out at that very moment to be notified if any plane, train, or boat tickets were placed under that name."

That key I thought had been my salvation, was actually my downfall it seemed. I thought I'd been so careful. I got the information from someone who wasn't connected to Tommaso or his family. I stayed clear of his usual suppliers. But his reach was further than I could have ever imagined. I should have known, should have taken more care to get the passport out of the city. But where would I have gone? I was barely able to escape him for an afternoon to go to the seedy underbelly of the black market without him traipsing behind me. I'd thought getting out of the country was the first step, but I would need to be more cautious next time, get the documents out of his clutches first before fleeing the country.

"I knew the moment you booked that plane ticket, along with the cruise to Alaska." He smirked smugly, lowering his face closer to mine. Only inches separated us now. I could smell the crisp citrus and deep mahogany of his aftershave. I knew the smell would haunt me for years to come, even if I eventually escaped him. "It was so fun watching you squirm—listening to the lies spilling from those pretty lips."

His mouth stilled so close to mine—too close. I knew leaning back would do no good. He'd only close the distance between us again, just as he'd done when he pinned me against the door in the interview room. His breath feathered across my skin, and the smell of whiskey curled in my nostrils.

"You better think about how you'll use those pretty lips to make it up to me," he whispered, the warm scent turning sour as his words sank in. An unbidden, indignant gasp left my mouth, and I reeled back. He grinned maniacally at my reaction, mistaking the heat in my cheeks as desire rather than anger. There'd always been a thin line between anger and lust with us, but not anymore, not when he hurt someone innocent in a jealous rage and forced me to watch.

He stood to his full height, and before I could drag my eyes up, his hips were in my eyeline, the zipper of his pants now bulging, clearly showing the outline of his cock hardening at the idea of what he wanted me to do. I swallowed the curses I wished I could spew at him, knowing it would only make matters worse.

To my relief, he slid back into the seat across from me with a lascivious grin splitting his face. His eyes trailed up my form, taking in my curves and the low neckline of my summer dress. A shiver of fear ran up my spine at his attention. Instead of acting on that lust, he pulled out his phone and leaned back in his seat, his legs spreading wide to encase mine within them. Even when sitting here, his phone in his hand, he needed that sense of control to make sure I didn't move.

"Father? Yes, we're on the plane now," Tommaso said, his attention on the conversation even though his eyes stayed locked on mine.

A leaden weight sunk in my stomach at the mention of his father. He was part of the reason I didn't want to go back home. He was worse than Tommaso and had taught him everything he knew of power and control, fostering the need for it in his son long before I'd been dragged into this dark world.

"Is the house set up for us? Perfect. We'll be settling in for the next few days, but we'll plan dinner for the end of the week."

That promise had dread pooling in my stomach. Dinner with his family was the absolute last thing I wanted to do. I couldn't be there, see his parents, an image of what would likely become of us. His father was a ruthless man. He needed to be to run this empire of drugs, sex, and guns—they really had a hand in everything. My skin crawled at the thought of being near him, remembering his leering gazes. We'd always been in public spaces with his parents since Tommaso and I left for New York, and I couldn't shake the stories I'd heard whispered about how Angelo Barone preyed on women.

And his mother ... she was a shell of the woman she must have been before. Her vacant gaze was cold and haunting. She'd had to retreat so far into herself long ago, something I already felt happening to me. But she could never leave him, escape his grasp. And being legally wed ... that was something I couldn't let happen to me. I would rather die than become any version of her. That piece of paper would be like the order for my execution. There would be nothing left of me then.

"See you then," he announced, disconnecting the call and sliding his phone back into his pocket.

"You have a house in East Haven?" I asked hesitantly. *How did I not know that?* We left when I was eighteen and he'd lived with his parents before that. We'd flown back a few times over the years, but usually only for a few hours, needing to go to some sort of stuffy event with his father. He never told me about a house or any sort of plans for leaving New York. He took the opportunity of me wanting to move out there for school to solidify his father's business in the city, and I figured that would be something that was permanent with their crime empire always expanding.

"*We* have a house, mi amore. You and me. We're about to be married now after all," he said darkly. "We were always going to go back, you just sped up the process."

A weight I hadn't realized was there lifted at his declaration. I thought it was my actions that triggered this move and he just solidified it. But it was always going to happen. I was living on borrowed time, and I was sure Tommaso wouldn't have been happy to wait for much longer. Especially since I'd been putting off the wedding for six years now. I came up with excuse after excuse—college, my career—but now there was nothing left to hold off this inevitable ending.

A wedding and marriage were supposed to be exciting, the start of something new. But to me, it felt like the final nail in my coffin, the penultimate piece of the puzzle before the last of my willpower slipped away.

He leaned closer, his fingers trailing over my knee again and tracing circles on the soft skin of my thigh, easing my dress upward.

"If you knew this the whole time, why didn't you stop me? Why did you let it get so far?" I asked, my lips tingling as fear and excitement rushed through me.

I knew I had to forgive myself for feeling any lust toward him. It was purely human nature, it had always only been that deep for the six years we'd been together. He'd been the only person I was with since I was eighteen. He would never have my heart, but my mind couldn't seem to forget what he could do to my body.

"I needed you to feel that hope slip away, to realize just how useless it is to run from me," he whispered, his voice soft and filled with lust.

His words crashed over me like a bucket of ice water, freezing me to my core, and the tendrils of desire that flickered to life inside of me at his touch turned to ash. Any time I felt anything for this man, I needed to bring up this moment, replay it in my mind like a record on repeat. All he wanted was to own me, to use my body as he saw fit, and to claim the right to call me his.

"I needed you to finally give in completely and realize that we're meant to be. You're mine, and I don't let what's mine slip through my fingers." I wrenched my leg from his grasp—every stroke of his fingers had churned my stomach. His eyes hardened at the slight, but to my relief he let me go. Leaning back in his chair, he swirled his glass of whiskey, bringing the crystal to his lips to take a long pull, his eyes shuttering as he let out a groan of pleasure.

"Why can't we just stay in New York?" I asked, knowing the answer, yet I had to try. If I thought things were bad in the city, they would undoubtedly get worse with his father's influence. I hadn't missed the slight tinge of purple that shone through his mother's makeup beneath the right light during our last encounter. No matter how hard she tried to hide it, I could see the subtle winces of pain. Tommaso hadn't hit me, not yet, but he came close, which was why I knew I needed to get out of there, out of his clutches.

"We need to go back home for your safety. I can't just have you wandering off, you're obviously not well and there's too many dangers in the city," he jeered in a mocking tone of concern. He knew full well there was nothing wrong with me. Well, there might be, but if anything, he was the cause not the cure. "My family can watch after you back home, you know just how many eyes we have."

And that was exactly what I was afraid of. Because I knew the underlying meaning to his seemingly caring words. I saw them for the threat they truly were. Despite us living in one of the wealthiest towns in America, there was still a lower class, and men like Tommaso preyed on those he could buy, those he could own, wielding his money like a weapon. At the end of the day, that's what it was. That was the way with the Barones, anyone that crossed them either got paid off or killed. Everyone knew that, so most just took the money and looked the other way.

Families with wealth and riches guarded it like dragons hoarding their treasures, not because they'd ever spend it all. No, because it kept everyone else down, kept them subservient. Men like Tommaso craved power, and money was the best weapon they had to achieve it.

"I emptied your account too," he proclaimed, chasing my lingering inner thoughts away. My face burned with anger as I stared back at him incredulously, hating that he'd insisted to be put on my account to begin with. But before I could get out a word he continued. "We'll be getting married, so there's no need for you to have a separate account. But you've also lost the privilege of having a job after this. I decided to indulge you and it backfired. I won't let that happen again."

I couldn't get a job? He gave me a self-satisfied grin, clearly reading the loss and despair across my face. I shut down my emotions at that, letting him think he'd won.

"I might let you go back to work once you earn back my trust. But for now, you'll stay at home. You'll go to parties and wear pretty dresses," he explained nonchalantly, as though he had the final say. Which he did, for now. "Can someone get my fiancée a drink? We have a lot to celebrate," he called out and the third guard rushed to the drink cart to pour a glass of rosé. Just the sight of it turned my stomach, having become the symbol of the life I was trying so desperately to escape.

The guard handed me the drink and I took it without argument. I could do this. I could let myself slip into this role once more. Let him trust me, let him think I would be an obedient wife.

"Cheers to our upcoming nuptials. I love you, mi amore," he professed, his face softening. I didn't let myself fall for it though. Instead, I gave him a sweet smile, willing my eyes not to show the venom coursing through them, and took a long pull of the wine.

He'd caught me, and I thought that would've broken me. I thought I'd be an empty vessel right now, ready to retreat into myself just to numb the pain, but to my surprise, that fire still lingered inside of me. It only grew hotter now that I was about to be plunged back into East Haven. I couldn't allow him to chip away another piece of who I was. I had a taste of freedom, however brief it was, and I couldn't let go, not now.

"Oh, and don't you dare let me catch you near them, otherwise I'll slit their throats and make you watch." I internally balked at the casual declaration, but he just continued sipping his whiskey, completely unperturbed by the thought of murdering two innocent people.

Rage burned in my veins as my grip tightened on the cool wine glass, reminding myself not to show my emotions openly mere seconds before I'm sure the glass would've shattered in my hand. This would end, one way or another, and this time, I was willing to die to escape him. I would build myself up piece by piece, becoming the woman I once was. The me from yesterday was dead now, but I couldn't let him see that, not yet.

And I would kill him before I let him touch them. I'd get away from Tommaso on my own, no matter what it took. In the end, one of us would not be walking away.

CHAPTER THREE

GIANA

SIX YEARS AGO ...

"ORDER UP." GREG'S GRAVELLY voice echoed out the small pickup window while placing two plates of burgers and fries down.

I glanced around the small diner and grimaced when I caught sight of the only table with customers seated around it. *Of course Pam is nowhere to be found,* I groaned inwardly as I tied the apron around my waist. My jaw clenched in anger when I saw her on the other side of the large glass windows, smoking what had to be the last of her pack. Her thin frame was illuminated by the flickering, fluorescent lights above the door. But knowing her, she had a stash squirreled away somewhere in the storage room.

She was supposed to be watching the front while I cleaned up in the back, but of course, she had to take every opportunity for a break that she could, especially when she had me here. Huffing out a breath of annoyance, I stomped over to the window and pushed down the irritation clawing its way up my throat.

"Where's your mom?" Greg grumbled, the annoyance clear in his own voice ... and that was another reason why I couldn't say anything. Greg and Pam were my parents, not that they acted like it most of the time. Using their first names was my small act of rebellion against both of them. They treated me more like an employee than a daughter most of the time anyway so it was only fitting.

"I'll give you one guess," I muttered, grabbing the ceramic plates off the metallic counter. His eyes narrowed on me as though he was about to reprimand me for the disdain in my tone but he muttered something under his breath and stalked back to the flat top.

"Table ten," he said over his shoulder, as though I wouldn't be able to figure out that the two meals went to the only two people in the diner. Turning on my heel, I attempted to collect myself as I maneuvered around the sage green and chrome counter, my white sneakers squeaking on the aged linoleum floor. My parents hadn't decided to do many renovations to the old diner when they bought it over twenty years ago, choosing to leave it as a retro throwback. They still took care of it though, keeping up with the maintenance, but only so that they wouldn't have to open their pocketbooks for a massive remodel anytime soon.

They thought the matching sage green booths and tables were an ode to simpler times, but in reality, it just looked dated, sterile, and lacked character. Just like them I supposed.

I inhaled sharply as I approached the two men seated at our only table, steeling myself for having to deal with sleazy Jim. Forcing my best customer service smile on my lips, I slid the food before him and his friend, creepy Bob. *Sure, my nicknames weren't the best, but they were accurate.*

"Good evening. Here are your usuals," I said as sweetly as I could muster, before stepping back out of their reach. It wouldn't be the first time one of them had tried to grope my ass while pretending to whisper something to me, and I really wasn't in the mood for their sexual harassment tonight. Especially knowing my parents wouldn't say a word to their best customers.

"Well now, I thought it was supposed to be dinner before dessert," Jim slurred, apparently already drunk off his ass at nine o'clock at night. *Lovely.* His glassy eyes leered at me, and I suppressed my shudder of disgust as they dragged their way up my form. Giving a weak chuckle, I took another small step away from them, not willing to take any chances.

"Are you still *ssseventeen, sssweetheart*?" Bob asked, slurring. He clearly had more to drink than his friend, especially since he could barely sit up straight in his seat.

Fabulous.

My smile widened, teeth clacking together with strain, and my skin crawled at their lascivious looks. Judging by the way Bob's face blanched slightly, I'm sure the expression looked like I was baring my teeth at him more than a friendly gesture. This wasn't the first night they'd been overly ... friendly, and I didn't want to have my parents berate me again or potentially take this job away from me. Despite relying on me almost every night and weekend, they held this position over my head, knowing I needed the money for college and to get the fuck away from them. Pulling in an exaggerated breath through my teeth, I willed my jaw to relax. *Only a few more seconds and I could back away*, I reminded myself.

"Yes, sir," I ground out, doing my best to keep the repulsion from my tone.

"That's a damn shame," Jim said, drawing my attention back to him. "You be sure to tell us the minute you turn eighteen."

Another uneasy laugh escaped my lips, and I took a step back, having noticed Jim's outstretched arm looming closer. His lips parted, about to say something equally as degrading, I was sure, until a chime at the door interrupted him.

I sent a silent thank you to whatever higher power sent Pam through the door at that moment. But when my eyes landed on the two people who had just walked through the door, a genuine smile slid across my face, overtaking the fake one.

"Enjoy your food," I said, not bothering to look back at the two abhorrent excuses for men. "My mom will be back to check on you in a few minutes."

I hastily made my exit, grabbing two menus from the front counter to give to the newcomers, not that they would need them. They'd been here often enough that they had their own table, which they wandered over to now. I didn't bother to wait for Jim's or Bob's response, not caring what they had to say—not when the sole reason I still put up with this town had just walked through the door. Not Pam, no, she was still dragging on her cheap cigarettes, butts littering her spot by the door. *Fucking bitch.*

Jim and Bob grumbled under their breath about something, but I tuned them out, grateful to have some reprieve now.

"Are they giving you a hard time?" Merrick asked before I could even greet my two best friends, his dark, hazel eyes narrowed on the two drunken bastards. The muscles in his chiseled jaw pulsed, his hands clenched into fists on top of the sage green table as though he might use the two wastes of space as punching bags regardless of my answer.

"Nothing I can't handle." I giggled, willing my voice to portray the calm that washed over me when the two of them stepped foot inside the small diner. But it drifted away with the tide, tension radiating through my chest in response to the fine line I walked. If I ever told either of them what happened when they weren't here ... Well let's just say I wouldn't want to stick around for the aftermath. And since I needed this shit job and a roof over my head, at least for the next few months until college, I would rather just stick it out. Because there was no doubt in my mind that my parents would disown me if I lost them their best customers.

Besides, I wouldn't be able to live with myself if Merrick got locked up for beating two worthless assholes into a bloody pulp. He just turned eighteen two months ago, so it wouldn't even be juvie this time. He was just starting to put his life back together.

Merrick dragged a hand back through his short, cropped, golden-blond hair, and my eyes fastened on the way the muscles in his forearm rippled at the simple movement. *No, Giana, he's been your best friend since you were five years old. No checking out his sculpted body.*

"I better be the first phone call you make if they ever try anything," Merrick demanded, folding his arms on the table and cracking his knuckles. The sound echoes across the otherwise silent diner in what I had no doubt was a subtle warning to creeper one and two.

"I can handle it Merrick," I repeated, giving him a pointed look. At my insistence he huffed out a breath of exasperation but thankfully stayed seated. He knew how badly I needed this job, needed to keep my parents happy just for a little while longer. Three more months until college. I chanted the countdown in my head like a mantra. It had been one of the only things able to keep me sane for the past few years since we made the plan—that and these guys.

Kellan just watched me with his keen, sable eyes, as though he could read the thoughts that passed behind my own amber ones. My cheeks burned at his attention, knowing he could read me like a book. I pushed back a lock of my dirty-blonde hair, a few pieces coming free from the tight bun I normally had it in, giving me something to occupy my hands. Otherwise, I would end up playing with the fabric of my skirt like a schoolgirl with a crush. *Snap out of it, Giana.* We'd all been friends since kindergarten, and I wouldn't let my feelings break up the friendship we'd worked so hard to maintain over the years. These guys were my safety net and I refused to ruin it. Besides, it wasn't like either of them would ever return those feelings. But even if one of them did, that would completely mess with our dynamic. No, it was easier to keep my emotions to myself and hide the burgeoning attraction blooming within me for my two best friends.

"Sit with us," Kellan said, his long fingers wrapping around my own to tug me onto the bench beside him. Some of the tension in my chest eased at his gentle touch. It was impossible to resist him sometimes. He had such a calmness about him, the perfect match to Merrick's brutal fury. That's probably why we all became such close friends—that and our fucked-up family lives.

"I have to put in your order though," I argued weakly, not wanting to get up now that they were here. I worked since the moment I got out of school this afternoon, barely taking a break to scarf down a plate of fries.

"We hardly see you anymore, Gi," Merrick grumbled, his eyes hurriedly glancing down to stare at the speckled pattern on the light green table as though that would distract me from what he just said. A small, sad smile stretched across my lips, the same lonely pang echoing in my own heart. We were all busy lately, we had our classes and final exams coming up, plus we all had jobs now. *But this was part of the plan,* I reminded myself. We were saving up for our big move together in three short months.

"I get that," I murmured, letting the seclusion and loneliness I too felt, coat every word. "But I know you both must be starving. Growing boys and all that." I chuckled, attempting to insert some levity into the conversation.

A deep rumble emanated from Merrick's chest, and I almost choked on the gasp that escaped my lips. "I'm a man, don't forget that."

Fuck, fuck, fuck. How the hell was I supposed to stay only friends with him when he did shit like that? I suppressed the urge to cross my legs at the lust that flooded straight to my core. "You better be right back or else I'll come collect you, and then I'll definitely have to kill those two donkeys for seeing me carry you over my shoulder in that skirt." I sucked in a shocked breath at his warning, not exactly sure what to make of it. Was he checking me out too? No, he couldn't be, could he ...

"Take your time." Kellan laughed, his hand reluctantly slipping from mine to push back his black curls. Thank fuck he broke up that conversation because I had no idea what I would have said to Merrick. Lately I could sense a flirty undertone to our conversations, but it never went this far. If I had the chance to speak, I'm not sure I could have stopped myself from needling him, pushing that invisible boundary between friends and more. And that would be *very* bad.

Deciding not to let my mind linger on that, I slid from the booth, almost stumbling in my haste to put some distance between myself and the very confusing situation that was developing before me.

"Kiss ass," Merrick groaned out lowly. The impact his fist made with Kellan's arm was audible as I walked back to the counter to write up their usual order.

"Those boys are back?" Greg grumbled, appearing in the small window, his voice hoarse from all the cigarettes he too smoked.

"Yes," I sighed in exasperation. It was the same thing every time they came in, which was becoming less frequent each week. But we made sure every Friday night to hangout, no matter what.

"You know I don't like you hanging around with those two."

I choked down the laugh that threatened to burst from my lips. Of course he had a problem with my friends, the two people that had always been there for me through thick and thin. Meanwhile, he cared so little about me that he continually made me interact with customers who were inappropriate with me, if I was lucky, and sexually assaulted me if I wasn't. Yup, because that makes so much sense ...

I bit back the retort on the tip of my tongue before handing the ticket order to Greg. He grumbled something unintelligible under his breath and snatched the paper from my outstretched fingers before trudging back to the grills. *Fuck you too.*

My gaze swiveled to the door as a chime tinged throughout the quiet diner. Finally, smokey the dragon was back from the twentieth half hour break.

"Check on your table, Pam," Greg shouted over the sound of meat sizzling on the flat top. Thank fuck, because there was no way I was about to go and check on those nasty men, especially not in front of Merrick and Kellan. Because if they saw how the two of them acted toward me, I guarantee there would be blood splattered over the floor tonight, and it wouldn't be my friends'.

Kellan was normally the calm one, but that didn't mean he was entirely passive. His muscles were finely honed, despite the fact he was an artist, not a fighter ... Well, that wasn't exactly true. He'd gotten in plenty of fights alongside Merrick as a last resort.

Pam muttered something under her breath before heading over to the two pieces of trash, a waft of smoke blowing my way from the door closing behind her. My nose scrunched up at the foul smell, and I hurriedly made my way back to Merrick and Kellan, grateful for Pam's distraction.

"Did I make it back in time, sir?" I asked in a mocking tone, my eyebrow raised in an attempt to provoke the asshole across from me as I slid back into the booth beside Kellan. His hand automatically found mine again, playing with my fingers beneath the table. I expected some sort of retort from Merrick, but it didn't come. Instead, his jaw tensed, muscles working as he gripped the edge of the table in a vise-like grip.

My brows furrowed in confusion at the strange behavior, but Kellan's voice cut through my thoughts before I could voice them. "Have you decided what we're doing for your birthday?"

"Nope, but it's my birthday after all, I think you two should plan something for me," I declared with a self-satisfied grin. If I was being honest, I would have told them that I really didn't care what we did, as long as we were all together.

"I'm sure we can come up with something." Kellan laughed, his thumb rubbing circles on the back of my hand. A shiver ran up my spine at the comforting touch. That line between friendship and more was becoming fainter and fainter by the second ... at least to me. I was sure they were only trying to be nice though.

A sound of disapproval left Merrick's chest in a low rumble, but before he could say anything Pam traipsed over, her sneakers squeaking with every step. She swayed as she stopped beside me, her hand reaching out to clutch the table to steady herself. She'd obviously been into more than just cigarettes judging by the scent of cheap whiskey mixing with the stale smoke on her breath. I bit my tongue, knowing I'd be in more trouble for saying anything in front of customers.

"You finish up in the back?" Pam slurred, leaning against the side of the booth. I sucked in a deep breath, needing to center myself before I lost it on her. She's been outside for the past half hour yet had the audacity to ask me if I'd done my work.

"Yes," I said in a clipped tone, internally cursing myself for letting my annoyance show. I knew she was about to let me have it, and that wouldn't be good for any of us. Her face twisted in anger, her lips already curled into a sneer.

"Mrs. Bardot, you look stunning tonight. Did you do something with your hair?" Kellan cut in, stealing the words from her mouth. She sputtered for a moment, her brow gradually smoothing out. Merrick made a choked sound of amusement and my foot automatically twitched to kick him in the shin.

"Ouch," Merrick whispered, and I narrowed a derisive look his way, silently willing him to keep his mouth shut. Looking back at Pam, she was smoothing a hand over her hair, messily thrown up into a claw clip. I'd seen pictures of her and my father when I was a child, and she was an attractive woman before the weight of this town fully settled on her shoulders. But ever since they moved to East Haven, hoping for a small-town life, the pressure of running a business here and dealing with the gangs and the Barones took a toll on both of them. This was part of the reason why I had to get the hell out of here as soon as possible. I didn't want this life to drain my will to live just as it had for them.

"I started using a new conditioner." She beamed at Kellan, her shoulders losing some of their earlier tension and her amber eyes softening.

"I can tell. I'll have to get the name of it for my mom," Kellan responded, clearing his throat at her continued attention. "Say, would it be possible for Gi to get off a bit early today? We've all been so busy with graduation coming up and me working at the community center and Merrick at the garage, it feels like we haven't seen each other in ages." Kellan threw on the charm, his voice coaxing her and putting her at ease, along with his bright smile.

Pam's lips pursed but to my surprise, the dreamy expression didn't completely lift at the mention of me leaving early.

"Order up," Greg announced, slamming the tray of foam takeout containers down onto the counter. I never wrote takeout on the orders, but it never failed, Greg always packaged them to go, not wanting them to stay a moment longer than they had to.

"I guess it's okay," Pam said, twirling a stray piece of hair around her finger, her eyes going distant for a moment before they hardened into a glare on me. The fog of Kellan's charm had clearly started to lift. "Just remember not to stay out too late. You have a shift tomorrow morning."

"I won't," I rushed to assure her, not allowing her any time to change her mind. Kellan's smile must have been magic because she'd never let me off early otherwise, not even when I was soaked in sticky, iced tea from a toddler's temper tantrum. One night, I sliced my hand open on a can and she still kept me twenty minutes late that night.

I rushed to the counter, nearly knocking her over in my haste to get the food from the window. Despite Pam being in a half-decent mood, I had no doubt that by the time I turned around she would be collecting their money. Because even though they treated my friends like garbage most nights, they never forgot to make them pay their bill. Not that either Merrick or Kellan would ever let me give them their meals for free, but it was the principle.

"You get those boys out of here. They're bad for business," Greg muttered under his breath, slapping his meaty palm down on the boxes before I could slide them into my hands.

"They'll be leaving as soon as I give them their food," I said pointedly, eyeing his hand until he reluctantly lifted it. His fingers combed back through his thinning russet-brown hair and he huffed out an irritated sigh before waddling back to the grill. I didn't bother telling him that I would be going with them, knowing he would just say no regardless of anything Pam already said.

Turning back to the counter I slipped the containers into bags, catching the guys handing crisp bills to Pam as they slid from the smooth, pleather booth seats. I cast a furtive glance over at the two creepers, making sure they weren't paying attention to me as I met the guys by the front door. Thankfully, they were too engrossed in their bottles of beer Pam must have given them, not that they needed any more booze ... but I guess she wasn't the best judge of that either.

I kept my eyes fastened on the metal door handle, begging the fates to continue to shine their good fortune down upon me. My muscles tensed when a slurred "Sweetheart" rang out behind me from either Jim or Bob. Only a few feet separated me from the sanctuary of the cool night air. My heart pounded in my chest when I noticed Merrick still beside me, his feet cemented in place and his body rigid as he stared at the two clowns, and I could only imagine the lascivious, leering looks they must be pinning me with.

"Merrick, don't," I warned, my slender fingers wrapping around his massive bicep in a feeble attempt to keep him by my side. Kellan eased the bags from my hand and opened the door. The breeze washed over Merrick and me, and I hoped it would cool the anger boiling just below his surface. His muscles strained under my touch, begging to pound into their withering faces, and I could see the leash he held on that fury straining under the pressure. "Please," I whispered, glancing up at him, my eyes pleading. His gaze flashed to me at the sound of desperation in my tone and the rage fled almost immediately, his jaw relaxing as he nodded begrudgingly.

Wrapping my arm around his, I pulled him alongside me and out into the nearly empty parking lot, a sigh of relief slipping past my lips. Thankfully, the sound was swallowed up by the wind brushing through the leaves in the towering oak trees, their boughs casting ominous shadows over part of the parking lot. To my dismay, that happened to be where Merrick's 1962 Chevy Impala was parked, the weathered red paint barely visible in the poorly lit area. He was able to get the coveted antique car cheap from a family friend and was slowly restoring it to its former glory. It was a feat in itself it was even running. Only a few rickety lamp posts lined the sides of the parking lot, my parents unwilling to sink any more money into this place than was necessary.

I tugged Merrick closer, craving the feel of his thick arm wrapped around mine. He huffed out a breath of amusement but slid his arm around my shoulders, pulling me into his side and cocooning me in his warmth. An excited giggle slipped out, and I tucked my chin into him so he couldn't see the giddy smile that plastered itself on my face.

The flash of headlights from an incoming car cut through the light flutter in my chest, the easy feeling slipping away and replaced with a nervous twist of my stomach. Merrick pulled the keys from his pocket and tossed them to Kellan with his other hand since he was already waiting by the driver's side door. I stiffened against him, and he wrapped his arm tighter around me as though it could shield me from the terror behind the steering wheel of the blacked-out sedan driving past us. Keeping our eyes focused on the back of the car, we don't dare stare after them. It was best to ignore them, to feign ignorance of what was about to happen.

Some of the tension eased from my chest as Merrick opened the passenger door for me, and I hopped into the back seat, with Merrick taking the front once I was settled. Kellan turned the key in the ignition, having waited until we were both safely inside the vehicle just in case it drew any more attention to us.

"Scumbag," Merrick muttered under his breath. Watching in the rearview mirror, I waited with bated breath as the figure, clad in a black suit, slammed his car door behind him, striding to the front of the diner. "Someone needs to take care of the Barones."

My throat dried at Merrick's hissed declaration. Not because I didn't agree with him, I just couldn't give him any ideas. No one stood up to any of Barone's men and lived to tell the tale.

They were the main reason this town was so soul-sucking. Everyone lived under Barone's iron thumb. They were the ones who made the rules, and demanded a cut from every business in town in return for their protection, because they weren't the only gang, far from it. They controlled the mayor, the city councillors, the governor, and any government representatives in our area. It didn't matter who was voted in, as soon as they were nominated, they were on the Barone's payroll. Because no one said no to the Barones ... not unless they had a death wish.

Kellan put the car in reverse, pulling back just enough to angle the car toward the exit, clearly not wasting any time getting us out of here.

Inhaling sharply, my eyes darted to the road as the man looked back at us. It might have been common knowledge that the Barones controlled everything but they weren't keen on attention. And staring too long could be the last mistake you made.

My heart jackhammered against my chest as we turned onto the quiet road. The night was always the most dangerous time here, meaning nothing much was still open in East Haven this late except the few bars. Not many wanted to risk getting mixed up with the sordid business that happened after dark.

It wasn't until Kellan pulled onto a side road that I was able to lift my gaze back to the mirror. Some of my anxiety washed away in the absence of the blacked-out car behind us, and I slumped back in my seat.

"We'll be out of here soon," Kellan reassured us, reciting the words we'd each repeated more times than I could remember. His knuckles stiffly gripped the steering wheel until we drove a few blocks farther without any sign of them. With a hitch of his breath, he flexed his fingers, clearly attempting to dispel some of his nervous energy.

Three more months and we'd be free of this hellhole. We just had to make it that long.

CHAPTER FOUR

GIANA

NOW

THE AFTERNOON SUN BEAMED through the window, beginning its descent in the early evening hours. Families strolled down the streets of downtown East Haven, indulging in ice cream from the local shop. Couples and groups of friends laughed and embraced while heading to the few restaurants and shops along the main road. The shops hadn't changed much, though a few new ones had popped up here and there, new victims for the Barones to sink their teeth into after draining the last owners dry.

My stomach twisted as I realized what we were about to approach. Greg's Diner ... my parents' diner. Chewing on my bottom lip, I debated turning before we reached the place that evoked so many memories, a place I vowed never to step foot in again. But I squashed down that thought, knowing my discomfort would only draw Tommaso's attention, something else I really needed to avoid right now. Knowing him, he would ask the driver to pull over just to make me squirm.

The buildings slipped past my view, as though each were a second ticking away on a clock, shoving me closer to the edge. My chest tightened as we passed the last bar, leaving a clear view of the open parking lot just beyond it. I clenched the edge of the door, attempting to hide my reaction at the dilapidated exterior. My heart panged at the loss of a carefree childhood, of parents who weren't able to care for me, and the friends I left behind. Pulling in a shuddering breath, I internally scolded myself at the show of weakness at that last thought. I rarely allowed them to cross my mind but seeing these familiar places had all the repressed memories rushing to the surface.

I felt no loss from the people that Greg and Pam were, only for who they could have been if it wasn't for this town, for the Barones. They were on the list of people I wished I could never see again, right after Tommaso and his father. But East Haven was a small town and I was having serious doubts about my luck right now, especially after my hopes and dreams were crushed earlier today. I held on to the small sliver of defiance that remained, though that stemmed from my desperation to escape, to not become the lifeless being who was an empty vessel of the person I used to be.

The car came to a stop right outside the rundown diner, and I glanced up anxiously, checking to see if he was about to make me get out, but exhaled a sigh of relief at the red glow of the stoplight that must've been installed in the past six years.

"Do you want to go in?" Tommaso asked, his voice betraying the wry smirk on his lips. Schooling my face, I turned to him, realizing my mistake. He clasped my thigh, his thumb rubbing circles on the sensitive skin in what was supposed to be a comforting gesture. Bile climbed up my throat, but I pushed it down, willing my expression to remain void of any emotion.

"No," I answered, my voice hard as I met his eyes, and his grin creeped wider, growing at the declaration.

"But, mi amore, we're about to get married, surely you'll want to invite them to the wedding," he pried. But to my relief, the driver hit the gas the moment the lights turned green. The tension slowly seeped from my shoulders with each foot of distance we put between us and the ramshackle diner that I'm surprised was even still open. Greg and Pam had allowed the diner to go into disrepair over the years judging by the brief glimpse I got of the overgrown greenery, tilted flickering halogen sign, and thick layer of dirt coating the windows. I would've thought they'd have closed for good if it wasn't for the few cars and movement I could make out through the streaked glass.

"They won't be coming," I muttered, slouching back in the seat. My legs spread wider with the movement, and he took the opportunity to slide his hand up farther, teasing closer and closer to my center.

It would be easy to let him take away the stress of seeing this town, to forget he was the reason we were back here. He knew every inch of my body, knew exactly how to make me weak. I could let him do it here and now, in the back of the blacked-out sedan like we'd done so many times before. A shudder ran over my body at his touch, both repugnance and longing swirling within me as my panties grew wetter. My body craved the oblivion he could bring me, the only thing he was good for in my opinion, the release of my pussy clenching around his fingers, imagining they were another's.

But they weren't. This was Tommaso, the man I'd just tried to escape from a few hours before. The man that could bring me both pleasure and pain. But was the ecstasy really worth it? Was it worth the mind-numbing soul-sucking nothingness I would be plummeted into if I continued down this road? Was it worth his wrath, his brutality? There'd only been two men before him that made me feel anything close to what Tommaso did but we hadn't had a chance to explore that side of our relationship. But it gave me hope—hope that I could leave and find someone who both lit that fire within me but also was someone I could love. Because I'd never loved Tommaso.

So I closed my legs, swallowing thickly to clear my mind from the fog of lust that had settled over me. Tommaso released a derisive snort as his hand fell from my leg, a chill sweeping in at the absence of his touch. He shook his head in exasperation, but I didn't miss the spark of excitement that lit in his eyes at the challenge. The look chased away any lingering passion I had, cold dread settling in my stomach instead.

"Really, Gi?" He wrapped his arm around my shoulders, his fingers digging into my flesh until I leaned closer to him. I gingerly rested my head against his shoulder, my body rigid. "You're really going to punish me after all that you've put me through today?"

"Punish you?" I asked incredulously, springing away from him as though flames had just sprouted from his skin, and his hand fell away. "You knew all along, you could have stopped me at any time. Instead, you chose to wait until I got to the airport and past security, just to show me how powerless I am—just to exert your control."

I didn't care if the driver heard us. I was done staying quiet and playing by his rules. I glared at him, my breaths coming out in quick pants from the rage burning inside me. I waited for him to say something, to scold me for speaking so loudly, to attempt to make himself look like the victim—anything. But a look of amusement was plastered on his smug face, declining to refute anything I just said.

"You used it as an excuse to move us back here, to tighten your chokehold on me." My anger cooled as realization came crashing over me like a bucket of ice water, chilling me to my bones. "How long have you had this planned?"

"The past three years, ever since you graduated college," he admitted, his chest puffing out with pride at his careful manipulation coming to light. "I increased the severity of your repercussions when you disobeyed me and gave you small opportunities, giving you the illusion that I wasn't watching, hoping you would take one of them. But you never did ... until now."

"Why didn't you just bring us back here then if that was your plan all along?" I pressed my body as far away from him as I could, my arm plastered against the tan, leather interior of the door. "Why bother waiting three years?"

"Because you needed to break, to see that there's no running away from me," he said casually with a shrug, reiterating what he had already said on the plane. His blasé tone grated on my nerves, but I wasn't surprised, that was what his family did. If someone didn't bend to their will, they broke them. He shook his head in disappointment, as though I should have already guessed that. "I had to finally get you to accept that you're mine so that I knew you wouldn't dare try anything here and embarrass me or my family."

The car came to a stop just as his words trailed off. The light squeak of the brakes followed by the mechanical whirring of wrought-iron gates opening, signaling we'd arrived. I glanced up at the long cobblestone driveway stretching beyond the entrance, toward the towering mansion. The exterior was covered in stone, and knowing Tommaso and his family, it was most likely imported from Italy. A marble statue stood in the center of the roundabout, artfully carved bushes in the shapes of waves surrounding it. Light glinted off a metallic surface, drawing my gaze up to the entryway where a large door stood, which I could only assume had been honed from gold.

I pointlessly wondered how long it took him to have this built, but I didn't want to know, not really. Because judging by the size and intricate details that were put into this place, it had to have been started before we even left for New York ... six years ago, when I was only eighteen.

"We're home."

Home. That word hadn't existed for me in over six years. And even then, no house had ever felt like home.

"STUPID BOX," I MUTTERED, crouching down to push the massive thing across the hardwood floor. Sweat beaded on my brow, and I paused my movements to swipe a hand over it. I went from packing a small bag to run away with to now having to unpack all my worldly possessions. Things that clearly meant absolutely nothing to me since I was willing to do away with them all. I scowled down at the brown cardboard, internally scolding myself for accumulating this much junk over the years. But especially after high school, having access to the kind of money I could never have even fathomed was my only escape. I spent and spent, to fill the hole inside of me, or perhaps it was my own little rebellion against Tommaso and his family. However, it never really helped since everything I bought had to be from one of the luxury brands Tommaso approved of so I "portrayed their level of wealth." I had no idea just how much had been in the condo in New York until I was faced with unpacking it all into the massive house.

At least I hadn't been the one to pack it all up. No, Tommaso took the liberty of having everything packed and sent over from New York. It had all arrived the next day, and I had no doubt the timing was so close just to show how stupid I'd been to believe I would get away with it. But desperate people do desperate things, and my need to escape him, to escape this town, only grew with each day I spent locked away in this fortress.

"You're going to scratch the floor if you keep doing that," Tommaso said, huffing out a sigh of exasperation from behind me.

"Why don't you lift it for me then?" Turning to face him, I plaster a mocking, saccharine smile on my face. My hands clenched at my sides, pushing down the urge to strangle the fucker. He helped—some—but his excuse was that he was busy tying up loose ends in New York ... which was *my* fault of course.

"I wish I could, but I'm heading out for the night to meet with a few business associates," he said in a dry tone, leaning casually against the bedroom door. I schooled my face, not letting the jolt of excitement that ran through me show. My pulse pounded in my ears, and I fought to remain focused, pushing the plans rushing through my mind onto the back burner. "Can I trust you on your own?"

"I'm not a child," I ground out between gritted teeth, but I bit back the rest of my retort, not wanting to push too far. This was the first opportunity I had to be on my own since we got here five days ago, and I couldn't instill any doubt within him.

He quirked an eyebrow in question, but his contemptuous look turned lascivious as he scanned my body, taking in the tight, matching black sports bra and yoga pants clinging to my skin. "No, you aren't," he drawled, his dark tone making my skin crawl. I suppressed the urge to shudder and gave him a pointed glare. "I see you're still frosty." He chuckled, pushing off from the wall to stalk over to me, like a lion closing in on its prey.

My stomach sank at that thought—I never wanted to be the victim, to be weak, powerless, like a lamb to the slaughter. The embers flickered inside of me then, as though reminding me that I could still fight, that I could still get out of here. I wouldn't let him break me, mold me into some brainless fuck toy for him. Because soon enough, that's all I would be—that's all I would crave, the moments of pleasure between the emptiness of it all. I realized I was heading down a dark path, by embracing that desire but sometimes they were the only thing that had made life bearable. I hated that I'd fallen headlong into using that release to cope with my bleak future, but that all changed the second his jealous rage finally exploded. The spell had broken enough for me to take that leap.

He closed in on me, his fingers gently clasping my chin and tipping it up so my eyes met his half-lidded gaze. My pulse hammered in my ears, half in fear and half in anticipation. I sucked in a shuddering breath, the blood draining from my face as I attempted to fight against the weakening power he held over me. Grinding my teeth, I pushed back from him, pulling every ounce of willpower I had to put some distance between us.

His brow furrowed in confusion, watching me intently as though I were some sort of puzzle he was trying to figure out. I pulled my shoulders back, willing my spine to go ramrod straight, not allowing him to catch any sign of weakness. A spark of intrigue glimmered in his eyes and a grin stretched his lips. My defiance apparently amused him.

"Don't wait up for me, mi amore." With that, he gave me one last parting look before straightening his suit jacket and striding out to the hallway. Waiting with bated breath, I stood deathly still, not wanting to make a sound. His movements echo through the expansive house, footsteps reverberating on the marble tile in the entryway. I slowly slipped my phone from my pocket, the screen immediately illuminating the time for me. It was five forty-five, and judging by his parting words, not only would he be out for dinner, he'd be going out with his father's men afterward.

But it could all be a ploy; he could be waiting to see what I do. He hadn't technically told me to stay inside, so if he gets home before me, I can always say I went out for a bite to eat. I fought the urge to fidget, needing to hear the door close and see the car pull from the driveway to truly believe it. As though he could hear my thoughts, the hinges squeaked on the front door, his muttered curse following it at the quality of materials, and he slammed it behind him. The sound reverberated off the walls, and although I'd expected it, I jolted from the crash, my phone clattering to the floor in front of me. I didn't bother picking it up, instead I eased over to the bedroom window, my steps silent in case he hadn't left the house. I would believe it when I saw it.

Pulling the curtains aside, I peeked through the small gap, my ears peeled for any noise inside or outside of the house. A breath of relief slipped past my lips as his car came into view, easing around the cobblestone roundabout as the gate opened. My eyes narrowed as I attempted to make out the form behind the wheel because I wouldn't put it past him to have someone drive his car just as a scheme to see what I'd do.

His eyes lifted to the rearview mirror, and I hurriedly stepped back, the curtain swinging closed to shutter out the thin stream of light that beamed into the room. I slumped back against the wall, some of the tension slipping off my shoulders now that I was alone.

The silence pushed in on me, and although waves of relief washed over me, a different sort of pressure began to mount. I hadn't thought I'd get this opportunity, especially not this soon, so I had to make this count.

Thankfully not only did Tommaso not trust me, he also didn't trust his guys near me. Meaning there were no staff on site, no guards at the gate. There'd be cameras though, that's for sure. He'd know that I left, I'd just have to make it quick enough that he'd believe I just went out to eat.

Rushing back over to where I dropped my phone, I stooped down and plucked it up, the face recognition automatically unlocking my home screen. My finger shook as I rushed to click the maps button. I may have known every inch of this town once upon a time, but six years could change things. I scanned the screen, my foot anxiously tapping the floor as I rack my brain for somewhere to go. I had to get a job, that was number one on my list.

Now that Tommaso emptied my account, I'd need to either open another or make sure I get paid under the table in cash. Not many places would do that though—not many places would even hire me with my connection to the Barones. East Haven was a small town and word traveled fast. I had no doubt in my mind that most people already knew of our arrival even though neither of us had left the sprawling estate yet. Tommaso conveniently had everything delivered to us, not that I was complaining, there wasn't a single soul in the place I wanted to run into again. My mind drifted to the two people I'd do anything for, and my heart panged at the thought of seeing them again. I wished more than anything that I could go back, that I could change things, but after what I did, I knew any run-in would not be pleasant. It would crush my soul even further to see the disdain in their eyes, to see the hatred in their sneers.

I scanned the map again, pushing those thoughts from my mind and searching for somewhere not controlled by the Barones. Before I left there were a few gangs that stood up to them that held some territory near the outskirts of town. I pushed the map over in that area and paused when I found a bar named The Inferno. Chewing my lip, I clicked on it but not much information popped up, only a generic image, not even a phone number.

Hell, I could be walking straight into an abduction. My only hope at escape may just be my undoing. Who better to hold hostage than *the* fiancé of Tommaso Barone? I grimaced at the thought, but what choice did I have? If any place would be willing to give me a job, it might be them.

Frowning back down at the screen, I attempted to do another search but still nothing came up about the bar. Who knew, it could very well have changed hands in the last six years, and I could be walking straight into an establishment run by the very people I was looking to escape. But as I shook, attempting to dispel some of the tension radiating through me as my desperation mounted, I knew that I had to take that risk.

I huffed out a breath and tossed my phone on the bed, conjuring every ounce of courage I had. These were gangs we grew up fearing, seeking the safety of the Barones' rule rather than being terrorized by them. And now I was going to them for help. But after the past six years, I was used to being surrounded by dangerous men and women, so this wouldn't really be any different ... would it?

Out of the frying pan and into the fire as they say—or I guess The Inferno. I could only hope I wasn't exchanging one demon for another ...

CHAPTER FIVE

GIANA

NOW

I TAPPED MY FINGERS against the steering wheel in a steady staccato, needing something to dispel the anxious energy spinning around me like a tornado. The heavy squeal of the wrought-iron gates made me wince as they creaked open for me. Thankfully Tommaso gave me the gate code and the keys to a brand-new car as a peace offering earlier this week. Despite his need to control me, he knew I would need to leave the house at some point. I could only hope that this wouldn't be the tipping point to strip away these last vestiges of freedom from me.

My foot eased on the gas pedal, and I maneuvered the car onto the street slowly, still remembering how to drive after years in the city. I grimaced as I looked out over the hood, my stomach turning at the bright cherry red that shined back at me in the last rays of the setting sun. Of course, not only did he have to get me the most obnoxious and memorable car ever, he also had to get another jab in there since it was the same shade as Merrick wanted for his Chevy. The thought brought up memories both wistful and painful since I never got to see it fully restored. I idly wondered if he still had the car, wishing, despite myself, that I could see him again. *No Giana, you're the last person he'd want to see,* I reminded myself, focusing back on the road as I rolled to a pause at the stop sign.

The engine purred beneath me, nothing like the deep rumble of Merrick's restoration project. Leave it to Tommaso to get me a car that no one would be able to ignore, ensuring I would have eyes on me at all times. It was obvious from the stares I was already receiving that anyone would be able to tell the Barones if they saw my Porsche 911 Carrera Cabriolet driving past.

The movements came easy to me despite my lack of experience at driving. I hadn't really driven many times, other than when Merrick would let me drive his car—my own parents not caring whether or not I ever got my license. If it hadn't been for him, I'm not sure I ever would've been able to learn. This damn place, every street, every shop reminded me of Merrick and Kellan, and I could only hope I would be able to keep my distance from them, for their sake and for mine. Because, although things ended badly between us—our friendship severed by my actions—I still held on to the good times we'd had. Imagining what could have happened if all our dreams came true was one of the only things that helped me get any sleep at night, until my dreams turned to nightmares.

Glancing at the car's internal tablet screen, I selected a number I had saved before I left, needing someone to take my mind off the thoughts plaguing me.

"I feel like this is bad news," Sophia answered hesitantly on the first ring. Although I told her I would let her know how everything went, her and I knew that was a lie. I would've gotten rid of my phone if I'd made it to Vancouver. Of course I had her number written down, but it wouldn't have been safe to contact her for a few months at least.

"He knew," I sighed simply, and I filled her in on what happened. The airport, the plane ride, and the move back to East Haven. I held a few things back though, like how dangerous Tommaso truly was and how we ended up together in the first place. After I told her the truth about how he treated me and hinted at what he was willing to do to keep me in line, she made me promise to not keep any more secrets. But there were some things I just couldn't voice. Some things that showed how weak I'd truly become, and I couldn't bear to hear the pity in her tone, not to mention the danger she could be in if I divulged everything. That was part of his power over me too; I lived in constant fear he would hurt those I cared for, especially since he never missed the opportunity to threaten them. And I knew if I told her, she'd get her father involved, and I couldn't risk their lives.

"That fucking bastard," she seethed. The echo of what sounded like her fist hitting something came through the speaker, punctuating her anger. "I'm on my way there now, no arguing. I should've done this in the first place. We'll leave together."

"I can't let you do that, Sophia, you know how dangerous he is. Besides, he drained my account, transferred it all to the joint one, so I'd have no money to get us anywhere," I explained, hoping she could see reason before she did something brash. I couldn't live with myself if anything happened to her because of me.

"I have money," she groaned, but she and I both knew it wouldn't be enough. She worked with me in marketing and made a good salary, but with the cost of rent in Manhattan we both knew she didn't have enough for a new start for both of us, and I didn't want her to have to borrow anything from her family. I did, before he wiped my cards, but there was no way to get that back now, not with my name on the joint account. There'd be no proof that he was holding it from me, and no one would be willing to listen, not when it would be their life on the line. "I'll save up," she amended, knowing exactly what I would've said.

"No, Sophia, I—I can't talk freely," I groaned, glancing around the interior of the car. I wanted to tell her what was happening, but I couldn't risk it, not if he'd planted a listening device in here. "But as soon as I can I'll tell you the rest."

"Giana," she warned, but I wouldn't risk it. I smacked my palm against my forehead, cursing my desperation once more. How had I only now thought about a listening device or a GPS? Technology might be convenient but the world was developing into a scary place with how easy it was becoming to stalk someone's every move.

"I promise, I'll tell you as soon as I'm able to, but I have to go," I urged, attempting to keep my voice as calm and steady as

I could, but even I could detect the slight tremor there now that the thought crossed my mind.

"Stay safe, Gi," she sighs, her voice slightly muffled, and I could just picture her scrubbing a hand over her face in frustration. "Love you."

"Love you too." I didn't give myself a moment to reconsider and immediately pressed the end-call button.

My free leg bounced in apprehension, doubt clouding my mind as though my confidence was setting along with the sun. Thankfully I didn't dare pull up the route on either my phone or the car GPS, at least that would be one less damning piece of evidence against me. My stomach churned as conflicting thoughts rushed through my mind, and I pulled to the side of the road, not trusting my ability to maneuver the car through the narrow streets while fighting off a panic attack. My breaths came in ragged pants, my throat so dry I choked against the sensation.

I put the car into park and leaned back against the headrest as I attempted to control my breathing. My eyelids closed and I counted to ten, holding each breath and shoving every other thought from my brain. I reached for the water bottle I knew was placed in the cup holder and guzzled down the cool liquid like it was a lifeline, helping to ease the ache in my throat.

This wasn't me. I wasn't this person. I'd spent every moment of the past six years just surviving. This life was making me become this person I barely even recognized. The old Giana wouldn't have cared if he found out, would've rattled his cage each chance she got. But I grew complacent, abiding by his rules to keep others safe. I tried to convince myself I could handle it, that this was what I deserved for one stupid mistake. The old me was chipped away bit by bit, until all that was left was this shattered version of myself.

I had to do this. I needed to get out of here, away from him. My eyes popped open, as though that realization was the key to the lock. I inhaled a startled breath when I examined where exactly I'd stopped. The old firehouse just on the edge of town, the one place of refuge I used to have. It was abandoned long ago, the Barones paying for a new state-of-the-art facility in the center of town—and closer to their house—made this one obsolete. And rather than wasting the money on demolition, they just left the old building as it was, boarding up all the doors and windows to keep people out ... well most people. We took it over as soon as the dust had settled, and it became our place to escape, to tune out the family drama at home and just be us.

Judging by the overgrown weeds climbing up the sides of the brown bricks it hadn't been used in quite some time. Probably not since our graduation ...

I ground my teeth against the memories that flooded to the surface and focused on myself. I needed to get back to the person I was before. Hell, even then I was still under my parents' thumbs, ruled by their constant threats to take away my job, the sole source of income I had. I pushed down my feelings then too, letting others push me around, harass me, take advantage of me—but not anymore. A few more months of this and I would save up some money, just enough for first and last month's rent on an apartment and then get another job. I just had to put some distance between me and the Barones, find somewhere to disappear under the radar until I could trust a supplier to get me the documents to travel abroad. But the first step was tonight. I might get caught, but the alternative would be to accept this life, to accept this empty person I'd become.

I glanced at the firehouse again and steeled myself, accepting that there may be consequences to my actions tonight, but I'd rather that than sink into this pit of self-pity and doubt. The embers of independence and defiance flickered inside me—brighter this time—as I put the car back into drive and headed straight to The Inferno.

I FROWNED AS I pulled up to The Inferno, my eyes scanning the line of motorcycles parked out front before examining the bar itself. It was only a few minutes' drive past the firehouse, and I idly realized how much danger we'd inadvertently put ourselves in as teenagers. We were so close to a known hangout of the Demon Riders, the local motorcycle club that was known to be even worse than the Barones for their brutality. They didn't have the cash flow or influence to overtake them though, not six years ago and not now judging by the ramshackle bar. Dirt kicked up as I pulled into a parking space, and I grimaced knowing it would stick to the unblemished paint.

A few men lingered outside, leaning against their bikes while they cast curious glances my way. I again cursed Tommaso and his ostentatious car choice, wishing I could've gotten a beater somewhere, but that wasn't an option and it wouldn't be, so my focus had to be on rent money, that's it. I could purchase a last-minute bus ticket to the next town over and switch buses until I got where I needed to be. I'd be traceable but that was a risk I had to take. Once I got a job, I had to give myself a time limit on getting out of here to avoid falling into the same traps as last time. I wouldn't be complacent, not anymore.

I drew in a calming breath, steeling myself for this. I could be walking into a number of scenarios but I had to do this. Pushing open the door, I gingerly stepped out of the car. Heels were probably not the best choice, but I did at least choose wisely with the tight jeans and low-cut black top, not too flashy and not over-the-top sexy but enough to show off my curves. Swinging my crossbody purse over my shoulder, I patted the bulge there as reassurance that I remembered my taser.

I closed the door as silently as possible, not wanting to draw more attention to me than I already had, and made sure to lock my car. I honestly wouldn't have been surprised if I came back out here to an empty parking space or no wheels. Training my eyes on the entrance, I strode toward it, pulling on a mask of cool confidence. A whistle sounded from one of the men leaning on their bikes, but I ignored it. I could put up with this for a few months. I used to do it all the time as a teenager, what was the difference now? As I closed the distance, a squealing guitar solo was cranked up from inside the bar, drowning out whatever else the men behind me had to say. I pushed open the door and immediately fought to keep the wince off my face as the amp screeched, the sound nearly deafening.

The stench of stale beer smacked me in the face as I stepped in, my shoes sticking to the thick varnish of the dark hardwood floors. The bar was packed inside, men clad in thick leather jackets took up almost every seat in the place with a few women within the groups. A few patrons were sitting on the dark-brown wooden bar stools. The inside looked clean, but I could tell it hadn't been updated in years. Pictures of antique cars and bikes lined the walls, along with license plates and hub caps as though they were pieces of art. I pushed down my thoughts of the place, it didn't matter what my impression was, money was money, and I definitely was not in any position to judge.

"Get off the stage," a man shouted and stood as a chorus of boos echoed around the bar. My gaze slid over the stage at the far side just as the band paused their playing, and the loud twang of their instruments reverberated off the walls, piercing my eardrums. I fought back the urge to slap my hands over my ears, not wanting to offend anyone.

"You wouldn't know good music if it hit you in the face," the lead singer jeered, throwing the microphone to the ground and stomping over to the grey-haired man.

"I sure as hell know what bad music is, my ears are fucking bleeding," he quipped back, stepping into the narrow walkway to confront the singer now foaming at the mouth in rage.

"Kick his ass," someone else shouted, and I took that as my cue to get the hell out of the way. Ending up thrown into the middle of a bar fight was not the way I wanted to start off my night. Especially not when that would mean someone was going to get zapped.

I sidestepped over to an empty space at the bar, leaning against the cool varnished wood rather than taking a seat. The last thing I wanted to do was let one of these guys think I was open to being chatted up. The muffled sound of grunts and fists meeting flesh sounded behind me followed by a round of cheers, but I kept my gaze trained on the woman behind the bar.

"Mike," she called out, briefly glancing at the brawling men as she huffed out a breath of exasperation. She turned to grab a bottle of liquor off the back wall and her long black hair swung out around her small frame. Her dark-brown eyes were lined with thick black eyeliner, and she had a seemingly permanent derisive curve to her lips. I mean, I guess I would too if I worked here.

A burly bouncer stomped out from the back drawing my gaze back to the brawling men. His shoulders were massive, and he reached out to pluck both men up by their collars, holding them back with barely any effort.

"Get the fuck out, both of you," Mountain man—or Mike I'm assuming—growled, pushing them both toward the door.

"It was all in good fun." The heckler chuckled nervously, but his attempt to dissuade Mike was only a weak one since he was already retreating toward the exit.

"You can't kick me out, our band still has another set to play," the lead singer argued, crossing his arms over his slender chest. He was younger than most of the men in this bar, probably in his late twenties, but he looked much older than that under the harsh overhead lights that Mike switched on before handling the two clowns. He had deep, dark bags lining his eyes and pock marks littering his too-pale face. He looked like a toothpick compared to Mountain Mike, who merely lifted his lip in a sneer. If looks could kill, I'm sure they would have already skewered the sorry excuse for a singer.

The singer wasn't deterred though, despite his bandmates already packing up their equipment. "We had a deal," he insisted, planting his feet wide on the sticky wood floor.

Mike stepped forward, but instead of pushing the singer again, Mike scooped him up under his shoulders and carried him out the front door. The audible slap against the pavement must signal Mountain Mike flinging the man to the curb since a moment later he stomped back empty-handed, his heavy footsteps vibrating through the bar. Everyone averted their gazes as one when he scanned the room, so I did the same, ducking my head to avoid his wrath. I really didn't want to be thrown out like a sack of potatoes just for looking at him wrong.

"Happens all the time," a woman drawled in a bored tone. My head snapped up from the bar top and the bartender gave me a wry smile. I couldn't help but return it, somehow knowing she didn't offer many up.

"I have no clue why, especially with ..." I trailed off, biting my tongue before "Mountain Mike" could roll off my tongue. Probably not the best idea to fill her in on the nickname I'd just given him in my head.

"Drunk idiots never learn." She chuckled, idly wiping the bar with her towel and slinging it over her shoulder. I cleared my throat awkwardly, almost choking on the laugh I stifled at the totally cliched bartender move. "I'm surprised to see someone like you here."

She quirked a brow, not in accusation but in confusion. And I couldn't really blame her, I really wasn't the bar's normal clientele, that was for sure. I pulled myself up straighter and squared my shoulders, needing to exude as much confidence as possible. I'm sure a place like this could chew someone up and spit them out, but I'd dealt with it all before, hell I probably served some of these guys at my parents' diner without their club jackets on.

"I'm looking to see if you have any openings, I have experience as a server and I'm a hard worker," I said, keeping my voice clear of the desperation sinking like a leaden weight in my stomach. She eyed me curiously, scanning me from head to toe as though she could see every fiber of my being with her discerning gaze.

"Okay, I'll go get my manager." She shrugged and turned toward the door Mike had come out of as though she hadn't just been intently examining me head to toe. "It'll be good to have some fresh meat here," she threw over her shoulder while sauntering away.

Swallowing thickly, I wiped my hands on my jeans, attempting to dry the clammy moisture that had gathered from my nerves. I took it as a good sign that she didn't recognize me, that no one seemed to recognize me, yet. Hell, I might even be able to come up with a fake name. I could take a cab here and sneak in and out of the house if Tommaso was out just to make sure there was no way to trace me back here.

Movement drew my attention to the backroom the bartender disappeared into, and I fought the urge to chew on my bottom lip.

Lights glinted off a head of golden hair, styled with a seemingly effortless tossed-back look. My breath caught in my throat, and I instantly wished I could sink into the floor when he turned the corner, his dark-hazel eyes wide with shock as they locked onto mine. I would know those eyes anywhere, could sketch his wide jaw and thick muscles with barely a thought. That was what happened when you knew someone for an eternity, had harbored feelings for someone that now all came back, rushing to the surface as a sob racked my chest.

My greatest dream and my worst nightmare—that was what tonight was turning out to be. My heart both jumped with excitement and panged at the loss. I had craved to see Merrick Ford again with every ounce of my being, but judging by the cutting look he pinned me with, the feeling was definitely not mutual.

CHAPTER SIX

GIANA

SEVEN YEARS AGO ...

"GET IN." MERRICK'S VOICE boomed over the other students' conversations as I descended the school's front stairs. The hum of voices was silenced around me, and I huffed out a breath of exasperation at his brusque tone. Merrick must've skipped his last class again. He drummed his fingers impatiently while leaning against the worn paint of his red Chevy Impala. I strode over to his passenger side door, and was just about to scold him when he cut me off. "Driver's side."

I stared at him incredulously, my mind wrestling with either questioning his sanity or just ignoring him and sliding into the patent red leather seats he'd just refinished.

"You can't be serious." I settled on something in between, still mindful of the students filing out the front doors and the wary glances they were directing his way. Merrick had built a reputation for himself both at school and around town. He'd throw a punch first and ask questions later and was unfairly judged for it. He was one of the sweetest people I'd ever met, but he didn't let anyone else see that side of him.

"I'm dead serious, Gi. Get in the driver's seat, now," he growled, his hand still propped on the hood. I swallowed thickly, my eyes scanning up his lean muscled form. He'd built up his athletic build even more since he got out of juvie a few months ago, and I couldn't help the way my eyes were drawn to his chiseled arms. I bit down on the side of my cheek to dispel the lust for my best friend.

"Are you trying to get someone killed?" I hissed, stepping closer to him, not wanting anyone to overhear us now.

It was almost my seventeenth birthday, and I still hadn't truly learned how to drive. I got my learner's permit at sixteen but rarely had the opportunity to between work and my parents not letting me use their car. He quirked a brow in response, glancing at the students passing by as though he was asking me if I really wanted him to announce I couldn't drive in front of everyone.

"Fine, but let's just go to a parking lot or something." I sighed, my lips jutting out in a pout I knew he wouldn't be able to refuse.

"You're evil," he said resignedly, and I leapt to the passenger seat, unwilling to give him a chance to change his mind. "You're not getting out of this though," he warned, grumbling something unintelligible under his breath as he slammed the door behind him.

"Why did you skip last period?" I asked, changing the subject. I clipped the seatbelt into place, and he pulled out of the lot, heading away from town.

"I had something to do." He flexed his knuckles on the steering wheel, and only then did I notice the redness there.

"What did you do?" I reprimanded, tugging one of his hands off the steering wheel and cradling it between my own to inspect the tender flesh. It was close to being broken open. The idiot would need to ice it soon, but it would most likely still bruise.

"Don't worry about it." He winced as I touched his hand but he didn't move it away.

"You need to stop this, Merrick. You've already had charges against you. What happens if you're picked up next year and you're eighteen? It won't just be a slap on the wrist then," I explained, hoping I could get him to see some reason. I knew he wouldn't tell me what he was really doing, but hopefully he would heed more warning. "I don't know what I'd do if you were sent away again."

I let the admission slip from my lips and glanced away, allowing his hand to drop from mine. My stomach twisted just at the thought of him being locked away again. He was able to get a deal the last time, his assault charges would be wiped from his record, but I'm not sure they would be so lenient again. Not to mention it would only get worse if he was arrested after he turned eighteen. I sucked in a shocked breath when his fingers gripped mine again, holding them tenderly.

"I know, Gi. I'll be careful, I promise," he assured, giving my hand a tight squeeze to draw my attention back to him. Just like he couldn't deny my pout, I couldn't refuse his sweet, caring, and gentle words. So I slipped my fingers between his, gingerly holding his hand in my lap and leaned against his shoulder. The tension that had radiated through my chest eased at the contact, his touch reassuring me that he was here, that he was safe. "Cuddling up to me isn't going to save you from learning to drive though." He chuckled, breaking through my thoughts. I gave his hand a little squeeze and he sucked in a pained gasp.

"Why do I need to learn how to drive all of a sudden?" I groaned, pulling back to look up at him.

"Because it's a good skill to have and it's the perfect day for it; you finally have a day off work and Kellan is busy at the community center," he explained, his chest puffing out a bit in pride at his plan coming together.

"I don't even have a car though," I argued, trying everything I could to get out of this.

He sighed in exasperation and eased on the brakes, the car rolling to a stop just in front of the old firehouse. We came here to hang out in the parking lot a few times over the past year after it was shut down. There was a wide stretch of pavement out front where they used to park the trucks, not to mention the street was pretty much abandoned. Now that the fire station had a new location at the center of town, there really wasn't any need for people to venture this far out.

"Switch places," he instructed, slipping his hand from mine and opening the car door. I groaned in frustration but slipped off my seatbelt. My hand felt cold and bereft at the absence of his strong fingers entwined with mine, and I suppressed the disappointment that washed over me. That was dangerous territory I couldn't dwell on. I guess I'd been putting this off long enough. This wasn't the first time he tried to get me to drive. Sure I did the classes but never bothered to get behind the wheel after that. I figured having that skill might keep me from the city, where I didn't need to drive with all the subway lines. And I desperately clung to that escape, needing it to get through school and dealing with my parents. The promise of a better future was the only thing that drove me to deal with this fucked-up life.

I reached for the door handle, but before my fingers could grasp the chrome lever, Merrick was there. His arms scooped me up and scooted me over to the driver's seat, drawing a shocked gasp from me. He sat in the passenger seat and closed the door then leaned over me—my mind still reeling from the sudden shift—and closed the driver's side door too. He pinned me with a devious look, our faces, our lips mere inches from one another. His warm breath caressed my face, and it took every ounce of willpower I had not to lean forward and place my mouth softly on his.

"No excuses now," he said triumphantly, easing away to sit back in his own seat. I could feel every thump of my heart, every shallow breath as my body was paralyzed with anticipation at his closeness. My heart sank with dismay for just a moment until I reminded myself we were just friends. We couldn't cross that line, it would only complicate our dynamic, along with our future plans for the three of us to all move to New York together.

"Fine," I relented, pulling on my seatbelt as he did the same. I had to get over this irrational fear. Driving wouldn't make me lose my determination to get out of this town. My hands gripped the hard red steering wheel, thankful that this car was automatic. "Teach me."

We spent the next few hours going over basic things like parking and turns—just getting me more comfortable behind the wheel. It would take a few more tries until I'd chance driving on an actual roadway but we made good progress. A warm satisfaction spread through my chest and I turned to face Merrick after putting the car in park, a wide smile stretching across my face. His expression instantly mirrored mine, his eyes fogging over as he studied me. We just stayed like that for a moment until he shook himself out of his daze, his lips pressing into a thin line in annoyance.

"Why are you smiling?" he asked hesitantly. I couldn't help but giggle at the apprehensive look he gave me, as though scared there may be some hidden meaning behind the giddy smile.

"Thank you for forcing me to do this," I admitted, slumping back in my seat as my hands slipped off the wheel. We'd found a spot at the back where the firefighters must've parked their personal vehicles so we would be out of the way in case anyone drove by. It was rare for anyone from town to come out this way, but there were known gangs on the outskirts, and we didn't want to take any chances. Especially now that the sun had set and the stars twinkling in the sky were the only light we had.

"See, it wasn't so bad," he goaded, chuckling at the tongue I stuck out at him, the sound morphing into a groan. His strong fingers slid back through my hair, pushing a few stray strands back from my face. Leaning into the touch, I relished the feel of his calloused fingers against my skin. Their trail sparking like fire, warm and comforting, yet dangerous. The line we toed so often lately was becoming thinner and thinner.

"I have an idea," I exclaimed, easing back to look at him. I needed to put some distance between us or else I might just give in to the tendrils of lust scorching through me. His brow knitted together in confusion, but before he could get a word out, I swung open the door and bolted out of the car, rushing to the firehouse.

"Giana," he hissed, following after me, but I didn't bother waiting for him as I hurriedly searched for an entrance to the boarded-up station. "What are you doing?"

My legs pumped as I searched frantically, knowing if he caught up to me before I made it inside, he would definitely throw me over his shoulder and take me back to the car. But I wanted some fun, and I needed some small form of rebellion. Besides, the fire station was just sitting here, abandoned. No one would notice if we were inside ... hopefully.

My eyes caught on a small window parallel to the pavement, just big enough for me to squeeze through. All of the other windows were boarded up, which would make it difficult but not impossible to get through. I just didn't have enough time to attempt to pry one of the large panels off, especially not with Merrick closing in. I slid to the ground, careful not to scrape my knees too hard against the rough pavement—the last thing I needed was a full day of waiting tables tomorrow with both legs bleating in pain. My fingers gripped the window's edge, dirty from the year of disuse, and pulled but nothing happened. Trying again, I put my entire body weight into it. I hadn't seen a lock, but there could've been one on the inside. All I knew was this was my last shot.

The pane groaned under the pressure, giving way one inch at a time, so I kept pushing until it slid the final inch.

"Giana Bardot, don't you dare—" Merrick growled but his words cut off as I slipped my legs through the opening, followed by my torso, my hands gripping the windowsill; the only thing keeping me from falling since my feet hadn't found any purchase yet. "You're insane."

His hands clasped around my wrists and he attempted to pull me up, apparently thinking I'd just give up now that he caught me. I was so close though. Hell, half of my body was already inside, so I counted to three, gathering my courage before I let my hands slip from the edge. He wasn't ready for my sudden drop, and despite his attempt to catch me, gravity won this round. My sneakers hit the hard pavement sending a jolt of pain up to my knees. Thankfully the drop hadn't been too far, maybe a foot at most.

"Giana," he scolded, his tone incredulous, yet I could hear the note of fear. "Are you okay?"

"I'm fine." I glanced around the room I just dropped into. The stream of moonlight that filtered in through the open window illuminated the outline of sheets, draped over bulky shapes I could only assume were furniture.

"Don't you dare," he grunted, stopping me in my tracks. I was one hundred percent about to wander off and check out the room. I choked on a laugh as I caught sight of him wriggling through the small opening. His muscular form struggled to fit through, and he grunted in pain as his shoulder got caught.

"Are you sure you don't want me to—"

"I'm fine," he snapped back, groaning as he finally squeezed his shoulders through.

"I could've just unlocked the door for you ..." I trailed off, holding back my laughter. Although most of the windows had been boarded up, there was a steel door at the back that was clear. I knew it would've been locked, but I was sure I could've unlocked it from the inside.

"No, you stay right there you little devil," he wheezed and dropped to the floor, his thick shoes reverberating off the concrete ground. I snorted out a laugh at the nickname, which usually only came out when I came up with some sort of reckless idea. My life was boring, and monotonous as it was, I needed a bit of excitement and adventure to make sure I was still alive sometimes.

"I'm not the devil," I pouted, my bottom lip pulling down into the look I knew he couldn't resist. He growled, my face illuminated by the small light streaming in through the window, and scrubbed a hand through his hair.

"You have no idea just how devious you are, little devil," he groaned, wiping off the dirt from his blue jeans and tan T-shirt. I let loose a mischievous giggle, just to punctuate his point, and turned back to the furniture.

"Hold on," he grumbled, his hand clamping down on my shoulder to hold me in place. Instead of letting go, he wrapped his arm around me, tucking me into his side as he brought out his phone from his pocket and used the flashlight to illuminate the expansive space.

"Woah," I exclaimed at just how much was down here. "Why wouldn't they donate all of this?" I asked, wrapping my hand around Merrick's back to pull him along with me. The basement was too dark to chance wandering around on my own ... or at least that's what I told myself.

"Who knows, maybe just in case the Barones went back on their deal," he sneered, and I attempted to change the topic knowing how the subject of the crime family that ruled the town soured his mood.

"This should be our place," I declared, slipping out of his hold to spin around the space, my hands wide to encompass it all.

"What?" He seemed to choke on the word, and he cleared his throat, his cheeks reddening slightly from what I could see in the dim light.

"You, me, and Kellan, this should be our place to get away to forget our families and all the other bullshit," I explained, wandering over to one of the couch-shaped mounds. I pulled off the sheet covering it, sending a cloud of dust billowing up from it to smack me in the face and invade my airway. I sputtered and coughed as I attempted to suck in a breath of clean air and expel the debris.

"Oh," Merrick murmured with a hint of disappointment. I turned back to him, my eyes still watering from the dust explosion, but his face was neutral, not a hint of any emotion there. "I thought you didn't want me to go to jail," he quipped, washing away any thought that he'd been upset.

"No one comes out here," I assured him. The police barely even patrolled the town and were paid to look the other way most of the time. They wouldn't take the time to search around the back of this building just based on their fear of catching one of the gangs in town. Even though they were firmly under the Barones' control, the other gangs paid off the cops to look the other way as well. East Haven PD was a joke, but unfortunately Merrick had hit the wrong person a year ago, which was the only reason he got charged.

"Okay, fine, you convinced me," he grumbled, acting as though it really took that much to sway him. "You really are the little devil on my shoulder."

"If anyone's the devil, it would be you. At least I tell you not to fight people." I shrugged, turning back to face the furniture. My mind was already working to figure out how we would rearrange this. Excitement sparked within me at the prospect of this place being ours, and I let loose a wistful smile.

"No, you're the devil. You're my little devil," he declared, stepping up to my side. His rough finger tipped my chin up to meet his dark-hazel eyes, so warm, so full of devotion. "I'm your demon Gi, and I'd destroy anyone for you."

And I knew he meant it. Despite how comforting that thought was—that he'd always be by my side—it also scared the life out of me. I used to love watching him fight, watching his skill and finely honed muscles dominate his opponent, but I wouldn't be able to live with myself if anything happened to him. I swallowed thickly as memories of that night floated to the surface, but I shoved them back down, not wanting to relive that horror again. Because if he picked a fight with the same person he had before ... I'm not sure they'd let him live long enough to even be sent to jail.

I begged and bargained for him to be spared the last time, and I'd never let him know that. But I'm not sure if it would work again.

CHAPTER SEVEN

GIANA

NOW

HIS LOOK OF SHOCK quickly transformed to one of blinding rage, his jaw grinding as his dark-hazel gaze scanned me up and down. Those eyes I once saw so much care and devotion in now held nothing but contempt and hatred. I sucked in a startled breath as he stomped around the bar, his sights on me, like a bull charging his target. I glanced at the door debating whether I should've just bolted then and there, if I should have attempted to outrun him like that first time at the firehouse.

But I knew I'd never reach the door in these heels before he closed the distance. I stepped back from the bar, wondering whether I could endure his tirade while slowly escaping out the front. But it was too late. I only managed a few steps before he was on me, his large palms wrapping around my biceps, pushing me to the empty corner a few feet away.

“What the fuck are you doing here, Giana?” he seethed, no note of concern in his question. No, just pure vitriol leaking from every word.

I suppressed the flinch, not wanting to give him the satisfaction of the pain he could cause me with just a few scathing words. It would take more than that to crack the mask I’d mastered. I wanted to sob, I wanted to let the tears welling in my eyes stream down my cheeks and mourn the loss of this person who used to be so important to my life. But I couldn’t do that. I refused to give anyone that power, not anymore.

I was about to answer him, but he cut me off, his face blazing red as he dug his fingers in deeper. “Is this some sort of sick joke? Did Tommaso put you up to this?” he hissed. I glanced around nervously but besides a few curious stares it didn’t seem like anyone was really paying attention to us.

“Boss,” the black-haired girl interrupted. I peered around his massive bicep, and she stood just behind him casting a wary look at us.

“Leave, Evelyn,” Merrick ground out, his jaw working as he attempted to suppress his growing frustration. Her eyes flicked to me, asking me a silent question and I nodded. He wouldn’t hurt me, not if he still held a shred of the man I once knew before. Besides, there wouldn’t be much she could do, that anyone in this bar could do, if he tried. “She’s fine,” he snapped incredulously, his glare never leaving my face.

With one final look at me she made her way back to the bar, leaving me alone with one of the men I used to love who now looked at me like I was the devil he always claimed me to be.

He cocked a brow in a silent question, his breaths coming in ragged pants as he barely leashed his anger.

"Merrick," I breathed, my instinct to calm him down, to comfort him taking over.

"Don't you fucking say my name like that," he barked, a pained look twisting his face before he could shove it back down. "Like you still care."

"I was looking for a job, not that it matters anymore," I huffed out on a frustrated sigh, attempting to twist out of his grip, but he only tightened his hold.

"Why would you need a job? Let alone in a place like this. I thought you had some high-paying job in Manhattan the last I checked," he ground out between gritted teeth, his eyes going distant for a moment. My heart skipped a beat at that admission, and he let loose a string of curses, obviously not meaning to let that slip.

"It's complicated," I started, not sure what to even say. There was no way Merrick would give me a job, not with everything he already knew. If it had been a rival gang, at least I could tell them I wanted to get away, and that would be that. But Merrick would need to know why ...

"It's always complicated, Giana," he muttered, shaking his head in disgust. "I was an idiot to think you'd start explaining now."

"Think whatever you want, Merrick, you always did," I jeered in a weak attempt to protect my heart. Right now it was crumbling piece by piece with every glare, every harsh word he flung at me like a whip.

I knew this would happen if I ever saw him again, but still a small piece of me had held on to some ludicrous shred of hope. My chest felt lighter than it had in years when our eyes first locked, my foolish heart believing there was a chance he'd forgive me, that he wouldn't let what had happened between us cloud his judgment. But even then, I couldn't tell him, because I knew what he would do. If I told him why I left, let alone told him why I needed a job, he would kill Tommaso. And despite how much I wished that was the answer, Tommaso was just a small cog in the machine and his father wouldn't stop at retribution until all of us were six feet under.

"What the hell does that mean?" he shot back, giving me a small shake to jolt me from my thoughts.

"It means, I never would've come here if I knew you were here, Merrick," I challenged, needing him to get mad, to hate me, to let me go—just like I needed him to back then. The only difference is now he already did hate me, but his hands were still banded around my arms, not too tightly, but I couldn't get away even if I wanted to.

"Good, because you aren't welcome here. And not just by me—if any of these guys get wind of who you are it won't be pretty," he hissed. I swallowed thickly, wishing I could tell him the truth. The fact that my name was synonymous with Tommaso's, with the Barones', caused bile to rise in my throat.

"So let me go," I demanded, fighting past the sorrow that began to creep in my tone. I didn't want him to, but that didn't matter. I wished he'd draw me into his chest like he used to, his arms both cradling me against him and caging me in, protecting me from anything bad in the world. But that was impossible now, too much had happened between us, too many secrets and lies.

His eyes widened a fraction and he glanced down at his hands as though he'd forgotten he was still touching me. Pausing, he drew in a shuddered breath, like the thought of letting go pained him as much as it did me. I couldn't let myself think like that though. It was better if we both forgot about each other, even though I had a million questions for him poised on the tip of my tongue. Like how he got mixed up with the Demon Riders in the first place? He'd always wanted to work with cars. I never pictured him running a bar for a dangerous motorcycle club. My chest tightened with regret at the dreams we both lost.

But there was a reason for that, just like there was a reason I had to leave ... immediately. If he didn't let go of me right now, pinning me with the same vicious glare as he had before, I might not have the willpower I needed to go back to the cavernous mansion that held as much warmth as the Antarctic.

I gently pulled from his grip, jolting him from whatever was going through his mind. The sorrowful dip of his lips curled into a scowl as though he just remembered everything that happened between us.

"I'd warn you again to stay away, but that's what you're good at, isn't it, leaving?" he snipes, and despite all the armor I'd built up over the years, I flinched at that. His barbed retort stung so much more than I thought it could, draining all my energy. I just wanted to go back to that empty house and crawl into bed, pretending to be asleep when Tommaso got home and begin planning for tomorrow. Although tonight hadn't worked out, it didn't quell the fire burning inside me. I needed to get out of here now more than ever because I wasn't sure I'd be able to handle another run-in with Merrick or worse, Kellan. I could take Merrick's jabs, or at least I could take most of them, but my sweet friend, I'm not sure I could keep the truth from him, not with how he could read me like an opened book. *Was he here too? Did he somehow get mixed up with them right along with Merrick?*

I didn't dare look any farther down the bar, out of fear of seeing his familiar face too. Instead, I strode to the door, not letting Merrick get in another sneer or insult. I'd had enough of being his punching bag for tonight.

"Gi," Merrick called out, the vitriol having left his tone. He sounded like the man I used to know for the first time tonight, the one that used to only show his caring, vulnerable side to me. My steps faltered, now only two feet from the door. I stared at it, indecision swirling around in my mind. I wanted to turn around more than anything right now, I wanted to tell him the truth and have him wrap me in a comforting embrace like he used to and battle my demons for me like he'd always promised. But I have to remind myself for what seemed like the thousandth time what a bad idea that would be. I left for them, went with Tommaso for them. I couldn't bring my problems to his doorstep now, not after everything.

My shoulders shook with a silent sob, but I swallowed it, refusing to let anything show, and closed the distance to the black steel door. I stepped out into the cool night air just as a crash of glassware erupted behind me. The click of the door closing was like a lock snapping closed, shuttering that chapter of my life for good. This is what I wanted, wasn't it? I wanted him to hate me, and it looked like I just got my wish. I let that thought push me forward, giving me the strength to walk to my obnoxious red Porsche, which surprisingly was still there. I nearly tripped stepping onto the gravel parking lot at the force crushing my chest. I rubbed at the ache, needing to make sure there wasn't a gaping hole where my heart was supposed to be.

Pulling in a ragged breath, I blinked the moisture from my eyes in an attempt to focus, but it was too late. A boney hand gripped my shoulder, freezing me in my tracks.

My heart jolted in fear, my pulse racing as adrenaline pumped through my veins. I reached across to my taser, but before I could flip open the clasp, the person spun me around. I stumbled at the sudden motion but his hand on my shoulder steadied me, keeping me pinned in front of him.

"What is a pretty girl like you doing out here?" the man sneered, a cruel tilt to his lips. I blinked away the lingering moisture clouding my vision and recognized him immediately. It was the horrible singer who was tossed from the bar.

The dim lights from the entrance cast his face mostly in shadow, but judging from what I could see, that was a good thing. He pulled me forward, close enough for his breath to wash over me, the putrid stench curling in my nostrils. Bile rose in my throat, and I swallowed it back, knowing puking all over the unhinged man's shirt probably wasn't the best idea if I wanted to get out of here unscathed.

"I'm leaving," I ground out between gritted teeth, stepping back to break his hold, but his hand only tightened on me, his fingers digging into the exposed flesh.

"Not without me you're not." The malicious glint in his eyes made me pause, and I assessed my options as he continued.

"See, I've had a bad night. I didn't get paid for my gig and my band dropped me as their singer because of it. So I'm not going to let a pretty thing like you just slip away now, am I?" His finger curled around a lock of hair and an unbidden hiss escaped my lips. My hand eased toward my purse, but I had to keep him distracted.

"I'm taken unfortunately, maybe you'll have better luck with the next girl." I smiled, hoping he would just accept the brush off, but I knew deep down he wouldn't. Desperation makes people do stupid things. I knew that firsthand after all. My pulse hammered in my ears, moisture pooling in my hands.

"Not tonight you aren't," he chuckled, his other hand reaching up to brush my hair over my shoulder, giving him a clear view of my cleavage. My skin crawled at his leer, and I flipped the clasp open on my bag, my hand slowly reaching inside to grip the taser. But before I could pull it out, a glint of steel caught my eye. But it wasn't pointing toward me, no, the blade was pressed to the garbage singer's throat, a masculine arm clad in a black leather jacket wrapping around him from behind.

I glanced up at the man, needing to assess him to see if he might be an even bigger threat than No Balls here. My breath caught in my throat as I took in the thick halo the light cast atop his nearly white bleached hair. His features were masculine yet softer, almost angelic. But I could tell by the delight in his violet eyes he was far from an angel. More like the handsome predator ready to lull his victim into a false sense of security before he snapped their neck. I could make out the black outline of tattoos along his neck. My fingers itched to explore them, to trace along the smooth skin of his jaw, feeling his plump lips pressed against mine.

"I guess your horrible singing killed a few too many brain cells," the newcomer drawled with a hint of amusement. The metal ball of his tongue ring reflected the muted light as he spoke, distracting me for a moment before my attention was drawn back to the glinting steel at the singer's throat. Garbage singer stiffened, letting loose a pained grunt as the edge of the dagger pressed farther into him, opening a thin slice along his neck. Drops of blood beaded on his skin before sliding down the steel. I couldn't help but be riveted by the sight, my excitement growing with each rivulet that cascaded down. "Did you really think she would be interested in a loser like you who's too stupid to understand the meaning of the word no?"

"Of course not, Spade, I was just asking her for a ride home," the garbage singer stammered, his eyes desperately clinging to me, begging me to back him up.

"Of course she wouldn't be," the man—Spade—continued, completely ignoring the singer's bullshit story. "What happens to people who touch others who aren't theirs?"

He slid the knife closer, and the singer hissed in pain, his body trembling uncontrollably now. Spade's violet eyes sparked with delight at the sound, a deep rumbling laugh vibrating from his chest. The sound was dark and seductive, promising pain and passion. I swallowed thickly, my heart pounding for a completely different reason this time. The laugh must not have had the same effect on the singer, and I leapt back, letting out a groan of derision as I noticed a wet spot growing in the front of his pants.

"I—I don't know," the singer whimpered, biting back a cry as his movement sent the blade slicing even deeper.

"That's the wrong answer," Spade declared in a singsong voice. "Hmm, the question now is, should I kill you?" Spade mused, humming to himself as though the decision to take this man's life was no more important than choosing what to have for dinner.

"Please, please, no. I'll do anything."

"I wasn't finished," Spade scolded, humming as he sliced deeper. "Or should this lovely lady exact your punishment first?" I blinked in surprise as his eyes met mine, mischief dancing in their violet depths. I couldn't help the wave of giddy excitement that washed over me, as though it was contagious. "Something tells me you weren't reaching for lipstick in that purse."

At his prompt, I pulled the taser from my bag, not bothering to ask how he'd seen the movement I attempted to keep concealed. Something told me he saw far more than most did.

"Excellent!" Spade proclaimed. I could almost picture him clapping his hands in excitement if he hadn't been hindered by the blade in his hand.

"I don't know," I said hesitantly, glancing around the parking lot, but there was no one else out here. No witnesses other than the three of us. And something told me people were purposely keeping their distance because of Spade.

"Yes you do," he laughed, brushing off my hesitance. But he was right, I wanted to do this. I wanted to see this man's body convulse in pain, writhing on the ground as helpless as he'd made me feel just moments before.

He took my silence as his answer and kicked out the garbage singer's legs, his knife moving to the side just in time to avoid slicing him farther.

"Please," the singer cried, but neither of us heard his pleading, our eyes locked on each other instead. My breaths came in shallow pants, my body lighting up at his attention.

Intrigue glinted in his eyes as he scanned me from head to toe, my skin heating as he did. When our gazes finally met again, he waggled his eyebrows, glancing down at the sorry excuse for a man shaking so hard his teeth were chattering.

I brought the taser up before me and glanced down at the garbage man. How many men like him had touched me like that, had leered at me and made me feel powerless? I couldn't even keep track of how many there had been. I had to put up with it all my life, as did countless women all over the world. And this was my chance to fight back. Not to defend myself and run, but to take control, dole out his punishment, and revel in the satisfaction of one less predator roaming the streets.

I pressed the button and a spark zapped across the metal prongs. The spark of electricity brought a smile to my lips as I glanced down at the whimpering man before me.

"Help," he pleaded, but no one would come to his aid. I knew that now, not with the anticipation vibrating off Spade right now.

I took a tentative step closer to the garbage singer, his sobs racking his chest now that the knife wasn't against his throat. He slumped farther down as though he could somehow melt into the gravel and slink away from the mess he found himself in. I drowned out his frantic bargaining, my mind already set on the retribution I was about to serve to him—for me, for the countless women he'd done this to before, who weren't able to get away or fight him off, for all those women whose stories were forgotten.

My hand lowered to his neck, the bolts of the taser mere inches away from him, but he jolted away—only to find the cool press of Spades blade there again, pressing in even harder this time.

"You really don't listen, do you?" he tsked. "Stay still or I'll slice your skin off in ribbons right here in the middle of the parking lot."

The singer's spine went ramrod straight at that threat, and Spade huffed out a breath of amusement. Apparently satisfied that he wouldn't put up a fight any longer, Spade drew the blade away again, stepping back for me to take over. I didn't hesitate this time. Pressing the pins directly against his slick skin, I pushed down on the button, watching his body jolt with the first shock. His teeth clacked together as his body shook, my hand compensating for each tremor. A sick keening sound left his lips as I pressed it harder against him and Spade's laughter erupted in the background in response.

A surge of exhilaration lit my body on fire as the singer slumped to the ground, his body still convulsing with each wave of electricity I sent through his unconscious form. I wanted to dance, to sing with the hyper energy lifting me up like an endorphin rush. It took me a moment to fully register he was out cold, the constant shocks weren't having the same effect as they had before, and I backed away, my finger sliding from the trigger and losing that hum that had vibrated through my hand.

"He'll be out for a bit now." He shrugged, his foot swinging back to land a swift blow to the singer's torso. "I'll kill him after you leave, unless you'd like to do it yourself?" He smiled, tilting his head as he examined me.

"I think that was enough for me tonight," I said, chewing on my bottom lip as I looked down at the unconscious man sprawled out on the gravel. I couldn't help picturing how it would've felt to press the knife against his neck as Spade had done. Excitement rushed through me at that thought and I knew I would revel in that power of having the control I lacked for so long. When I glanced back up to meet Spade's violet eyes, a knowing gleam sparked in them, as though he could read every thought that just crossed my mind.

"Is it too early to tell you I love you?" Spade asked curiously as though he was truly contemplating it, completely catching me off guard.

"Well seeing as our only interaction has been you saving me and tasing this piece of shit—" My own foot landed a kick to his abdomen too, not even caring about the pain that radiated through my bones from it. "I'd say it's a bit too early. Maybe tell me after the next man we bring to his knees." I chuckled, tucking the taser back into my purse.

"That's what I was afraid of," he sighed wistfully, a dreamy look crossing over his face. "I'm not sure I can wait that long, especially not when you say things like that."

His head tilted to the side, like he was mulling something over, a thought on the tip of his tongue he wasn't sure he should voice.

"What is it?" I laughed. God, I couldn't remember the last time I laughed this much, the last time my chest felt this light and carefree.

"I would ask you about what you said to Merrick to make him go berserk back there, but I don't want to ruin the moment," Spade admitted, taking a step closer to me. That name brought my head out of the clouds a fraction, but Spade's presence drawing nearer distracted me from the sorrow that begged to sweep in like a wave crashing on the beach, washing away any sandcastles built from joy.

"Ruin the moment? I'm not sure I'd consider this romantic ..." I trailed off, huffing out a breath of amusement. But I couldn't deny the attraction that sparked between us, that mutual understanding like even without words we already knew one another. Swallowing thickly, I pushed that thought down, it wouldn't do me any good to get attached to anyone right now.

"Isn't it?" he asked, his hand reaching out tentatively—giving me enough time to bat it away if I wanted to—and reverently trailed his calloused fingers through my hair, pushing it back to cradle my cheek in his warm palm. I couldn't help but lean into the comforting touch. Something about this man just reeled me in. "What is an angel like you doing in the devil's black heart?" he mused, the question so soft it was as though he voiced the thought aloud unbeknownst to him.

"I'm definitely no angel," I scoffed, my old nickname springing to mind at his mention of the devil's black heart. If he only knew how wrong he was.

Garbage singer groaned beside us, breaking the moment between us. Spade stepped back and we both pinned the man on the ground with an incredulous glare. "I guess I better take out this trash," Spade groaned, but he couldn't rid the eager glint in his eyes. "I'll be seeing you though," he promised, giving me a wink before hauling the singer's limp form up.

"Yeah, I'll see you," I murmured back, knowing there was a good chance that wouldn't happen, not if I planned to get out of this hellhole, which I still did. If I couldn't have either of the men I'd loved what seemed like a lifetime ago, I wanted to have at least that chance to start over. Tonight reminded me of that.

As I strolled to my car, I couldn't help the pang that racked my chest at what I was leaving behind, the loss of an old friend, a love that never got to flourish, and the chance at something new, someone that sparked a new excitement for life in me. I pulled open the car door but before I could climb in, Spade's voice stopped me.

"I *will* be seeing you." The determination that hardened his voice drew my attention back to him, sparking an ember of hope that I could have it all. The singer's limp form was tossed over his shoulder now, and he gave me a wry smile and winked before he turned, sauntering to the back of the building with a spring in his step. I idly realized there wasn't a crest on the back of his jacket like the others, and my lips quirked to the side, my curiosity mounting.

Sliding into my car, I turned the ignition, the purr of the engine rumbling under me. My mind was still with the mysterious Spade, imagining what could've happened if I did see him again as I pulled out of the parking lot.

CHAPTER EIGHT

GIANA

NOW

EACH MILE BACK TO the house felt like another weight slipping back onto my shoulders. My mind was still a rollercoaster of emotions from the bar, and meeting Spade felt as though it was a dream. I bit the corner of my lip, needing that sharp pain to prove this was reality and I hadn't dreamed up the whole thing. Glancing at the clock, I couldn't believe that all happened in one night.

The strength I found from wrestling back that moment of control over my life slipped away with each second that ticked by. I tried to grasp onto that feeling, to clasp it close to my heart to steel myself against dealing with whatever fallout awaited me. Despite the risk I took tonight, I really didn't have much to show for it. Sure, tasing that piece of shit singer had allowed me to reclaim a part of me that had been broken for some time now, beaten down for years of being treated like I was less than a person, controlled like a puppet with threats and violence. I wished I could have gone with Spade and helped him carve into that man ... the thought shocks me from my daze as though a drape had been pulled back, illuminating the dark thoughts. I'd never been one to revel in causing pain, but I couldn't shake how I felt tonight—like I took the first breath of fresh air I had in a very long time.

My run-in with Merrick seemed so long ago now, and the way he spoke my name just before I left still haunted me. His tone had been so much like the old Merrick, the one who was always there for me, who taught me how to ride a bike, how to drive, how to fight, and how to shoot a gun ... The confidence I had just a few minutes ago was whittled down as I pulled up to the house. But I held on to what little power remained, tucking it away like my own little secret.

I pressed the remote as I neared the wrought-iron gates and they rattled open for me. I couldn't help but picture them as gates to a cell, my life with Tommaso suffocating the last of my freedom. Glancing around the driveway, I sighed a breath of relief at the empty spot where he usually parked his car. Hopefully he wouldn't notice the dust clinging to the side of the car before I had a chance to wash it off tomorrow. Although he'd know I left, I wouldn't be able to use the excuse of going out for dinner if he did. All of the restaurants were situated in the downtown area, one of the "safest" places to be according to his family. Hell, even my parents' diner didn't have that much dirt and debris despite the disrepair it had fallen into over the years.

Closing the car door quietly, I walked to the front entrance, my chest tightening with each step I took. Worry clouded my mind despite his car not being in the driveway. *He had other cars in the garage*, I reminded myself. There wouldn't be any room to park in there. But I couldn't seem to shake off the feeling of unease that creeped over me. There didn't seem to be any lights inside the house from first glance, so I eased the front door open, a high-pitched squeal setting my teeth on edge.

Shutting the door softly, I glanced around the dark entrance way, scanning the sitting room and into the kitchen. Only the faint hum of the appliance lights illuminated the kitchen. The tension in my chest eased at that and I turned to the light switch by the door, some of my earlier giddiness resurfacing.

Slipping my phone from my bag, I glanced down to check my messages and stepped into the sitting room. Sophia's name had me pausing.

Sophia: You need to tell me what your plan is, otherwise, I'm coming there myself.

I read it and hurriedly deleted it, not wanting any evidence of our conversation from the car. If Tommaso read that he'd have men at her apartment within the hour. I took another step forward, so engrossed with my phone the crash of glass beside me startled a scream from my lips. The phone dropped from my hands, and I scrambled to the side, putting as much distance between me and whoever made that noise.

I frantically scanned the area again, freezing when my eyes locked on a pair of mahogany ones that haunted my every waking moment and every nightmare. Red splotches dotted his face and neck, and his chest heaved almost uncontrollably.

My breath caught in my throat at the rage rolling off him, the massive room shrinking in on itself as panic clouded my mind.

His fingers gouged into the arms of the chair he sat in, the indentations so deep I wouldn't be surprised if he punctured the fabric somehow. I glanced at the wall needing to see what happened in case there was another threat. Liquid rolled down the wallpaper only inches from where my head had been a few moments earlier, and a crystal tumbler laid in shards scattered across the hardwood floor. The warm scent of whiskey invaded my nostrils and I fought against the wince, knowing this wouldn't be good. Tommaso was bad enough on a regular day if he was upset, but who knew how long he'd been sitting there sipping on his whiskey and preparing for me to walk through that door. Who knew how many ways he came up with to punish me as he'd waited.

"Where have you been?" he growled out between gritted teeth, the sound so animalistic, I almost stumbled back. But I forced my feet to stay planted where they were, even though every fiber of my being begged for me to run.

"I went out for dinner," I hedged, attempting my excuse, but judging by the state he was in, there wasn't any answer I could give that would appease him.

"Dressed like that?" he sneered, his lips curling in disgust as he scanned me.

"This isn't New York, Tommaso. I would look out of place if I wore a designer dress to a local pub," I sighed, still clinging onto some shred of hope I'd convinced him my story was true. I just couldn't back down, I couldn't let him see any glimmer of fear. It was easier after tonight, after having that man convulsing on the ground because of me. I had the power to do that. And if I got the chance, I'd do worse to the Barones.

"You look like a cheap whore," he barked, bolting up from his chair to stalk over to me. My jaw clenched at the insult, but I kept my chin high, refusing to back away regardless of the menacing set of his shoulders or his clenched fists tensed at his side. I could handle anything he threw at me. *This is only temporary*. I would be out of here soon after I found a job—just a few months.

"I'm wearing jeans and a blouse Tommaso." Biting back the retort I wanted to fling at him, I remained as calm as possible. I couldn't let him get me worked up, otherwise we would just keep pushing each other until one of us snapped, like last time. My mind went to the taser tucked into my purse. It would be so easy to slide it out and do the same thing I did to the piece of shit singer. But this—this would have consequences, ones I wasn't ready to deal with yet.

"Your breasts are almost all the way out, Giana," he spat, closing the final few feet between us. I took in just how disheveled he looked before I forced myself to look up at him.

He was usually so put together in a full suit, but his jacket was tossed over the back of his chair, and the long sleeves of his shirt were rolled up to his elbows. His signature red tie was nowhere to be found, his shirt half unbuttoned, and this close it looked like he'd ripped half of the buttons clear off.

"Do you do this just to test me, mi amore? Do you really think I won't slaughter whoever you met?" He pressed his chest against mine, his warm skin burning against my own.

"I d-didn't meet with anyone," I stammered, swallowing thickly. I thought he'd assume I was trying to escape again, not that I was meeting with a man behind his back.

Dread pooled in my gut as I remembered the last time he'd assumed I was with another man. He'd moved from threats to violence after the last time his jealous rage had gripped him when he'd met me at my gym and caught my fitness instructor flirting with me. Before I could even get a word out, Tommaso's men had dragged Ryan into the alley and had swiftly bashed his right leg with a tire iron until an unmistakable crack echoed around us, audible even over the ear-piercing screams they'd tried to muffle with a hand clasped over his lips. I'd been powerless to do anything to stop them, as Tommaso had held me against him, his hand covering my own mouth as he whispered in my ear that it was my fault and they'd kill him if I moved a muscle. It was later that night that he'd lifted his hand but came to his senses just in time with his knuckles poised mere inches from my face. That was what made me plan for my escape, because that would've been the first step down that dark and dangerous road. The abuse would only worsen from there.

His palms ran up my arms and he inhaled deeply, his eyes closing as though touching me helped to calm him. Well as long as my arms were the only thing he wanted to touch that would be fine with me. I may have indulged in the physical aspect with Tommaso before, but after seeing Merrick and meeting Spade, I couldn't stomach being touched intimately by this man despite all the years we'd spent together. His need for me was toxic, it had always been toxic. It was like I was a drug he couldn't refuse and for a while he was mine too. He made himself the only thing in my world and although I never loved him, I couldn't deny there had been passion between us.

"Oh, then you won't mind if I check the GPS on your car, would you?" he asked, a smug smile stretching across his face as his eyes drifted open. The last of my hope came crashing down around me, laying on the floor like the shards from crystal glass he'd thrown. My pulse pounded in my ears, drowning out all the background noise.

"You're really tracking me, Tommaso?" I forced the accusation past my lips, my throat drying as fear twisted my stomach. I had to try everything I could to dissuade him from looking at that GPS. He couldn't know where I went or who worked there, because he'd definitely kill Merrick if he found out, regardless of whether I went there to see him or not.

"Do you blame me?" He trailed his fingers up and down my arms as though attempting to soothe me. But I could still see that mistrust and wrath barely caged in his eyes. "You just tried to leave me less than a week ago."

He stepped back abruptly, and before I even had a chance to say anything, he pulled his phone out and tapped a few times on the touch screen. The blood drained from my face, and I attempted to school my expression, not allowing the sheer panic coursing through me to show.

"Hmm," he hummed absentmindedly, feigning a nonchalance I knew he didn't feel. He scrolled through something, and I pushed down the urge to step behind him and look over his shoulder, suppressing the urge to come up with an explanation until I saw proof. I knew the games he played, and I wouldn't let myself admit anything too soon. "Are you sure you didn't go to see anyone?"

"I already told you I went out for dinner. Stop playing games," I huffed, continuing to feign ignorance.

"I didn't know they served dinner at The Inferno," Tommaso announced as though that information was the smoking gun he'd been looking for.

"I wanted to go somewhere that was out of town, somewhere I wouldn't recognize anyone," I shrugged, raising a brow in challenge. "I unfortunately found out when I got there it was just a bar filled with low lives, so I stopped by a café downtown on my way back." Pretty little lies, that's what they were—something I'd grown accustomed to fabricating. The thought of a tracer had stuck in my head on the drive home so I made sure to do just that, weaving lies together into a beautiful tapestry for him. I could only hope it worked this time too.

"How convenient," he said in a mocking tone, his brow lifting to mimic my own. A game of poker was what this was, he had the winning hand and all I had was my bluff. I just had to hope he didn't call me on it. "So you didn't run into anyone at The Inferno?" he asked seriously, catching me off guard. I shuttered my true emotions and drew my brows together in confusion.

"Of course not. Who on earth would I meet at a place like that," I said with a derisive snort. "Need I remind you I don't have anyone who is even willing to see me anymore," I spat, adding a bit of bite to my words, knowing he wouldn't believe it otherwise. He knew exactly why I didn't have anyone in East Haven—because of him.

"Oh, so you're telling me you didn't know that Merrick Ford owns The Inferno now?" he asked in a condescending tone, any lightheartedness there had vanished the moment he spoke that name. "You just so happened to go to the bar he owns out of any other place you could've gone." Venom leaked from every syllable as he pocketed his phone.

I sucked in a shocked gasp, for once not feigning my surprise. I'd thought that he simply worked there, not that he owned the bar. *What the hell is he doing mixed up with the Demon Riders then?*

"Save the theatrics, Giana," he sneered, pinning me with a look of contempt. "What did I tell you would happen if I found out you were seeing either of them?"

"I honestly had no idea that he owned the bar, Tommaso," I assured him gently, wrapping my fingers around his. I needed to cool the anger simmering just beneath the surface before he did something stupid. "I never would've gone there if I knew that."

"You really expect me to believe that?" he asked in disbelief, but he didn't pull his hands from mine; that was a good thing.

"Yes I do. You know what I've done to protect them, why would I put them in danger now?" He stiffened at my question, and I immediately knew I said the wrong thing.

"Still after all this time?" he spat incredulously, ripping his hands from mine. "After everything I've given you, the life I've tried to build for us. Is it still not enough?" My eyes widened but I bit back what I truly wanted to say. He knew this wasn't what I wanted, but he couldn't hear that right now. He might do something brash and stupid just to get back at me.

"Is it not enough that I'm here?" The question slipped out before I could clamp my mouth shut. We were in dangerous territory now. He was still holding the airport over my head.

"Are you really?" he barked out a sardonic laugh. "Because last I checked you tried to leave last week."

"We should wait till tomorrow to talk about this, Tommaso," I sighed, attempting to walk past him.

"Don't you dare walk away from me," he snarled. His arm wrapped around the front of my shoulders, catching me and shoving me back.

My heels twisted and I scrambled to keep myself upright but I couldn't find any purchase on the tiled floor. I flew back and my body smacked against the hard stone. A cry slipped past my lips as agony radiated along my spine, my muscles spasming as they absorbed the impact.

"Look what you made me do!" he roared, stomping toward me. His hands clasped my biceps, and I flinched away from him, a sob racking my chest as the sudden movement sent another jolt of pain through me.

Ignoring my fear, he reached for me again, easily plucking me up from the floor this time. Tucking me against his chest, he carried me up the winding staircase, each step causing a jolt of pain. He turned to our bedroom and settled me gently onto the bed, much to my surprise. I bit back the wail I wanted to let loose and composed myself the best I could. Even the slight jostling sent shooting pain up my spine and stars sparked in my vision.

"That's nothing compared to what could have happened to you tonight," Tommaso grumbled, settling on the bed beside me. He eased the shoulder bag from where it had twisted around my torso and pulled my sore feet into his lap before easing my heels off. A hiss of pain escaped, and I winced as my ankle twisted, silently hoping it hadn't been sprained. To my surprise he massaged my tight calves through my pants in an attempt to soothe me. My muscles were still pulled taut, still on edge around him. "You can't go back there again, Giana," he breathed, some of his anger simmering.

I kept my mouth shut though, rather than continuing. There wasn't any point. He was still too worked up, and even on a normal day there was no discussing anything with him. His word was the law I had to abide by ... for now.

"They could've killed you tonight," he continues, unwilling to put this conversation to rest. "And if I ever catch you near either one of them again, I won't hesitate, Giana. Do you understand?"

I swung my legs over the side of the bed, gritting my teeth against the pain as I pulled myself up. Taking an uneasy step forward, I pulled in all of my strength. *I can get through this,* I chanted to myself. *Just get to the other room and you can let it all out there.*

"Where do you think you're going?" he demanded, shooting up after me.

"I'm done with this conversation for tonight, I'll sleep in another room. I just can't deal with this right now," I groaned, taking another step away from him. Every inch sent an agonizing jolt radiating through my muscles, but I worked past it, the need to get some space away from him mounting with every word that came out of his mouth.

"Don't walk away from me," he snapped, rushing in front of me in a blur.

Before I could even register what was happening, something barreled down on me, slamming into my cheekbone just below my eye. The force of the impact knocked me back, my feet slipping out from under me again. A scream pierces my ears, ringing out for a few moments before it finally registers that the noise was coming from me. He hit me, not like earlier, he actually struck me—backhanded me in the face.

Tommaso caught me before I crashed to the floor, scooping me up and flinging me unceremoniously onto the bed. My hands immediately flew up to cradle my face in shock, the tender skin already swelling. He stepped forward and I flinched back automatically this time.

"You think that was bad?" he asked incredulously, looking down at me in disgust. And at that very moment I vowed never again. I didn't care if I had to live on the street. Two weeks was all I had to get out of here. I wouldn't let this sorry piece of garbage put his hands on me a second time. The throbbing in my face and the stabbing pain in my back wrestled for control, the agony melding together into something nearly unbearable. "That was nothing compared to what the Demon Riders would've done to you if they found out who you were." He shook his head, looking down at me in a mix of revulsion and pity. "Get some sleep," he instructed, walking off toward the closet to get changed.

So I laid back and closed my eyes, and in place of the nightmares that usually haunted me I pictured the singer convulsing on the ground, my taser firmly placed against his neck. A tremor ran through his body with each shock that vibrated the weapon in my hand. But instead of the singer's mottled face, I imagined Tommaso was the one writhing in pain, and despite the agony still stabbing through my body, I drifted off to sleep with a faint smile on my lips.

CHAPTER NINE

GIANA

SIX YEARS AGO ...

I FLOPPED BACK ONTO the brown leather couch and relaxed back into the thick cushions, thankful for the reprieve. After a long day at school and a seven-hour shift at the diner, I seriously could've passed out right here. But I fought off the wave of exhaustion that washed over me as I finally took a moment to relax today. This was one of the only times we all had to spend together. The rest of the weekend we would all be at work, saving up for our big escape. It would all be worth it in a couple of months—we just had to get through it.

I wished we had more time to enjoy the last summer before adulthood, but in reality, we were already there, dealing with adult problems while still being treated like kids. But at least during the summer we wouldn't have school on top of our already full schedules. Luckily, I already got my acceptance to

NYU, including a full scholarship and financial aid. I just had to keep my grades up, but I crammed most of my courses into the beginning of the school year so I could have more time to work now and less pressure with homework. My dorm room was being paid for by school but we all wanted to split a place. We'd been inseparable throughout our childhoods, and there was no way we would go to the big city and be separated.

"Have you thought about coming to work with me at the community center?" Kellan asked, settling down on the other side of me. I couldn't help the grin that spread across my lips just at his proximity. He'd been over the moon when we showed him the place, excited to finally have a place to call ours. He'd even pulled all the boards off the back windows in his excitement, to give us some extra light, and a heads-up if anyone was coming. Even though we cleaned up the firehouse over a year ago and organized the furniture into our own little hangout, the guys usually both crowded around me on the one couch. They claimed it was because it was the most comfortable, but I wasn't so sure.

"No, she's going to work with me at the shop," Merrick offered, squeezing in on my other side. I groaned in frustration and scrubbed a hand over my face. It had been like this ever since I told them I wanted to get a second job for the summer. My parents promised they would keep me on evening shifts for July and August, meaning I could get a second job during the day.

Sure it would suck, but I had to take some money with me. Kellan had a paid internship lined up at a tattoo shop in Queens, and Merrick would be doing an apprenticeship in an automotive shop. He probably knew more than anyone else already, but our society cared more about if there was a certificate or diploma hanging from your wall than actual knowledge. But they both had jobs to help pay for the rent, and I had no idea what my workload would be yet. They assured me they could take care of it, but I couldn't do that to them. We found a place, and it was affordable—or more affordable than most places there—but I didn't want them to take care of me, not with the cost of living already so high there.

"I haven't decided yet." I chuckled. "Maybe I'll have to find something else if you two keep arguing about it."

"Us, arguing? No, I don't think that was us, you must be mistaken." Kellan gasped, clutching a hand to his chest as though my words physically wounded him. "Besides, Merrick, do you really want her to work with you at the shop? You realize she wouldn't just be working with you, right ...?" Kellan trailed off giving Merrick a pointed look.

Merrick's brows furrowed for a moment as he thought it over, and his lips pursed a moment later, the look of confusion transforming into a glower. "You're right," he grumbled, his look turning apologetic as he glanced at me. "Sorry little devil, you'll have to work with Kellan."

"Again, who said I was working with either of you?" I reminded them, pinning them each with a glare. "And why exactly can't I work at the shop?"

"Don't worry about it." Kellan chuckled, wrapping his arm around my shoulder and pulling me into his side. I huffed out a breath of annoyance but allowed him to pull me over. Nestling into his warmth, I closed my eyes and relaxed into him. Merrick grumbled something unintelligible from my other side and my lips tipped up into a grin. Reaching out, I slid my hand onto his leg in a reassuring gesture.

Kellan wrapped his other hand around the back of my head and placed a tender kiss on my forehead, his lips lingering there a few seconds longer than could be considered friendly. We were tiptoeing that invisible line more and more often lately. My thoughts were constantly consumed by thoughts of both of them ... and not in an only friends kind of way. But I could never act on it, just like I knew neither of them would. I wouldn't want to screw up the dynamic of our friendship. Besides, I could never choose between the two of them. My feelings were deepening each day, and I knew it was a dangerous path I was exploring, but I couldn't help it. I'd tried to distract myself by looking at other guys at school, but none of them could compare, none of them lit the same fire in my soul as Kellan or Merrick.

I sometimes caught the furtive glances they cast my way, the looks of longing for something more. But none of us ever said anything, we all locked our feelings down, refusing to let them bubble up to the surface. Was it healthy? Probably not, but I wouldn't say anything to either of them out of fear that I'd imagined it all, that they only thought of me as a friend and nothing more.

I hummed in contentment as Kellan rested his cheek atop my head and Merrick pulled my hand between his, warming the chilled skin between his large palms. I had no idea what would happen between us all in New York, but I couldn't give this up, I couldn't let go of either of these men.

"So what's the plan for my birthday?" I asked curiously. The thought had been rolling around in my mind for the past week since they brought it up. My birthday was two weeks away, and graduation was the week after that. Thankfully it fell right after exams, so we'd all be able to let loose to celebrate my eighteenth birthday.

"You left it up to us to plan, so it's a surprise," Merrick teased, squeezing my hand between his.

"That's not fair. Can you at least give me a hint?" I pouted, glancing up at Kellan. Between the two of them he would give in the easiest. His lips twitched with amusement, but his smile fell as I held his gaze.

"Don't do it man," Merrick warned, Kellan's gaze breaking with mine to look past me at Merrick. "Don't give into the devil." I dug my nails into his palm. He let out a hiss of pain but only squeezed my hand tighter in response rather than pushing me away.

"Don't listen to him, Kellan. Tell the devil all your secrets," I purred, lifting a brow in what I hoped was a seductive look. If the way his throat bobbed was any indication, I was almost sure I hit the nail on the head.

"She really is the devil, isn't she?" Kellan murmured, his eyes flicking from me to Merrick and back again.

"I told you, bro, she's pure evil. She could get you to sell your soul just by batting those long lashes," Merrick groaned, tugging my hand with him as he leaned back against the couch.

"Ha-ha, very funny guys," I said dryly, nestling back into Kellan's side and resigning myself to not prying any information from them.

A buzzing sounded beside me, and I reluctantly looked over, leaving my little cocoon of warmth to glimpse my phone which must've fell out of my pocket. I groaned in frustration, not wanting to move or pull my hand from Merrick's to check the message.

"Can you check my phone please?" I pouted at Merrick, batting my lashes just for fun.

"Don't give me that face," he growled, lifting his head up from where it had lolled back over the headrest. "See, not even two seconds later and you already have me doing your evil bidding."

Kellan's chest vibrated as he chuckled in amusement, but I refused rise to their prodding ... not until after he checked my phone. Then I would pin them both with a disapproving glare.

"Fine," Merrick groaned, sliding his hand from mine while the finger of his other hand took its spot to make up for the loss. With a satisfied grin, I leaned back against Kellan taking comfort in the rising and falling of his chest with each breath, assuming the text was probably a reminder from my parents about my shift tomorrow. I was friends with a few people at school but I wasn't really close to anyone besides my two guys. Honestly, there wasn't much time for anyone else, especially this year. I only spoke to most of them in classes or during lunch.

"Ouch." I jolted up from Kellan's chest as Merrick's hand squeezed mine uncomfortably. His grip relaxed slightly at my protest, but when I tried to pull away, he pulled it farther into his lap, turning me to face him fully.

My brows creased in confusion as my eyes locked with his dark-hazel ones, narrowing on mine in an incredulous glare.

Redness crept up his neck as he clenched my phone in his other hand. I glanced from it and back to my hand, confounded by his sudden change.

"I'm gonna fucking kill him, Gi," Merrick growled, his hand shaking beneath mine, his rage cresting.

"What's going on?" Kellan asked from behind me, his tone just as bewildered as I felt.

"Ask her," Merrick ground out, and despite his anger he kept his hand entwined with mine, no longer putting too much pressure.

"I have no idea what's going on," I admitted, giving him an imploring look. "Please Merrick, just tell us what happened, who are you going to kill?"

"You know full well who I'm going to kill," he huffed, passing the phone to me. My head tilted as I grasped it, the phone lighting up at the motion, and that's when I saw it.

My lips turned down into a scowl as I read the message.

Tommaso: So mi amore, when are we ever going to go on that date you promised?

I swallowed thickly and let the phone drop to the couch, the message and its sender meaning nothing to me in this moment or any one after. Judging from the sharp intake of breath behind me, Kellan must have read it too.

"You're not going to kill him, Merrick," I groaned, scrubbing a hand over my face in exasperation. I hadn't even given Tommaso my number, but I wasn't surprised he'd found it somehow. I didn't even want to know how he'd managed to save his contact without me knowing ... With his connections I wasn't sure there was anything he couldn't get if he really wanted it.

"Yes, I am," Merrick huffed, a look of determination crossing over him. "If he lays a finger on you, I won't hesitate."

And I knew he wouldn't. He tried the last time Tommaso hit on me at school, but that had been two years ago. Thankfully he hadn't had another chance since he was in juvie when Tommaso graduated, and their paths hadn't crossed since.

"You won't," I cautioned with a note of steel as I snatched my hand back from him. "Do you remember what happened the last time?"

"Of course I do," Merrick growled, his chest actually puffing out with pride. I clenched my hands into fists, my teeth clacking together with the effort it took not to lash out at him for that. "I beat his ass into the ground for coming near you, and he didn't even have the balls to go after me."

"No Merrick, you went to jail—remember that? You were lucky that was the only thing that happened," I seethed at him, actually sneering at the infuriating asshole. We danced around this subject for two years now. I begged him to stay away from the Barones, but whenever their name came up it was like he couldn't help himself. He had no clue what he was talking about. But the truth was, if he really knew what his actions caused that day, he'd never forgive himself, or worse he'd actually go after Tommaso Barone, the second most dangerous man in the state if not the entire East Coast. The only person more deadly than him was his father, and that was only because he was the leader of their family crime ring.

"Let's all just calm down," Kellan soothed, attempting to put an end to the argument that had been brewing for some time now.

"No," Merrick and I both barked at the same time, and I leapt from the couch and began pacing back and forth in front of it. The air had become too thick, stifling while wedged between them. I pulled in a deep breath and continued to dispel the nervous energy rushing through me.

He had no idea what I had to do to keep him safe. What I would always do to keep either of them from any danger. Thankfully it wasn't as bad as it could've been. He could've asked me anything at that moment and I would've given it to him. I had to promise Tommaso I would give him a chance—go on one date with him when I turned eighteen. I'd honestly thought he'd forgotten about it since he graduated shortly after the deal, but apparently not. But that was a small price to pay for Merrick's life, and I'd gladly take that deal over and over again if it meant he could live.

"Do you actually like him?" Merrick's tone was softer but no less deadly than before, like the rage was barely caged beneath the surface.

"No, of course I don't like him," I ground out, the relaxing mood from earlier completely lost, the night now grating on my last nerve.

"You could've fooled me," Merrick scoffed, crossing his arms over his wide chest like a petulant child. My jaw ticked at the fury I was holding back. I wanted to scream, I wanted to tell him everything that happened after he was carted away in the police car that day. How I had to get on my knees and beg Tommaso not to have him killed while he was in there. I had to beg for his life because Tommaso could've taken everything from me that day.

How could I ever have feelings for someone who would make me do that, who would threaten someone I loved like that. Was there a tiny bit of attraction? Yes, of course, he was good looking and the dark life he lived always sent a jolt of excitement through me, but that wasn't what I wanted. I wanted these two idiots in front of me who still refused to admit why they both were so pissed over this. Because although Kellan hadn't erupted like Merrick had, I could still see the hurt and disappointment creasing his eyes.

"And what if I did?" I blurted, the need to push them rising inside. "What would you do if I liked anyone?" We played these games, toed the line between friends and more for so long now. They both had to see how I interacted with both of them. At some point we either needed to admit our feelings and figure it out or I had to move on. Regardless of not wanting our friendships to change, if we continued this way it would eat at us bit by bit until there was nothing left anyway. I couldn't live my whole life not having a romantic connection to anyone because I was waiting to see if any of us would gain the courage to say something.

Both Merrick and Kellan prowled closer to me, their movements measured and deadly. Kellan was exuding that dark side he kept tucked away more often than not. I'd seen it a few times, when he helped Merrick in a fight or got ready for those jobs they sometimes did for the gangs on the outskirts of town.

They closed in on me, Kellan at my front and Merrick at my back, caging me in between them. The air grew thick again and my breaths came in ragged pants with their bodies pressed up against me. My anger died as soon as they touched me, my body melting for them. I wanted their lips on me, their hands exploring my every curve.

"Do you want him?" Kellan asked, his voice dark, yet there was a slight tremor in it, the only hint that our proximity had some effect on him as well.

"No," I breathed, the word slipping from my lips before I even had a chance to think. I inhaled a shuddering gasp, my hands tensing at my sides as I held myself back. This was very dangerous territory, and despite my urge to push them, I wasn't sure I was ready.

And as if I had voiced my thoughts aloud, they both stepped away from me at once, sending a cold rush of air to the place where their bodies used to be. They both walked casually back to the couch, flopping back down like nothing had happened at all. The only sign was a wry smirk on their lips as they shared a look, otherwise I might've thought I imagined it all.

Fucking men.

CHAPTER TEN

GIANA

NOW

A THROBBING PRESSURE POUNDED in the side of my face, drawing me from my slumber, and had my eyes flashing open as panic set in. My hand flew to my face and cold fear pressed in on me as I attempted to put the pieces together. Had he done something to me while I slept? I tenderly touched the swollen skin just below my left eye as the events from last night rushed back to me.

He hit me. He backhanded me for ... walking away from him, for not wanting to argue anymore. I winced as I sat up, my back twinging at the movement. I completely forgot about the fall too. Too much happened last night, and it took a moment for the fog of sleep to lift completely. So many ups and downs happened, along with my worst fear. I didn't want to be this person, trapped in a loveless, toxic, and abusive relationship

… and if he got his way it would be marriage. I shuddered at the thought and a sharp pain sliced up my spine. *Okay, note to self—don't move.*

I groaned as I laid back down, contemplating whether I wanted to venture downstairs for some ice, or just stay in bed, when the door creaked open. I hurriedly glanced around me, only then realizing Tommaso hadn't been in the room. My hands fisted as anger boiled in my veins, my fingers itching to wrap around his throat and watch the life fade from his eyes. That would be justice, the eyes that haunted me in both life and nightmares fading before me. The beginning of my dreams flashed through my mind where I pictured Tommaso's face in place of the singer's, his body twitching in agony on the gravel. Oh Tommaso would hate that, the humiliation of rolling around, piss stain on display, helpless in the gravel on top of the pain would be perfection.

I let that thought strengthen me as he pushed the bedroom door open. Sucking in a breath, I pinned him with a glare and prepared myself for whatever he could throw at me. Who knew what sort of mood he would be in? I didn't want to be his punching bag for the next couple of weeks, but I couldn't bear cowering to him, not now. My stomach clenched at the sight of him, and I pushed down the urge to launch myself across the room at him. The glare slipped from my face when I caught sight of the tray he carried in with him as he pushed the door closed with his back. My brows creased in confusion at the turn of events. I knew he'd been drunk last night, but I hadn't expected such a complete switch this morning.

Head hanging as he approached, he was unable to even look me in the face as he propped the tray above my lap. My eyes flicked from him to the tray, taking in the breakfast he had brought for me. Fresh fruit sat in a bowl next to a plate of various pastries, along with a plate of sausage and eggs. A glass of orange juice and a mug of coffee accompanied them, along with two ice bags. My stomach soured at the spread, suppressing the urge to toss it across the room. I really didn't need another bruise on the other eye, not if I was going to go out searching for a job again anytime soon.

The bed dipped beside me, and I reluctantly turned my attention to him. Somehow I was able to keep my fingers from gouging the fake remorse from his face.

"I'm so sorry, mi amore," he pleaded, his brow creasing as he gently took my hand in his, cradling it as though he actually cared. I swallowed the snort that begged to leave my throat and clamped my lips shut. "I just needed you to understand how dangerous it was to do what you did. This isn't like New York; everyone here knows you, knows that you're mine, and will use you just to get back at me."

I sat completely still, schooling my face from my innermost thoughts. My brows itched to knit together at his explanation, unsure how hitting me could possibly convey all that.

"I couldn't live with myself if anything happened to you, Giana." My hand twitched in his, and he squeezed it in response, interpreting that as a gesture of understanding rather than me attempting to hold myself back from clawing his eyes out. "I know it will take time for you to forgive me, but I promise I will never hurt you again."

I hoped he choked—choked on his lies, on his promises I knew he wouldn't keep, on a dick—I really couldn't care less what it was, but I wanted to see that light leave his eyes more than anything.

He didn't wait for me to say anything, apparently assuming correctly that I had nothing to say. Instead, he reached under my arms and helped me sit up, the muscles in my back groaning in protest with each inch. He continued, gently propping me up with pillows and placing the ice pack behind me.

"Anything you need, mi amore, I'll get it for you—you don't have to worry about a thing," he assured. I couldn't do anything more than nod, because if I opened my mouth I wasn't sure what would have come out. Who did he think he was fooling after six years? I knew this wasn't him, I knew there was something else going on other than his feeble attempt to turn back the clock to before he struck me. "You just focus on icing that eye today. Because we do have that party tomorrow and you know how my father is." And there it was, it was all about optics, of course. He couldn't have me going to his parents' house, or wherever the hell we were going now, hobbling around with a black eye. He was right though, I knew how his father was, and that wouldn't be an excuse not to show up, especially after how many times his own mother showed up to functions with bruises peeking out from beneath her dresses and worn-down makeup.

I didn't even bother asking about the party, last I heard it was just supposed to be a family dinner. But of course, the Barones didn't do anything halfway. They'd welcome their son back with a huge party and announce our wedding date while they were at it. And why wouldn't they, it's not like I would need to know anything like that.

I just hoped it wasn't in the next two weeks while I put my plan in place, because there was no way in hell I would ever chain myself to a man like him.

One of us would be dead by the time the church bells rang.

HE KEPT TRUE TO his word, letting me stay in bed while I rotated the ice on and off my back and cheek, and by the end of the day, I was actually able to walk somewhat normally and the swelling had gone down in my face.

Once the pain had subsided in my back, we switched to a heating pad to help relax the spasming muscles. Luckily the damage hadn't been too bad so there weren't really any bruises. My face, on the other hand, was another story. Despite icing it off and on throughout the day, it really only helped the swelling, and my cheek was still a purple mottled mess. Thankfully he didn't hit too close to my eye so the impact hadn't affected it, but there was no way I could leave the house without layers of makeup on, which I'd have to apply carefully since pain still bloomed there every time I touched it or made a facial expression ... So needless to say, I still hadn't really spoken to him since yesterday, other than one-word answers to his questions.

I pulled myself up in the bed as the door cracked open and Tommaso carried in a tray of breakfast for the second morning in a row. I had no doubt in my mind that after today his apologetic behavior would end, and he'd switch back over to attempting to suffocate and lock me away.

"Breakfast, mi amore," he announced, a faint smile on his lips as he placed the tray above my lap with the same spread from yesterday. I knew he hadn't made it for me, we had a chef come in to make our meals for the day, but there was no way he'd allow her to bring it up to me. No, because then she'd be a witness. "It's looking a lot better today," he announced, but I could tell from the crease between his brows he was just saying that to make himself feel better.

I picked up a croissant, breaking a piece off and placing it on my tongue, letting the buttery taste coat my mouth. It also helped that now that I was eating, he couldn't expect me to talk to him. I just wondered how long I'd be able to keep him at arm's length. Probably just long enough for the bruise to heal, for the evidence of his abuse to fade from my face, then the guilt-tripping for my "behavior" would start up again.

"I have everything ready for you. Your dress and jewelry are all laid out so all you need to worry about today is resting and icing that eye," he announced in a chipper tone, smiling as though he had already forgotten he was the cause of the bruise adorning my cheek.

I hadn't asked yesterday but he explained on his own that his parents had thought it was best to throw us an official engagement party tonight rather than a simple dinner, just like I expected. So rather than the Barone mansion, they rented out the massive hall in town, and unfortunately, most of the town would be in attendance tonight, including my parents.

If I hadn't wanted to go to the party before, that information alone made me want to argue I wasn't going. But there was no way that was going to happen, especially not now that tonight was supposed to be an engagement party for the two of us. My chances of getting out of the dinner would've been slim to none, but the embarrassment of me not showing up with the whole town watching, wouldn't be tolerated.

"I have to go set up for tonight, but don't worry, I made an excuse for you so you have more time to relax." I fisted my hands in the sheets to keep them from throttling him. "I love you," he murmured, looking down on me tenderly. He placed a soft kiss on the top of my head and bile rose in my throat at the show of affection, souring the taste of croissant that was still in my mouth. *I swear I could kill him just for ruining that for me, fuck everything else. Pastry is life.*

He looked at me expectantly, and I swallowed the scream of frustration that bubbled up. The fucking nerve—he thought I would say I loved him after everything? So I just gave him a tight-lipped smile and pointed to my lips pretending to still chew the piece of croissant I'd already swallowed, along with a halfhearted wave. His brow lowered into a glower for a brief moment until his eyes locked onto the bruise he'd given me.

"I'll see you tonight ... don't be late," he added, turning and straightening his suit before striding from the room.

I sat there in silence for a few more moments, breaking off pieces of my croissant as I waited for him to leave, the telltale squeak of the front door signaling his departure. I took a deep breath, finally able to breathe without his suffocating presence looming over me for the first time since I walked through that door the other night.

I knew what I needed to do now, and it wasn't sleeping or icing my cheek—well maybe a little ice wouldn't hurt. But I had to get back out there, knocking on every door I could until I found a job. One thing I knew for certain was I wouldn't be going back to The Inferno.

I PULLED UP TO the main street and glanced down the road at the various shops and restaurants lined there. Most looked the same as they'd been six years before, but I'd need to make sure the owners were the same before taking any risks. There were a few businesses that, while they still begrudgingly dealt with the Barones, they weren't pleased with it. With Greg and Pam being in the business community, we heard whispers of different shop owners wanting to take a stand. So I'd have to gauge them to make sure they were still resistant. I couldn't let anyone know too much, just in case they went to the Barones. This was dangerous and something I'd wanted to avoid. At least with The Inferno I knew they weren't allied with the crime family but to be in town you had to abide by their rules, so everyone here was reliant on them in some way.

I put the red Porsche in park at the end of the street, deciding to leave it here. With Tommaso able to track my movements it would look too suspicious to keep starting and stopping the car at multiple places. It also wouldn't look great to show up in an obnoxious red Porsche and beg for a job ...

There was a small ice cream shop that was first on my list. The owner was an older woman, Francine, who used to chase Barone's men off with a broom after they collected their cut. If there was some idiot around town harassing someone, she was the first to run them out and was always there with candy and a friendly ear if you had a rough day. That was one of the main reasons her shop was so busy year-round. People went there for her first and the ice cream second, but admittedly the treats were delicious too.

I caught a glimpse of myself in the rearview mirror and frowned at my reflection. I put on foundation and concealer but didn't go too heavy, I would save that pile of makeup for the party later. A faint shadow was still visible under the thick layers, proving just how much I would have to cake on tonight to hide it from the guests. For now I would slip on a pair of oversized sunglasses that covered up the spot nicely when I positioned them part way down my nose. I'd be in even more trouble if I didn't cover it up tonight, but this afternoon was a different story. Let the town see the too-big sunglasses, see the faint shadows as I frantically made sure they stayed in place. It might just be the only thing that got me a job around here.

I stared at my reflection for a few moments longer, taking in just how exhausted my amber eyes were. Besides the bruise, I had bags under my eyes from the tossing and turning, never getting a good night's sleep. *A few more weeks,* I reminded myself, letting that bolster my willpower. One step at a time. If I thought about everything I needed to do right now it would overwhelm me. If I started to plan now, I might leave some sort of trail, and I'm not sure my heart could survive another disaster like the airport.

I smoothed out the few stray strands of my sleek ponytail and slipped on the sunglasses, pulling on my game face as I stepped out of the car. Straightening my pink blouse and black dress pants, I gently closed the convertible's door, not wanting to call too much attention to myself. I'd go see Francine first, but even that could go either way. Her hatred for Tommaso's family ran deep, but the question was whether or not she considered me part of that now too. She might just chase me out with the broom too.

I strode over to the small ice cream shop. With it nearing summer there were more people out and about on a Friday afternoon, enjoying their treats and the local shops. My low-heeled open-toe sandals clicked on the pavement as I passed a few other shops including a stationery store and the bank. I knew neither of those was an option. Even though I was more than qualified to work as a teller, they were very public and squarely under Barone's thumb. His men went in there daily to make deposits and would notice me in a second. And the stationery store ... well, everyone knew that was owned by Luann, who was married to one of Barone's higher-ups, so that was a definite no.

I paused before the ice cream shop and glanced in the window, checking to see if there were any customers. Thankfully it was still the second to last week of school so the children would still be there about now. I had no doubt in my mind the place would be packed with families in just a couple of hours as they went out for dinner and a walk. Taking a deep breath I gathered my strength, preparing for the worse, while still holding on to the sliver of hope for the best.

The bell chimed as I pushed open the door to the retro ice cream parlor. Unlike Greg's, the shop was curated to have a nostalgic feel while not looking run down. A large wooden bar ran along the front with freezers on the side. Red stools lined the bar and wooden tables sat in front of the windows.

Francine glanced up from her book by the register and did a double-take, taking her glasses off and putting them back on as though she couldn't believe her eyes. She recognized me despite the large black frames covering most of my face, even after all these years. She was most likely in her seventies now, lines creasing her wise face, and her back arched from the years of scooping ice cream from the deep freezer.

"Well now, I wasn't sure if I'd see you in here," Francine said, crossing her arms over her chest as she examined me, her expression unreadable. "At least you didn't bring that man in here with you," she sniped, and my chest tightened at the dig. I'd always gotten along with Francine; she was a key fixture of my childhood.

But her frostiness would make sense since she was important to Merrick and Kellan too. The three of us used to come in here with the spare change we collected around the house as children, but she never charged and seemed to always know we needed a place to just be ourselves, to be kids without all the extra pressure at home.

"I—" The word froze on my tongue, my mind searching for something to say, something to explain my actions without putting her in danger, but I came up blank. What could I say when the whole town thought I'd fallen into bed with the enemy, for no reason other than attraction, greed, lust, power? I couldn't do this—face the people from my past and have them judge me based on their assumptions when my cheek still throbbed from Tommaso's blow. I took a step back, about to reach for the door, but she stopped me.

"Oh come on now Giana, come over here and give an old woman a hug." She stepped out from behind the counter and motioned me with her arms already spread wide. I hesitated for a moment, unable to remember when the last time was that I truly hugged someone. Most likely Sophia, but it wasn't the same as someone who had an almost maternal role in your life. "I'm not getting any younger," she griped, glaring at me impatiently.

With that, I closed the few feet between us and stooped down to embrace her. She wasn't a tall lady, maybe five-foot-two at best, so she had to reach up even with me ducking low since I had about eight inches on her. I breathed in and inhaled her familiar scent, coated in the sweets she was surrounded with each day. Her weathered hands rubbed my back in a soothing motion, and I fought back the sob that racked my chest. I couldn't cry, not here, not now.

"So something tells me you came in here for more than a hug." She stepped back, assessing me as her hand rubbed my arm in a comforting gesture. "And I'm assuming it has something to do with the family you have yourself messed up with."

"I—I came to see if you'd give me a job," I breathed, deciding to cut straight to the chase. I couldn't endanger her by telling her anything that had gone on, especially not if she was willing to let me work for her. "I could stock stuff in the back for you, stay out of the way."

Her hand stilled on my arm and her head tilted to the side in confusion before her eyes snagged on the too-large glasses. I could see the moment everything clicked as her eyes hardened. Her boney fingers gripped my arm roughly and she pulled me along into the backroom, taking care to shut the door behind us.

"How long," she demanded, cold fury in her voice as she let go of my arm.

"I—" I paused. "I can't exactly tell you everything, I don't want to put that burden on you, but I could really use a job right about now." I sighed, my hand shaking slightly as I pulled the glasses from my face, revealing my halfhearted attempt to cover the bruise on my cheek. It wasn't fear I felt in that moment, but rather shame that burned through me—shame I hadn't tried to get out sooner, that I'd let him catch me off guard like that, that I couldn't be the woman I knew I had the power to be just yet.

"Giana," she gasped, her hands trembling as she reached up on her toes to graze the mottled mark that bloomed on my cheek. "Do they know?" she asked thickly, pulling her hand back reluctantly.

"No, and they can't know." I shook my head, dreading the thought of either Merrick or Kellan seeing me like this. I'm not sure I would be able to stomach their reaction, whether it was pity or satisfaction that I'd reaped the consequences of being with a man like Tommaso. If they were still the men I knew, still held a spark of the feeling they'd held for me back then like I saw in Merrick the other night, I knew it wouldn't end well for anyone.

Francine chewed at the corner of her lip, the indecision twisting clearly on her face as she wrestled with the information. My heart dropped into my stomach at her hesitation. My legs itched to turn back now, to get out of this shop and run, to get in the car regardless of the GPS tracker and drive as fast and as far as I could before ditching it.

Her sigh rang out, so deep with exhaustion as she scrubbed a hand over her face. "I'll trust you for now, but they might be able to help, more than you think—"

"No," I cut her off, not wanting to hear the rest of her sentence. I left for a reason, put myself through this for a reason, and I wouldn't let it be for nothing. I wouldn't let them get themselves killed.

"I wish I could help you, Giana, I really do," she groaned, and fear slithered its way up my spine. Sure this was only the first place I tried today, but out of everyone, Francine would have been the most likely to help me. No one else stood up to the Barone family or his men more than Francine, so if she was unwilling to help me, I doubted anyone else would. "My kids were grown before, but well, my youngest ended up in prison recently—got too much of his mama's spunk I guess." She chuckled sadly, her hands twisting nervously in front of her. "And now I'm the sole guardian of his boy, my grandson. So this place is all I have and I can't risk him getting mixed up in all of this. His safety is my first priority."

I nodded in understanding, forcing a small smile onto my lips, but before I could say thank you for her time, she cut me off.

"Wait—" She held up a weathered finger and hurried to the back of the storeroom. That gesture alone reminded me of just how old she was, and she was the sole provider for her grandson now. My throat dried as guilt twisted inside me, already reaching back for the brass doorknob of the storeroom, ready to sneak out, when she rushed back toward me. I never should've come here, especially now knowing her situation. "I might not be able to have you work for me, but I can still give you something." Reaching forward she snatched my hand, pressing a bundle of paper into my palm. Her other hand curled around mine, forcing me to grip the wad tightly before jumping back, as though she already expected my protests and was getting out of the way before I could force her to take it back. My mouth parted in shock for a moment both at her movements, which were much sprier than I'd thought they'd be, and at the gesture itself.

"I can't—"

"Yes you can," she barked, taking another step back from me as though she was scared I would tackle her just to give it back. "It might not be much, but just in case you can't find anything else." She paused, her eyes drawing back to my cheek as though on reflex. "You need to get out."

I slipped the sunglasses on, grateful for her concern, but the constant reminder made bile rise in my throat as the memories from that night slammed back into me. I nodded at her statement—not a question but more like a demand.

"Put that in your pocket, before you lose it, and no more hugs. I don't want you getting sneaky. I'm not broke so don't you dare try anything," she scolded, and I shoved the bills into my pocket at her command. "Come back again ... before you leave?" she asked, and I too was unsure if I truly should. If I came back here too close to when I left that would leave a target right on Francine's doorstep, putting both her and her grandson in danger.

"I will, and thank you, Francine. You really didn't have to do that." I tried my best to smile past the sorrow at never seeing this kind soul again and past the foul taste that lie left on my lips. Because I couldn't come here again, I couldn't put them in danger, just like I couldn't do that to my guys. It would be different if she still wanted to take a stand against the Barone family, but her grandson came first. "I'll find some way to get you the money back one day."

"I don't have a clue what you're talking about, dear." She grinned, giving me a wink. "And don't give up, there may just be some people along this street that have had enough and are willing to take a stand."

My brows knitted in confusion, but I nodded, opening the storeroom door and striding back out to the shop floor. She followed me out, taking her place back behind the register as I paused at the front door, my hand hovering just over the handle.

"Goodbye, Francine," I said, glancing with a sad smile on my lips. Grateful for what she's done for me but also sad this would be the last time I saw her or this place again. When I left for New York, I always knew that there would be a chance to come back, at least to visit, but once I left, there would be no turning back this time.

"Goodbye, Giana," she sighed with a wistful smile, a wry tilt to her lips that made me pause for only a moment until an approaching family just outside the window caught my attention. So I slipped out the ice cream parlor door, holding it open for them as a boy and girl excitedly ran in, rushing past their parents and over to Francine. As the door swung closed, I just caught her smiling down on them, the joy clear in her light-brown eyes as she handed them each a small candy.

I glanced down the street, my mind still on Francine as I made my plan for where to try next.

I SPENT THE NEXT few hours going into stores to gauge their reactions, and for the most part ... people were terrified. Their reactions caught me off guard—the same people I grew up with, went to high school with, were trembling as they greeted me, handing me free things, and rushing me out the door. No one sneered in my direction, nothing to make it clear they despised the Barones, or even took a second look at my glasses.

After what Francine said about the business owners, I figured at least one of them would've shown enough disdain to allow me to trust them, but not a single one did. I had a latte in one hand, a bouquet of flowers in the other, and bags of food and baked goods hanging off the crook of my elbow.

Each time I stepped into a shop or a restaurant, I held my breath, with one last shred of hope flickering inside me that I might be able to trust this next person, but it was all the same thing. I pursed my lips as I exited the decor shop with Teresa, the owner, ushering me out while promising to send over a package to the house with a beautiful set of aqua glass bowls I'd pretended to look at while I waited for her to finish up with another customer. The bell chimed behind me as she swung the door closed, apparently not bothering to wait for the automatic weight to close itself.

I had half a mind to stomp back to Francine and ask her why exactly she'd been so sure I'd find someone to help me, so giddy when I left. Glancing down to the end of the street, there was only one more storefront to go to, and I couldn't make out the name from where I stood. I took a step in that direction, not wanting to stand in front of Teresa's shop any longer in case she came back out to shoo me away or offered to send me throw pillows. But my steps faltered as I glanced at my watch. It was already four in the afternoon; I'd have to head back to the house soon to reapply a pound of makeup under my eye. Was it really worth it just to be disappointed again?

I pulled in a deep breath, steeling myself for more of the same, but I couldn't leave, not with what Francine had said still ringing through my mind. What if this last shop was who she'd been talking about? Could I really just walk away without trying?

With the last of my strength, I strode toward the last storefront, my mind barely managing to remember what had been here before. The outside looked different than it once had when it was a salon, the crisp white paint around the trim now black. I turned around the corner to where the front entrance was and glanced up at the large sign that read "Tattoo" in bold lettering. My lips thinned into a line at that; what sort of help could I offer here, perhaps cleaning up the stations or helping with bookings? I couldn't really sit out front, not with the location and the two walls lined with windows that showed off every square inch of the small storefront. Judging by what I could see there was only one station, the black patent leather bed looked as though it had been freshly cleaned, the ink and gun arranged meticulously.

Frowning, I considered my options again, but this might be the only chance I had. I could use the money Francine gave me to book a bus ticket, but I wanted to leave that as a last resort. At least some of the tension had eased from my chest with that lifeline in my back pocket.

I threw the now empty coffee cup into the garbage can at the corner and pulled open the glass door. The name of the shop was plastered to the front door, but I barely caught it, my nerves ratcheting up too high to focus on it—Something About Ink, which would make sense for a tattoo parlor.

I stepped into the store and took in the dark interior. The walls were a deep violet with black velvet armchairs stationed by the door as a waiting area. Tattoo designs were hung on the walls, some as samples while others were framed as decor. The front desk sat empty, a computer and phone sitting at the corner, along with what looked like a booking calendar.

"Be right there," a masculine voice called from the partially open curtain leading to the back, his voice muffled as though he was attempting to speak around the food in his mouth.

"Take your time," I called back distractedly, something on the desk catching my attention. A small photo sat framed on the desk almost tucked away, out of sight. I placed the bouquet of yellow tulips on the counter and sat the bags on the floor before grasping the edge of the silver frame. My fingers smoothed down the edge, my sunglasses slipping down my nose a fraction, needing an unobstructed view of the photo. It was a pencil sketch, the detail exquisite, every strand of hair placed perfectly, the smile stretched from ear to ear, a look of hope, of joy on her face, so full of life. A sob racked my chest and moisture flooded my eyes, my hand lifting to stifle the sound. I blinked furiously against the tears now blurring my vision, unable to look away from that drawing, from the girl who used to be so carefree and so full of love, from the masterful artwork that sent memories of that night racing through my mind.

"Giana," Kellan breathed from behind me, my name not a question—it was more like a prayer, like something he never thought would touch his lips again. I couldn't hold back the next sob as the frame slipped from my hand, clattering back onto the counter. Cracks spiderwebbed through the thick glass, mirroring the ones spreading through my heart.

CHAPTER ELEVEN

GIANA

SIX YEARS AGO ...

"IT FEELS SO WEIRD to be here in the middle of the day," I admitted as Kellan unlocked the steel door to the firehouse. With the help of some of Merrick's underground friends, we were able to get a key made for the back door, which was much more convenient than slipping in through the narrow window. Although I was able to slide through easily, both of the guys ended up getting stuck every so often. Despite having the entire station to ourselves, we still chose to stick to the basement area, our little home away from home. The rest of the place was eerie, the space so open with all the furniture underground, plus it helped in the summer heat with no air conditioning where the upstairs was stifling compared to our cool cavernous den.

"Yeah, I really hope no one notices us here." Kellan frowned, looking back at the abandoned parking lot as though someone was about to pop up out of the bushes.

"We'll be fine," I chuckled, placing my hand over his, still poised on the door handle to pull it open. We both paused at the light touch. We so often held hands without even thinking about it, but lately—with my feelings drifting further and further away from being friends—there was an electricity that sparked between us, something that promised more. Heat flooded my body as I glanced up to find his sable eyes already on me. They were so warm, so full of love, of joy, I couldn't help the way my heart fluttered at his attention.

My other hand itched to trail along his jaw, to grip the back of his neck and bring his deliciously lickable lips down onto mine. Would he take control of the kiss, searing his mouth to mine, or would it be soft and gentle, so full of care and love? Or would he push me away ...? Would he tell me he didn't feel the same and our friendship would be completely ruined?

With that dark turn of thought, I cleared my throat, letting my hand slip away from his to fall back limply at my side. I already missed the warm feeling of skin against mine, but I pushed that thought aside and stepped back as he pulled the door open the rest of the way, not willing to meet his eyes again just yet out of fear of what I would see there.

Because even if he felt the same, there was still Merrick, my bullheaded, stubborn, hotheaded friend, who lit the same flames of desire within me. I pushed those thoughts from my mind and stepped into the firehouse. Muted sunlight streamed in through the window highlighting all the dust drifting through the air up here. I tried not to look too closely at it and opened the door leading to the lower level, descending the stairs as fast as I could.

That was another reason why we stayed in our own little cave, the entire house was way too huge to clean. It took us long enough to dust and sweep downstairs, besides it would look way too suspicious if any of us tried to take a vacuum from any of our parents' houses to clean all the worn carpet upstairs.

I rushed over to my favorite couch, leaping backward onto it with a big "Oomph," when my side bag flopped down onto my lap. Kellan laughed softly as he closed the door behind him, leisurely walking down the stairs and settling onto the couch across from me. I couldn't help but childishly stick my tongue out at him, giddy excitement bubbling up now that we were truly in our cave. "I can't believe I actually got out of work early," I mused, pulling my textbook from my bag along with a notebook. Exams were next week, so I needed to get a few more hours of studying done before then. Greg and Pam usually didn't care, but this time they surprisingly let me off work early. So eager to get here, I was still clad in my work clothes, a pair of yoga pants and a simple white T-shirt, my hair pulled up into a messy bun to keep it out of my face.

"Yeah, I seriously can't believe it either. Greg and Pam must actually care about your education." Kellan laughed, pulling his sketchpad and pencils from his bag. Kellan's art class he taught at the community center was canceled for today since the administrator was off sick.

"I seriously doubt that," I groaned, flipping open my textbook to the page I left off on. "They probably just want to make sure they don't have to deal with me for another year if I fail a class."

"I'm sure they'd love for you to stay," he huffed out, the pages of his books flipping as he found a spare page. "It would mean they could keep having someone else do all the work for them."

"Mmhmm," I hummed in agreement as I scanned the pages of my marketing textbook for important passages to write in my study notes. This was the one class this semester I really had to focus on with my reduced course load. It also was what I planned to major in at NYU. Searching for a major had been one of the easiest decisions I made. Ever since I was sixteen, I knew I wanted to get into business. Not because I was passionate about it—sure I found it interesting, but in this world money was power. People spent their whole lives in search of making more, and after seeing what happened to this town, to Greg, Pam, and all the other business owners, I knew I never wanted to be in their position. The world was set up so the rich got richer off the hard work of the working class. So I wanted a degree I could use to keep me out of this small-town life. Sure we were all answering to someone, but I would find a way to break free somehow.

"What are they going to do anyway without you there?" Kellan asked, his pencil scratching idly at the paper.

"You know them, they wouldn't hire someone else," I huffed out on a frustrated sigh, not wanting to think about it. They'd been laying the guilt on thick over the past few months, but I really couldn't care less after everything they'd done. They wouldn't hire anyone else because no one else would put up with how they treated them ... or half their tips being stolen. But in a town like this, there weren't many job opportunities.

"Well even if they did, no one could compare to you," Kellan said, the compliment so out of the blue I couldn't help the giggle that slipped from my lips as I glanced up at him.

An electronic snap went off just as my eyes met his, and Kellan smiled at his phone screen, the soft glow illuminating his face. Soft beams of light streamed through the small basement windows but they didn't allow for much to filter in.

"What was that?" I asked hesitantly, my hand smoothing along my cheeks to check if I had something stuck there. That would've definitely been embarrassing since I hadn't eaten for a while. I was about to scold him for not telling me sooner, but I froze when I didn't feel anything there.

"Look." He laughed, picking up his sketchbook and supplies to carry over and sitting beside me on the couch. He tilted the screen in my direction, and there was a picture of me on it. Not of my look of confusion, but just a second before. A goofy grin stretched across my lips, my amber eyes so full of amusement, full of adoration for the cheesy compliment he said just to brighten my day. Because that's what Kellan did, he always made sure I had a smile on my face, and kept my head from spiraling to that deep dark place inside of myself. He was like the sunshine, undeterred from the dust and buildup on the windows, shining brightly through despite it all. Just like the ray of sunlight that brightened my face in the photo, his comment had the exact same effect.

"I look gross, my hair is still up, I barely have any makeup on," I murmured, chewing on my bottom lip. I glanced toward those windows, my self-conscious thoughts bubbling up inside me.

Society constantly made women feel as though they had to have a full face of makeup and their hair perfectly done to be viewed as beautiful. I could see it though—what he saw in that photo to make me beautiful—but my brain was so focused on my imperfections that they seemed to overshadow the rest of me entirely. So despite his picture proving otherwise, it still made me feel uncomfortable to have that piece of myself saved forever in his phone.

His finger curled beneath my chin, gently turning me to meet his sable gaze. His eyes were tinged with concern as they met mine, frowning as he scanned over my face.

"You don't actually believe that, do you?" he questioned, his head titling in confusion as though he was attempting to reconcile his image of me with my own.

"Yes," I whispered. "I worked most of the morning, I'm sure I have coffee stains on my shirt, and ketchup in my hair, plus my face is all shiny," I explained, fighting the urge to turn away from him again. It was too much to list out everything I saw wrong with myself while his face was so close to mine, his perfect jawline, plump lips, and soft eyes watching me as though he could see every single inch of me with just a look.

His finger slipped away from my chin, and I almost made a sound of protest at the loss, despite it feeling too real and raw for him to be so close. He brought the phone up for me to see again, the screen still on the photo of me.

"Do you want to know what I saw?" he asked calmly, and I nodded slightly. My stomach was tied in knots as guilt ran through me. I didn't say it to make him pay me compliments, but I could see with his hard look that he needed to say this ... and I probably needed to hear it. "Even though we were talking about Greg and Pam, I couldn't get over how perfectly the beam of sunlight looked swathed across your face. It highlighted every single one of your beautiful features. But there was something missing ..." he trailed off.

I put up a shield around my heart, in case he was about to say attraction, but I'm not sure anything would protect my heart from that blow.

"Your smile." He laughed. I instantly relaxed, sighing a breath of relief. "Your happiness makes you glow from the inside out, matching the sunlight already bathing your skin. You are the most gorgeous, exquisite person, both inside and out. I don't care about the makeup and neither would any real man. You look beautiful with or without it, because it's your inner light that makes you shine so bright, Giana." I took a deep breath, blinking away the moisture pooling in my eyes. Kellan always knew the right thing to say, like he could read every thought that crossed my mind, keeping me in the light. "It's how you feel about yourself that makes you beautiful, this smile is the most breathtaking thing I've ever seen in my life," he murmured, his thumb trailing along my bottom lip now lifted in a grin I couldn't help from spreading across my face.

I leaned into his touch and his palm cradled my cheek tenderly. The touch that was soft and caring turned heated with each swipe of his thumb against my lip. Shivers of ecstasy went up my spine, our faces too close to each other. The touch was so teasing it made me crave the press of his lips against mine.

"I need to sketch you," he murmured, as though it was partly to himself, and reluctantly eased away from me, his own lips quivering as his hand slid from my face. I swallowed the protest that begged to slip out, my mouth desperate to taste him, my hands itching to run over his soft skin. But I didn't, both out of fear and admiration for the spark of passion that lit up his eyes as he opened his sketchbook, his pencil already poised between his fingers. I could see what he saw in me as I watched him. Despite how handsome and perfect I already thought he was, as the inspiration hit him—joy brightening his face as he got lost in something he loved—I understood just how much that added to his appeal, to my attraction for him.

I took a deep breath, needing some air to cool the fire blazing within me. I wanted to rip the sketch pad from his hand and let him trace his hands along my bare skin rather than sketch my photo onto the page, regardless of how incredible an artist he was and how stunning I knew it would turn out.

"I'm going to give it to you for your birthday, so you can always be reminded of how I see you," he announced excitedly, but his lips pursed as he realized the thought slipped out. "That was meant to be a surprise." His mouth quirked to the side in disappointment.

"Then I won't look, not until you're ready to give it to me," I assured, stretching my arm out to rest across his broad shoulders. "It will still be a surprise then."

"You're perfect," he whispered on a wistful sigh, immediately engrossed with his sketch again. His hand moved over the page, skillfully starting right where he left off. Keeping my hand on his shoulder, I pulled my book closer, not wanting to lose his comforting heat so soon when his words still rang in my ears.

I'm not sure how much longer he'd think that for though as I'm reminded of my eighteenth birthday drawing closer every day. It was now officially one week away, and my stomach clenched at the thought. Ever since I got that text from Tommaso, the day I thought would be full of fun and excitement, casting off the chains from my parents as we prepared for our big move, now filled me with dread. My chest tightened just thinking about the texts he'd been sending me recently. My plans to move to New York seemed to be crumbling by the minute, with each inch Tommaso kept demanding while holding the lives of my friends over my head. And I just prayed he had an ounce of decency left in him not to take too much. Because if push came to shove, I would give into anything he demanded if it kept Kellan and Merrick safe.

CHAPTER TWELVE

KELLAN

NOW

"TAKE YOUR TIME," a feminine voice sounded from the front of the shop, and I paused with my sandwich poised just before my lips. I had back-to-back appointments all day, and this was the first time I had a chance to grab a bite to eat so I'd had a mouth full of the delicious bread when the door swung open, a fresh gust of the summer breeze following in after them.

But that voice, I would recognize it anywhere. I still heard it in my dreams, pictured her sweet amber eyes gazing back at me every morning just before my eyelids fluttered open. But she was never there, the other side of the bed still cold, the sheets missing her lilac scent. My fingers itched to push her long dirty-blonde hair from her face, letting me see her perfect cheekbones and luscious lips, an artist's dream honestly. But when those lips curved into the most delicious scintillating smile, that was when the work of art became a masterpiece.

My breath caught in my throat and my pulse became a rapid fluttering in my neck. *Would she look the same as she had six years ago? Would the inner light be shining through as a result of her new life or had that monster broken my little devil, fallen from heaven?* I placed the sandwich back down, the thought of eating now turning my stomach. I wanted nothing more than to draw back that curtain to sweep her into my arms like I had so many times before. But six years of distance stretched between us...

So I stood from the small workbench and gripped the side of the black curtain, each second stretching on like an eternity. I craved to see her again but so much had happened. She left with him of all people, and everything we'd worked for came crashing down around us in one day—one day she was there in my arms, fulfilling my greatest dreams, lighting my soul up like she always had, and the next she was gone.

I drew in a deep breath, steeling myself for the next moment when I would finally come face to face with the woman who crushed my heart. I slid the drape open, the afternoon sunlight beaming in through the wide-open windows, drenching the woman that stood at my counter in the bright light. My eyes scanned over every inch of her, drinking in the sight as though I'd been starved. Her dirty-blonde hair was pulled back into a sleek ponytail, not a strand out of place, and her cheeks looked gaunter than they had before. Hands clenched at my sides, and my mind raced to fill in conclusions of how this could have happened. Had he made her not eat as much, or was the stress of that life eating her away from the inside?

I pushed that thought from my mind, not wanting to get ahead of myself. I had no idea if she was even unhappy but my heart screamed that it was the truth. Because despite her being swathed in the sunlight as she had been in the picture she was now holding clutched in her palm, that sparkle she had once had, was gone, snuffed out for one reason or another.

Her full lips pulled down into a sad nostalgic smile, the too-large sunglasses masking her face, hiding away her true feelings from me. My hands itched to take them from her face so my eyes could trace every inch of her, unhindered. When I had looked into her eyes before, it was as though I could read every thought like pages of a book. I wondered if it would be the same now. If I even could after all this time. But I knew I would because even though she'd been gone, she never truly left my heart. She was with me every day, haunting me with the goodbye I never got and all the words left unsaid. Like a ghost she was there one minute and gone the next, her presence never leaving my side, even when her physical form had fled.

Her hand flew to her mouth, attempting to hold back the sob that escaped her lips, but I still heard it. My mind scrambled with everything I thought I knew, everything I assumed battling for supremacy. I began to reach out to her, needing to wrap tightly around her to comfort her and soothe the pain and sorrow that twisted her lips. Her sunglasses slipped down her nose slightly, giving me the briefest glimpse of her eyes, moisture flooding them as she blinked back the tears.

"Giana," I breathed, my arms dropping to my side, and I internally scolded myself for how close it sounded to a prayer that had just been answered. Especially when the picture slipped from her fingers, cracks running along the glass like a reflection of the ones that had been there ever since she left, festering like an old wound refusing to heal. Her face blanched as though she'd been so consumed by the drawing, her mind hadn't fully pieced together that this was my shop, that it was me behind the curtain. Her lips parted in shock as she stared back at me, and she hurriedly pushed her glasses back up, covering what little glimpse I had at her amber eyes behind them.

She squared her shoulders as though the tension vibrating there now pulled them taut. I had to keep her here, keep her talking because right now it looked like she was about to bolt any second. But what was I supposed to say, after all this time, after how she left, and who she left with? The blow she dealt to my heart was still gaping. What could I say to keep her here? What could dull the ache still pulsing in my chest?

"Are you here for a tattoo finally?" I asked, attempting to keep my tone casual but even I recognized the note of panic that rang there. I wanted to slap my palm over my face at that comment and retreat to my backroom, but my momentary embarrassment fled at the snort of laughter that erupted from her. I smiled as I pushed the pain from my mind and focused on the here and now. Because she was standing right in front of me—she may be a ghost of herself, but maybe if I could get her to stay ...

"Kellan," she breathed, some of the tension easing from her shoulders. The sound of my name on her lips made me want to pull her into my chest like no time had passed. *But it has,* I reminded myself. Her lips quirked to the side as though she too was debating if she should approach me, nestling her head against my chest as she'd always done.

"Can I interest you in one of our pre-made designs or do you have something in mind?" I continued. I had to keep it light, not get too into the topics my heart really wanted to dredge up. I had no doubt in my mind if I did, she would bolt, and I couldn't risk that, not when she was so close. So I swallowed all the questions and all the accusations and walked to the other side of the counter, pulling out the large black binder filled with my designs I had for customers to choose from or get inspiration from.

"I—" She paused, her mouth opening and closing as though she was attempting to figure out what to say. *Just play along*, I silently begged her, my face falling slightly at the thought that she might run. So I continued getting out the samples, like I would if she were a client. Last night Merrick told me what happened, how she walked through that door ... and how he smashed up half the bar because of it. My chest had burned after hearing that, wishing I'd been there to see her ...

I couldn't let her go, not now, and I couldn't afford to slip back into the deep dark well of despair, not when we finally had our chance to get her back. "I'd love to see them," she whispered, as though she was fighting herself too—her instinct to run warring with her need to stay, for the illusion of normalcy between us.

Turning the binder to face her, I flipped open the cover, my heart hammering against my chest at every second that passed between us. I knew that at any moment she could walk out that door and there wouldn't be anything I could do to stop her. I wanted to lock her away, to throw her over my shoulder and take her back to my place so she would be out of *his* clutches. But I knew I couldn't. That would make me just as much of a monster as Tommaso Barone.

Her hand reached out hesitantly to turn the pages, and my breath caught at the slight tremor as it shook lightly. The tension was palpable between us, but it was as though neither of us could let go. Like this could have been something that actually happened if she hadn't left or if we all went to New York together like we'd planned. Tingles ran over my skin as she turned the first page, both excitement and anxiety churning within me at the thought of her seeing my artwork. The first few pages were simplistic designs, but after those I had samples of my other work, of the personal pieces I'd sketched out and had etched into my skin. I both wanted her to see them and dreaded her getting that far. They were like snippets of my life, of my heartbreak with her gone, and I knew she would understand as soon as she saw them. It was as though letting her see them was like putting my heart right back on that table, barely beating, and holding on by a thin thread that stitched it together, waiting for her to either heal it or smash it to pieces again.

I tugged at the long sleeve plaid shirt I wore over the black T-shirt that covered up most of the designs inlaid into my skin, my very soul, and wondered if she would notice the one peeking out over the shirt's hem right above my heart ...

Silence stretched between us, becoming so charged, I had to hold back all the words poised on my tongue. She pushed the glasses on her nose again, her hand shaking lightly as she held it there. Only a few more minutes, I told myself, glancing at the clock on the wall. Merrick was supposed to meet me here any minute to discuss our plans.

I nearly killed that stubborn asshole last night when he said he'd let our girl walk out that door, destroying the bar in a fit of rage rather than chasing after her, but I understood why. She was too closely connected to the Barones and in a bar filled with bikers who loathed them, it might have turned into a bloodbath if they found out who she was ... and we still needed them.

I understood there wasn't much of anything we could've done to keep her there, just like I knew there wasn't anything I could do now. But it still didn't stop me from hating him for being the one to see her, to have her fall straight into his lap and then he let her go. But now with her standing in front of me, paging through the binder of my art, I wasn't sure how I would handle it if she left right now. Because despite the fact we were in my shop, I had no doubt that someone could be watching us. Maybe not even one of Tommaso's men, but it could be anyone in the town that was loyal to them. There were still some that believed the Barones were the good guys they pretended to be, that they kept the town safe from the thieves and thugs that hovered just on the border of town, waiting for an opportunity to pounce. But there weren't any gangs like that anymore, not for the past four years, and the Barones had absolutely nothing to do with that.

I glanced nervously at the glass door, the only sound the turning of the plastic page covers as she skimmed the book. Hopefully Merrick would have a better idea today now that his anger had waned because my head was an absolute mess right now.

A pang sliced through my chest when I noticed where she'd stopped—the first tattoo I'd designed after she left, the one I had tattooed over my heart to remind myself of the woman who was so ingrained there, so entwined in my body, mind, and soul her imprint would stay there forever. It was the same sketch that was held in the frame which laid to the side still shattered, but I'd taken some artistic liberties—the side of her face that had been bathed in light was surrounded with tiny lilacs, and my nostrils flared, that same scent flooding my senses now. The other side, that was shrouded in darkness, had flames dancing around it as though she controlled them, resting close but not enough to burn. Over the top of her head was a halo, casting down the light onto the one side, along with two small devil horns, barely peeking out through the wisps of hair along her crown.

The angel and the devil that dwelled inside her were equally beautiful. Her innocence and carefree, wild streak mixed to create my Giana—perfect in every way. It also held a deeper meaning of the emotions running through me at the thought of her just after she left. I couldn't let go of how I felt for her and how much love I had—still had—for her in my heart, and that made me hate myself. I despised that I still cared for her even though she threw us away and everything we could have had together. She was both what lit me up and tore me down in that moment.

But six years passed—six years where I was left analyzing everything that happened leading up to that moment. My eighteen-year-old-self wanted to hate her, to believe that she'd lied to us, and strung us along all those years when her real plan had been to leave with Tommaso the whole time. I'd let anger cloud my judgment and sour what I knew of the woman I loved. For two years I tried to forget her, had focused on my art, and turned to anything I could to help drown out her voice, her scent from my memories. Until one day, when I got the courage to pull out that drawing I'd made in seemingly another lifetime and designed that tattoo sitting between us. I truly let myself remember everything, who she was as a person and how she'd acted leading up to graduation—and pieces began to click together. I couldn't be sure, not without seeing her, what her motivation had truly been, but in that moment, as I filled in the final details of those eyes, that she was my devil and she was always up to something.

But perhaps that was a good thing, that both Merrick and I were so full of rage we believed the web of lies that had been spun for us. Because if we'd had any shred of clarity in that moment we would've gone after her, killed every person in our way, and probably gotten us all killed in the process. Merrick had always been skeptical, but I'd known in that moment I couldn't let her go, not then and not ever. We weren't eighteen anymore, and we could fight back.

Her hand trembled on the page, our faces lifting to look back at each other at the very same moment. The silence was too heavy, too charged with everything that happened between us. This close I could see the faintest hint of her eyes behind the framed lenses. My breathing became heavy as we both stared at each other, our breaths, our hearts coming together as one. I had to see those eyes, read the emotions that she was keeping locked away, knowing I'd be able to read every thought that was crossing her mind with a single look. My hand reached out as though it had a mind of its own, inches away from easing away those black frames from her face.

My heart leapt in my chest, and I jerked my hand back as the door swung open violently, the warm summer breeze sweeping through the sleek strands of her ponytail as we both turned to see who was there.

Merrick stood in the doorway, his towering form taking up almost the entire opening, his legs spread as though he was blocking it—blocking her from running, I realized.

"What are you doing here?" he growled, his lips curling into a sneer as his dark-hazel eyes trained on Giana in a menacing glare. The moment we had was now shattered around us like the broken shards of our hearts, the cold hard weight of reality settling in its wake and sucking every particle of air from the room.

This was it, the moment of truth.

CHAPTER THIRTEEN

GIANA

NOW

I SCANNED THE DRAWING taking in every single detail, the way the shading signified the light that had shone down on me that day, and the halo casting that light. My attention snagged on the two small devil horns that peaked out, almost unnoticeable through the wisps of hair from my messy bun. He captured the two sides of myself perfectly, the dark and the light, not separate but mixed and melded with each other.

I could be upset by the personification of myself as the devil, but I knew it had a deeper meaning. Sure, it was their nickname for me, but I could see the underlying grief I'd caused him had made him cast me in that role too. Pain sliced through my chest at that thought, at causing either him or Merrick any heartache, but a broken one was better than a silent, unmoving one.

My eyes trailed up his form, taking in how much he'd changed. He'd always been a few inches shorter, six-foot-two compared to Merrick's six-foot-five frame, his muscles leaner than Merrick's bulky form. He could fight but more often chose not to. The curve of his abs showed through his tight black shirt, highlighting how toned he'd become in the past six years. My Kellan—the one I used to snuggle with so often, now had a hard chiseled torso, but I had no doubt his embrace would be just as comforting as before. Drawn in by the only piece of ink visible beneath the collar of his shirt, I studied the lines wishing I could tear down the center of it to examine the intricate design in its entirety.

The curve of that line looked so similar though, so close to the picture in front of me. The part visible was the curve of the halo, but I couldn't mistake it, not when I had just burned it into my brain. Despite everything that happened between us, he got my face—the very essence of me—tattooed on his chest, right over his heart it seemed. But was it because he still held some feelings for me, or was it a reminder to never let the devil into his heart again ...?

My gaze drifted up to meet his, our eyes locking onto one another as though pulled by a magnetic force. His sable orbs bore into mine, and the world faded away from us. For a moment there was no Tommaso, no crime family controlling me, the town, the state, hell even half the country had disappeared. It was like no time had passed at all, like he saw every inch of me and knew my scars like the back of his own hand. There was so much fire left between us, so much to say, to explain. But I couldn't wrap my head around any of it, I couldn't voice a single syllable.

Fear churned in my stomach as the door crashed open, and I readied myself to jump in front of Kellan to shield him as best I could from Tommaso. But it wasn't his menacing form shadowed in the doorway—no, it was the bulky, towering one of Merrick, glaring down at me as though I was the bane of his existence. *Fuck, I have to get out of here.*

I'd been so caught up in the moment between Kellan and me I hadn't noticed his hand subtly reaching for my glasses, not until he snatched his hand back. That was close—too close and for all of our sakes I had to get out of here before they figured anything out. I hadn't meant to stay here this long; I had no idea what time it was. Selfishly, I wanted more time soaking in Kellan's reassuring presence, the sense of normalcy he'd attempted to create for me. I got so lost in what could've been, the fantasy of a life where my greatest worry was which incredible design Kellan was going to tattoo on me next, that I completely forgot about the threat my presence caused to them.

Now I'm not even sure if Kellan had wanted to spend the time with me or if he'd just been biding his time until Merrick came—letting him be the bad guy rather than telling me off himself. Well I already had enough of Merrick yelling at me the other night. And despite how horrible I felt for all the pain I'd caused them, I would kick his ass if he gripped my arms like that again, not after what Tommaso just did...

"What are you doing here?" Merrick sneered, his brows lowering into a glower. And I'd had enough—enough of these men playing games, trying to intimidate me, trick me or whatever else they were up to. The moment had been nice while it lasted but reality came sweeping back in like an icy wind, shocking me from my daydream. This was real life, and I had real problems I had to deal with, like how my very presence here was a threat to both of these men.

"I was just leaving," I shot back. I was no one's punching bag, not physically or verbally and the next person that took either one of those shots would get a fist to their ribs ... *Well, if it was Tommaso I might switch that out for a knife,* I mused to myself, the thought lighting a spark of sadistic satisfaction in me.

I took a step forward, about to brush past him, but before I could take another, Kellan was there, his large palm cupping my shoulder and holding me back. The touch distracted me until the crash of the door against the frame and click of the lock had my gaze snapping back to Merrick. A protest was poised on my lips until a metallic clang cut me off. Kellan's hand had slipped off my shoulder, and he was already over at the windows shutting the blinds. I hissed out a breath of irritation. It seemed both of them worked in tandem to trap me here and shutter out any spying eyes, forcing this confrontation that we all knew was long overdue.

"This isn't funny, I have places to be," I huffed out indignantly, pulling on the mask of who they were supposed to think I was now. I'd let it slip, both the other night with Merrick and here with Kellan today. The feelings I still held for them came bubbling up to the surface, muddling my mind and throwing me off kilter. But now especially, with the bruise on my upper cheek as evidence of what Tommaso had done, proof that all was not as it seemed, I couldn't let my façade drop now. I had to make them think I was the cold unfeeling girl who left them six years ago and not the desperate woman who was trying to escape.

"Giana," Kellan breathed, turning back from shuttering the last window. The space had been so bright just a moment ago, but the sudden shift to the thin streams of light filtering in through the cracks sent a chill running up my spine. Every time he said my name like that, both like no time had passed and like he was desperate to have it on his tongue again, made my heart splinter.

Fuck, I wanted to scream at him. Was that all he could say? Just repeat my name in that pleading tone that made my chest want to cave in, that made my legs want to buckle beneath me and stop being strong, at least for one minute. But I couldn't—this was why I left in the first place, why I went with Tommaso and fell into this life where I numbed the pain of loss each day until it almost suffocated me, where the only pleasure I felt was with a man I swore I hated on top of me, making me forget just for a second I was frozen, trapped, suffocating ...

I pulled in a ragged breath at that thought, reminding myself I could, that I was still here and I was going to get out. *Never again,* I promised myself. I wouldn't let him touch me like that again, let myself slip into that place of complacency again. Not after what he did ...

I pulled myself from that dark place, realizing both of their stares were hard and heavy on me, as though they sensed my mind had drifted off.

"I have to go," I snapped, forcing some irritation into my tone. I didn't want to go, not really, but I knew I couldn't stay. "So get out of my way."

"Why, you have to get to your engagement party?" Merrick sneered and Kellan sucked in a sharp breath from beside me. His jab sliced through me like a knife, but I didn't let it show, pushing it far down to examine later along with the cold gleam in Merrick's eyes. "Is that the real reason you came to the bar the other night, and why you came here today, to shove it in our faces?"

My hands clenched at my sides and I pinned him with the same hard glare he was giving me, though mine didn't have quite the same effect with the glasses on. He was lashing out at me, regardless if he believed his own claims or not, he was in pain and throwing barbs at me to hurt me back. But I couldn't rise to his baiting, I had to keep my irritation in check, because I couldn't let anything slip.

"Believe what you want, Merrick. I don't give a shit," I gritted out. Lie—lie—lie. The truth was, I cared too much, but I couldn't help it, I had to throw his words back at him, I had to make him believe I didn't. I started forward again, attempting to shoulder him out of the way, but he stepped into my path, his chest puffing out in defiance, his muscles taut and poised to intercept me at a moment's notice. "What the fuck are you going to do?" I spat, crossing my arms over my chest in frustration.

"I'll throw your ass over my shoulder if I need to, but we're long overdue for a chat. About six years, to be precise," he snapped, his arms folding over his chest to mirror my own. "You at least owe us that much."

"I don't owe you anything," I said with a derisive snort, venom leaking into my words. Not because guilt didn't twist at my gut over what I'd done, but because of how blind he was—how well I'd apparently played my part that he couldn't see past the betrayal. I'd set out for them to hate me, but at least a small part of me had hoped they might've seen through my cracks, that they would've known me better after all the years we'd spent together, that they'd be able to see this wasn't me.

"I think you do," Kellan said, stepping beside Merrick, both of their muscular forms now crowding the doorway. "After everything that happened, I think there's a lot to discuss ..." he trailed off letting the meaning of his words sink in. Memories of my eighteenth birthday flooded my mind, and I pushed them down, knowing I wouldn't be able to keep my cool with both of them in front of me with that night playing like a movie before my eyes.

"Fine. If you want to talk so badly, then talk," I huffed out, steeling myself for this. My eyes flicked between both of them, memorizing their features as though this was the last time I'd see them. My heart wrestled with the idea, but after striking out today, I had to come to terms that there was nowhere else for me to turn. I had to leave, I had to take the cash Francine gave me and run. I didn't want to let them go, not again, but I knew if I didn't run or if I took them with me, Tommaso would kill either them or me. I just had to play the part for a little longer, endure them hating me even more, and pretend as though the distance that stretched between us didn't pierce my soul.

Kellan's face fell at my curt reply, rocking back as though I'd dealt him a physical blow, but what else was I supposed to do?

Silence stretched between us; the tension so thick it was almost palpable. Merrick stiffened in front of me, his muscles so taut I could've sworn they were vibrating. My brows furrowed as I studied him, attempting to piece together what caused the sudden change. Sure, he'd been pissed before, but now it was as though flames blazed in those dark-hazel eyes, his jaw working as he ground his teeth together.

"Take off the glasses, Giana," Merrick growled harshly. My heart jolted at that demand, sending my mind into a tailspin as panic flooded my body. Eyes flicking from him to the door, I attempted to form a plan, some way to get past him before they asked any more questions.

"What are you talking about?" I snapped, swallowing down the quiver that vibrated in my throat and praying they hadn't noticed it. I worked to keep my face schooled, pushing down the panic. I couldn't let him know how close he was.

"It's pretty fucking dark in here, Giana. Yet you're still wearing sunglasses," Merrick retorted snidely. "I saw you the other night and you weren't wearing them then, so I know it's not a new style. Take them off." His face turned a darker shade of red with each word, his hands clenching and unclenching at his sides. He knew.

"Why should I? I was just about to leave anyway, so if you'd kindly—"

"Take them off, Giana." Kellan's deep voice cut through my feeble attempt to dissuade them. His voice was calm, yet so lethal, like his fury was as sharp as a blade, while Merrick's was explosive.

"Stay out of this," I hissed, unable to keep the wobble out of my voice. I sucked it back, wishing I could take back the plea, but it was no use. They both knew. My plans for today backfired so fantastically, only I could fuck something up this badly. The last thing I wanted was for either of them to find out and that was exactly what happened. My plan to convince anyone who was against the Barones to help me was a complete and utter disaster and now there was barely any makeup to shield the mark I knew would be the end of us all.

I couldn't help but realize this had been why Francine had been so sure, so smug. She knew if I continued down the street I'd end up at Kellan's shop. And if I broke down and showed him what I'd revealed to her, she knew they would help me no matter the cost. Whether it would be out of pity or some deep feelings they still held, I wasn't sure. All I knew was that couldn't happen. Because despite Kellan and Merrick being older now, they still weren't any match for Barone and his men, and it would take an army to wrestle me from Tommaso's clutches.

I took a step back, and then another, hoping I might be able to find a way to escape out the back. But I didn't know this place. I had no clue if there even was a door that was accessible, let alone where it was. They knew though, they'd be on me the second I bolted for the back.

I took another step, needing to put some distance between us. I couldn't let this happen, everything I put up with for the last six years had to be for a reason—it just had to. I tried to block the other voice from my mind but it was there, reminding me that after all this time, they might not even care. Sure they might be mad, but what would I do if they truly hated me so much that they just let me go? That's what I wanted—to keep them safe—but I wasn't sure my heart would be able to survive the blow of them no longer caring about me. And I'm pretty sure that would knock the last of my will to flee out of me, plummeting me into the dark abyss I'd barely clawed my way out of.

Both Kellan and Merrick followed after me, each step mirroring my own as though they were attempting to block in a wild animal.

"Just let me go," I whispered, internally screaming at myself for sounding so vulnerable. I'd thought that part of me had been stamped out long ago. My tender foot wobbled on my next step back, and that was when they pounced. Merrick closed in on one side and Kellan on the other. I glanced behind me, but instead of the curtain I expected, a thick wall blocked any chance I had at fleeing.

"Not in this lifetime or the next, little devil," Merrick murmured. My lips parted in shock at the conviction in his tone, but it was as though he hadn't even noticed he'd said the words aloud. His hard glare softened when he looked down on me, reassuring me his rage wasn't directed at me. But I knew, I always knew that it wasn't, even the other day when he'd gripped my arms, he'd loosened them as soon as he knew it had caused me pain.

Kellan moved closer to me now, and he reached out tentatively, just as he had before. But his jaw was tight this time as if he was straining to keep a leash on his anger. And I knew exactly how they felt, because even though time had passed between us, if someone hurt either of them, I'd tear them to shreds. His thick fingers gently wrapped around the chunky frames and drew them slowly off my face, revealing the half-covered, healing bruise beneath.

He sucked in a sharp breath as our eyes met, his face twisted with anger. My gaze hardened into a steely look of determination. I didn't need their pity, and I sure as hell didn't want their help.

A string of curses left Merrick's lips, and I couldn't help but turn to him, but he was already gone, striding over to the back wall to unleash his rage. His fist pulled back and smashed into the drywall, dust billowing and debris crumbling in its wake. I wished I could soothe that anger burning within him, to let him comfort me as well ... but I couldn't.

Kellan turned toward Merrick, and I knew this would be my only chance. As he strode past me, I debated whether or not to grab the glasses, but he'd know as soon as I took them that I was about to bolt. So I waited until he was almost to where Merrick struck another hole into the wall to make my move. I sprinted toward the door, my sandals slapping against the tiled floor. I pushed down the discomfort as I reached the door, unlocking and swinging it open. Merrick and Kellan both shouted for me, their own steps thundering behind me, but I was too fast.

My feet pounded on the sidewalk, ignoring the pain with each stride as it radiated up my ankle and twinged in my back. These shoes sure as hell weren't made for running and after Tommaso pushed me the other night, my back and ankle were not healed enough for this. But I pushed on, needing to put as much space between me and the two men cursing behind me.

"What am I supposed to do, chase her down the street and throw her over my shoulder in front of the whole town?" Kellan snapped incredulously, and I sighed a breath of relief as I drew closer and closer to my car. I rushed past groups lingering on the sidewalk, darting around them as quickly as I could and praying none of them noticed the bruise beneath my eye. But if any of them recognized me, I'm sure they wouldn't say a word. Because if I learned anything today, it was just how terrified the town had truly become of the crime family.

I frantically dug in my purse, and I whipped out my keys, preparing to hop in as soon as I reached the door. Some of the tension eased as I neared the obnoxious red Porsche and leapt off the sidewalk to the driver's side door. Yanking it open, I dove inside and slammed a hand down on the locks. I started it and put the car into drive, not trusting myself to sit here for too long. I didn't even dare drive past the tattoo shop on my way back to the mansion, both out of fear that Tommaso's GPS would know I was there and worry that I might not have the strength to drive off if I saw them again.

It was too late to leave town now. There were no buses running until the morning in any of the nearby towns, and Tommaso would be hot on my heels if I left tonight. I'd have to endure the party tonight, but tomorrow I'd leave—I'd get away before there was any time for Merrick or Kellan to get involved. Because if they went after Tommaso, I knew how it would end, and I couldn't lose them now. I'd rather leave them behind for good and let them have a chance at a normal life without me in it.

CHAPTER FOURTEEN

GIANA

NOW

GENTLY APPLYING THE YELLOW concealer, I did my best to cancel out the deep purple hue while attempting to not make the mark any worse. A pained hiss escaped my lips as I got to an especially tender spot, my face throbbing under the pressure, but I had to continue. I took my time, ensuring each layer of makeup was applied perfectly, and didn't allow a speck of the purple mark beneath it to shine through before moving on to the rest of my face. And as I curled my dirty-blonde locks, I stared back at the woman that sat before me in the vanity's mirror, my stomach twisting in disgust at the invisible mark and at the fact I covered it up. I wished I could stride into the room tonight without a stitch of makeup on, allowing every person there to see what he'd done to me, to show who he truly was. But it wouldn't do any good, they already knew, and that was why no one stood up to them, out of fear of him and his family doing even worse to them or their loved ones. I couldn't blame them—not really—not when I was doing the same thing.

My thoughts kept drifting off to this afternoon, to Kellan and Merrick, at seeing them once again, and the rage that had filled them at seeing the mark plastered across my face. But thinking of them would do no good now. I just had to get through tonight and leave before they had a chance to do anything brash. That was the only way I could keep them safe.

I glanced over at the clothes hanging for me in the closet, and just below them a note was nestled atop a new lingerie set. Its mere presence sent a rush of anger searing through me. I could only imagine what was on it … a reminder to hide the mark he'd left, or another apology? I crumpled the note and threw it in the garbage, not wanting to read the lies inked in black. Sliding my robe off my shoulders, I pulled on the lace bra and panties, my teeth gritted in frustration. I hated that he controlled me so entirely, even choosing what to wear beneath my clothes, that only he would see … maybe before, but never again. Not after the other night. I'd cut off his fingers before he slipped another piece of clothing off me. *One more night,* I promised myself—I'd make sure to take off my makeup as soon as we got home, let him be reminded of what he'd done, and then I'd leave tomorrow.

I slipped on the black evening gown that Tommaso had picked out, the soft silk of the underskirt sliding against my skin. A shiver ran up my spine at the sensation, and vitriol rose in my throat at having anything that man had touched on my skin. My skin crawled as I imagined the fabric as his hands sliding down my body, possessively running over my curves as though he owned me. I swallowed down the bile, pushing that thought from my head. I'd been so torn between the desire and disgust his touch elicited only a few days ago, but now after he struck me all that remained was revulsion for the man I'd spent the last six years with—the man who at one point I'd resigned myself to being the only option. The neckline of the dress came down low enough that it made me wonder if I should wear the bra under it, but I wouldn't allow the asshole the satisfaction of having me there without a layer of clothing on, wearing it as part of my armor.

I strode back over to the vanity to collect my things and paused when I caught my reflection, scowling back at the woman in the full-length mirror—the bright red lipstick and perfect skin, it was all a lie. But it was one I wouldn't have to live with for much longer. Tommaso already told me he'd be having brunch with his father tomorrow morning, so that would be my chance. I couldn't look anything up though, I couldn't let there be any breadcrumbs to follow, not this time. My fingers gently clasped the wad of bills sitting on the counter and slid them into the clutch I'd have with me tonight. I couldn't let there be any trace of it, couldn't risk Tommaso finding it sometime during the night. This was my only ticket out of here, so I had to keep it close by my side, guarding it like the dragon hoards its treasure.

My phone chimed on the vanity, pulling me from my thoughts and back into reality. Grimacing, I reached down for it, knowing it could only be one person. The screen lit up with a preview of the text and moisture coated my palms as soon as the name popped up.

Tommaso: The car is waiting for you outside, mi amore. Don't keep us waiting too long ...

My hand clenched around the case, and I suppressed the urge to chuck it across the room. The screen was already cracked from the other night when it had dropped from my hands, and I couldn't let go of the only form of communication I had with the outside world. Sure, I'd have to get rid of it tomorrow before I left, but I couldn't let the small illusion of a tether to the outside go, not yet. I'd have to leave it here to keep from leading him directly to my whereabouts. I had no doubt that he'd catch on pretty quickly, but hopefully by then I would've switched over to another bus. Or I could always drive as fast and as far as I could, and ditch the car, even sell it off to a chop shop. But that would leave too many witnesses ... too many people looking for a quick buck who could recognize me.

I pushed those thoughts from my mind, I could think about all of that later, while I tossed and turned tonight, because there was no way I'd be getting a wink of sleep, not with the anticipation thrumming through my veins. For now I had to focus on getting through tonight alive. I could only hope neither Merrick nor Kellan would try anything stupid before then. But judging by how they hadn't tried to stop me this afternoon, they knew it would be suicide to stand up against the Barones. And with me gone, there wouldn't be any reason for them to plan anything, and they could get back to their lives with a clear conscience and forget about me ... and that was a good thing, right?

EAST HAVEN WAS ALWAYS a small town, and we didn't have most of the extravagant places that were found in the city. Quaint shops and restaurants were the most abundant, some in good condition like the ones I'd visited today, and others in a state of disrepair like Greg's Diner. The class divide amongst its residents was worlds apart, either you owned a business here, you worked for one, or you worked for the Barones. But either way, it didn't matter, everyone was beholden to them in some form or another. Because of the strong hold they had, many of their wealthy associates and politicians lived here while owning businesses in neighboring cities, their connection to the crime family giving them free rein to whatever they'd like.

They even had some legitimate businesses, like the place the long-armored stretch limo was about to pull into. Le Jardin des Roses was the place to hold anything in East Haven, but no one other than the Barones themselves and their partners could afford it. The driveway was similar to the house Tommaso had bought—to all of their properties for that matter. The sand-stoned cobblestone led up a steep hill, with a fountain in the center of it. Marble figures were posed within it and water flared around the couple embracing, their blank eyes staring at each other, appearing to most people that they were in love, but to me it looked different. The man's arm was clasped around the woman's waist, clutching her to him as she leaned away, like she was trying to break free from his clutches. He stares down at her with the hard edge of possession in his eyes while she glances off to the side, in a move that I knew was meant to be demure, yet her gaze looks vacant to me, numb while attempting to flee, her hope dwindling with every moment that passes. *Or maybe I'm just projecting.*

Blocking the statue from my view, I turn to the wall of smooth stone, hewn from large blocks imported straight from Italy. Why do I know this ... because I'd heard the story plenty of times before. This place was his family's pride and joy, and I'm sure they'd live in the enormous castlesque estate if it wasn't for the notoriety of having an equally jaw-dropping home in addition to the space they saved strictly for large events.

The Barones never did anything halfway, so I was sure there'd be no expense spared with tonight's party. A lavish event to remind both the town and their wealthy associates who was in control and who had the power grasped within an iron fist. My thoughts were confirmed as the limo came to a stop, the brakes squeaking lightly in front of a red-carpeted walkway. Red roses and peonies decorated the entry along with artfully shaped shrubs at the bottom of the wide, carved stone stairs leading up to the towering front entryway. The doors were splayed open, revealing the twinkling lights of the chandeliers just beyond them. Their real show of force though wasn't their wealth. No, it was the twenty guards armed to the teeth scattered along the driveway. They all were outfitted in crisp black suits, their clear earpieces visible as they turned their heads. Some had semi-automatic rifles strapped to their shoulders and others had handguns holstered to the outside of their suits, stationed there to keep any undesirables at bay.

Drawing in a deep breath, I stole a few more minutes of peace before heading into the lion's den, simply watching the guests walk up the sidewalk beside us and up the stairs. Of course I didn't know any of them, and why would I? This was only supposed to be *my* engagement party after all. But really, who would I even want to be here? Sure as hell not the guys or anyone from our old school.

My thoughts were cut short by a gust of the humid night air blowing into the limo's interior as the driver pulled open the door. I internally scolded myself for letting my guard drop, I didn't even hear the front door open or see him walk back to me. Swallowing back any lingering unease, I slid from the seat and wiped all emotions from my face before I faced the horde of gossiping busybodies inside.

"Have a good evening," he murmured, and I thanked him in return. I wasn't sure who he was, probably one of Tommaso's parents' staff, but it wasn't his fault that he worked for them, not when those were some of the only well-paying jobs in town.

In this world you were either a predator or prey, and although some of the guards in New York had seen the way Tommaso treated me, I never let myself look like a victim, not in front of them or anyone else. I couldn't allow them to see me as any less of a threat than the family they worked for, especially when I was supposed to become one. The only exception had been the two guards that caught me at the airport. They had seen me at my lowest point and savored it. I hated that they'd seen any weakness, but they would pay for their cruelty, especially now that I had a taste of that darkness. The devil within was no longer satisfied with the thrill of danger or watching others shedding blood. I wasn't sure how I'd do it, but once I got away, once I started my new life, I'd find those two guards and watch their faces drain of color, the sick smell of their fear permeating my senses.

I pulled on that tendril of darkness I'd felt before, that sadistic glint that reveled in the pain, the fear, and took joy from it when aimed toward the right people. I let the feeling of satisfaction I'd felt when I pressed the taser into the singer's skin wash over me, the excitement I felt knowing what Spade was about to do with him, his knife still gleaming with the deep red tint of blood. I imagined carving off a slice of his flesh with the knife, his face transforming to the two guards from the airport in my mind's eye. I wished I could take turns with them, soaking in their screams and terror. A smirk tilted my lips as I strode up the stairs, wicked delight gleaming in my eyes. I locked gazes with each of the guards, picturing them watching me dismember their colleagues. Each guard who met the barely caged bloodlust on my face glanced away, shivering at the violence emanating from me, despite them being armed to the teeth. I clutched my bag tighter, my hands picturing the hilt of the knife in place of my phone tucked within it. I watched as grown men literally shuddered at the brutality rolling off me, my satisfaction brimming.

I let the pictures playing through my mind fade to a close as I passed the last guard, holding on to a piece still as I walked through the open doors. I couldn't let Tommaso see that, not just yet, not until I was ready to slide a dagger between his ribs. He too would be subjected to my wrath if I was able to ensure Kellan's and Merrick's safety first. That sort of defiance, promise of outward violence toward him or his family, might just land me in deeper trouble than staying would. Because if they thought I could be some sort of asset to them—aside from his son's infatuation with me—there wouldn't be anything in this world that could keep his father from using every resource to find me.

The interior was a wide-open expanse of wealth, with wood beams carving along the cathedral ceiling. The walls were covered in a red baroque wallpaper in the foyer, and a large oak table sat in the center with a massive floral bouquet perched atop it, mixed with peonies, roses, and greenery. The soft hum of a string quartet filtered through the murmured voices in the hall in a soft, lilting tune. A waiter approached me with a tray of champagne and before they could even get a word out, I slipped one off the silver platter and let the bubbly alcohol slide down my throat, my head tilting backward in a rush to get at least one drink in me before I had to see Tommaso and his parents.

"Thanks," I breathed, placing the glass on the table where a few others sat ready to be collected and took another one to sip on. I'd have to nurse this one for the next hour or so to keep a straight head, but at least I'd have something in my system.

"No problem," he chuckled, sliding his tray onto the table now that I took the last two. "I know how boring these events can be. Do you want me to stick by your side for the night? I'll be sure to keep my tray fully stocked," he whispered, winking at me as his dark-brown eyes slid up my body. The poor guy obviously must be somewhat new to town, otherwise he wouldn't be caught dead insulting one of the Barones' events or hitting on me.

"Not if you want to keep your head," Tommaso purred from behind him, and I huffed out a breath of exasperation as he stepped beside me, his arm slipping around my waist and jerking me possessively into his side. The poor waiter's mouth dropped open as he realized exactly who had just spoken, his lips trembling as he took a few uneasy steps backward. I guessed he must have some self-preservation then since his face instantly blanched.

"I—I didn't know," the waiter stammered, stumbling back a step. His hand still clutched the edge of his tray though, and in his haste to retreat he ended up knocking over the glasses strewn across the oak table. Glass shattered all around us as they crashed to the floor, the chiming gritting against my nerves as the entryway went silent, everyone's gaze darting in our direction. His eyes widened, looking from us to the mess of glass littered across the floor and back to us, fighting his instinct to flee. I wished I could give him an apologetic look, but I merely cock an eyebrow, watching him with barely disguised contempt, knowing that every eye was watching us now. I couldn't show any weakness, not to Tommaso and not to the vipers waiting in the winds, surveying any weak spot to strike.

"Get this cleaned up," Tommaso spat, sneering back at the man.

Despite the brusque reply, the waiter almost seemed relieved as Tommaso guided me away, since he now wouldn't have to decide between his job and running for his life. Tommaso's hand on my waist tugged me alongside him, not allowing any space between our bodies. I suppressed the groan that bubbled up, cursing the man who'd tried to be kind, because that flirty banter would now mean I'd barely get a moment to myself tonight.

"Are you having fun?" Tommaso hissed, and I worked to keep a bland, bored expression on my face. I wanted to push him away, to scream at him that I hadn't asked for his advances, I'd literally just walked in the door. But that—that would only direct his anger toward the waiter. "Didn't you learn from the last time?"

"Nothing happened, Tommaso," I whispered, a shiver of fear creeping up my spine. Despite how useless I knew it was, I had to say something. His jealousy had no limits. I could point out the fact that I hadn't said a word to him, hadn't gotten the chance to politely turn the server down since he swooped in before I could. But he wouldn't care, not with the tension I could feel vibrating off him right now. I had no doubt that he'd seen the entire conversation. He would have been surveying the door for the moment I arrived.

My head swiveled around at the groups of people gathered, signs of their wealth dripping off them in the form of diamonds, designer gowns, and suits. They cast wary glances in our direction, not missing a moment of the action. Everyone here was waiting for one slip, one momentary lapse to pounce, and I wouldn't give the satisfaction. I realized I didn't know any of them so I let my lips curl into a slight sneer, allowing a glimmer of that violent intent to show.

Silence stretched between us then, as he did the same, both of our contempt-filled glares making guests avert their curious looks and move away from the entrance. I looked up at him then, at those mahogany eyes I loathed so much, with my brow arched in question. I didn't want the waiter to be killed for something so small, but if it seemed like I cared too much, I might just make it happen faster. He held my gaze and we paused amid the room full of strangers milling about from the entrance to the main room. The buffeted ceiling rose up at least fifteen feet above us, with massive crystal chandeliers hanging from them. The walls in here were covered in an ivory wallpaper, inlaid with an intricate gold design, which made the enormous space look even larger. He huffed out a breath of frustration but placed a kiss on the top of my head in what I could only hope was agreement.

"I'm sorry, mi amore. You can't blame me for being protective though," he murmured against my hair, his warm breath sinking into my skin with every word. I suppressed the shudder that begged to run through my limbs, my hands clenching with the effort it took to not push him away. Everything about this man repulsed me, and I realized I truly didn't know what hate was until now. I wished I could slide a dagger into his throat and watch the blood flow down his neck and soak into the crisp white collar of his shirt.

I let that image play through my head as my lips tugged up into a grin and rested my hand on his back in a way I hoped he'd interpret as a tender gesture. And it must've worked as he instantly relaxed against the touch, his muscles losing some of the strain at the reassurance.

"What would I do without you?" he murmured, placing another kiss atop my head before drawing away. *He'll have to figure out the answer to that question sooner than he thinks,* I reminded myself smugly, letting that bolster my strength as he led us forward again and into the ballroom.

There were small tables set up around the massive room with two bars on either side. Waiters milled about to each group, offering the hors d'oeuvres and passing out glasses of champagne. The string quartet was set up on the far side on a small platform and out of the way from the guests as their soft classical notes vibrated through the room. I surveyed the distance, searching for anyone that I knew, including his parents, not wanting to be caught off guard.

My heart hammered in my chest as my eyes locked with a familiar amber pair, the exact same shade as mine with deep dark circles beneath them, her dirty-blonde hair streaked with grey pulled into a tight bun. Her hand lightly patted her husband's, drawing his attention our way. His lips pursed at the sight of Tommaso and me, but he didn't dare say a word. I pinned them with a glare as we approached, the rest of my face relaxed as though they were only a minor inconvenience, a pest that needed to be swatted away.

"I didn't think they would actually come," I ground out between gritted teeth, my lips barely moving as the two people I never wanted to see again stared back at us. My gaze flicked to the other side of the room as we glided past them, not wanting to give them another moment of my time. The two of them were honestly lucky to even be alive at this point. I might've saved them once but never again. I wouldn't step in if they made fools of themselves tonight. They lost any claim on being my parents the night they abandoned me, the night they disowned me as their daughter.

"They are your parents after all, and with us moving back, they should at least be present for our engagement party," he murmured, guiding us along without a look back. The cruelty was gone from his voice when he brought it up this time, and my mind revisited our conversation in the car from when we first drove through town. Then he'd wanted to throw them being invited to the wedding as a way to hurt me. But I caught the note of disdain in his tone at their inclusion, leading me to believe this was more his parents' sentiment than his own. The irony was that he'd been ready and willing to kill them for laying a finger on me before we left for New York—when he'd now done the same thing, leaving a mark much worse than they ever did.

I didn't bother fighting him, knowing it wouldn't do any good, not if it was something his father had declared and not when I was so close to leaving. He could have whoever he wanted, because there wouldn't be a wedding if everything went according to plan—or at least what little I had of a plan. I did a double check on my posture as I knew exactly where we were heading now. It would be disrespectful not to see his parents as soon as I got here, especially since they were hosting the party. My stomach twisted at the thought of seeing them again, but I held my head high, not letting any emotion slip past my mask. It was a tight line I had to walk with his father, respectful yet not weak. I couldn't show any of that threatening glare I'd been clinging to, not with Angelo Barone.

He stood near a grand fireplace on the opposite side of the entrance, allowing him and his guards a view of everyone around them. Nothing would escape their keen eyes, and I was now sure they'd also seen everything that happened with the waiter. I swallowed thickly as he came into view, past his crowd of gathered admirers pandering to his every wish, tendrils of fear skittering up my spine as his mahogany eyes latched on to me. His gaze was so similar to his son's, I couldn't suppress the shudder that ran over my skin at this attention.

Angelo Barone was one man you didn't want taking an interest in you. Unfortunately, as someone close to their family, it meant I was subjected to that cold, calculating glare more deeply than most. That was one of the good things about New York, we were far enough away I hadn't been subjected to his scrutiny very often. *I won't have to deal with this for much longer. I can get through tonight,* I reminded myself, not allowing my mind to swirl out of control with thoughts of the future. I could do this, I could deal with this for one night, and tomorrow I would be gone. His leer slithered over my skin, taking in every inch as though it was him and not Tommaso I was meant to marry. My lips twitched as they attempted to pull down into a grimace but I caught myself just in time. Tommaso's hand tightened on my waist like he too noticed his father's attention, but he would never say anything, never stop him if his father ever tried anything.

Glancing around the gathered crowd, I spotted Rosa Barone, Tommaso's mother, perched gracefully on one of the burgundy wingback chairs settled near the fireplace, smiling serenely as though she was holding court for all her adoring fans. Her beaded navy floor-length gown spilled out around her feet, acting as a barrier between her and the women crowded nearby.

Most would see a wealthy woman enjoying the company of those who looked up to her for her money and power, envisioning her life as their own. But I saw the truth, I saw those subtle sideways glances, where she just needed a second to breathe without the suffocating presence of the so-called friends who would stab her in the back in a heartbeat. I could see the vacant look behind those tawny eyes, retreating so far into herself to drown out the attention, the pain, the soul-wrenching despair as this life threw her through the ringer. Her name was supposed to mean rose, a sweet and delicate flower flourishing into full bloom, but the years had sucked that from her until she became merely a stem adorned in thorns, a shadow of her former self.

Maybe it was the same as with the statue and I interpreted her pain as my own, a kindred need to flee, to break free from the control, the abuse. But I didn't think so. Not when I'd seen the barest light flicker in her just to be extinguished in the next moment by Angelo. Not with the waiter poised next to her just as the man at the front had asked to do for me, polishing off the glasses of champagne almost as fast as he could pass them to her, using alcohol to numb the pain of her existence she'd never escape—the same road I'd felt myself stranded on before I woke up a few weeks ago.

"Leave us," Angelo bellowed simply, cutting off what another man was about to say. No one argued though, the men and women scattering, as though Angelo would put a bullet between their eyes if they hung around for a moment longer, which honestly was a possibility. He didn't wait for us to approach, instead he turned to the fireplace and sat on the chair on the opposite side as Rosa. They looked as though they were the king and queen, the servants and court surrounding them in the castlesque building. Even the waiter with the tray filled with flutes of bubbly retreated as Angelo sat, much to Rosa's dismay. "We need to have a chat about your behavior, Giana, and your position in this family," Angelo addressed me, venom coating his every word, cocking a brow in silent challenge, daring me to speak against him. But judging by the slight curl to his lips, he knew I wouldn't. No one would stand up to him and even fathom living to tell the tale.

The guards stood with their backs to us, keeping a barrier around us and the guests. No one could hear us, not with his murmured tone pitched so low to draw you in closer just for him to slit your throat. Although they couldn't hear the conversation, I could tell by the furtive glances they were casting our way they had no intention of not watching, trying to glean whatever they could for an advantage.

"You ruined my plans, Giana," he said cryptically, his tone dark yet his face bored. "I'd kill most people for interfering in my business deals, you know?"

Rosa silently sipped on her champagne, nursing this one as if she needed to prolong every sip just for something to distract her.

"Yes," I breathed, knowing from experience that it was always best to answer Angelo, even when he was being rhetorical.

"Do you know why I haven't killed you?" he asks. And my lips parted, about to answer, but he cut me off. "Because you foolishly walked right into our plan. Sure it was nice to have my son further our business in the city, but the plan was always for you both to come home, and now we can all be one happy family," he concluded, clapping his hands together as though because he decreed it, it would be so.

A shiver of fear ran up my spine at the look he gave me as the waiter rushed back in to refill everyone's glasses. The waiter frowned at my still full glass before continuing on to Rosa, who greedily downed the few remaining drops before shoving her glass toward him impatiently.

There was a reason I never wanted to spend any time alone with the man in front of me, why even Tommaso never left me alone with him. My stomach turned at the leering look he gave me as he lifted his glass, prompting us to do the same. Tommaso pulled me closer and for once this evening, I was glad to have him by my side if it kept his father from putting his hands on me.

"Cheers, and welcome to the family. I have so much planned for the two of you," he announced, his mahogany eyes glinting with a malice I hadn't even seen in Tommaso's yet, and dread sank like a leaden weight in my gut. But I pressed the crystal glass to my lips and sipped at the crisp bubbly, only allowing a few drops to slide down my throat.

I had to stay on guard tonight, even more than I'd thought before, especially with the keen intrigue glittering in Angelo's eyes and the malicious grin curling on his lips as his own flute lowered.

My chest tightened as panic gripped me. The only thing keeping me sane at this moment was the idea of escaping tomorrow, because I knew I'd never survive the torment Angelo was ready to unleash if I stayed.

CHAPTER FIFTEEN

GIANA

NOW

"WHY DON'T YOU RELAX, mi amore?" Tommaso murmured in my ear, his hot breath washing over the sensitive skin and the small amount of food I was able to force down now churning in my stomach. I internally cringed, unable to jerk back, knowing all eyes were on us. Angelo had set up a head table before all the others in the massive ballroom, and of course it was poised on a platform, making the four of us the spectacle while everyone ate.

Thankfully I was sitting at the end of the table with Tommaso beside me and his father and mother next to him. I wasn't sure I could've forced myself to choke down anything if I was beside his father. I pushed his lingering stares out of my mind and forked up another bite of the creamy mashed potatoes. Though

I was sure they were supposed to have flavor, they tasted like ash on my tongue as my other senses were on high alert.

My champagne sat close to me, and I didn't dare to take another sip out of fear a waiter would come to refill my glass. Taking a flute at the door was one thing—no one knew which one I would take or even when I was going to show up—but now I couldn't trust anything that was put in front of me, which was another reason why I barely ate any food.

"I am relaxed," I whispered back, my hand covering my lips to mask our conversation. He just stared back at me with a pointed look, silently calling out my lie. I hate that he could see through me, that he knew me at all. I wished I could just forget the past six years, but I couldn't, because they weren't something I could take back no matter how hard I tried. "Maybe I'd be able to relax if we weren't the entertainment," I ground out, pushing some more food around my plate before taking a hesitant bite of my steak. I had to walk a thin line right now, between not wanting to eat, and the possibility of offending Angelo.

"Oh, Giana." Tommaso chuckled, his hand rubbing circles on my back in an attempt to comfort me, but the gesture only put me further on edge. I stabbed another piece of meat with my fork just to avoid skewering his thigh with the sharp prongs. "Everyone's here to celebrate us and our love, not to judge. So relax and enjoy the party."

I forced a smile on my lips, hoping he believed the weak attempt and swallowed the laugh choking me right now. The entire thought was preposterous, not only was there no love between us, only possession and infatuation, these people were not here to celebrate. They were here either out of fear or responsibility to his parents. Either it was an attempt to climb the social ladder or avoid being found in an alley. I forced my fork to my lips, his hand still resting on the exposed skin between my shoulder blades, setting my teeth on edge.

I sighed a breath of relief as the waiter came back out and began collecting plates. Others began to push back from their tables, and I decided to do the same. I had to get out of here for a minute at least, otherwise I wasn't sure I'd be able to keep what little composure I still clung to for much longer. As soon as the waiter came by the table, I lifted my plate for him, ignoring the quizzical look he gave me at the barely eaten food.

"Please excuse me," I said loud enough for his parents to hear me and began to slip off my chair, grabbing my clutch off my lap.

"Where are you going?" Tommaso hissed, his hand wrapping around my shoulder with enough force to hold me back.

"I have to go to the washroom," I whispered back, glancing back at him with knitted brows. Tommaso reluctantly let his hand slip away, his fingers lightly grazing my arm as he did. Suppressing the urge to bare my teeth at him for all the subtle touches he'd been giving me, I did my best to turn it into a small smile. I stood and stepped off the platform in the next moment, not wanting to stay there for a second longer, fearing what I might say to him. Working to keep my face neutral, I glided through the ballroom with my head held high. I wanted to claw at his hand when it gripped me, the movement so full of control and possession. A waiter passed by me with a tray filled with champagne, and I just wanted to flip it over, taking my anger out on anyone or anything that I could ... but I held it in.

One more night, I promised myself, grateful for the decision I'd made before I came here tonight, otherwise I wasn't sure how I would've gotten through this farce.

"Giana," a gravely woman's voice called out, breaking through my thoughts. It took a moment for it to register, the shock bringing me out of my anger for a moment until I locked eyes with the amber ones that mirrored my own. "Can we talk, please?"

Her hand closes over my arm, and I immediately wrench out of her grip. I had to put up with this from Tommaso for one more night, but I didn't have to with her. I couldn't care less what anyone thought about it or if they saw, but this woman would not dare touch me like I owed her anything.

"Don't you dare put your hands on me," I hissed, stepping closer to her. I'd always been a few inches taller than her, but with my heels on I towered over her, allowing me to look down on her like she deserved. I wasn't that same teenager who had to follow everything she said out of fear my escape would be snatched away from me. The fact that they held that over my head at all showed what type of people Greg and Pam were, and after what happened on my last night in East Haven six years ago, I'd never let her lay a hand on me like that again.

"Giana," Greg warned, stepping up behind Pam and placing a hand tenderly on her shoulder. If he thought he could intimidate me he was dead wrong. Because I'd lived with one of the most dangerous men in the country for the past six years, and if I was still willing to run from him, to stand up against him and not just accept my fate, I'd never let a man as pathetic as Greg scare me.

"Don't you dare say my name. You lost that privilege six years ago," I spat, turning away, wanting to leave them behind me just like they'd turned their backs on me.

"Please, we want to apologize," Pam sniffled, her voice muffled. I internally cursed myself for what I was about to do, but against my better judgment I spun around, my brows raising as she buried her face in her hands, her shoulders shaking lightly. Glancing around the hall, I found a small alcove that was out of view from most of the room. Although most had probably already seen the altercation between us, I couldn't have this woman sobbing in the middle of the room and attracting even more attention.

"Fine," I ground out, lifting my chin to indicate the small alcove behind them. They silently nodded and scurried over there with me reluctantly following a few feet behind them. This was the absolute last thing I wanted to deal with right now.

They huddled into the small corner, and I stood off to the side, at an angle that would both block off anyone's view of the conversation and allow me to see anyone approaching. There was no way I'd let my back be exposed to anyone looking to take me by surprise ... After all, who knew what any of the lions in sheep's clothing had in store for tonight.

"This is your chance to say your piece, after this I don't want to see or hear from you again," I huffed out on a breath of irritation, and Pam jolted back as though my words had landed a physical blow. Not once in six years had they even bothered to contact me. I saw right through her little act though; I spent my childhood with these two and knew every single one of their childish games. Pam had never been as good an actress as she thought and judging by the begrudging look Greg was giving her, I could tell this wasn't his idea—he'd be just as happy to forget about me as I would about him. That was one thing I guess I could be grateful for; I'd rather have his stubbornness than the lack of backbone Pam had.

"We just wanted to apologize for everything that happened between us, for how we treated you. We should've tried to find a way to help you more," Pam sobbed, clutching at Greg's shirt dramatically. He patted her hand awkwardly, his unease showing he wasn't really sure what to make out of her theatrics either. "You'll always be our daughter, Giana, and we'd love to be closer."

"So you've decided that after six years, now you want me to be your daughter again?" I asked, quirking a brow in question. "You had six years to reach out, to try to find out where I was and make amends, but you didn't. Why was that?" I asked skeptically, not letting her crocodile tears sway me in the least. I wasn't the same girl that had left this town. I wouldn't be the daughter they treated more like an employee while they looked for ways that I could help them rather than being supportive parents in any sense of the word.

"We wanted to, but we had no way to contact you," Pam cried, letting a little annoyance creep into her tone. Did she really think so little of me, that she thought I wouldn't see straight through her bullshit and just forgive them instantly?

"I'm sure you could've found a way," I huffed, tired of her excuses already. "What's the real reason?"

"Don't give me that tone, Giana," she snapped, her eyes narrowing on me in a glare, but she slapped a hand over her mouth a moment later, her brows smoothing out as though she hadn't meant for that to slip out. There was the true Pam.

"We're your parents, we don't need to answer to you," Greg grunted, taking a step away from Pam now that their charade was up. "We've run into some problems the past few years and we could use some help from the daughter we fed and clothed for the first eighteen years of her life."

A giggle crept my throat, slipping out before I could clamp my lips shut. Greg's face soured immediately, but I couldn't help it—once that single chuckle escaped it was like the floodgates opened and I allowed my frustration and anger to be washed away by the laughter that slipped out. The sorrowful look Pam had tried to revert to vanished in an instant, both of their faces contorting into indignant sneers, apparently dropping their act completely now that the truth was out. All they wanted was money, so they could continue on with their ways, letting their diner crumble around them while drinking away their problems.

"The fact that you actually thought I would help you is laughable in itself," I huffed out on a breath of amusement, my laughter tapering off. "But to try to make me feel obligated to do so out of some sort of loyalty to you, for doing the bare fucking minimum as parents, is disgusting," I spat, my eyes narrowing to slits in a cutting glare. They balked at the sudden change. I'd never truly shown them this side of me, instead choosing to abide by their rules, counting down the days until I could leave.

"But we—" Pam stammered, but I cut her off.

"No. You're not my parents, you haven't been for years now. Not after what you did. So don't try to act like it all of a sudden—like I owe you anything just to get something from me." I didn't let them get another word in and turned on my heel, striding off to the bathroom. I needed a breather, a moment of fucking peace to myself.

The truth was, they'd stopped being my parents long before that. Which was one of the reasons why I started calling them Greg and Pam. I honestly couldn't even pinpoint the time that had happened. I started working in the back at ten, when they'd gotten tired of me "taking up space without being productive" as they'd said. Before that I was either left to my own devices, forced to play or do homework in the dusty old supply closet in the back of the diner so I would be out of the customers' way. That way they wouldn't have to pay for a babysitter.

I knew it was partially the fault of the crime family I was supposedly marrying into. They'd stolen my childhood with the iron grip they kept on this town, the constant threat they posed, physically and financially on the residents and business owners. But it was also my parents' fault as well. I'd let them off the hook too many times by focusing on their hardships and excusing any they'd let fall on my shoulders as a child because of it.

There were people like Francine, who were able to not only raise her grandson with the kindness and compassion she'd always had, but in her gesture of giving me that cash today, she did more than my parents had to help me get out, despite being put under the same pressure. She showed more kindness to the children who wandered the streets, forgotten by their parents, than Greg and Pam had done for me or my friends. She showed me we didn't have to be beholden to our circumstances, that we made the conscious choice on how we would treat others every day. So the truth was ... Greg and Pam were not only shitty parents but shitty people too, and regardless of me leaving tomorrow, I didn't need people like that in my life, despite their blood ties.

I blocked out the staring faces, watching me as I passed, my lips pulled into a tight line, my head held high. My gaze hardened, letting any of them know that if they got in my way they would have to deal with my wrath. That seemed to get the message across as most backed away and averted their gazes, while others at least tried to disguise their curious looks now.

I strode down the hall and found a bathroom with its door ajar, and slammed the large oak door behind me, locking it immediately. I leaned back against the smooth varnish for a moment as I caught my breath. I swear if I saw them again, I'd throw their asses straight out, consequences be damned.

Some of the tension slipped from my shoulder at the brief moment of respite and I walked to the mirror and slid my clutch onto the counter, gripping the edge of the cool marble in my palms. I wanted to turn on that tap and splash some cool water onto my face, but I couldn't afford to do that, not with the makeup piled on my bruised cheek. Instead, I stared back at myself, seeing the fatigue on my weary face, but despite everything that had happened tonight, my lips twitched with a small smile.

Although I hadn't wanted to confront Greg and Pam, I was almost glad they'd pulled me aside tonight. It gave me the chance to say what had been on my mind for years now. I had the chance to show them I was fine without them, and it gave me strength knowing what I would face in the coming days, weeks, months, and years ahead as I scraped by while escaping the Barones' clutches. I'd persevered before, and I would continue to, no matter the circumstances. Glancing at the clutch, I could almost see the few hundred dollars nestled inside the inner pocket, my safety net, my beacon of hope. My proof that despite everything I'd been through, the world wasn't filled with only people who wanted power and prestige, who wanted to pick the bones clean of anyone who stood in their way. There were good people out there, hardworking people who were willing to help their fellow humans in need.

Letting that thought lift my spirits, I drew in a deep breath, preparing to brave the lion's den once more, and strode to the door. I unlocked the deadbolt and pulled open the heavy wooden door, closing my eyes for a moment at the bright chandeliers shining directly in them—and that's when a masculine hand clamped over my lips, dragging me the rest of the way out the door. My sight attempted to focus as I blinked against the light, but the man had my head tilted up toward the ceiling still.

Screaming against his hand, my teeth gnashed, desperately trying to pierce his skin while I bucked against him. He clutched me closer, his arm banding around my stomach as he pulled my back against his chest.

"Shhh, it's just me, sugar," the man's voice lilted in my ear and my body stiffened as I attempted to place it. His grip on me eased as I halted bucking against him, allowing me to turn my head back to see him. My eyes lit on his gaze glowing like a halo under the bright lights, my breath caught in my throat at the sight of the man I barely knew yet already felt such a kindred connection with; the man who showed me the adrenaline spike that came with exacting pain, violence, and punishment with my own hands. His violet eyes sparkled with delight as my own lit with recognition.

Spade.

"Buckle up, babe. You're in for quite the show." He smirked, tilting his chin back toward the ballroom.

The words barely left his lips when an explosion jolted us back, his grip on my stomach the only thing keeping me upright as the floor shook under us. Smoke billowed up at the end of the hallway, and the power flickered from the blast, the crashing and shattering of a chandelier echoing through the screams of the guests just outside.

Spade chuckled at the chaos erupting around us, but my gaze was riveted on the ballroom as two figures emerged from the smoke. Their forms still shrouded in darkness were the only thing I could make out past the thick dust clouds as another explosion rocked through the building.

CHAPTER SIXTEEN

GIANA

NOW

SPADE'S ARMS BANDED TIGHTER around me as the force of the explosions rocked into us. His tall form cocooned over me, his thick corded muscles shielding me from most of the shock. The few remaining lights blinked out and screams echoed throughout the ballroom. A creaking sounded over us, and Spade scooped me up in his arms, dashing out of the way just as the chandelier above us began to groan at the shockwaves it'd been hit with, ominously rocking back and forth in the dim glow of the emergency lights. I frantically clutched my arms around his neck as the thick chain snapped, sending the chandelier hurtling toward the ground. Spade dropped to the floor midstride, his body folding around mine to shield me as crystal smashed against the hardwood floor, sending shards of glass shattering around us.

His warm breath skated across my neck, and despite my rapid heartbeat hammering against my chest, warm tendrils of lust coiled up my spine and I arched into his touch. Fuck, this wasn't the time to get turned on, but I couldn't help it with the pressure of his hard chest against my back, protecting me, shielding me from danger. My adrenaline was already pumping from the peril surrounding us, and that on its own was enough to send waves of lust straight to my core, even without his selfless act. I fought back the urge to turn my head to the side, knowing his lips would be right there, reminding myself this wasn't really the time nor the place for that.

"Careful, sugar, if you keep rubbing against me like that, I'll throw caution to the wind and pin you down on this floor right now," he groaned in my ear, his promise making my breath catch. His lips brushed the shell of my ear, sending waves of heat through me and my back arched again, searching for some friction. Only then did I realize I was indeed grinding against him as I felt his hard length against my backside. I sucked in a sharp breath—fighting against the little voice inside that wanted to push him, to see if he really would lose control—and reluctantly lowered to the ground, turning in his grip to face him. I might've also forgotten about the shards of glass littering the floor because his hand clasped my wrist a second before it landed on a stray piece. He used that hold to pull us both up, glass cracking under his thick black loafers. I stepped gingerly on the glass, careful to miss any larger pieces that might scrape the exposed skin from my open heels.

He didn't let go of my wrist, instead, he clutched it to his chest just above his heart, his eyes glittering with mischief as he looked down at me. A grin curled on my lips as I met that look and I could almost see all the trouble the two of us would get into in that moment, two kindred spirits, craving the dark, relishing in the danger, and taking every moment of pleasure in between. I drew closer to him, completely forgetting where we were, his violet eyes trapping me like a moth to a flame until I noticed the rips on his white buttoned shirt and the spots of blood seeping through the fabric.

"You're hurt," I accused, scolding him as I gripped his arm and turned him around to inspect his back. He'd taken the brunt of the impact from the falling glass and some of the sharp pieces had managed to slice open the shirt of his waiter uniform and through to his skin. They all looked superficial though, most of them already clotted now.

"It's not my fault." He chuckled, raising his hands up in a pleading gesture. "I can take a little pain, especially when I have a gorgeous woman pinned beneath me." He winked, pulling me against his side. He wrapped an arm around my shoulders, and we stared out toward the chaos in the ballroom.

I had completely forgotten about the two figures that stood at the end of the hall. Even now I could barely make out their forms in the shadows. Their faces were covered in black masks, the emergency lights gleaming off the hard plastic surface. The face coverings gave them both a menacing look, but I guess that was the point—you didn't blow up a building just for funsies. I glanced up at Spade and he waggled his eyebrows at me—well maybe some of us would.

"Spade," one of the men growled, drawing our attention back to them. There must have been a voice distorter hidden in the mask because it was deep and robotic. My gaze flicked between the two men and a million questions popped into my mind. Spade had been at Merrick's bar the night I went, and his black leather jacket didn't have the Demon Rider's crest embroidered onto the back. Was he with them? Was I about to escape into a fate possibly worse than my life here or maybe ... maybe he had nothing to do with them, or maybe he'd been there for the man that was sending glasses hurtling across the bar at the same moment we met.

I cupped a hand over my mouth to keep the sob in, pushing down the urge to run to them to pull off their masks and see if it was really Kellan's and Merrick's familiar faces beneath them. But I couldn't do that, not yet. If it was them, they were here for me, and that sent both a shiver of fear and a buzz of excitement through me.

"She's fine, now get on with it. We don't have all day," Spade shot back at the two hulking figures, his grin spreading from ear to ear as he clutched me closer. I couldn't help but lean against his side, carefully winding my arm around a section of his back that wasn't cut.

They both gave him one more hard look, unreadable because of the masks, and stepped out from the shadows and into the ballroom. I scanned their forms beneath the grey hoodies and jeans they wore, analyzing their build and the way they walked, looking for any sign of my guys. One of the men was taller than the other, his shoulders wider, and biceps bulging against the tight fabric. The other's thick corded muscles were almost as large, but he held himself with a lethal calm, each step measured and sure.

I stepped forward, the need to follow them to make sure they were safe building within me, but Spade's hand kept me back. "You're a troublemaker aren't you, sugar?" He chuckled. "I'm already going to be in a shitload of trouble for not getting you out right away but this is something you need to see."

My brows knitted together, and I glanced up at him, reluctantly taking my eyes off the two forms striding into the lion's den, thick smoke now curling around them and masking them from my sight.

"Just watch," he whispered, his violet eyes brimming with glee helping to take some of the edge off. If they were in danger, Spade wouldn't be this excited ... right? I tried to convince myself and looked back into the ballroom. Countless laser beams shone through the thick smoke, and my breath caught in my throat, about to rush forward, to knock them out of the way, until I noticed they were pointing everywhere ... except at the two of them.

"Put the guns down," one of the robotic masculine voices boomed, his voice echoing out through the ballroom and sending chills up my spine—not of fear but of yearning. The pure venom and malice that radiated off him made me forget where we were for a moment. "The guards outside won't be coming to save you either."

At that, the clatter of metal thumped against the ground in a sea of sound, but the lasers remained, trained on shadowed figures in the distance. They were completely surrounded. These men had brought enough back up to make even the vicious crime family back down.

"I want you to remember this moment, Angelo. We could kill you all right here and now," the other man said, his electronic voice booming. Spade vibrated with excitement beside me at that thought, and I couldn't deny the grin that tugged at my own lips. "But we'll spare you tonight, under two conditions."

They must know how the operation worked because I'd more than guarantee that Angelo was wearing a bulletproof vest, as I'd felt the bulky form beneath Tommaso's suit. Even so, there were still a few members of their family, including his brother, Lorenzo, who were missing tonight. We might be able to get away tonight, but only if not a drop of blood was spilled. Otherwise, even if they were able to get a headshot on both Angelo and Tommaso, the rest of his family wouldn't stop until they stomped out every last one of us.

"As of this moment, your engagement to Giana Bardot is officially over," the first man, whom I could only assume was Merrick, growled, his hands clenching at his sides as though he wished he could strangle the last breath from the man he directed that statement toward. His declaration held no room for argument, but Tommaso's roar of outrage still boomed throughout the hall.

"Your options are you die right now or you shut your mouth and accept that," the other man—Kellan—said, his tone calm yet deadly, as though he was only barely holding himself back from putting a bullet between Tommaso's eyes. "I should kill you right now for what you've done to her but I won't."

I wished I could wrap my arms around him right now, for putting that blood lust aside for now so we could get out. Because they'd all die, one way or another I'd make them pay, but we'd need a plan to cut off every single one of their heads so that they wouldn't spawn back to life. The Barones would die, even if it killed me in the process, but I'd make sure to take every single one of them with me deep down to the fiery depths of hell.

"The second condition," Kellan continued, regaining a slice of his composure. "Is for you all to empty wallets. Cash and jewelry all go in the bags, and if anyone tries anything we'll put a bullet through your head."

Ten figures emerged from the shadows at the mention of bags, the smoke still so thick I couldn't make out anything more than the outline of semi-automatic rifles pointed at the crowd, the beams of the lasers shortening as they approached. Judging by the amount of red light beams that remained unmoving, I could only imagine how many others they had with them. The figures circulated through the crowd, the click of metal and jewels audible through the gasps and whimpers of fear emanating from the guests.

I could only register the movement of those figures through the ballroom, still unable to make out the faces of who they approached. Finally they stepped back into the shadows, their lasers rejoining the others as they steadily held the crowd at bay.

"We're the Devil's Demons, and you'll never put your hands on her again, Tommaso Barone. If you try, I'll take my time breaking you—day by day, piece by piece—until you're begging for us to take mercy upon you and end your pathetic existence," Merrick declared, stepping forward and pulling something from his pocket. "But even then, just know our devil doesn't do mercy, doesn't feel remorse. Our devil feeds on violence and mayhem and now that we're at their side, you'll be seeing a lot more of it."

My breath caught in my throat at his declaration, at the claiming, at the promise of retribution. Because although he hadn't said my name, hadn't even revealed that the devil was a female, I knew these were my guys. This was Kellan and Merrick and the three of us would turn this town upside down—four of us, I amended, glancing up at Spade. With his white hair glowing in the faint emergency lights, face split in a childlike glee at the promise of violence. I couldn't help but mirror his expression, as hope bloomed in my chest—even fuller and brighter than it had been even before the airport. Running had been my last resort. I didn't stand a chance at standing up against the Barones, but now—now we just might. Curiosity bubbled up inside me as I looked back out to them, wondering what had happened since I'd left that got Kellan and Merrick to this point. They had connections with some of the gangs as teenagers, were part of fighting rings and other illegal activities, but I never thought they would've amassed this sort of power, especially under Angelo Barone's nose, to be able to pull this off.

"This is a remote detonation. Those explosions before, those were just to get your attention," Merrick's disguised voice sneered. "If anyone tries to come after us, I'll blow this place without a second thought with everyone trapped inside." He paused as screams erupted. His head swiveled around the room and the cries cut off immediately at his pointed glare. I could only imagine how eerie and terrifying that mask looked in the pale emergency light shining through the thick smoke still billowing in the air as chunks of drywall crumble to the ground in the distance.

"And don't even try to call anyone. We've jammed the towers, so you won't be able to get through," Kellan chimed in, pulling something from his pocket as well. At that an electronic beeping sounded somewhere above us, the sound constant like the ticking of a timer. "You have thirty minutes before the bombs automatically disengage, if no one attempts to leave in that time. If someone does, let's just say there won't be much left of this building by the time all the detonations we set up go off."

"That's our cue," Spade whispered in my ear. And before I could make a move, he scooped me into his arms, striding toward the emergency exit at the end of the hall.

"You know I can walk?" I asked dryly, but I didn't put up much effort to get away, enjoying the feel of his strong arms tucking me in against his chest. Sure, I might have daydreamed of slitting people's throats open, but that didn't mean a bitch didn't like cuddles every once in a while.

"I can't let the devil slice her feet open on the glass now, can I?" he quipped back, the crunch of crystal under his feet punctuating his excuse. "I don't think your other demons would let me live if I did."

I clamped my lips shut, not wanting to draw attention to him including himself in my demons, hoping it hadn't been just a slip of the tongue. Because I wanted him to be. After so many years apart and after being forced into accepting a relationship with Tommaso, I was done playing by society's rules. I wanted what I wanted—who I wanted, and I instantly knew Spade was someone I craved.

With that, he turned, using his back to press against the bar of the steel door, giving me one last look at the wreckage of the Barones' pride and joy. Light filtered in past me to illuminate the hallway, cracks running along the drywall, the shattered chandelier lying in broken shards littered along the hall, and the thick smoke that still clung to my skin, and my clothes, hanging thick in the air. Muffled sobs and coughs were still audible from the hall, but I didn't care, every last one of them could rot in there, as long as my guys got out.

I could only hope the destruction caused here today was symbolism for what would happen to them and their empire. Because now that I was out, now that I was free, I wouldn't stop until their world came crumbling down around them for everything they'd done to me, to the childhood I never got a chance at, and for the people of this town, of this country, who scraped by day by day just to put food on their tables while the Barones raked in cash they could never possibly spend in a lifetime. Their lavish lifestyles were built upon the backs of those they took advantage of.

Spade paused as though he knew I needed a moment to let it all sink in, and only when I turned my head, unable to stomach looking at it anymore, did he step back through the opening and let the door slam shut on the past six years of my life that I'd fought tooth and nail to escape. I drew in a long, deep inhale, my lungs expanding so much it felt as though it was the first real breath I'd taken in years. A weight lifted off my chest in that moment, the invisible iron shackles I'd felt pressed against my skin for so long vanished too. I was free. But still, some anxiety remained, and I knew I couldn't truly bask in this feeling or fully work through the trauma of the past and recover until my guys were out too, not until we were speeding away from this godforsaken place—not until every last one of the Barones were dead.

I wiggled in his grip as he turned to walk down the pathway and toward a waiting black armored vehicle idling at the back, attempting to see the mayhem they'd caused on their way in. With the number of guards out here before, they'd had to have done some serious damage not only to have them all taken out but to do so without anyone inside being tipped off. I could just make out figures clad in black, masks obscuring their faces, prodding bound, suited guards forward with the barrels of their rifles into the front doors.

"Now, now, I promise there'll be plenty of time to see and cause your fill of death and destruction, sugar. But we're in a bit of a time crunch right now." Spade chuckled, and his fingers wrapped under me to pinch my ass lightly. I jumped at the sting of pain that radiated there, sending a wave of both annoyance and arousal through me. I attempted to pin him with an incredulous glare but judging by his smirk even he knew it was halfhearted. "Don't act like you didn't like it."

Fuck, Spade was dangerous. I knew what was at stake right now, the enormity of this situation wasn't lost on me. But it was almost as though he knew I was barely hanging by a thread right now, that the emotions of relief, suspicion, and dismay all warred inside of me, fighting for dominance. I had no doubt that his teasing was genuine, yet he knew I needed something to take my mind off fully going through all of the clashing feelings, and I had no doubt he wouldn't take advantage of me, not in this state. My mind was still reeling at the sharp turn of events that tonight took.

Spade continued to carry me to the car and I didn't complain one bit. Honestly, with everything that happened, I wasn't even sure my legs would support me right now. Though when we got to the car, I had to push down my disappointment as he eased me out of his arms to open the door of the SUV for me.

"Get in," Spade whispered, gesturing to the interior of the SUV before he focused on the rear of the vehicle. He drew a Glock from the holster at his side and eased forward silently. His face was drawn in concentration but there was a faint smile there, betraying his excitement as he stalked whatever threat he'd sensed.

I was about to get into the back when I paused, registering the faint crunch of shoes on the pavement as someone approached. My heart leapt in my throat as my adrenaline spiked. I glanced out of the car window, thankful for the blacked-out windows as another figure advanced, a gun in his meaty palms.

I swallowed against the lump that formed as I saw that gun pointed right toward the back of the car, prepared for any movement Spade may make. My panic ratcheted and I glanced at the floor, desperately searching for any sort of weapon to help him.

A metallic glint caught my eye under the back seat, and I hurriedly reached for it, attempting to do so silently. The cool feel of steel pressed against the pads of my fingers as I wrapped them around the middle of the bat and a sense of calm took over while the complete helplessness slipped away from the hefted weight of it. No one was going to take away my opportunity to leave if I had a say in it, and tonight was the best chance I'd been given in years.

I slipped my shoes off and placed them gently on the car floor, wanting to be as silent as possible as I stepped toward the front of the car. Ducking down to make sure the figure couldn't see me, I stopped at the passenger's side of the hood and watched him approach the rear of the vehicle. I clutched the bat to my chest with both hands to keep it from knocking against anything and giving me away.

"I wouldn't take another step if I were you," Spade said in a singsong voice. I glanced over my shoulder just as he stepped around the taillight, his gun already raised. I sighed a breath of relief at his words, grateful he hadn't rushed forward with the other man's gun drawn.

I eased around the front of the car, making sure he was facing Spade before I rounded the corner. My footsteps were silent on the asphalt, rocks and sand gritted against the soles of my feet, but I pushed the discomfort from my mind as I brought the bat up and over my shoulder.

"I saw you bring her out here," a familiar male voice sneered, and my mind searched for where I recognized it. "Give me the boss's useless slut and I'll let you go."

Useless. That word rang in my mind as I truly took in the guard's face for the first time. I was so focused on helping Spade, on making sure he was safe, I hadn't scanned the man's features.

"I'll take my time gutting you for that," Spade said gleefully, and I could only imagine the sadistic grin splitting his face.

It was one of the asshole men that had stopped me at the airport, had thwarted my attempt at escape, sending all my dreams swirling down into a dark abyss of despair. *He isn't going to do it again, that's for sure.*

I set my sights on his gun, knowing what I had to do. I closed the distance between us, my footsteps light and swift, my muscles bunching as I swung the bat. The hard metallic surface clanged as it collided with the fragile bones of his outstretched hand, sending the gun flying in the opposite direction.

A shot rang out, piercing my eardrums and echoing over the cry of pain that burst from the soon-to-be-dead guard's mouth as he snatched his hand back, clutching it to his chest. I didn't let myself lose momentum, no—I brought the bat back and swung again, putting my hips into it as I aimed for his face. Bones crunched as I made impact with his nose with a sickening, wet smack.

Blood spurted from his nose, gushing down his lips and chin as I readied for another strike. An agonized scream pierced my ears, slightly muffled by his hands rushing up to assess the damage. The sound brought a wicked grin to my lips as I swung again, this time landing a blow to his abdomen.

"Fucking bitch," he cried, doubling over from the pain that must've radiated from his middle now. I vaguely registered the red smears coating the silver bat, the smattering of it sliding off his face, landing in thick drops against the pavement.

I brought the bat down on the back of his head, letting all of my pain, fear, and anger funnel through the slap of metal against flesh. He fell to his knees, his hands rushing away from his battered face to hold himself up.

I turned my head over my shoulder at the sounds of the car door opening behind me. The driver stepped out, his gun raised, seemingly hoping to help us out ... until he took in the entire scene, the guard already sprawled out on the ground. He scratched his light shaggy brown hair in confusion before he shrugged and got back into the vehicle, clearly convinced we had it handled.

"Now, now," Spade chided, causing me to whip my head back to the asshole guard. "I already warned you about your language toward my sugar."

He stepped forward and pressed the barrel of his gun to the guard's forehead. The guard heaved in a deep breath, his body trembling as he held himself up, blood still dripping from his bent nose.

"Please," the guard whispered, the sound barely audible over his panting breaths.

"As much as I'd like to see you beat this asshole to a bloody pulp, we might not have time for that right now," Spade grinned, completely ignoring the waste of space in front of him as he glanced at me. Some of the bloodlust cleared from his violet eyes as his gaze slid to the exit we came from. My stomach twisted and some of the fog cleared from my own mind as worry for Merrick and Kellan swept in.

"One more swing?" I asked sweetly, glancing up at him from beneath my lashes. "We have ... history." My eyes lit with violent delight as he met my gaze and a visible shiver of desire ran over his body.

"I can't say no to you," he beamed, both of our gazes slicing back to the guard. He looked between us, and a whimper slipped from his lips as he glimpsed the same wicked delight on both of our faces. “Make it a good one.” Spade winked at me and stepped back, his gun easing away from the guard’s temple but he still kept it trained on him.

I’d felt overwhelmed by emotions just moments before, and I knew that would all come rushing back in as soon as this adrenaline subsided and my heart calmed to its normal pace. But I needed more—I needed to see his blood flow again by my hand. I had to make him feel the way I had at the airport, bask in the icy shards of fear that caused him to tremble. I’d pay him back for his heartless man handling, the enjoyment he took in crushing that last shred of my hope as he’d marched me back to Tommaso. I hadn’t forgotten about his friend either, his face ingrained into my memory. His time would come too.

It was fitting that the start of this journey, returning to East Haven with Tommaso, would start and end with this man. But this time, I was the one with the power, and I already knew there was no way he’d be able to live after seeing Spade’s and the driver’s faces.

“Useless,” I sneered down at him, repulsion coating the word that had echoed in my ears as he shoved me into that room, stealing away the last seconds I’d had before shoving me back into Tommaso’s net. I pictured his smug laugh and dark look as he and the other guard had given Tommaso and me space on the plane, remembering my promise to get my revenge.

And with that I lifted the bat over my head and brought it down with all my strength. The metal smashed against the back of his skull with a satisfying *thwack*, a gash splitting the skin from the impact as blood sprayed. His hands gave out beneath him, sending his already battered nose slamming into the asphalt, his body going slack as his consciousness fled. His back still raised in shallow breaths though—he was still clinging to life.

"I fucking love you," Spade breathed, heat pooling in those violet eyes as they held mine before he pulled the trigger.

Warm blood splattered onto my bare feet, pulling me from my trance. My pulse pounded, the cool breeze sweeping through my hair as the shot rang through my ears. The faint tension that had radiated through the guard's body after my hit fled the moment the bullet sunk into the back of his head, blood and gore sprayed out around him. My chest lightened at the sight of his unmoving form on the ground and excitement bubbled up in me.

My brows furrowed as Spade's words registered, drawing me from my thoughts. I dragged my gaze up to look at him.

"What?"

Spade's black dress shoe collided with the now lifeless guard's head, the wet *thunk* echoing off the pavement before stepping over him, like he was nothing more than a piece of garbage littering the ground. He closed the space between us and holstered his gun again.

"You said I could tell you I love you the next time we brought a man to his knees." He glanced back over his shoulder, pointedly eyeing the dead guard's lifeless body on the ground, blood pooling around him.

He swiveled back to me, a wicked, mischievous grin spreading across his lips, seemingly daring me to disagree. I sucked in a startled breath as his arms wrapped around me and hoisted me up against his chest again, the sudden movement catching me off guard. He strode around the front of the vehicle and back over to the still open-door, basking in the delight of either his kill or getting to tell me he loved me, I honestly couldn't tell.

"But what about ...?" I trailed off. I was certain it had been Kellan and Merrick back there, but what if it wasn't? I honestly couldn't believe this was real until I saw them sitting in front of me peeling those masks from their faces. All of this felt way too good to be true. Could this be a dream, just a figment of my imagination? Had I fallen in the bathroom and this was my mind playing tricks on me, showing me something that could never come true?

"They'll be right out," Spade promised, his hands gently placing me down and turning me to face the interior of the car. "But I promise if you don't get in before they get out, they're going to kick my ass or at least try to." He chuckled, his hands sliding down to rest under my biceps to help support me as I climbed in. My heart hammered in my chest in a mix of apprehension and excitement, but what choice did I have? Did I really want to stay here? Hell no—I couldn't even imagine how bad things would get after this. The small freedoms I thought I had before would be nonexistent now.

I glanced up at the front as I took a seat, the shadowed driver seated in the driver's seat didn't bother to glance back as Spade climbed in beside me and tossed the bat under his seat. There were four seats in the back, the two we sat in faced the front, while the other two faced the back. Meaning, I would get to see them as they took off their masks, see my guys after everything they just did for me and everything that happened between us earlier today. My breaths came in ragged pants, and I attempted to calm them as my pulse pounded in my ears. Spade's hand slid along the smooth skin between my shoulder blades, helping to calm me a fraction.

"There was a reason I wanted you to see that, why I refused to take you out before you heard what they had to say," he murmured, some of the usual mischief fleeing his violet eyes. "Just trust me."

And for some reason I did. I barely knew the man, had only met him once before, but something about him had called to me even then. And even though it was way too soon for him to be proclaiming his love for me, there was just something about his confession that made me actually believe him. It was as though he'd awakened something within me that had been forced to slumber for years. Two kindred spirits that were ready to dance together again. To weave mischief and mayhem into the hypnotic dance of life and revel in every minute of it. I dipped my head in agreement, our eyes locked on each other, drawn in like a moth to the flame, so unaware of the death that loomed so near.

Hurried footsteps pounded against the pavement, drawing my attention to the car door still left ajar. My heart skittered as fear and excitement mixed in my chest. Spade chuckled as he sat back in his seat, his arm draped over my shoulders as he turned to watch as well. Two figures emerged from the direction we'd come, clad in grey zip-up hoodies and black jeans, the menacing thick black masks still covering their faces. They hopped into the back with us and my breath caught in my throat as they strapped themselves into the two seats opposite from us, and Spade pulled the door closed.

"What the hell happened out there, Spade?" one of the masked men demanded.

"Oh just letting off a bit of steam." Spade chuckled, waggling his eyebrows as he gave me a secretive grin.

"Drive," the same masked man ordered, slamming the separator closed. I gripped the armrests as the car jerked into motion, peeling down the cobblestone driveway to the exit. "Goddammit, Giana, put your seatbelt on," he snapped as I swayed to the side, Spade's hand on my shoulder the only thing keeping me upright.

"No," I whispered, the unbidden word slipping out before my brain could even wrap around what I was saying.

"No?" the robotic voice growled, and I could even imagine Merrick's brow lowering into a glower. But that was the thing—I didn't want to imagine it. I wanted to see it with my own two eyes. I needed proof this wasn't all some dream and I was really here, in a car with the two guys I'd loved my entire life, who I tried desperately to protect, who I never thought would forgive me for the lies I'd spun—that I was finally safe.

"Take off the masks." That was all I could say, all I could focus on right now. Spade's hand gripped my shoulder to keep me from toppling sideways as the SUV turned onto the main road. I felt as though I didn't have full control of my body, my mind so focused on the two men in front of me, on everything that just happened, that I couldn't will the strength into my muscles.

Both men glanced out the window, clearly making sure we weren't being followed before slipping off their hoods. I clasped my hand over my mouth at the mere sight of their hair, one golden strands and the other black curls. They pulled off the masks, their faces hard and coated in beads of sweat, their breaths coming in ragged pants, but it was them. Merrick and Kellan had threatened the largest crime family on the East Coast, had basically held them hostage and taunted their inability to fight back ... for me.

A million thoughts buzzed around my mind at the sight of them. I wanted to ask them how they'd done it, why they'd done it, what was the plan now? But as my eyes flicked down to my lap, I took in the clutch, somehow miraculously perched in my lap, and the dress Tommaso had custom-made for me. I had to get it off—now—I had to get rid of every last possession I had from him. Not only because who knew if he had a tracker on my phone, or in my clothes, but because the only thing I could think of now was the slide of that silk against my skin, reminding me of his hands caressing me possessively. Bile rose in my throat, and I fought to keep it down, to not spill my guts all over the inside of this car.

My eyes widened and my muscles went rigid as panic set in. My hands shook lightly, my breaths coming in rapid pants as I attempted to fill my lungs, but no matter how many inhales I took it was never enough. It was as if his presence still lingered on me, sticking to my skin like the cloying scent of his aftershave. I needed to get it off me, to wash it all away, but I couldn't, not yet. So the next best thing was getting these damn clothes off me.

"Giana, what's wrong?" Kellan asked, his sable eyes creasing in concern as he lunged forward. He attempted to take my hands but I pulled them out of his grasp, unable to have something else touching my skin right now. Spade's arm eased away from me at that, and I sighed a small breath of relief at the ease of pressure, but it still wasn't enough.

"Clothes," I gasped, my throat closing in on itself with each second that dragged by. I gripped the armrest tighter, suppressing the urge to claw at my neck. "I need clothes."

Merrick and Kellan both stared back at me, confusion creasing their brows, until Spade began pulling off his ripped white shirt, spots of blood dotted along the back. But I didn't care, I needed something, anything else.

"No," Merrick growled, scowling at the shirt like it had personally offended him, unzipping his grey hoodie. It just went to show how bad the panic attack was since I wasn't mesmerized by his bulging pecs and abs on full display, instead my focus fully on the sweatshirt he extended to me.

Immediately I slipped off the black dress, gritting my teeth against the feel of the fabric sliding against my skin, and flung it off as quickly as I could. Merrick cursed under his breath, clearly not expecting me to shed the clothing so suddenly, but I didn't care. The windows were blacked out and the partition between us and the driver up front was closed. At this point I couldn't have cared less if the entire town saw me naked just as long as I got this off me.

I flung the fabric to the floor, uncaring of the blood that still speckled my feet, and gently took the hoodie from Merrick and slipped it on. As soon as I zipped it up, I slid off the lace panties and unhooked the bra through the sweatshirt, maneuvering it to pull it out of the opening. I had to get rid of everything. I didn't care that I was sitting here in front of these three guys with the chilled air-conditioned breeze flowing up the hem of the hoodie—I didn't care if I had to go commando in front of anyone else either. Every piece of clothing had to go.

The entire car sat in silence, all three of them watching me intently as I gathered the clothes off the floor, found the clutch beneath them and pressed the button for the automatic windows. Merrick inhaled as though he was about to warn me to stop, but I didn't care. Not only did I need it out of my sight, but if there was a tracker, I couldn't let it lead them to wherever they were taking me, not after everything they just went through for me, not ever.

I threw the clothes out first, not caring where we were. I could be throwing it in the middle of the sidewalk for all I knew, it just needed to go. I put all my anger, fear, and frustration into it, a scream ripping from my lips as they launched from my hand. I opened the clutch next, tossing the phone with all my might, the crunch and shattering of glass bringing a faint smile to my lips. *I hope he finds them, especially that phone. I hope he finds them and that final slice of hope slips away like he stole mine from me at the airport.*

Next I fished the money out of the hidden pocket, clutching it in my hand as though it was my good luck charm. And it was—it was Francine's goodwill and kind heart, not to mention her meddlesome nature, that put these events into motion. If she hadn't convinced me to check the entire street, perhaps I would've given up after the first few shops and never saw Kellan or Merrick today. And they never would've known what Tommaso had done to me ... With that I tossed the clutch out the window, a weight lifting off my chest as the final remaining item I had from him flew away.

I hunched over in my seat, staring at the wad of bills clutched in my hand and thinking of what had almost been. I'd almost left tomorrow morning with two hundred dollars in my pocket, a generous donation from Francine, but not much to live off of. I hadn't allowed myself to think about what I was willing to do to get away, what I almost went through just to survive.

A sob racks my chest at that thought, mourning for the life I almost had to turn to, the woman I almost became and the girl I used to be—her life upended too soon, her dreams smashed in one day. But most of all my tears were ones of joy, of hope for a better future. Something I never even dared to dream of happened today, and my mind was still trying to wrap itself around my new reality. Spade's hand rubbed tender circles on my back as we sat in silence, the only sounds piercing through the night sky were my ragged breaths as tears streamed down my face, blurring my vision. I slowly raised my head, sitting up in my seat, and wiped away the tears drenching my cheeks, the spray of blood now coating my hands catching my attention, and I winced as I pressed too hard on the bruise hidden beneath the layers of makeup. Uncaring that I may have wiped some of it away, I finally pulled on the seatbelt that I knew they were itching to buckle themselves.

My gaze flicked to each of them, my chest lighter now than it had felt in years. I knew it would take time to work through everything that happened, both mentally and with Merrick and Kellan, but I was so grateful to have this chance. To not have to lose pieces of myself by either living with a monster or on the streets. Merrick gripped his armrests just as I had before, the muscles in his jaw twitching with the effort it took to hold himself back. Kellan sat in stunned silence, and I could see that internal struggle within him as he debated whether he should push Spade out of the way to be the one comforting me. And Spade, he gave me an approving nod, his violet eyes full of rage, understanding, and just a hint of menace as though silently promising that we'd bring them all to their knees. His look made me wonder what had happened to him in the past, what had he gone through that made it seem as though he could read every thought crossing my mind right now.

"Thank you," I breathed, capturing each of them in my gaze. The sudden words caught them off guard, Merrick and Kellan looking back at me with confusion and a faint smile played on Spade's lips. "You didn't have to do this, help me get away. Any of you or your friends could've been hurt or worse ..."

I didn't want to allow myself to think about how horribly tonight could've gone. They had no idea what was going on past the bruise covering my cheek and had no obligation to me.

"Giana," Kellan said, disbelief thick in his tone, but I couldn't hear whatever he was about to say, not while my head was still reeling from everything that happened tonight. I couldn't chance the tiny flicker of hope that they came for me to be snuffed out just yet. We would never get the six years that we lost back, but we might just have a chance to make up for them now.

"I was going to run, tomorrow morning," I murmured, some of the lingering tension easing at that admission as I held the cash up for them so they could understand the desperation and how close I'd been. It was the first time I said it out loud. I hadn't been able to tell a soul, not until now.

Merrick's hands shook, his knuckles white from the effort it took to hold himself back. "I'll rip his throat out," Merrick ground out, the muscles in his jaw ticking as he forced the words out.

"No, you won't," I breathed, a lethal calm sweeping over me. This wasn't like when I'd warned him from keeping away from Tommaso in high school, attempting to keep the peace and protect Merrick—no, my proclamation had a very different turn this time.

"Even after all this?" Merrick asked incredulously, mistaking my intentions. "I'm going to choke his last breath out from his pathetic, vile mouth."

"No, you won't," I declared, my eyes slicing between each of them, Merrick's anger fading at the hard look of determination in my gaze. "Because I want to—no, I need to. I deserve to be the one who steals his last breath from him after all he's done."

"Fuck yeah," Spade exclaimed with a fist pump, breaking the tension that had stretched through the car.

CHAPTER SEVENTEEN

GIANA

NOW

TO SAY THINGS WERE tense for the rest of the drive would've been an understatement. A sense of unease had settled over us. The emotions hung thick in the air, and none of us knew where to start. We all had a lot to discuss, I knew I would need to tell them what happened that led to me leaving, but I couldn't handle that right now. I felt as though I'd been in survival mode for the last six years—hell, most of my life—waiting for the next thing instead of truly appreciating and living life to its fullest. My body still thrummed with nervous energy as I attempted to reconcile how drastically my life had just changed.

I watched as the car sped along familiar roads leading out of the town of East Haven, past a few of the surrounding towns and into the neighboring one of Fallpond. This must have been one of the reasons they flew below the Barones' radar, operating their gang just beyond the town's limits. They had some connections here still but they saw it as too small, too poor to bother with for the most part.

We pulled into a long driveway, surrounded by wrought-iron fencing, and a line of five more cars followed in behind us before a large gate rolled closed, the clang of the metal reverberating through the car. I hadn't even noticed the other cars on the drive here, my mind too preoccupied to even think to look behind us. I squinted out the windows, attempting to get a better view of the surroundings but the tinting on the windows made it almost impossible in the dark night. All I could make out were the glow of headlights.

The SUV rolled to a stop just outside what looked to be a separate garage. Six large doors lined the front of what looked larger than most mechanics' shops. I glanced at Merrick, but he had his phone pressed to his ear, barking orders to the rest of their team from what I could make out. Deep exhaustion weighed on me, now that I was finally away from Tommaso my body needed a reset—to shut down and recuperate from being on high alert all the time. But that was wishful thinking. I hadn't missed Merrick's and Kellan's furtive glances, the way they had almost asked a million questions on the drive but held themselves back.

Spade pushed the door open almost immediately and climbed out the back. He clearly had some sort of idea what the tension was about and had no wish to be part of it. I bit my tongue, holding back the annoyed grumble that begged to slip out. I just wanted to go to sleep, to let my mind and body rest and process everything in the morning. But judging by how Spade approached the other cars lining up behind us and directed them off toward the far side of the garage, I knew that wasn't going to be happening anytime soon. Despite my need to know how they pulled tonight off, I didn't want to deal with the questions I would get in return.

Kellan stepped out of the car next and waited near the door, silently reaching out a hand to help me down. I frowned down at my bare legs. Sure the hoodie was long on me, but it only reached about mid-thigh, plus I didn't even have my shoes anymore after Spade had passed them to me and I tossed them out of the window too. I met Merrick's gaze as I glanced up and grimaced at the brow he cocked in response. He didn't even need to say anything—that look said it all. Either I got out now or he'd heave me over his shoulder, and with the length of this sweater I was not very keen on giving the rest of his guys a show.

I muttered unintelligibly under my breath, not even sure what I was saying at this point, and crouched over, holding the back of the sweater against me to keep from exposing my bare ass and pussy to Merrick. A shiver of desire went up my spine at that thought, and I almost let go of the thick grey material ... almost.

I reached out with my other hand and Kellan grasped it, our eyes locking at the touch. We both stayed frozen for a moment, and I took in the minor differences in the feel of his palm against mine now. His skin felt rougher than it used to, calloused from the hardships he'd had to face along the way. I sucked in a sharp breath as his other arm wrapped under my legs, catching me off guard, and cradled me against his chest. I suppressed the urge to snuggle into him, the movement so instinctual, but there was so much still between us, so much left to discuss.

My breath caught in my throat as I looked up at the large Victorian-style house. It wasn't dilapidated like I would have expected. No, the exterior looked pristine, as though it had been completely refinished.

"Where are we?" I whispered tentatively, not wanting the others to hear me as they gathered after climbing out of the other vehicles. I wasn't sure why; they'd helped tonight too. But after living in a crime family, I learned you could never be too careful. What if one of them worked for the Barones? I pushed down that thought, since if they had, tonight would've never happened. There were so many important government officials and businesspeople there tonight that if Angelo had been able to stop it, he undoubtedly would've. Tonight made them look weak, something that could spell death if they didn't take quick action. At least that was one good thing, they'd be so preoccupied with fighting off their rival gangs that they wouldn't be able to come after us immediately. But they would come, that wasn't a question. Because even if Tommaso was able to let go of his obsession, they would never just let me go, not now, not after they'd been shown up tonight. It would be a matter of pride to Angelo.

"It's, uh—" Kellan murmured, glancing back at Merrick behind us, a silent conversation passing between them. "—It's our house."

I chewed at the corner of my lip and held back any more questions. There was obviously something they were hiding from me, and I'd rather not keep asking questions just to get vague answers. Merrick brushed ahead of us to open the bright red door. If it wasn't for the thick iron fencing and gate, I would've thought this was a normal historical home as I looked inside the now open hallway. Kellan eased me out of his arms just past the doorway, my feet hitting the cool hardwood floor. My gaze swept around the quaint entryway. They'd kept it true to its original form rather than knocking down all the walls for an open floor plan. Glass-paneled double doors sat on either side, one leading into what looked like an office, a dark-stained wooden desk on one side of the room with a computer atop it and a fireplace decorating the opposite wall, while the other was a dining room. A long antique table spanned the room with velvet-upholstered dining chairs around it.

"Let's go upstairs," Kellan said, just as I took a step forward, my curiosity getting the better of me. He looked back at the group with Spade before joining me in the foyer. Merrick closed the door behind us, shutting out the pale starlight that had illuminated the small entryway. Kellan flicked on a light beside him, and the faint hum of electricity flickered on from a chandelier just above us. I immediately scooted out of the way, dashing up a few of the polished-wood stairs in order to not stand under it for longer than I had to, the memory of the one in the hall crashing around me still fresh in my mind.

I continued to climb the long staircase since I'd already leapt up and didn't want to just stand there. Especially not when they obviously didn't want me on the lower level. Their shoes echoed on the wood behind me, and I clutched the smooth varnished railing. Kellan moved to my side, his arm resting on my back, and I instantly knew it was to direct me rather than comfort me. My mind wandered to what they might want to keep hidden from me, but I pushed those thoughts aside, not needing another thing to worry about, not with the weight of the long overdue conversation looming over me. We'd spent six years apart, of course there were things they couldn't trust me with, not when they were running a gang this large that could stand against the Barones … and they weren't entirely sure if I could be trusted at all.

Frustration tensed my muscles, but I understood it. They never would've gotten to where they were today if they weren't careful. A hallway stretched along the top of the stairs leading in two different directions with white wooden doors lining each side. There had to be at least five in each direction as Kellan led me toward the right. He swung the first door open and gestured me inside, but I hesitated for a moment, sweeping my gaze around the room to make sure it was clear before I stepped in. My own hesitation proved I had my own reservations. It all seemed too good to be true. Everything in my life had gone so wrong for so long, it was hard to trust, and I had to believe this wasn't all a dream.

The space looked as though it was a small living room, with two couches and a large tv propped on the wall. Kellan's drawings decorated the walls, along with a few photos of cars, but it remained largely plain, lacking in décor, even something as simple as side tables. The sofa caught my attention, something snagging in my memory as I stared at it. The brown leather looked more worn than it had been in my memory, speaking to its recent use.

"You took the couches from the firehouse?" I asked in disbelief, glancing back at the two of them huddled just in the doorway, their bulky frames looking strange in the small space. Kellan stepped forward after a moment and rubbed the back of his neck, his eyes darting around the room and looking at everything but me. Merrick stepped forward too and closed the door behind him, shifting his weight from foot to foot.

A burst of laughter bubbled up at the image of these two men so nervous before me, while less than an hour before they were threatening to blow an entire building to the ground.

"It's not like anyone was using it," Merrick muttered, refusing to meet my eyes. A wry smile split my lips at that, and I knew then that even though we had six years of baggage to unload, we would be okay. These two men, one gentle, one gruff, were both lethal in their own ways. But that's what I loved about them, every facet of them, just as they loved my soft side mixed with the wild danger-loving side. The devil reunited with her demons once again.

I slumped back on the brown leather couch like I'd done so many times before, leaning back into the plush cushions. My eyes slipped closed as I relished in the moment I never thought would come again and felt the sofa dipping on either side of me, the two of them taking their positions as though the past six years had been a distant memory and no time had passed between us. But as I opened my eyes and saw their guarded looks, I was reminded of how much had happened, not only to me but to them too. We'd all gone through our own trials to get back to this moment here together, and it would be a disservice not to acknowledge that. They had to know what I went through just as much as I needed to know about them.

"I guess we have a lot to talk about," I gauged, sucking in a deep breath and steeling myself for the conversation I never wanted to have. I knew what would happen though if I told them everything. "Can you tell me first?" I asked, needing to hear their stories before I delved into my own. I had to hear the truth, without the guilt and regret that would undoubtedly come when I told them why I'd left first.

They both looked over me at each other, checking in before they said anything. My lips quirked to the side at the instinctual glance, making the distance seem even greater between us. We all used to be on that level, able to read each other's thoughts without a word passing between us. But now I was an outsider looking in.

"Giana," Merrick sighed, scrubbing a hand over his face.

"Please?" I whispered, letting some of the sorrow I kept buried deep down seep into my tone. I had to focus on something else, anything else. That breakdown in the car was still fresh in my mind, and I knew I would crumble if I had to speak now.

Kellan pulled in a deep breath on my other side, and Merrick's shoulders slumped slightly, his head dipping in agreement.

"Well, after you uh ... left," Kellan hedged, his hand rubbing the back of his neck as he grimaced. "We really didn't know what to do. We both sort of fell in with the gangs more, gaining a reputation and a name for ourselves."

I pursed my lips, not wanting to interrupt them, but I hated that they'd gone down that road, putting aside their aspirations and dreams, at least for some time.

"I continued working at the shop, but after a while they let me go because of the guys I was bringing in there," Merrick explained. "With the money I was getting from there and with my fights, I had enough to open up my own chop shop, and things sort of escalated from there."

"I found a tattoo shop a few towns over that was willing to take me on, but it was harder then because of our affiliation with the gangs," Kellan added. "So I ended up distancing myself from that life."

"The Demon Riders didn't like that, though. Kellan had become one of their best enforcers so they ended up sending me to rough him up," Merrick said with a derisive snort.

"Why would they send you of all people?" My brows furrowed in confusion, glancing between the two of them.

"We lost contact for a year or so, because honestly it was hard sometimes not to think of you when we saw each other," Kellan explained, his lips curving down into a frown. The few inches between us felt like miles at this point. I wanted to curl into his side like I'd done so many times before, resting my feet on Merrick's lap and reassuring them with my presence, but I couldn't.

I hated that I got between them like that, made them unable to maintain their friendship because thinking of me was such a heavy weight on their chests.

"I'll be honest, Giana. We were both fucked up for a long time. We were reckless, fell in with the wrong crowds, even turned to drugs and alcohol to numb the pain," Kellan murmured, his words cutting deep. I pulled in a ragged breath but refused to let anything else show. I wanted to know the truth and this was it. Raw and real, they were holding nothing back, and I had to respect that for what it was.

"I went to Kellan and told him about what the Demon Riders had planned and that's when he told me about his theory," Merrick said, glancing off to the side and refusing to meet my gaze. His mouth pulled down into a deep frown.

"We weren't able to see past what you'd done after graduation, enough to really put the pieces together. Our anger had clouded our vision. But things didn't add up," Kellan explained, playing with the hem of his hoodie. "But after a few years some of that haze had cleared and despite how hard I tried to find the signs, that you were slipping away from us because you loved him—"

A rumble emanated from Merrick's chest at that, cutting off Kellan's explanation for a moment before he continued.

"—but I couldn't. There were signs that something wasn't right, that you were hiding it from us. But not that your feelings had changed."

"Honestly, I wasn't as convinced. I hadn't had that moment of clarity yet, but I decided to trust my old friend," Merrick huffed out on a sorrowful sigh, and I could almost tell by the far-off look he got that he'd wished he could go back to that moment and change his outlook.

"So we came up with a plan; instead of working for the gangs, instead of fearing them, we would take them over," Kellan declared with a steely glint in his gaze. "There were enough people that we knew who weren't happy with the small gangs or living with being second to the Barones that we gained allies and started taking them over one by one."

"The last one was the Demon Riders. They were by far the largest gang of all of them and the most prominent to Angelo and his men," Merrick explained. "So we knew if they went missing, questions would come up about who had taken them out."

"So we made a deal," Kellan announced. "We let them live and in exchange, the older members and leaders would still wear the crest on their backs, still act like they were the ones running the show so no one in the crime family would think any differently. They'd think that the Demon Riders had run off the smaller gangs and that they were the only threat. Meanwhile, we lurked just behind the curtain, waiting until the moment we could strike."

"And that's when you came strolling into my bar, looking for a job," Merrick sighed, scrubbing a hand over his face and shaking his head as he clearly replayed everything that happened that night. "It just caught me so off guard. I couldn't help considering if we'd done this for nothing, just for you to throw it back in our faces and take off with him again."

"How long?" I choked out, my mind still racing to piece together the snippets of their lives they'd revealed. "How long have you been planning all of this?"

"It's been two years since we overthrew the Demon Riders and started planning to get you away from them," Kellan admitted, pinning me with an unreadable look. "We'd originally planned to go to New York but we moved everything up once you came back."

I pulled in a shuddering breath and let that admission play through my mind. For two years they'd been working on gathering enough force to go against the Barones, to give me the shot at fleeing, when they weren't even sure if that was what I wanted.

"So we have to know, Giana. Were we right? Did you have a reason for leaving us the way you did? Or did you leave because you had feelings for him and it just recently turned bad?" Kellan pleaded, his eyes creasing with pain. Clearly he knew either way would splinter his heart. "It won't change anything; we're still going to help you either way—"

"We just need to know," Merrick blurted, like he had already figured it out but just needed to hear the words come from my lips. I wished I could lie, to ease some of that guilt weighing heavily on his shoulders but I couldn't. I owed it to them after all this time to clear the air and tell them the truth.

I'd only told Sophia about how Tommaso had treated me, what he did to others to keep me in line, and what he'd nearly done to me. I hadn't told her all the details about how I got to New York in the first place. That would've put her in even more danger and I couldn't do that. Not when telling her the small amount I had already put her in peril.

"It all started with those texts, two weeks before my eighteenth birthday," I breathed, the words floating out of me and freeing me like a boulder being shifted from my chest. "Reminding me of a deal I'd made two years before."

Tears sprung to my eyes at the admission, something I never wanted to do. I never wanted Merrick to know that this all stemmed from that day. Merrick sucked in a sharp breath; his lips pressed together in a thin line as he pieced what had happened just after my sixteenth birthday.

"You got into that fight with Tommaso, trying to keep him away from me," I paused, swallowing down the lump that had formed in my throat. I kept my eyes focused on my lap, my fingers curling.

Tommaso was two years older than us and a few months before he was about to graduate, he took an interest in me. He would follow me home, lurk at the diner until I got off ... I was mildly interested in the fantasy of him but had made it clear I wouldn't go out with him. Despite everything, my heart had always laid with my two friends, even before I'd realized it.

"And after the police took you away, he showed up at my house that night," I said, not letting my voice falter, not even with the muttered curses leaving Merrick's lips. "We made a deal, I had to go out with him when I turned eighteen, and in exchange he wouldn't get his guys in the prison to jump you."

"If I'd known—" Merrick blurted, but I cut him off, my head whipping to look at him.

"If you'd known you would've gone after him and he would've killed you and just forced me to do it anyway. He would've threatened me with Kellan's life next. That's the kind of person he is, Merrick," I exclaimed, taking and clasping his hands in my own. The motion drew his gaze up to meet mine. "He gave the illusion of choice, had kept it up for over two years, but it had always been his plan."

"We could've helped," Kellan said weakly, as though he wanted to believe it but knew deep down there was nothing they could've done at the time that would've kept Tommaso away. If we'd killed him, his family would've destroyed us. Hell, we were just kids, barely eighteen.

"No, you couldn't have," I said with a sad smile. "I'd honestly hoped he'd forgotten about it all after leaving for college. So much so I had completely wiped it from my mind, grateful that you were still alive."

"So that's why you always convinced me not to go after him," Merrick mused, and I nodded. We both knew that it was suicide to go after the Barones then, but it was as though I had to keep reminding him of that since they hadn't come after him before.

"I guess I should've told you then, at least about his threat," I admitted, my fingers clammy in his and sweat beaded on my brow. I hadn't imagined this would be so difficult. "But I knew I'd have to admit the deal I'd made with him then and I just couldn't. I didn't want you to have any more reason to go after him."

His eyes creased with pain, his lips quirking to the side, but he didn't say a word. He knew I was right. His anger and protectiveness would've gotten the best of him.

"But the texts started two weeks before my eighteenth birthday and they didn't stop." I sighed, letting Merrick's hands slip from mine as I leaned back against the couch cushions. This was something they both needed to hear. "I convinced myself it was just going to be one date. That I'd go out with him once and that would be it."

"What happened, Giana?" Kellan asked. I could tell he was trying to hold back his own anger, directed at Tommaso, not me, as he pieced everything together.

"He was waiting for me, at my house the morning after my birthday—had apparently been waiting for me all night it seemed ..." I trailed off, memories of the three of us on my birthday night playing like a film on repeat in my mind like they'd done a million times before. "And he snapped, told me that no one touched what was his and revealed his plan all along was for me to move in with him in New York."

They both swore, and I drew in a deep breath, grateful for the brief moment of reprieve before I continued.

"He threatened to have you both killed of course. He'd even gone as far as to wait while I packed my things."

I winced at the memory, unable to tell them everything that happened with him yet. If I did, I knew they wouldn't hesitate to make him pay. And that was a debt I needed to repay, not them.

"So at graduation, I knew I had to make you hate me. I had to make it seem like I was going with him because I wanted to," I admitted, and stared at my lap again, unable to meet their eyes and see the echoes of anger in them. "So I made it believable, to make you hate me, and convince him he had nothing to worry about and wouldn't just kill you for the hell of it."

It had been my choice to make them believe the lie. To commit to the role so fully that they would hate me. And that's exactly what they did.

"Because that's who he is. He was never going to take no for an answer. I've come to terms with that. There was no choice, no way to get out of it except running ..." I trailed off, meeting their gaze briefly before I continued, dredging up everything from the past six years.

I poured my heart out for them, not sparing the details, not for them. Not when I kept everything buried deep inside for so long. Not now when I didn't need to be scared. Because in their grief, they'd built something strong enough to stand up to the ruthless, nearly unstoppable crime family. And I knew one day we'd all laugh as we watched their world burn before our eyes ... or die trying. Because we had a shot now, we had something worth fighting for now that we were back together. And after everything they'd done to us, and this town, we had to take it.

CHAPTER EIGHTEEN

GIANA

NOW

I PACED ACROSS THE floor in the large bedroom, the fluffy white carpet tickling my feet with each step. My hands clenched at my sides and my teeth ground together as I held in the frustration mounting inside me. It had been two days since the engagement party, two days since they helped me escape from Tommaso, and two days that I'd been held up in this room by myself.

I needed them to give me space though, to be by myself for some time to process everything that happened. Honestly, I had to process more than the last six years. I'd been in survival mode for most of my life, never enjoying life, always on guard whether it was with my parents or Tommaso. The only moments of reprieve were with Kellan and Merrick. And I could tell that they too needed some time on their own.

Everything they'd known had been completely turned on its axis. Sure, they had their suspicions once time healed some of the wounds from me leaving, but they never actually knew what happened until I told them. It had felt like my lungs could expand for the first time, in who knew how long, once I finished my story up to the moment when Spade had caught me outside the washroom. I didn't spare any details from them, despite the guilt that creased their eyes as they sat absorbing everything. If there was supposed to be any hope for the future, we had to start on a clean slate.

So for the past two days I laid in bed, allowing my mind to register everything that happened—to accept that I did the best I could under the circumstances. I tried to protect Kellan and Merrick in the only way I could and I survived, and that was what was important. Despite how many times I wanted to give up, the weight of the world seemingly resting on my shoulders, I persevered, I kept breathing.

I mourned for the girl I used to be, for all the life and experiences I missed out on—on the life that could have been. I mourned for the woman I almost became—I knew the two hundred dollars, although generous, wouldn't have kept me off the streets. I hadn't admitted it to myself but deep down I knew what I was willing to do to get away from Tommaso, had even begun to mentally prepare myself for what I might become, what might be done to me. That was the hardest weight to let go of, to remind myself I didn't have to endure that life anymore.

Through my reflection I realized that although Tommaso claimed his reasoning for breaking me was so I knew my place, his jealousy and insecurities had peaked the closer we'd gotten to coming back to East Haven. He'd wanted to show me just how far he'd go for an innocent flirtation to make sure I knew he'd kill Merrick and Kellan if I ever approached them.

I knew he wouldn't let this go so easily, not only because of his obsession, but everything he'd worked for, each layer of manipulation he'd meticulously woven over the past eight years would be for nothing. His ego would never allow him to give up, not now, not when he'd look weak for losing me to men he'd consider "lesser," and not when he'd lose that self-satisfaction he'd built up by "helping lift me from poverty" as he liked phrasing it to his business contacts.

I began to process the trauma, both growing up as well as my time forced by Tommaso's side. I poured my heart and soul into a notebook I'd found, writing until the pen ran dry, until the words became mere scratches on the page. Tension lifted from my chest, leaving me feeling freer than I'd ever felt before. It was cathartic to get all of those inner thoughts written down, as though writing the words onto the page took the burden of the past off my shoulders with each stroke, each mark like a scar I was transferring from my soul and into the book. And as that pen died, it felt as though I was done—I was done with that chapter of my life. It was real, it had happened, but I no longer had to hold on to that pain and trauma. I felt validated having my thoughts and feelings laid on the page before me, like for one of the first times they really mattered.

But I couldn't stand to look at these four walls anymore, not after everything that had happened. The same duvet and soft white drapes that had seemed warm and comforting a few hours ago now sparked rage in me, and I wanted to claw at them and rip them to shreds. This space had been a safe haven for me to release and process the grief and come to terms with it—I'd never be able to turn back the clock or wipe the memories away, but I could accept them for what they were, forgive myself, and figure out how to move forward. I always knew I'd want to get revenge on the Barones and I would, but I couldn't allow that to cloud my mind. We had to come up with a well-laid plan, a game of sorts and have them play straight into our hand.

I knew I could leave; I hadn't been told to stay put, but they had understood that I needed some time to myself and had brought me food for every meal. I could go downstairs if I wanted to, right? I could go explore the house. Deep down I knew that was true, Merrick and Kellan had never been the type to lock me away, to keep me like a prized trophy on display. But I couldn't help replay the warning from the first night here, the insistence to go straight upstairs rather than explore the rest of the house. I'd been too exhausted both mentally and physically to fight back then, to assert I wouldn't be shut away or kept out of the loop—but I wasn't now. If anyone knew who I was, it was them, and they'd have another thing coming if they thought I'd be content to remain the damsel in distress.

Although I knew who they used to be, I couldn't shake that distrust that had built up like a wall around me, keeping me on my toes and protecting me from all the dangers of the past. *Did they want to keep me away from their guys for some reason? Did they not trust them, or did they not trust me?* I pushed those thoughts aside, knowing they'd do no good. There was no point in overthinking, for building everything up in my mind that may not even be true. Besides, if they didn't trust their guys, they wouldn't have brought them to the party the other night, right?

I had to go see them eventually, because I was tired of barely living, of going through the motions and never really enjoying myself. I mourned the time I had lost with Merrick and Kellan, but what was I doing now? I was wasting even more time and if I'd learned one thing in my life, it was you never know what the next hurdle will be. Despite my best intentions, I'd lost six years and I refused to lose another moment. I may have been unsure about what I wanted before, scared to take that leap, so worried about what society may think—but now, I couldn't care less. I knew what I wanted, and that was Merrick and Kellan … and Spade.

I knew as soon as my eyes locked onto those mischievous violet orbs that a spark connected us, like a twin flame. I knew I wanted him too and after being at Tommaso's will, I wouldn't let him claim another part of my mind, body, or soul for a moment longer. I was going to claim what I desired, what I craved …

But maybe I was getting ahead of myself. They could all have girlfriends—or wives—and had only helped me because that was the type of men they were. My lips pursed at the thought and I worked to push down the anger that boiled in my veins at the notion of them with another woman. I had no real claim on them, not after all this time, not after the lies I'd spun and the act I'd played to make them believe.

The only way to find out the truth was to pull on my big girl pants and go face them. So I took a deep breath, steeling myself for my new reality, and reminded myself I didn't have to be on guard all the time here. I didn't have to watch each reaction, looking for any sign of hostility and tiptoeing around so I didn't get hurt or lose my freedom. With that, I padded to the large wooden dresser and pulled out a pair of sweatpants. There weren't too many clothes here, and at least I could be grateful that there weren't any women's clothes, even if there was a lot of pink in the bedroom ... The pants seemed to match the hoodie I was already wearing that smelled just like my memories of Kellan. I pulled on the pants and tied the drawstrings taut on the too-large garments, hoping they wouldn't fall.

The nightstand caught my attention and I grimaced at the thought of leaving it unguarded. It was just a simple light-stained wooden table, with a white and silver lamp atop it and a glass of water by the bed—but it was what was inside the drawer that twisted at my stomach. Leaving the two items tucked inside was a huge step, a massive vulnerability I wasn't sure I was able to take. Both the notebook and the wad of bills from Francine were hidden within and both shone like beacons to me, keys that I wasn't sure I could stand to lose right now. My heart had splintered under the pressure of living with Tommaso, and although I'd begun to piece it back together, there were some cracks aching to be healed completely.

The notebook both gave me a sense of relief, to have those thoughts off my chest, but it sent a new wave of fear through me at the thought of someone reading it. It was one thing to relay events but my innermost thoughts and feelings were another thing entirely. The cash was another story—I wanted to give it back to Francine, to both thank her for her generosity and scold her for her meddling. But I knew I couldn't, not when Tommaso and his men would be looking for me. There was no way I could show my face in East Haven right now and expect to not be picked up straight away. But also that small crack screamed at me to keep it for now, just in case the guys weren't the same as I'd remembered and I again needed a way out ...

I forced myself to reach for a pair of socks in the drawer and pull them onto my bare feet, only then registering how cold my toes had gotten, and pulled on the new pair of running shoes, the tag still hanging from the laces. They must've gone to get them for me because the guys' shoes would've looked like clown shoes on me, and these fit perfectly. My pulse thundered in my ears at the step no matter how small it may seem, of distancing myself from these two items, but I knew I had to. I needed to build that trust back up, brick by brick, and this was the only way. So I put one foot in front of the other, pulling open the door to the empty hallway.

THE WARM SUMMER BREEZE flowed through the foyer, ruffling my hair lightly as I opened the front door. I'd searched the entire main floor and came up empty, my footsteps were light on the squeaking hardwood floor as I explored through the dining room and into the kitchen. It looked as though it had been remodeled recently, and while most of the original finishes remained, the cabinets were a bright white and the appliances in stainless steel, a stark contrast to the wood tones throughout the house. It was almost like they'd just hired someone to do what was necessary without really putting much of themselves into it.

But they got the furniture from the firehouse and now in the daylight the rest of the wooden furniture looked similar too. The dining room table, chairs, and the desk in the office had all been there. We'd kept most of it covered but I could place it all now. My heart panged at the nostalgic touch, an homage to our old hideout ... and perhaps this house would become the same now, our escape from the world, where we could just sit back and be us.

So I took a step out onto the porch and closed the red door behind me, breathing in the fresh summer air. It was so clean compared to the city, so vibrant and full of life. There the sun beat off the asphalt, the fumes clinging to your nostrils ... along with other things. Before, I'd wanted to escape the small town I was in for the city so badly—and just the thought of returning had sent bile rising in my throat—I never realized how much I missed it. It was easy to get lost in the bustle of people rushing past. I was able to forget my own troubles, my thoughts drowned out by the blaring horns and constant hum of people chattering. But with some of that tension slipping off my chest already, I was able to finally appreciate the quiet calm that came with a small town.

I glanced over at the garage, sure that I'd find Merrick there, and headed off in that direction. Thankfully there wasn't anyone else around to witness me standing back and inhaling the floral breeze that trickled past like I'd never breathed before. The entire house was abandoned from the looks of it. But if I knew Kellan and Merrick, there was no way that one of them wasn't here to look after me. The gravel crunched under my running shoes as I strode to the separate building. But as I neared, I noticed a glass door around the side, with large paned windows surrounding it. I almost continued, but pulled up short, nearly tripping over my own feet as a movement through the door caught my eye.

So I changed direction, heading around the side rather than to the red steel door in between the wide garage ones. Because the glass panes, reaching nearly to the top of the building, reminded me of somewhere else, somewhere the windows line the entire shop, the beaming sun illuminating even the darkest corner of the tattoo parlor.

I reached for the door tentatively, grasping the cool metal handle, shaded by the position of the sun against the towering Victorian house. I pushed aside any lingering worries and pulled the door open, the cool air from inside hitting me in the face as it rushed out. Kellan spun on his heel at the electronic chime that clanged through the silent shop.

His eyes widened as he scanned my form, and a shiver of desire slithered up my spine at his attention, at the concern creasing his brow. I took another step forward and let the door close behind me, the movement breaking the trance that had fallen over Kellan.

"Is everything alright?" he asked hesitantly, inching forward, his arm barely lifted as though he wanted to reach for me but he hesitated.

His concern for me warmed my chest, but at the same time, I didn't want to be coddled, didn't want to be seen as breakable.

This was not what I had wanted when I told them my story. My goal had been to tell them the whole truth so nothing laid between us, not for them to see my past, my trauma, before they saw the real me.

"Of course, everything is," I scoffed, downplaying my change in routine. Turning to look at the wall, black and white sketches and watercolor work displayed in frames. This art seemed more personal than what was in his shop in East Haven. It was just as beautiful of course, but that was more commercial, examples that people could have tattooed on them, art that showcased his talent at tattooing. This though, the detailed lines and vibrant colors were straight from his soul. Just as I had poured the essence of myself into that notebook, I could tell he'd done the same with his art.

"You've been through a lot, Giana," he soothed, stepping beside me, a hand tentatively brushing over my shoulder. I gritted my teeth at the light touch, the uncertainty in it. I was not breakable, I would not—could not allow what happened to destroy the person I was, the woman I could be.

"Stop," I barked, jumping away from him.

He needed to hear this; they all did if they were going to treat me like some broken doll rather than the bloodthirsty woman I was.

"You don't think I know that?" I asked incredulously. His hand slowly dropped to his side, his lips parting, but I cut him off. "I know what I went through. I'm done barely living because of that man."

"Giana," he murmured, as though he was trying to calm a wild animal. I took a deep breath, attempting to calm myself.

But as he took a step forward, I knew what I needed to do, what I wanted to do, to clear up all those lingering doubts, to show the love that never truly left and to chase away six years of memories of Tommaso's lips on mine.

I wouldn't be the damsel needing to be comforted by a man—I was the devil and I needed to start acting like it.

So I closed the distance between us, and before he could stroke my arm in that hesitant way he had before, I fisted my hands in his black T-shirt, and yanked him toward me. His hands gripped my biceps to keep himself steady, lips parting with a question on his tongue, but I smothered them with my own. My mouth captured his in a searing kiss, conveying all the emotions swirling around inside me like a tornado.

It was hard and unyielding, and he paused for a moment, his lips still beneath mine. Uncertainty coiled around my chest, and my hands loosened a fraction, about to back away when a ragged sob racked his chest, the sound vibrating through me as he kissed me back with just as much fervor. The kiss was rough and wild, filled with passion, pain, and relief. My friendship had always been soft and gentle with Kellan, but this was as though we were both releasing the hurt and the trauma of the past six years. Our tongues wound together in a dance that tied our souls back together after they'd been ripped apart so long before.

His hands slid from my arms, one reaching up to cup the back of my head, fingers winding through my messy hair, while the other slid to my back, pressing my body into his. The thick material of the hoodie grated on my nerves, and I needed it gone, needed to have my bare skin pressed up against him. Warm waves of ecstasy flowed through me, straight to my core, and I gripped him tighter, wanting to feel the hard press of more than his chest against me.

But before I could beg him to throw me down on the desk and strip the sweatpants off me, he pulled away, drawing in a ragged gasp of air, his chest rising and falling rapidly as he fought to compose himself. A chill swept over me in his absence, leaving me feeling bereft without the warm press of his muscled chest against me. Heat still lingered in his eyes, but there was a hint of hesitance that cut through the lust. Seeing that lifted some of the fog from me and brought me crashing back to reality. Still, I shoved aside all the whispering doubts that clawed their way back to the surface, reminding myself that I'd felt his need for me, just as hard, hot, and desperate as my own.

"Giana, are you—"

"Stop," I cut him off, not wanting him to ruin what just happened between us. That same frustration I'd felt up in the room set in, and I just wanted to flip over the desk beside us, to kick and scream, and to crawl into a ball and let all the rage and hurt flow freely from me in a stream of tears.

He rushed forward, arms grasping me just as my knees gave out, and I fought against all the emotions raging inside of me, cursing myself for being this weak. I thought I'd blown through this, had weathered this storm the last two days, but I hadn't seen the part that still lingered beneath all the bluster. But Kellan had, he'd seen right through the façade. I wanted none of this to affect me but it did, and it would for a long time. This was a wake-up call that I just had to take everything day by day.

So as I let all that frustration, pain, and anger flow freely—sobs racking my chest so hard I thought my ribs might splinter from the force—I let Kellan soothe me, and nuzzled into his chest as his fingers stroked down my hair.

"There's no rush, Giana," Kellan murmured. "You're safe. You'll always be safe with us."

My chest warmed as I looked up at him, blinking away the tears still blurring my vision. I hadn't realized how much I needed to hear that, that I was safe, that I could take my time healing. Because as much as I didn't want what had happened with Tommaso to take up anymore of my life—to cloud the now bright and sunny future I could finally picture, so close I could almost taste it—I couldn't just expect myself to completely recover in a couple of days.

I reached up, my fingers teasing along his smooth jaw, and traced the hard line, pulling strength from the muscles beneath it. He shuddered at the light touch, his face pressing into it like he needed more. My brows creased as I studied every line, every curve of the face I used to know so well, cataloging all the differences the years had made. But he still looked the same really, more defined almost, but despite all the emotional turmoil of the last six years, he was still my Kellan. I raised on my toes, and his hands tightened on me, as though he feared I might lose my strength again, but that was impossible with him by my side. My lips lightly brushed his in a tender caress and he groaned at the contact, his own capturing mine immediately this time.

I melted into him, our mouths coming together as one like a breath of fresh air filling up my starving lungs. My body hummed with pleasure at the sensuous kiss, and I moaned into his mouth as his tongue delved in to meet mine. My hand wrapped around the back of his head, smoothing over his black curls—needing this pressure, his touch like I needed air to breathe. How had I survived this long without him? How could I have ever thought I could live any semblance of a normal life without him?

"I just don't want to waste any more time," I whispered, as I leaned back, my lips still lightly brushing his with each word. "We've already lost so much, and I don't want another moment lost thinking about—"

His lips closed back over mine, stealing the words from me, showing me rather than telling me that everything would be alright. Because in that moment I knew it would—I knew despite the years between us, we didn't need to rush. I was safe now.

He pulled away much too soon, and I pushed down the urge to chase after him, reminding myself that we had time. His lips quirked up into a teasing smile, his hand trailing down the arm of the thick sweater as he took another step back. His fingers entwined with mine and he pulled me toward the desk.

My breath caught in my throat at that smile, that the slightest tilt of his lips made my heart flutter. I grinned back at him, my chest light as he tugged me closer.

"I wanted to show you this," he said, his other hand reaching for a sketchbook and flipping it open. He paused at a sketch ... of me.

I looked as I had the other night, my hair in the same curls, the hoodie on my shoulders rather than the straps of the dress, thankfully. My eyes were tilted down, drawn in sorrow, my lips slightly parted as if I was mid-sentence, and a swath of light stretched across my face, from moonlight that had been glowing down upon me at that moment. I expected my face to look broken but it didn't. I looked sad, the heaviness of exhaustion weighing me down, but there was something to my eyes. Despite the pain creasing them, there was a look of steel to them, a hardness that wouldn't be squashed so easily. And just above my hairline were two horns, they were shadowed and wreathed in flames. I knew then that it was to symbolize that ember that still glowed within, that was building into a burning flame with each moment the tension eased off my chest.

It showed not only how I had looked in that moment, but what Kellan saw within me, someone who wouldn't be broken and beaten down so easily. I glanced up at him then and he smiled back at me. He had never thought I was broken, merely bruised, in need of some time to heal so that the inner devil could regain her strength.

"I want a tattoo," I blurted, confusing both Kellan and me as the words left my lips. But as I turned them over in my mind, I knew it was true. I needed something to mark me, to remind me of that inner strength if times ever grew dark again. Something to remind me of the ties that bound me, the roots I had were so deep, so mighty that nothing would ever shake them.

Kellan studied me, like he could see every thought that passed through my mind. And without me even having to say a word he nodded, his hand reluctantly slipping from mine to grasp one of his example books.

"Then let's do it."

Chapter Nineteen

Giana

Now

"Just relax," Kellan soothed, placing a swift kiss on my cheek. I sighed an exaggerated breath and shook out my arms, hoping to work some of the tension out of them. "I promise it isn't too bad."

"I take it back, I don't want a tattoo," I squealed, wincing as though he was about to just start even with all my squirming.

"You don't have to if you don't want." He chuckled, about to put the tattoo gun back down. I pursed my lips and pinned him with a glare that burned into the side of his head. He knew exactly what he was doing. He knew I would relent if he backed down. And I knew he really would let me back out now, even after he'd taken the time to prepare his equipment and help me pick out the perfect design.

"Fine," I sighed, leaning back in the chair. "You promise it's not that bad?" I asked for the millionth time.

"I promise, it's not that bad." He laughed again, and I glowered at the amusement dancing in his sable eyes. "Besides, I'll be sure to kiss away the pain," he teased.

I lightly tapped his bicep and did my best to hide my blush as his laughter echoed around me. It hit me then how normal this seemed, how we'd slipped back into our usual banter like no time had passed. And despite my annoyance, I smiled back at him, my fingers itching to trace the lines of his lips and ingrain them into my memory.

We'd decided the best place for my first tattoo would be my bicep and he'd sketched out the design based on one in his book. When he stopped on one of the pages it somehow jumped out at me without even knowing its meaning. But when Kellan explained what it symbolized, I knew it would be perfect. It was called the Dara knot and was a Celtic design, the looping lines interconnected into a circle with four sections, all woven together with intricate lines. They were meant to symbolize the roots of an oak tree, so strong and magnificent it held up the massive sacred trees. I was immediately drawn to it for the beautiful design and the four different sections coming together as one. But when I heard that it was a symbol of strength as well, I knew it was exactly what I needed.

Getting this would be the perfect stepping-stone to the next chapter of my life. I'd be saying goodbye to the past, to the people that still tried to cling to me, to pull me back down into the abyss, and instead embracing my future, the one I could see with myself and the three men who'd saved me. Two of which had always been there for me, had been all I could think of for most of my life, and the third called to my soul. Although we hadn't known each other for long, I could tell he was meant to be part of my life. I wasn't sure how yet, but I knew I wanted to try, that I wouldn't choose or waste any more time on what society may think of us. They were never there to help me anyway, so fuck them.

The cool press of the antiseptic wipe shocked me from my thoughts and my gaze flashed to Kellan, an indignant huff slipping from my lips. I hadn't even realized how far my mind had drifted then, my vision hazing over so much, I hadn't even seen him approach.

"Are you ready?" he asked, some of the amusement slipping from his face as he studied me.

"Yes, just start already," I sighed, coaxing a laugh from him.

My head turned to face the other way, not wanting to watch as he pressed the tattoo gun to my skin. He didn't bother to count down, instead just starting right away, not giving me the time to tense up again. I suppressed the urge to move my arm at the feel of the needle buzzing into my skin. A moment later my nerves registered the sensation and I relaxed. It was more of a pinching rather than the searing pain I'd imagined and was surprisingly manageable. I kept my arm still, propping in on the armrest, but let my body recline back into the chair.

"What did I say," he chuckled, clearly seeing some of the rigid stiffness leave my shoulders.

"Of course, you were right—" A hiss of pain cut off the rest of what I was about to say.

"I mean I never said it would be relaxing." He shrugged, snickering under his breath as he went back to work.

"No, you didn't," I agreed, pushing past the throbbing that still lingered. "So I guess we need to discuss what happens next."

"No, you need to relax and let us handle it," Kellan murmured, his lips parting slightly as he focused on his work.

"That's not going to happen," I urged, unwilling to let this drop. "I'm not going to be hidden away. I need to be part of this, I need to hear the plans, help you make them, and make them bleed with my own two hands."

The tattoo gun stilled on my skin, and I could tell that he was about to pull away.

"No, don't stop," I blurted, and he stilled beside me. "If you stop now, I'm not sure I'll let you restart and I really don't want to walk around with a half-finished tattoo."

He looked between me and my arm, indecision warring in his eyes. I could tell from the torn look on his face that he wanted to devote all of his attention to this discussion so he could focus on countering all my points, but there was no way I was going to let that happen.

"I can't do it, Kellan," I whispered.

I didn't want this to be an argument. I understood where they were coming from. We were just reunited, and they didn't want to put me in harm's way. They wanted to protect me, just as I had done for them. But there was no way I could stand to be on the sidelines—not for this fight, not ever again.

"All of my freedom was taken from me before, and I won't survive it if that happens again."

"Giana, no—" he protested, but I cut him off.

"I know you wouldn't do it on purpose, that you're only looking to keep me safe. But part of being safe for me is having that freedom," I explained, wincing as he hit another painful spot.

"I get that, I really do," Kellan sighed, giving me a sympathetic look. "It's just hard. We just got you back, and to know that you did everything to keep us safe ... it's been tearing me up inside."

His shoulders slumped slightly, and I could see the weight of exhaustion, of guilt that bared down on him then as he let that mask slip. My hand itched to reach out, to comfort him.

"That's why we need to talk, to prepare, and to make sure we aren't taken by surprise, because they will eventually find us," I warned.

"We know that," he assured, easing some of the tightness from my chest.

My breaths stilled as I waited for him to continue but I didn't push him. Instead I watched him work, his mind concentrated on the intricate detailed lines of the knot. When he drew up the outline, we decided to just keep it simple to begin with and we could always add on later. I'm sure his artistic mind was already whirring with ideas on how to expand the design.

"You're right," he sighed, lifting the tattoo gun from my arm and the constant buzz that had hummed in my ears cut off.

My gaze flicked between him and my arm, a protest poised on my lips, until I realized he'd finished. My eyes locked onto the intricate design, and I vaguely wondered how much time had passed. He'd flicked on the overhead lights so that he could see what he was doing, but I hadn't even realized the sun had already set, the moon low in the sky still. The design felt like a part of me already, my soul connecting to it on a deeper level, signaling the start of something new. And reminding me of my inner strength, just as the roots kept the oak tree alive and grounded, this tattoo would remind me of my inner strength, that fire that grew each day.

"We have to include you in the plans," he sighed, drawing my gaze back up to meet his. He smiled back at me softly, but it didn't reach his eyes. They were creased with worry as he looked back at me, and I reached out for his hand now that it wasn't busy with the tattoo.

"It'll be fun," I teased, twinning my fingers with his. He scoffed at that but pulled my hand closer, a small grin tilting his lips. "Thank you for the tattoo."

My chest warmed at the thought of a piece of him with me wherever I went, just adding to the meaning of it.

"Of course, little devil." He grinned, and my chest warmed at the familiar nickname. His fingers lightly pushed a stray piece of hair from my face and goosebumps trailed in his wake, my nerves lighting up at the caress. I leaned into the touch, always needing more when it came to Kellan. Soft teasing touches were not enough anymore, not after I knew what he could do to my body—had pictured it for far too many nights tossing and turning in bed. He leaned in, taking his time as he closed the distance between us, his breath warm against my skin. His lips were inches from mine, but I wanted him to take control like he had the last time, to feel his passion for me with every brush of his mouth against mine.

"What are you two troublemakers up to?" a man's voice teased in a singsong tone from the doorway. Kellan's hands were already gripping me, about to pull me off the chair until we both registered who it was.

Spade leaned against the wall, the door slowly closing beside us as he watched us, his violet eyes twinkling in amusement.

"And what on earth are you wearing, sugar?" He chuckled, pushing off the wall to saunter over to us. His eyes traveled down my body and even with the bulky grey fabric hanging loosely off me, a shiver ran up my spine from the heat in his gaze. I'd unzipped the top of the hoodie slightly to pull my arm through the top, leaving the fabric hanging precariously just above my breast on that side.

"I think it's pretty obvious." I snorted out a laugh and his grin grew even wider at my response.

"Well there's no way you can keep wearing hand-me-down sweaters and pants," he hummed, shaking his head in disappointment when he looked toward Kellan.

"What?" Kellan asked incredulously, shuffling around for something on his workbench.

"Why didn't you get her some proper clothes before she got here?" Spade scolded, stepping up to my other side and placing his hand on my shoulder. I relaxed a fraction at his touch and stifled the giggle that bubbled up at his question. Clothes were probably the last thing on anyone's mind for the last few days, so it was completely understandable—but I couldn't help but let Kellan suffer under Spade's sardonic look.

"Spade," Kellan warned, and I turned to watch him gently pressing a cover onto my still-tender skin. He gave Spade a wary look once he'd finished, crossing his arm over his chest as apprehension creased his face.

"Come on, sugar," Spade said gleefully. "I'll take you shopping."

SPADE'S IDEA OF SHOPPING wasn't exactly what I'd had in mind. My brows furrowed and I gave him a sidelong glance as he pulled into the empty mall parking lot.

The small town of Fallpond had grown since the last time I'd driven out here with Merrick and Kellan. There'd just been a few strip plazas here before with suburban streets surrounding them, but it seemed even in the age of online shopping the town was large enough to have built a two-story mall, filled with a variety of department stores if the signs were any indication.

"I think they're closed," I offered hesitantly as he continued around to one of the service entrances, undeterred by the lack of lights illuminating the main entrance we just passed.

"I know," he answered, whistling along to the song playing through the sports car's speakers as he parked next to one of the loading docks. Spade had surprised me when he pulled a blue restored mustang out of one of the steel garage doors, beckoning me to hop in. It was a nice change from the blacked-out cars and ostentatious luxury vehicles I'd grown used to recently, reminding me of the old days in Merrick's Chevy when we used to cruise around to small towns like this one just to get out of East Haven for a few hours.

"I guess we'll have to come back tomorrow," I said, leaning back in the seat as I watched him curiously. But instead of turning the car around, he turned the key in the ignition and the rumble of the engine eased away.

"Why would we do that?" He chuckled as he swung the door open and hopped out, the frame thudding as he pushed it closed.

Before I could even register what was happening, the silent night breeze curled around me as he opened my door and took off my seatbelt.

"Spade," I say uneasily, not liking where tonight seemed to be heading. He reached for my hand, helping me from the car.

"You really think something as ridiculous as a closing time is going to keep me out?" he asked, huffing out a breath of amusement. "Just trust me."

He wrapped an arm around my shoulders and tucked me into his side, leading me to the service entrance. And despite my uncertainty at whatever he had planned, I couldn't help but lean into him. So I pushed my worries away, choosing to trust Spade in this moment and to allow the excitement humming just below the surface to wash over me. I was tired of playing by someone else's rules and doing what society expected of me. I always had to act a certain way, choosing my words carefully to not set Tommaso off or not draw too much attention to myself. But this seemed like it might be my chance to see what I really wanted, to be free and act with abandon—consequences be damned.

Before I could even ask him how we were supposed to get in, Spade reached for the steel knob on the service door which surprisingly yielded to him.

"I have connections," he boasted, giving me a wry smirk as he pulled open the door. I stilled, wincing in preparation for the screeching sirens I thought would pierce my ears, but they never came. "So little faith."

"How exactly are we able to just stroll into a mall after hours?" I asked skeptically, unable to shake the feeling we were about to get caught at any moment. Spade's arm slipped from my shoulder, but I swallowed the protest that formed on my tongue and followed after him into the dark hallway. The warm hum of the emergency lights washed over his face as he let the door close behind us, a mischievous grin splitting his face.

"That's for me to know and for you to stop worrying about." His fingers twined with mine, tugging me along beside him as he casually strolled down the hall to the double doors. Small windows showed the faint glow of lights illuminating the mall just beyond them.

"That's easy for you to say," I grumbled but didn't fight his hold on me as he pushed the door open. The sound echoed in the wide-open corridors, the normally bustling space now empty, void of life save for the two of us. "What about the security cameras?"

"They've all been put off-line, now stop fighting against this." Spade chuckled, catching me off guard at the seemingly abrupt change in subject.

I froze, waiting for some sort of explanation but he tugged me forward, spinning me on the freshly polished tiled floor.

Excitement bubbled up inside me as he pulled me against his chest, and I couldn't help the goofy grin that spread across my lips.

"You don't have to worry; nothing will happen to us. Besides, I can tell it excites you." He smirked, his violet eyes seemingly lightening with anticipation as he beamed down at me. I swallowed thickly at the full weight of his attention, capturing me like a fly in his web. I wasn't sure I ever wanted to escape the hunger and intensity in his gaze. "But there'll be plenty of time for some fun."

He pulled away reluctantly, but kept his fingers entwined with mine as he glanced at the flickering mall map beside us. Sucking in a deep breath, I took a moment to compose myself before following the trail of his finger tracing along the birds-eye view of the halls. He was right, my protests were mostly driven from that part of me that still clung to what others would think. I couldn't deny the thrill that thrummed through my veins at the idea of getting caught, of doing something I knew we shouldn't. But honestly, who cared. Spade and the guys must have had some sort of assurance we wouldn't run into any problems, otherwise I knew Kellan would've stopped him before he led me from his studio.

I shook my lingering worries aside and let myself fully be in the moment. This was exactly what I needed to shock me out of the sadness and uncertainty that still clung to me. I needed some excitement and adventure, and given that they technically ran a gang, this would probably be the tamest outing we could have. This was the perfect chance to live in the moment and not let life pass me by any longer.

I glanced up at Spade, watching him figure out where we were going in the maze of stores, and my chest warmed as gratitude flooded me. He'd suggested this not only as a way to get me new clothes—which I was thankful for—but he also must've realized I'd need some time out and away from the guys. There was so much we still needed to discuss, and we had only begun to scratch the surface the other night. But seeing them kept reminding me of everything that happened, how much I hurt them, how I'd done everything for them. And I could see that guilt weighing on them as well—well Kellan at least. I still hadn't seen Merrick at all today. My stomach twisted at that thought, but I quickly focused back on the map, not wanting my worries to sour this experience.

"So I picked out a few stores already, but where would you want to go?" Spade turned to me, and my lips parted as I turned his question over in my mind. *Where would I want to go?* It had been so long since anyone asked me what I really wanted. I was expected to wear certain clothes and brands with Tommaso that showcased their wealth. Most of the time he'd called up the designers and they brought over options for me to try on while he chose from them for me. And before that I didn't really have the money to buy what I wanted for myself, everything I earned went into saving for New York.

"I don't know," I murmured, my lips pursing at the vulnerability in that admission, the realization that I hadn't had any control over my life, let alone my clothes.

"Well good news is, the mall is all yours." He smiled, his eyes lighting with understanding. But there was also something else there, a subtle tightness that belied an ember of anger, and a steely glint that hinted what he would do to those who took that small bit of freedom away from me for so long. His thumb trailed along my bottom lip, easing it to relax, and his own tension flitted away as I exhaled a deep sigh. "We can go to every store until we find something you love."

It was more than just clothes; we both knew that. It was like a reclaiming of my identity, of the small pieces I'd tucked away for so long that made me—me. With that, he led me down the hallway, stopping to look into each store window that caught my attention. There were even more shops than I could've imagined, but Spade didn't complain as we explored each of them, peering through the windows until we found one I liked. They had a number of high-end stores there, to my surprise, but I didn't stop at any of them, just the sight of them turned my stomach, reminding me of the sense of obligation I'd escaped.

Escaped.

The word clung through me at that moment and my steps faltered. Reality smacked me in the face like a semi-truck barreling toward me at full speed. Spade skidded to a stop a few steps ahead as his hand slipped from mine. A question was poised on his lips, but it fled as he assessed me.

"I know how you feel." His eyes bored into mine then, seeming to narrow in on the fading bruise that still marred my cheek. "My parents used to abuse me when I was younger. It wasn't until I was sixteen that I finally built up the courage to leave."

"Spade." I stepped toward him, my hand outstretched to clasp his again.

"No," he blurted, shaking his head and taking a step back. "I didn't tell you because I wanted pity, just like I know you don't want my pity now."

My lips quirked, swallowing my protest. It was comfort I'd sought to give him, but I knew what he meant. He didn't want to wallow in the past just as much as I didn't. My hand fell to my side, and I looked back at him. Waiting for him to continue or not, wanting to absorb any piece of himself, of his past, he was willing to offer up.

"I just wanted you to know, I see you," he breathed, stepping closer and taking both of my hands in his, now that it was on his terms, on equal footing. Two people who had been through some fucked-up shit, sharing their mutual respect and understanding. "I know what it was like to finally be able to breathe, to make a decision for myself, and reclaim those pieces of me I'd thought had been lost forever."

My shoulders slumped at that admission, and the connection that thrummed between us, electricity racing through me from his touch. Although I barely knew him, I'd always felt as though he could see through me, could spot the broken pieces jumbled together, working their way to fit together again. And now I knew it was because he did—he had been through hell and understood some of the emotions clinging to me like storm clouds refusing to pass. But they would—and that was why he took me out tonight, to help show me that.

"We'll make them pay, sugar," he murmured, his violet eyes sparking with excitement and mischief. "You'll get your revenge, just like I did."

I had to be some sadistic bitch because rather than fear slithering up my spine at his admission—it was desire that curled around my core. I leaned into him, wishing his hands would explore more than just the light touch of my own. I couldn't help the smile that beamed in answer to his own, my mind flashing back to the parking lot, and the exhilaration that had buzzed through me when I'd tased that asshole.

I could already tell Spade was trouble incarnate, and I couldn't wait to see the chaos we would release on the unsuspecting world one day.

CHAPTER TWENTY

GIANA

NOW

"WILL THAT BE EVERYTHING today, sugar?" Spade asked, standing on the other side of the counter as he opened a paper bag and began folding and placing the pile of clothes within it.

We spent the last hour or so picking out clothes from the large store, and he didn't complain once about how long it was taking. Instead, he stood by me and made suggestions. But ultimately it was my decision. The store was well known but not luxury in the slightest, thankfully, and they had an array of everything I'd need, shirts, pants, dresses, skirts, shoes, and undergarments.

"I think employees would actually ring up a customer's purchases." I chuckled, folding a black printed T-shirt. My chest warmed at the now familiar nickname he'd decided to give me. "Besides I don't think they would call me sugar either."

"Well they better not because that's my nickname," he warned, giving me a teasing grin as he started on the lacy underwear he'd insisted on. Heat bloomed in my cheeks, and I glanced back down at the counter. He hadn't forced me to get a particular one though, merely suggesting it and letting me make the decision for myself. I pushed thoughts of Tommaso regularly laying out what he wanted to see me in from my mind, not wanting him to mar this experience.

"Why, though?" I chanced a glance back up at him as I folded a pair of jeans. His violet eyes were full of hunger and desire as he gripped the edge of the counter, his knuckles white as though he was physically holding himself back.

"Why do I call you sugar?" he purred, the sound vibrating through me straight to my core, sending tendrils of lust licking up my spine.

I swallowed thickly, and nodded slightly, unsure I'd even be able to form words at the moment with the heat blazing through me.

"Because you're like candy, delectable and addictive." He licked his lips, as though imagining the taste of me on them. A shudder ran through me, my mind picturing that tongue on me, savoring every inch of my skin until he reached my center, leaving me a quivering mess in anticipation of him. "Even from the first moment I saw you, I craved having you, tasting you to see if you're as sweet as you look."

My breath caught in my throat at that, words escaping me completely as my nipples hardened into peaks, my body craving the friction of his against me.

"I have an idea," he murmured. My mind was so lost in thoughts of him lifting me up onto the counter and stripping these restrictive pants from my body that I jolted as he swiped the bags from the counter and bounded around it. He took my hand in his and led me toward the exit, excitement hurrying his steps.

"Wait," I couldn't even believe the word slipped from my lips with the anticipation thrumming through my body. And judging by his hurried movements, I could only imagine what his idea entailed, and my body was one hundred percent willing and ready for him.

My hand trailed over the shoulder of a supple leather jacket I hadn't seen before. But something about it caught my eye. Sure it might be stereotypical, but I couldn't help but glance at the one Spade still wore, wanting one of my own. It was like a symbol, of a new beginning, of letting go of the past.

I reached out to pull the heavy material off the rack, but my hand faltered. Some of the fog of the excitement of the last hour fading as it hit me what we were really doing.

"What about the store anyway?" I asked. The question had been niggling at the back of my mind but I'd pushed it off to be in the moment. "Won't they call the cops?"

"Don't worry about it." He chuckled, dropping my hand to boop my nose. I blinked back at him in shock at the sudden playful gesture, but he was already sliding the jacket off the hanger and placing it in one of the bags he clutched in his other hand. "Don't let those responsible instincts taint our fun tonight."

My lips pursed, but I followed him out of the store. There honestly wasn't much I could do about it now. Not only did I not have any money, but I had to trust that he wouldn't put me in any danger. The door had been unlocked, after all, whatever connection he had wouldn't put their ass on the line if it was something that would get them fired. Besides, I had no idea what sort of arrangement they had with the authorities in this town. I knew they wouldn't hold them under their thumb like the Barones. No, not after everything us and our families went through growing up. They wouldn't be the men I knew if they held this small town in their iron fist.

Spade pulled the metal grate closed behind us and produced a key, locking it back up the way we'd found it. I hadn't asked him how he had the key either, knowing his reasoning for tonight. It was meant to pull me out of the haze of darkness still clouding my mind, no matter how hard I tried to deny it, some semblance of it still lingered.

"I have the perfect place for us to go next." He beamed back at me, taking my hand and pulling me after him. I stumbled a little but quickly regained my footing, speeding up my footsteps to match his.

"Don't we have enough clothes?" I asked hesitantly. He had three large bags packed to the brim with garments clasped in his other palm. It would be more than enough to get me through the next week or so, and then I could just do laundry.

"Yes, but this has nothing to do with clothes," he said excitedly, steering me toward a larger department store.

Dropping my hand, he went for the key again, the metal slider clanging as he pushed it back just enough for us to squeeze through. I bit back the question poised on the tip of my tongue, knowing he wouldn't answer it, and followed him in. The key clicked in the lock as I surveyed the locked glass cases surrounding us. Apparently the entrance from the mall led to the cosmetics section. The faint smell of soft floral perfume still clung to the air, the scent cloying in my nostrils as I waited for Spade.

"This is where we can have our fun." He grinned, dropping the bags by the entrance.

"What do you mean by fun?" I asked hesitantly, glancing around at the expensive locked cases around us. There was no way they didn't have silent alarms in them, and I highly doubted his contact could've disabled those as easily as the stores' internal alarms.

Instead of answering, Spade wrapped an arm around my shoulders, tucking me against his side. "This is the epitome of capitalism." He gestured around us, at the small luxury stores lining the sides of the sprawling store. "The system where they spend more on learning how to trick people into spending money that they don't have, rather than helping those who are struggling."

My lips quirked to the side at that, truly taking in the items around us. There were key dishes that cost as much as someone's grocery bill just past the glass cases. Bags that cost more than most people's rent.

"Haven't you ever just wanted to smash it? To take what little control you can in this fucked-up world?" he asked with a devious glint in his violet eyes.

Yes, I thought, but he already knew that judging by the subtle smirk that tilted his lips.

"I've made arrangements to pay back the other store already, but this one is the epitome of what is wrong with the world." He shot a defiant smirk up at the cameras as though someone was watching them. But if they were, I guarantee we wouldn't be standing here right now. "This will be our act of defiance for the night, the act of reclaiming that part of yourself that was forced to live in this world of excess."

"Okay," I said simply, rolling up the sleeves of the hoodie as I set my sights on the ridiculously expensive plates on the far wall. The ones that were the exact same as the set I knew were sitting in Tommaso's cupboards—not mine, not anymore. I'd scoffed at the ostentatious things, having wanted something more practical, but he'd insisted our guests' impressions mattered more than my thoughts.

He huffed out a breath of amusement, as if he hadn't expected it to be that easy to convince me. But as I glanced around at the luxury items, I could picture the people who would shop here, their designer watches, glinting in the halogen lights overhead. I could imagine their snide looks and sneering faces as they ordered the workers barely making a livable wage around them.

I let those lingering doubts slip away, and I decided to do what I wanted for a change. Fuck the consequences, if there were any, we'd deal with them then. But right now, I needed this—I needed this relatively small act of defiance to snap me out of the mask of impassivity I'd worn for so long. The adrenaline rush that accompanied danger had always sparked that love of life within me.

I grinned up at him, grasping the pieces of my old self that still remained, letting this act of rebellion feed those shards of my soul. And when his own smile broadened to match mine, I knew he could see the shadow of the devil that still lived within me, emerging, and he liked what he saw.

"READY?" SPADE ASKED, A plate clutched in his hand and muscles poised for my answer.

I shook out any lingering stiffness in my shoulders and lifted the bat, planting my feet wide as I took a few practice swings. "You know it." I was really starting to enjoy the feel of a bat wrapped in my grip as I unleashed violence and destruction.

"Three, two, one," he counted and threw the dish in front of me. I swung the bat, the metal connecting with the expensive dinnerware with a crash, shards scattering all over the place in its wake.

"Again." I laughed, pulling the bat back as I readied for the next piece. This time it was a coffee mug in the same red and gold pattern that I smashed with the bat, followed by the rest of the set. Luckily there'd been a sporting goods store next door that Spade was able to swipe it from. It just added to the satisfaction of watching the designer dinner set break into shards.

I'd already smashed most of them, throwing them against the walls, the floors, and practicing my swing on the display sets. My lips were tilted up into a permanent smile as we continued our crusade of destruction. The weight lifted off my chest with each piece of ceramic that crashed around me. I even let Spade get in a swing or two, out of the goodness of my heart.

"That's the last of it." Spade chuckled, striding up to me to ease the bat from my fingers and bringing it down on the display table. The glass shattered around us, and I couldn't help the giddy laugh that escaped at the pure delight radiating off him.

He tossed the bat back toward the entrance, and it skittered along the ceramic tiles before clanging against the metal grate.

"You're so fucking gorgeous, sugar," he murmured, and I nearly jumped as his thumb traced along the curve of my lips, his eyes glued to the smile that was plastered to my face. "I never want to see this smile fade, and I'll gut anyone who threatens to take it away."

I knew the threat was serious, he would kill anyone who threatened me or got in the way of my happiness. The thought should have sent tendrils of fear skittering down my spine. Instead, my chest warmed like the sadistic bitch I must be as I leaned into his touch, my eyes fluttering closed as I savored the feel of his thumb caressing the sensitive skin, wishing he'd replace it with his mouth.

As if reading my mind, his lips lowered on mine, the touch light and soft, letting me take the lead. I could back away from him if I wanted to, but I knew in that moment this was exactly where I wanted to be. I pressed against him, his chest hard against mine as his hand trailed along my jaw. His fingers threaded through my hair, deepening our kiss, and parting my lips beneath his. His tongue swept in long possessive strokes, tangling with mine as he devoured me.

I moaned into his mouth, my hands shaking slightly as I pulled him closer. My heart thumped against my chest as warm tendrils of need curled within me, urging my body on. Heat flooded my veins, and the thick hoodie and sweatpants became stifling. My hands itched to strip them off my body to find any surface, any position that might be able to find some release. I whimpered into his mouth, needing the friction of his body against mine. His answering chuckle vibrated through me, and I could've sworn it went straight to my pussy. His hand slipped under the thick fabric of the sweatshirt and caressed the smooth skin of my waist, the touch teasing as he played with the waistband of my pants.

I groaned in frustration and his tongue swept against mine as though playfully showing off his skill ... and now all I could imagine was the pressure of his piercing as his mouth stroked and sucked on my clit—

"I have an idea," he blurted, abruptly pulling away and jolting me from the fog of lust that had settled over me. My eyes flickered open, my lips still parted as I stared back at him with a bewildered expression. Undeterred by my shock and disbelief, his arms shifted to scoop me up, lifting me against his chest.

"That statement officially scares me." I giggled, squirming in his grip to get comfortable and wrapping my arms around his neck. I didn't bother to protest the sudden shift, especially since

I wasn't sure I'd be able to walk after that kiss. My body was still warm and languid from the desire pooling in my core.

"That's a lie, I know you love my ideas." He smirked down at me, waggling his eyebrows smugly as the broken ceramic crunched beneath his feet.

Yup, I really did, but I couldn't voice that, not just yet. Because who knew what crazy plans he'd concoct if he knew I was down for whatever he came up with next. So instead I stayed silent and relaxed into his arms, ready to roll with whatever he threw at me next.

"Can you hold this, sugar?" He shifted me in his grip and pulled a still packaged blanket from the top of a display. I chuckled as he placed it in my lap and secured his grip around my legs again, the movement so swift, I might not have noticed it if he hadn't said anything.

"Why do you need a blanket?" I asked, slipping an arm from his neck to secure the blanket against me.

"Oh, you'll see," he assured, his strides long and deliberate as he crossed the store. I stared up at him in wonder, wishing I could see inside his mind. Some I'm sure would balk at what they saw there but everything about this man fascinated me.

So I just shook my head, deciding to trust whatever clever plan he had up his sleeve now, knowing he wouldn't lead me astray.

"Perfect," he murmured, his violet eyes glinting in delight in the faint glow of light. He placed a swift kiss on my cheek before lowering me, the movement so distracting and sudden it took a few moments for my feet to fully register the hard press of the ground beneath them. He waited for me to regain my footing despite the anticipation radiating off him, barely restraining his urge to bound off to wherever he'd intended. I hugged the blanket to my chest and watched him curiously as he strode over to the wall with the TVs mounted them.

My own excitement built as I took in the leather sofas surrounding us, set up like small living rooms to give shoppers an idea of what the expensive items could look like in their own homes.

The screens all flickered to life at once and I blinked against the sudden light burning my eyes. Spade's tinkering with the cords echoed through the store, and my brows furrowed as my vision cleared.

"Are we going to watch a movie?" I asked before the image glowing on the bank of TVs became clear. They seemed to be hooked up to a camera that Spade was still adjusting, and my frown deepened as I stared back at the image of myself mirrored on at least thirty screens before me. The picture was dark but I could still make out my features illuminated by the faint emergency lights.

"Oh this will definitely be better than a movie," Spade said, cocking an eyebrow as he stepped back from the wall of electronics, apparently satisfied with whatever adjustment he had made.

My mouth dried as he stalked toward me, his mouth curved in a sensuous smile, his eyes glinting with mischief. All other thoughts fled my mind seeing the promise that look held. That this had only been a change of scenery and he had no intention of stopping where we had.

He closed the distance in a few long strides, my body already craving the teasing touch of his fingers playing with my waistband again. I couldn't help imagining how it would feel when they delved beneath them. My brows knitted together as his hands wrapped around the blanket instead, gently tugging it from my grasp. I frowned down at the bundle slipping from my grip, having completely forgotten I'd even been holding on to it. He ripped off the packaging in one swift motion and whipped it open with a flick of his wrist. Curiously, I watched him as he draped the soft material over the couch closest to us with a flourish.

"Now get that gorgeous ass on the couch so I can see if that pussy tastes as sweet as I've imagined," he growled, heat blazing in his look as he scanned my body. The way he looked at me, you would've thought I was already stripped before him, his gaze taking in my body leaving a trail of heat in its wake.

I couldn't help the burst of laughter that left my lips at the abrupt command, my eyes flicking from him to the row of TVs on the wall recording our every move. "You can't be serious."

"Oh I'm dead serious, sugar," he purred, crowding into me. His hands clasped the bottom of my ass and he squeezed tightly, fingers kneading into the soft flesh. Even though the thick material of the pants still stood in his way, I couldn't help the moan that slipped out at the delicious feel of his hands so close to where I craved him.

I gasped as he hoisted me up by my ass, my mind so overcome with thoughts of his hands on me, I hadn't even seen the movement coming. He smirked down at me as he pressed me up against his torso, my legs wrapping around his waist on instinct. My hands looped around his neck to keep myself from falling, and his mouth closed on mine. The kiss was hard and demanding as he picked up right where we'd left off. Lips parting beneath him, I craved the feel of his tongue stroking against mine. My body urged me on, needing the friction of him against me, my hips moving with a mind of their own as I ground my core against him, his cock already hard and straining against his jeans, pressing against me perfectly.

"Just trust me, sugar," he murmured, pulling his lips away from mine slightly. "This is for you and me only."

My hands slid to steady myself on his shoulders and I eased back from him. He cocked an eyebrow and eyed me curiously, but his silent question was answered a moment later when I slipped my hands down to pull the hem of the hoodie up and over my head. The cool open air sent a chill up my spine as I lifted the thick fabric off my body. I suppressed the shiver that ran over me as my skin pebbled into goosebumps.

Spade kept a hand under me, anchoring me to him while the other rubbed up my back, chasing away some of the chill. His lips were back on mine in the next instant, capturing my mouth in a searing kiss before leaving a trail of pecks along my jaw. I gasped at the caress of them as he made his way to my neck and sucked on the sensitive flesh, causing my hips to grind against him again.

I needed more—needed these damn clothes torn off my body, the feel of his fingers, mouth, and tongue exploring every inch of me before I did the same. I wanted to know every curve and every hard plane of muscle. I wanted to hear my name on a rasping groan as I drew every drop of pleasure from him.

His mouth trailed teasing kisses the rest of the way to my shoulder before his teeth lightly clamped down. The sharp pain and pleasure mixed perfectly, making me buck against him again. My clit throbbing with need, begging for just an ounce of friction.

"Spade," I groaned—no begged, for any relief he would give me. He ground his hips against me, his answering moan vibrating into my skin and causing a languid heat to roll through me.

Turning us around, he took a few short steps before lowering me onto the blanket. He leaned over me, his lips unwilling to leave my skin as he settled between my legs. I pulled in a shuddering breath and tingles spread along my body with every sweet, feathered caress. He continued, teasing along my collarbone before lowering to my breasts, his mouth clamping around one of the already hardened peaks. I arched into his touch, my fingers digging into his biceps, clutching him closer to me as his hand kneaded the other and he softly rolled them at the same time, coaxing a whimper from my lips.

"You say the word and we stop," he said, some of the lust fogging his eyes clearing with that as he drew away. I could see the thick hunger and lust in those violet eyes, but I knew immediately that he would stop if I wasn't ready for this step.

I nodded, a small smile curling on my lips as I shimmied the sweatpants and underwear down my legs in one go. He watched every movement hungrily, devouring every curve as he scanned my bare skin on display for him. I soaked in his reaction, loving the way he worshiped me like he would never be able to get enough. My body felt weightless from the joy and power that washed over me, like I was finally in control of my life, in control of my body.

It had been far too long since I was with someone I cared about. I needed this—the release, the memory of someone else's mouth on me, the reminder that Tommaso didn't hold my future any longer. The reassurance this was my body and I was in control of it. I got to choose who I was with, who I grew closer to both emotionally and physically. And I knew Spade would make this moment perfect. There weren't years of history between us. This was the beginning of something new—a fresh start. It was just him and me. Our mutual understanding of each other's scars and that twin flame connection that flickered between us.

He drew circles on my knees as I kicked off my pants and shoes. The light touch sent ripples of desire to my center, already wet and ready for him.

"I could just sit here and watch you," he sighed contentedly. I chewed on my lips, studying him as he gazed back at me reverently, the look tugging at my chest.

"Spade," I growled in warning, swallowing down the sappy emotions trying to make an appearance before they could ruin this moment. "If your mouth isn't on me in five seconds, I'm taking matters into my own hands." *Literally.*

Instantly I regretted the words at the intrigue that darkened his gaze.

"So demanding," he chided, stripping off his leather jacket, followed by his button-down shirt. My fingers itched to rip it off him, but I held back, not wanting to show him how impatient I truly was since he'd surely make me wait even longer.

I licked my lips as my eyes trailed along his lean-muscled torso, tracing down to his chiseled Adonis belt. I wanted to explore him, taste his skin just as he'd done to mine.

"You better be careful with that tongue, sugar. Otherwise I'll have you show me what it can do rather than demonstrating my own skills on you."

My mouth dried, my lips parting as he smirked up at me, clearly realizing he'd won this round. I was just about to retort when his mouth lowered onto my inner thigh, feathering light teasing kisses up the sensitive skin and stealing the words off my tongue. My fingers threaded through his short white hair, and I leaned back, my body shuddering with each brush.

My heart pounded as he inched closer, anticipation humming through my limbs. It seemed like he was moving in slow motion, each movement agonizing as I waited for his lips to close around my clit.

"So impatient." His voice vibrated through me, sending a warm wash of breath over my already wet pussy as he glanced up at me, those violet eyes sparkling with pure delight.

"Spade," I groaned, gently nudging him closer and silently hoping that wouldn't make him retreat.

I moaned as his tongue flicked out, running over my swollen clit. My body shuddered as pleasure coursed through me, the smooth metal of his tongue ring teasing over me, giving me a taste of the heightened pleasure that awaited me.

"Just as sweet as I imagined," he groaned, swirling his tongue around the sensitive nub. My legs shook at the increased pressure, but he roughly wrapped his hands under them, spreading my thighs open for him and sliding me closer. He wasted no time continuing, hungrily moaning against me like I was an all-you-can-eat buffet. My fingers clutched at his hair, gripping his soft strands as he switched between sucking and swirling his tongue, coaxing an array of curses and unintelligible pleas from my lips. It was like nothing I'd ever felt before, the piercing adding even more pleasure to his skillful movements.

My eyes flicked up, remembering the TVs along the wall, broadcasting his every movement between my legs. Keeping my eyes glued to the screen, my own desire ratcheted up as I watched Spade ravenously devour my pussy on the screen. I gasped as his tongue curled inside me, stroking me just as he had done to my mouth. My toes curled as he hit that spot with his piercing. Warm languid heat rolled through me as he built my pleasure higher and higher.

One hand slipped from my thigh, his fingers replacing his tongue as he slid two inside me. I bucked against his face, causing him to devour my clit, his movement desperate, ravenous, as though he couldn't get enough of me.

I watched myself on the multiple screens, how free I was with the pleasure coursing through my body—reassured that it was Spade between my thighs, Spade bringing me closer and closer to my climax with every swipe of his tongue and thrust of his fingers. My toes curled as waves of pleasure crashed over me, his movements pushing me over that edge. My pussy clenched around his fingers, claiming them just as much as the man wringing all this delicious ecstasy from my body.

His fingers and tongue worked me through the orgasm, my body shuddering from the force of it. But I already knew I needed more. His hands and his mouth weren't enough, I needed to feel his cock driving into me, our bodies coming together as one.

"Spade, I need you," I moaned. My fingers slipped down to replace his tongue as he eased away slowly, his fingers still lightly pumping into my soaked core.

"Fuck," he cursed, his eyes draw down to the movement, and watched my fingers circle my clit, drenched already from the climax he just drew from me.

"Spade," I whimpered, already feeling my body near that edge again. "I'm so close already, but I need the next one to be with you inside me."

"How can I fucking say no to that," he purred, his fingers slipping from me in one swift movement as he leapt to his feet.

I groaned at the loss of that friction, that fullness inside me, feeling bereft already, but I slid my own fingers down, alternating between sinking into my soaked core and rubbing my needy clit.

Spade kicked off his shoes, flinging them across the room somewhere. I vaguely registered the thump of one of them hitting something, but I didn't care, not when his fingers were already working at his belt. He torn his pants off next, his belt clattering to the ground, faster than I'd ever thought possible. His gaze didn't leave my center, watching every stroke, his hunger darkening his violet eyes. I was riveted by his hard thick cock before me, my pussy clenching just at the thought of him stretching me.

I blinked in surprise as a condom rolled on to his length, not even realizing he'd pulled it from his pocket.

"I know exactly how I want you." He grinned, and I could almost see the plan unfolding behind that look. I would never doubt another one of his plans again, not after tonight. This man could point me in any direction, and I'd follow in a heartbeat, because I knew it would be a hell of a good time.

My fingers stilled as he reached for me, lifting me off the couch. He hurriedly slipped in behind me, taking my place on the blanket over the couch, his hands sliding to my hips, easing me down to perch on his lap.

"Watch yourself, sugar," he whispered, his hand trailing up my side, tingles erupting everywhere he touched before he reached my chin, gently turning it to look at the monitors. I watched myself for a moment, a shiver of desire running down my spine as I saw myself, my dirty-blonde hair disheveled, completely naked, my nipples hard and desperate for his kneading fingers. "Watch yourself and see the woman that I see when I look at you."

His knees moved to the inside of mine, splaying my legs open for him. He reached beneath me, positioning the head of his cock at my entrance and nudging against me teasingly. I wanted him to thrust up into me, to fuck me with abandon, uncoiling that delicious pleasure in me once more, but I knew he wouldn't—not until I made the first move.

I swallowed thickly and glanced up at myself in the monitors, at the woman I barely recognized anymore. This woman wasn't the weak one that had laid in bed the last few days, the one who had iced the bruise on her eye, beaten and damaged by a partner she was trying to escape.

This woman was strong, she was taking what she wanted damn the consequences. She was seizing life in this moment and wouldn't let another day, another minute, pass her by.

"You're gorgeous, you're powerful, and you are the one in control," he growled, his breath caressing the shell of my ear and sending a shiver of pleasure down my spine. "Take the pleasure you crave."

I planted my hands on either side of my legs, using the leverage to slide down his thick length. A sigh slipped from my lips as he filled me completely. He groaned behind me, his strong palms gripping my hips as I adjusted to his size, and waited for me to move next, letting me take my time. My hips rolled on him and he helped guide me as we found our pace.

He kept one hand on my hip, helping to steady me while the other roamed around to the front, sliding teasingly up my side until he found the curve of my breast. Thrusting into me, he picked up our pace, hitting me deeper than before as his fingers rolled on my nipple. I whimpered as I looked down at him kneading my breast in time with his thrusts.

"Look at yourself," he murmured, nipping at my shoulder, and his fingers pinched the hardened nub. I gasped at the sharp pain coupled with the jolt of pleasure, my eye flicking up to the monitors in front of me. Tendrils of desire curled around me as I watched us on the screen, his cock pounding into me, building me closer to the edge of that cliff. I rode him frantically, chasing that release, the delicious friction sparking pleasure throughout my body.

My head rolled back, but I kept my eyes peeled to the screen, unable to look away. It heightened the lust fogging my mind, and like he could sense how close I was, his hand slipped from my soft flesh and down to my clit. His fingers slid expertly against it as that need built inside me to a crescendo. We both picked up our pace, my hips moving in time with his thrusts, both of us chasing our release.

He rolled his hips as he slid in, the friction hitting that spot inside me perfectly, sending me hurtling over the edge. My pussy clenched around him, pulse thundering as warm waves of ecstasy washed over me. I whimpered, unable to string together any sort of intelligible words just yet. My hips stilled but he continued to thrust into me, his fingers working on my clit and fucking me through my orgasm, sending me right back up that cliff, my body poised and begging for another.

"Spade," I moaned, no pleaded—for what, I didn't know—for him to never stop, for him to take some mercy on my body. But that wasn't what I wanted, I wanted more, needed more, craved more.

"I got you, sugar," he groaned, seeming to know just what I needed. His hand slipped from my pussy and grabbed my hips. His cock slipped out and a needy sound of protest left my lips at the sudden emptiness. But before I could say anything he lifted me off him, his strong arms depositing me on the couch in one quick motion. My knees hit the soft blanket, and my fingers sank in to catch myself as he positioned himself behind me, his fingers gripping against the soft flesh of my hips.

His cock sunk into me, a groan slipping past his lips as that delectable friction sparked again. He wasted no time, his length pumping into me, hitting me so deep I couldn't stifle the cry that slipped out. His pace grew frantic as he drove into me, and he kept one hand on me while the other moved between my legs. They swirled on me in time with his thrusts, and I glanced to the side, watching him fuck me, our bodies so desperate for each other like we needed this more than we needed air to breathe.

Pleasure rippled through me as his thrusts pushed me closer and closer to another climax. His hips rolling as he slid into me like he instinctively knew exactly what would make my toes curl.

"Spade," I cried, his name filling every crevice of my mind as another earth-shattering orgasm crashed over me, my legs shaking at the force as my core clenched around him. He thrusted a few final times before his length throbbed inside me, spilling his release into the condom. We stayed there for a moment, my lungs desperately attempting to fill themselves with the oxygen they craved, our bodies still together. I relaxed into the feeling of contentment spreading through me, the perfect feel of our bodies joined as one.

My arms quivered beneath me as I struggled to support my weight. The languid heat rushed through me, stealing every ounce of my strength. But thankfully I didn't need to for much longer as his arms wrapped around my torso, his hips easing away from mine before he pulled me to sit across his lap.

I curled into his arms that wrapped around me and relaxed against the hard muscles, his chest rapidly rising and falling in time with my own as we fought to catch our breaths.

"I'm not letting you go, sugar. Not ever," he murmured, his breath whispering over the top of my head before he placed a tender kiss there. His words were a promise, a declaration to the world and a warning to whatever forces may try to tear us apart. "I love you."

My chest warmed at those three words, and the sincerity and devotion that rang through them. It hadn't come from a place of infatuation, this time. I could tell they came from his heart, that he saw every jagged piece of my soul and loved me not despite the broken parts but for them.

"I love you too." And in that moment, I knew Spade had just ripped everything I knew to shreds. I was his just as much as he was mine, and we'd rain chaos and death upon anyone who got in our way.

CHAPTER TWENTY-ONE

GIANA

SIX YEARS AGO ...

"YOU BETTER NOT STAY out too late," Pam barked, slamming the door to the supply closet behind her, audible through the thin washroom wall. You would think she'd just got finished mopping the floors with the attitude she was giving—but no it was me, like always.

"God forbid I get a day off work for my birthday," I grumbled under my breath as I coated my lashes with another layer of mascara. "I wouldn't dream of it," I said with a derisive snort, letting some of my disdain seep through. She was only being pissy because I asked to leave an hour early, never mind I'd already mopped half of the restaurant save for the small section with the few remaining families.

"I mean it, Giana," she snapped back, heedless of the customers who could make out every word. "I don't want to hear you got up to some trouble with those boys. You have responsibilities."

I screwed back on the top of the mascara and let it clatter to the sink, my hand gripping the porcelain sides. I let the cool surface sink into my bones, chilling some of the anger blazing through me. *Two more months*, I reminded myself. The countdown became an internal mantra, that lately I had to repeat daily.

My phone chimed in my clutch, and I slipped it out, a goofy grin already curling my lips expecting a message from one of the guys. Exams were now officially over, I had my last one today, and I'd seen them at school—but tonight was different.

This was our first step to freedom, and soon we'd be leaving for New York, ready to put this town and all its residents behind us. Sure, the guys would still want to see their parents and visit home, but I'd be sure to not come anywhere close to this diner or my parents if I ever returned.

The screen lit up as I brought it to my face, the recognition unlocking the message preview immediately.

Tommaso: You can ignore me all you want, mi amore. But I can't wait for our date tomorrow.

The warm contentment and light giddy feeling that had lightened my chest a moment ago, now chilled to icy dread, pooling in my stomach. *It's fine*, I told myself, deleting the message before I shoved the phone back in my bag. *I'll just be incredibly dull and boring on the date.* It was only one date after all. I could get through it, then he'd leave me alone. There were plenty of other girls out there, many who would kill to go out with the wealthy, handsome heir to the largest crime family on this side of North America. *He'll get over his little crush when he sees I'm not worth the effort.*

I pushed all thoughts of him aside and swiped on some lipstick numbly, not even looking at the color before I coated my plump lips. I tucked it back into my bag and shoved the rest of my makeup into my overnight bag, hoping Pam and Greg wouldn't see before I snuck out the front door. They'd probably be too busy arguing or drinking to even notice me leaving. Not like they even wished me a happy birthday yet today ...

I eased open the door and breathed a sigh of relief when I didn't spot either of them in the main section of the diner. I said I wouldn't stay out too late, but I didn't say anything about coming home tonight. As one of the last nights any of us had before summer began and our work schedules picked up, we all decided to stay over at the firehouse tonight. A mix of nerves and excitement hummed through me at that thought as I glided smoothly through the restaurant, noticing Merrick's red Chevy already parked outside. Despite not wanting to ruin our friendships, I couldn't help where my mind strayed. There was no denying I was attracted to my two best friends and I'd dreamed of how it could be between us. But I had no idea if they felt the same way, despite all their small touches and flirty banter. Not to mention the fact I couldn't choose, wouldn't choose, between them. So where would that leave us?

I pushed open the front door just as Kellan opened the driver's side door, a beaming smile spreading across his face as his sable eyes lighted on me, his black curls freshly trimmed. He rushed forward, taking my hand in his and lifting the bag from my grip. It was moments like this that made all those rational thoughts flee from my mind, that made me think that we could be more than friends.

"Well hello to you too." I chuckled, my fingers twining with his as he guided me over to the passenger side. He swiftly opened the door, and my brows furrowed at the empty seat. "Where's Merrick?" I asked suspiciously.

He threw my bag into the back and turned to me, a hint of mischief glimmering in his gaze. My heart panged at that look, wishing I could tell him about the text and Tommaso but I knew he wouldn't be able to keep it from Merrick, and the two of them would end up going after him headfirst without any thought for the repercussions, and Tommaso would leave them in a bloody heap, that is if he didn't just kill them.

"Happy Birthday, Giana," he breathed, clutching me close to him and easing away the shiver that had run up my spine, chasing those morbid thoughts away. His strong arms enveloped me in a warm embrace, and I nestled my cheek against his strong chest, relaxing into the rise and fall of his steady breaths. His hand slid up from my shoulders to cradle my head against him and his face lowered to the top of my head. He inhaled deeply, as though taking comfort in the familiar scent of my lilac shampoo and placed a tender kiss there.

I melted into him, wishing I could lift on my toes and return that kiss, but this time in a soft caress of our mouths, rather than the chaste one he'd just placed. My arms wrapped around his waist and clutched him close to me, never wanting to leave the warm cocoon of his presence. But I knew I had to, just like I knew I couldn't break that wall between us, the one that teetered, so close to collapsing in on itself.

"Don't think you can distract me," I chided, pulling back from him and hiding my look of disappointment as his arms slid from my back.

"It was worth a try." He grinned, opening the door wider and gesturing for me to get in. "We're meeting him somewhere."

"That doesn't tell me anything," I grumbled, but obliged, slipping into the passenger seat. He closed my door for me, the click echoing in the silent car as I pulled on my seatbelt. Drawing in a shuddering breath, I attempted to compose myself. I'd been so close to crossing that line. Hell, if I was feeling this way already, what would I do when I was living with the two of them? How would I react if either of them brought another girl home? I knew they'd both hooked up with girls before, but it had never been serious.

My thoughts cut off as he opened the driver's side door and sat down. Wasting no time, he turned the key in the ignition and closed the door. He threw the car in reverse and then pulled out of the parking lot as I relaxed back into the seat, letting any lingering tension slip away. I wasn't going to let anything get in my way tonight, I was going to let loose and enjoy my eighteenth birthday. We were so close to leaving this town in the rearview mirror, and this day symbolized one of our final hurdles, the end of classes, exams, the legal age where I was in control of my future, not needing my parents' approval anymore, and that dreaded date tomorrow.

"ARE WE THERE YET?" I groaned, leaning my head against the cool glass window.

"You're impatient tonight." Kellan chuckled, glancing at me before focusing back on the road.

"Can you blame me?" I shot him an accusatory look and judging by the faint twitch of his lips I could tell he spotted it. "You still haven't told me anything."

Normally I wouldn't mind a nice relaxing night drive but anticipation thrummed through me. I knew they had something up their sleeves and I couldn't wait.

"We're almost there," he sighed, putting a hand on my knee. Since they hadn't given me a clue where we were going, I'd opted for tight black jeans and a low-cut top. I rarely ever splurged on clothes, so I figured I'd buy an outfit that could be worn again.

He rubbed over the material, his fingers snagging in one of the distressed holes. Just that small touch lit a fire in me, my mind drifting to how it would feel if I'd worn a skirt tonight and there was nothing in the way, no jeans to stop his path up my inner thigh. A shiver ran up my spine, and just as I thought he'd pull away or put his hand in a firmly platonic zone his hand delved farther. He slipped under the edge of the tear to rub against the sensitive skin of my inner thigh.

A sigh slipped from his lips, and I watched the effort it took for him to stay silent, the agonized longing that played across his face as he ran his fingers just under the edge of the seam, their soft pads gliding over my sensitive skin like silk.

I bit my bottom lip, willing my legs not to tremble, not to give away how good it felt, how much I wanted to kick dirt over that line and watch it dissolve into nothing. My hand trembled as I raised it, about to close over his, and push him higher … that was until headlights caught my attention.

"We're here," he breathed, his hand easing away reluctantly. The air was still thick with the palpable sexual tension that stretched between us. *That was too close.*

"Where is here?" Internally I scolded myself for how breathless I sounded. I kept my gaze firmly focused outside, unable to meet his, not yet. I couldn't bear to see if there was desire there, not when I still had no clue how I would react.

"Can't I keep it a secret for a little bit longer?" His voice wavered, as though there was some deeper meaning to his question. But when I finally gathered the courage to turn to him, he'd already wiped his face of whatever it had held a moment before, a weak smile now curving his lips.

I sucked in a long breath and nodded tightly, forcing a smile to match his. He turned off the engine, reaching for his door but I didn't wait and instead rushed to open my own door. I couldn't stand touching his hand after he led me out, not after that. My knees might just give out from under me if I let that happen.

The cool night breeze wrapped around me like a comforting old friend, shaking me from my inner thoughts. I truly took in where we'd parked this time. Floodlights were set up around the parking lot, weeds and small trees poking out of the crumbling asphalt of the long-abandoned area. We were past the edge of town, out where a few warehouses slowly decayed.

"You brought me to a fight?" I asked, my eyes lighting up with excitement at the prospect. The thumping bass was already audible through the thin sheet metal walls. The exhilaration that rushed through me should probably concern me—most eighteen-year-old girls didn't crave danger and violence, nor did they thirst to see the spray of blood splatter across the ground. But I honestly didn't care.

"There's my little devil." He chuckled, wrapping an arm around my waist and closing the door for me. "We know you so well." And they did—not only did they know about my lust for this sort of bloodshed, they enjoyed it, indulged it.

Anticipation thrummed like electricity through me. Both Merrick and Kellan participated in the illegal fight ring here from time to time. We'd been a few times, but I rarely got to go anymore, and they hardly ever participated either because of their busy schedules.

I couldn't help but lean into him, my chest light as a grin stretched my lips. He led me over to the front entrance where a large muscular twenty-something-year-old was checking IDs. My throat bobbed at the sight of him, unsure if I'd remembered to bring my fake, but he just ushered us in, nodding at Kellan as though they knew each other.

I looked up at him, my brow lifted in suspicion, but he just stared straight forward, his only tell the faint bouncing of his chest as he worked to suppress his laughter. We passed by the booth at the entrance, the line already curving around the side with people eager to place their bets.

Maneuvering our way through the crowd of eager people, the air was thick with anticipation. Patrons sipped on drinks and chatted in small groups, the throng already pushing toward the ring. A DJ booth was set up beside it with speakers wired along the roof. They must've struck a deal with the local authorities, because before everything was made to be peeled down at a moment's notice. Yet this looked permanent, as though they weren't afraid of being busted at any moment.

Whoever put on these fights apparently kept up with the maintenance inside much better than outside—which made sense. The inside looked to have been renovated since I was here last. They somehow managed to have enough electricity to run the lights spotlighting the cordoned-off area where the fight would happen, with muted neon lights washing over the rest of the space, casting a faint glow over everyone. Kellan led me toward a bar at the far wall. It was made of sleek metal that reflected the glow of lights off of it, causing it to flash back on the crowd gathered around it.

I tried to dissuade their fighting once Merrick got arrested, not wanting the cops to have another reason to take him in. But I loved watching them. It had been the highlight of my week, a place where I got to indulge in the violence, watching my friends pummel their opponents into submission. It gave me a thrill each time I saw how powerful they were, and I lived vicariously through them, wishing it was me landing those punches, having the spray of blood coat my face.

But unfortunately, I'd never been let in the ring before, but maybe ...

"Do I—"

"Nope," Kellan said, cutting me off, clearly knowing exactly what I was about to ask. I huffed out a breath of exasperation as we weaved our way toward the bar and past the few groups meandering their way closer to the stage.

"Is Merrick?" I asked, doing my best to hide my excitement. I leaned on the bar, the cool metal chilling my bare skin in the sweltering heat of the warehouse. They may have invested in some improvements, but unfortunately air conditioning was not one of them.

"I guess you'll just have to wait and see," he teased, his grin spreading slyly across his handsome face.

I huffed out a breath of exasperation, looking toward the bartender so I wasn't tempted anymore. I pushed down the urge to kiss that stupid smile off his face and smiled weakly at the bartender heading our way.

He flashed me a flirtatious grin, eyeing me up and down as he sauntered closer. He was handsome, sure—he had on a band tee that was hard to read in the shifting neon lights, and short brown hair pushed back in an effortlessly sexy style—but he wasn't one of my guys. He didn't make my heart skip a beat when I looked at him or light that fire in me, sparking an urge to draw nearer.

That look fell though as Kellan wrapped an arm around my shoulders and pulled me into his side. His eyes flicked between the two of us as his face sobered with understanding. I didn't bother to pull away from Kellan or correct the bartender though, and instead leaned into Kellan, walking that dangerous line once again.

"What can I get you two?"

"I'll have a beer, and she'll have a sex on the beach," Kellan said smoothly, tucking me even closer into his side.

I sputtered at the possessive growl in his voice and the bartender backed away to get the drinks, eyeing Kellan cautiously.

My pulse pounded in my ears, drowning out the sounds of the thumping beat vibrating through the room. I pulled in a deep breath before finally finding the courage to glance up at him, schooling my face into a look of exasperation I did not feel and cocking a brow at him in question.

"You know I can order my own drinks, right?" I huffed, needing to say something, anything to get my mind off that drink name coupled with the man beside me—our bodies entwined, with the crash of the waves in the distance.

"Why would you need to when I know just what you like," Kellan purred, dipping down to whisper in my ear. A shiver of desire ran through me as his breath caressed down the length of my neck, drawing goosebumps along the sensitive skin. He eased away slowly to meet my eyes. Our lips were inches from each other and neither of us pulled away, as though testing to see if the other would make the first move.

The smooth glide of glasses on the metal counter broke the trance we'd fallen into, both our gazes jerking to the bar and the man that had broken our moment. He grimaced, his eyes bouncing between the two of us, his brows drawn together as indecision creased his face. Only then did I realize I was glaring and a glance toward Kellan confirmed he was pinning the man with the same look.

Pulling in a deep breath, I stepped away from Kellan, the cold weight of reality barreling down on me as his arm slid from my shoulders. With all the looks and touches that had passed between us before, that was the closest we'd ever gotten to giving in to that temptation.

Kellan passed the bartender a few bills and handed me my drink, his eyes searching, scanning my face for any hint of emotion that still lingered. But I refused to meet them, scared of what might pass between us if I was finally truthful for once, if we both admitted those feelings lingered between us refusing to disappear no matter how many times I tried to push them away.

"Ladies and gentlemen, it's time for tonight's match-up," the DJ announced, cutting through the growing tension between us.

Kellan placed a hesitant hand on the small of my back as he led me toward the ring. His fingers trembling slightly on the thin expanse of exposed skin there. There was only standing room save for a row at the front where the fighters' friends usually sat—velvet ropes separating them from the crowd already so close they swayed together—fighting to get a closer spot to witness the violence and bloodshed. I glanced around the crowd, looking to see if I could spot Merrick. I still wasn't sure if he'd be fighting tonight, he could just be saving us a spot near the front for all I knew.

My suspicions were confirmed though when Kellan led me through the narrow aisle and toward the row of private seats. The guard placed at the entrance nodded at Kellan, just as the one at the front had done, and gestured up to the ring on the right.

"Is there something you need to tell me?" I asked, suspicion lacing my tone.

"Me? Of course not," he said innocently as he gestured to a seat closest to where the fighter—Merrick would be starting.

"Have you both been coming here without me?" I accused, narrowing a disapproving look on him. I was just as annoyed with him that they'd put themselves at risk for fighting still as I was that they came here without me.

"Maybe," he winced, giving me an apologetic look. "We didn't want you to get worried, but Sebastian has been slowly working to make this place legit."

"And let me guess," I hedged, giving him an unimpressed look. I didn't want them keeping things from me, just as much as I didn't want them to get arrested or worse ... "The only reason you've brought me here now is because it's all legal?"

"Of course." He smiled, huffing out an amused chuckle as I smacked his arm lightly. "I'm sorry we lied to you, but it's been one of the easiest ways to get money quickly, and we wanted to make sure we had enough for a few months' rent just in case anything happens."

My stomach twisted with guilt, and I leaned my head against his shoulder. His arm curled around me, drawing me closer, and he placed a tender kiss on the top of my head. I swear these guys were like drugs, no matter how much I knew I had to stay away to keep our friendship safe, I kept being drawn back in.

"Just don't keep stuff like that from me," I breathed, keeping my eyes focused on the bright ring before us as my chest panged, thoughts of my own lies drifting through my mind. It was a dangerous web we were weaving, all three of us, but I could only hope it would all work out in the end.

"I won't, I promise." He sighed deeply as though a weight was lifted off his chest. "No more secrets after tonight."

I swallowed down the lump that had formed in my throat, and nodded, my face brushing lightly against the thin material of his T-shirt—wishing I could promise the same.

"Let's welcome our opponents for the night," the announcer drawled, his voice booming through the speakers. "In this corner we have Tin Man Tommy."

I sat up straight in my seat and watched as a towering man, who had to be at least in his mid-twenties, strode from the opposite side and climbed into the ring. The crowd cheered behind us, and the man raised his arms and bared his teeth revealing a set of metal-covered teeth.

The crowd whooped at the sight, and he shook the ropes, soaking in the energy of his fans. Throwing his head back, he bellowed up at the ceiling in some sort of battle cry, and the crowd ate it up, mimicking him as shouts rang out around us.

"And his opponent, the one, the only Maniac Merrick," the announcer crooned, slamming his hand down to send a blaring guitar solo to amplify the hype. If Tin Man thought his welcome was warm, it was nothing compared to Merrick's. The crowd behind us screamed, and Merrick didn't even have to rile them up for it. He merely lifted a hand in greeting and thanks. The crowd surged behind us as though they thought they could push closer, but the bouncers kept them at bay thankfully, only a few knocked against the backs of our chairs before they were pushed back.

I was going to kill the man striding out from behind the black curtain for hiding this from me. How had they managed to keep this from me for over a year? How had they kept me from cheering them on and soaking in the violence and energy thrumming around us?

My eyes were glued to the obnoxious jerk as he swaggered over to us, his chest on full display, and glistening with the sweat from his pre-fight workout. I bit my bottom lip as I watched his every move, his abs rippling with each stride. I wanted to push him back behind that curtain and explore each inch of his strong chest with my lips, taste the beads slowly rolling down it, as though placed there solely to entice me further.

"There's my little devil," he growled, pausing before us leisurely like there weren't hundreds of people behind us watching his every move, their vocal cords growing hoarse with their screams. His eyes scanned up my body, searing me with the heat that blazed in that look alone. They scorched every expanse of skin they traced before he met my gaze. His eyes were dark with both longing for me and the promise of a show of violence. "Happy Birthday."

He didn't bother to say anything else and turned to the ring, expertly climbing through the ropes to face his opponent. After he slipped his mouthguard in, he tightened the straps on his thin gloves, meant to protect his knuckles. Something about the whole show of his movements just did it for me.

I swallowed thickly, my throat dry as I stared after him, and I swear I could make out a faint chuckle from Kellan beside me. Fuck, what were the two of them doing to me? Did they both get together and discuss torturing me with their advances tonight. We were so close to that barrier between friendship and more. It terrified me that the line drawn in the sand might become too blurred. At this point I wouldn't even have to kick the dirt over, it would only take a strong gust of wind to scatter the grains around, blurring it forever like it never existed in the first place.

"This fight will conclude when the first competitor either taps out or a knockout occurs," the announcer explained as both men took their positions. Merrick gave one last look back at us and had the audacity to wink at me before knocking fists with Tin Man. I rolled my eyes and huffed out a breath of annoyance, hoping the heat that bloomed in my cheeks wasn't noticeable. Both men readied for the bell to signal the start of the match, their fists raised and swaying on the balls of their feet.

"Make some noise," the announcer declared, stirring the crowd into a frenzy. A referee hurriedly climbed into the ring as though it was an afterthought, and the bell chime vibrated through the room, loud enough to echo over the chorus of chants from the crowd.

Merrick surged forward, his fist connecting with Tin Man's face. The blow echoed through the momentary silence; the crowd so entranced with the move they took a break from their frantic screams. Blood gushed from his mouth, spraying across the mat and down his bottom lip.

He seemed to sway but stayed on his feet, his hand moving automatically to shield his face from Merrick's following attack. He worked his ribs instead and Tommy grunted through the pain—apparently the only part of him that was tin were his teeth.

Merrick backed away, allowing him the opportunity to compose himself. I huffed out a breath of exasperation as Merrick allowed him to get close, dodging his few attacks but allowing to get a shot or two in on him. He was playing with the poor guy, or more likely he was earning his fee for his participation and putting on a show. Nothing drove away business to a maybe-le-gal-fight ring like a fighter that knocked their opponents out in two seconds.

I might not have liked these fights if there was a chance Mer-rick could be beaten. But knowing his level of skill allowed me to relax and enjoy the show, reveling in the poetry in motion of his cut muscles and nimble movements. Not only did he have strength on his side, but he was also able to maneuver around his opponents with ease, leaving them scrambling to fend off his attacks.

The bell chimed signaling the end of the round, and I sat up in my seat allowing for Kellan to go help Merrick out. Excitement coursed through me at the sight of Merrick striding back to his corner, pretty much unscathed. I knew he would never bother with fighting professionally, his passion had always been cars, but I didn't mind watching him, especially not when sweat beaded down his chiseled abs, making him gleam in the spot-lights.

Drops of blood had sprayed across his neck and shoulders, making the scene look even hotter. I chewed on my bottom lip, my thoughts moving into a firmly more than friends zone.

Kellan handed Merrick a bottle of water, which he greedily downed and murmured something in his ear. As soon as he drew away, they turned to face me, catching me completely off guard before I was able to mask the lust fogging my expression. Merrick's eyes darkened, ravenously roving over me, and Kellan grinned, something like relief washing over his face as he took me in.

Kellan murmured something else just as the bell chimed, signaling the start of the next round.

Merrick launched into action, a scowl curling on my lips as Kellan moved in front of me, blocking off my view for a moment. He chuckled and settled back in next to me. I could feel the weight of his stare on me but I didn't care—I was entranced by Merrick dominating the fight.

Merrick dodged a blow from Tin Man, his own fist striking the weaker fighter in the jaw. My lips parted at the smack of flesh, and blood sprayed again, coating Merrick's glove and face.

Tin Man stumbled back from the force of the impact, his body following the momentum and sending him crashing to the mats. A groan slipped from his lips as he attempted to get up, but Merrick was already on top of him, pinning him to the ground, his fists slamming into his face. Before he could land another blow, Tin Man reached out and frantically tapped on the mat, his other arm lifting to cover his face against any incoming blows. The chime of the bell rang out over the cheering crowd, signaling the end of the match.

"Our undefeated winner, Maniac Merrick," the announcer called as a medical team rushed into the ring to check on Tin Man. A wicked grin spread across my face at the energy thrumming through the warehouse and the man who dominated his opponent spectacularly, just like I knew he would.

Merrick stood as the announcer called his name, his eyes finding me immediately as though I was the only person in the room. The crowd roared behind me, chanting his name, but it sounded distant, my mind tuning it out as Merrick took up my entire focus. His lips curled into a smug smile as the referee raised his arm.

But it was as though he hadn't noticed either, his arm flopping back to his side as the referee dropped it, his attention zoned in on me.

"This place is about to be a madhouse. Let's just meet him back at the car," Kellan said, leaning close to be heard over the music now thumping even louder than before, mixed with the cheers of the spectators.

I blinked in confusion, my mind taking a moment to register his words. "But aren't we going to stay for the victory party?"

"Trust me, we don't want to get mixed up with some of these people more than we have to," he said, my body shuddering in response to his breath caressing down my neck. I did my best to suppress it, but I could tell from his light chuckle that he noticed. "Besides, we have something else planned."

And with that I followed him out of the warehouse and back to Merrick's car, my mind racing with what else they could possibly have in store.

MERRICK SLID INTO THE back seat right beside me, his chest still bare and glistening with the beads of water that clung to his skin. I was almost disappointed that he'd showered the drops of blood that had coated him. I must be some sort of twisted bitch because that turned me on more than I could even imagine. I was enthralled by the fight, the violence, the adrenaline, and fervor of the crowd, and the release as Merrick pummeled his opponent. But at the same time, I wanted to drag him out of there, take him behind that black curtain, and show him how I really felt—let him use those hands to bring me pleasure rather than delivering his adversary pain.

I let him wrap his arm around me and leaned against his chest, ignoring how my chest melted at the hum of contentment that rumbled through him. Silence pressed in on me, not uncomfortable, yet it was as though something lingered between us, something we were all holding back. Kellan maneuvered through the nearly abandoned roads and back into town and pulled Merrick's Chevy into the parking lot of the firehouse.

"So what is this second surprise you two have up your sleeves?" I asked, pulling back from Merrick as I opened the car door. I briefly glanced at his still bare chest, my throat bobbing as my attention lingered a few seconds longer than necessary.

Catching myself, I jerked my head away, attempting to hide the heat that blazed in my cheeks as I shuffled out of the car. I hurried toward the door but Kellan was in front of me before I could get to it, blocking off my path.

"Nope, nice try, but you have to close your eyes." Kellan smirked, his large form blocking off the metal doorframe. And as if there was any way to get past him, Merrick joined him, his wide chest taking up any inch I'd still seen of it.

"Fine," I huffed out on a breath of annoyance and squeezed my eyes closed.

The hinges of the steel door squeaked as they opened it, a rush of air washing over my face. Two hands gripped either arm and led me forward. I could tell by their touch that Kellan grasped one and Merrick the other. They led me through the now familiar pathway and safely down the stairs into our usual hangout in the basement. My lips curved into a small smile at how dramatic they were being. We were doing what we did most weeks, which was fine by me since it was always the highlight of my long, tiring day.

"Okay, open your eyes," Kellan murmured, their hands dropping away at almost the same time.

I gasped as my eyes fluttered open, taking in the transformed space. Red rose petals were strewn across the floor, leading to a large open space they'd cleared of all the furniture. Candles flickered around the open space, lining it as some sort of stage. Thankfully they looked to be fake though, since they must've been lit for hours now ... *I mean, it would be pretty ironic if we managed to burn the firehouse down.*

"You both did all this ...?" I trailed off, swallowing down the lump that had formed in my throat.

It looked just like the pictures of prom that we'd missed last week. I hadn't wanted to spend the money on the tickets or the fancy dress, not when we were still trying to save every spare cent. Besides I didn't really have anyone I wanted to hang out with other than these two guys here with me now. Everyone else would just be a long-forgotten acquaintance in a few years anyway but not Merrick and Kellan.

I hadn't thought I'd let on the sliver of disappointment I'd felt at not being able to attend. Not that I really wanted to, but it was just something that was instilled as a core high school memory and was something we'd all be missing out on.

"We're not really big on dancing but we figured we could give it a go," Merrick mumbled, glancing around the room almost nervously before he met my eyes. "For you."

With that, soft music played in the background, coming from the speaker Kellan must've just turned on, and Merrick extended a hand for me to take.

I placed my hand in his gingerly, my heart jolting at the light touch. Something about this felt different. We'd held hands so many times, hell I'd just been curled up against his naked chest, but this—this felt the most dangerous of all, like something was about to change so irrevocably we'd never be able to turn back.

But still, I allowed him to pull me closer and I inhaled a shuddering breath as he wrapped me into his embrace, slowly swaying me to the smooth melody. One hand kept hold of mine while the other slid to my waist. His throat bobbed as he looked down at me, my heart jolting at the look of open vulnerability he gave me. So often he hid behind his gruff façade, having to grow up far too soon when his father left, but this was the real Merrick only I saw. The man who could go from pounding someone's face in one moment, to swaying with me to the slow melody wrapping around our bodies, drawing us close with every lyrical note.

"Giana," Kellan whispered as he slipped in behind me. His chest pressed against my back, sandwiching me between the two of them. One hand curved around the other side of my hip, while the other rubbed soothing circles with his thumb on my bicep.

I closed my eyes and turned off my mind, relaxing into their embrace. A wave of euphoria washed over me at the feeling of both of their strong bodies pressed against me. I let myself be in the moment finally, and all the remaining tension slipped away.

"I love you, Giana," Kellan murmured, his lips brushing against the shell of my ear with how close he'd gotten. My lips parted as I sucked in a startled gasp, my eyes flashing open. Those words were raw and pained, a confession he wasn't sure would be received well.

My gaze met Merrick's, and rather than pain or betrayal, there was acceptance in his hazel eyes ... happiness.

"I love you, Giana," Merrick whispered, the words stealing away what little air remained in my lungs. "We always have."

My bottom lip trembled, and moisture welled in my eyes as I stared back at him and felt Kellan's breath on my neck, warm and reassuring just like him. I tried to speak, but my tongue felt thick in my mouth, my vocal cords shaky.

This was it—the moment I'd both wished for and dreaded. Do I question them and break this moment? Or do I lay my heart on the line and accept whatever may happen.

"Before you say anything," Kellan whispered, as though speaking any louder would pop the bubble surrounding us. "We've both known we each had feelings for you for a while. We don't want you to choose."

A sob racked my chest at his words, my brows creasing in disbelief. *I must be dreaming right now.*

My hand slipped from where it clasped Merrick's shoulder to cover my mouth, trying to hold back the tears that had already begun streaming down my cheeks.

"Giana?" Merrick asked, uncertainty clouding his gaze now.

I had to make a choice, and now. There was no going back from this, but would there really be any going back after their confession?

"I love you," I whispered, my hand dropping from my face to cover Kellan's where he was still rubbing my bicep. "I've loved you both for a while now, I just never wanted to ruin our friendship or choose between you two."

Merrick's shoulders slumped in relief, all the uncertainty creasing his face fleeing with my confession. His rough palm clasped the back of my head, fingers tangling through my hair as his lips lowered onto mine. He poured every drop of his emotions into me, his mouth hungrily devouring mine as if he'd been parched for far too long, and I was all the water and all the air he needed.

Kellan cleared his throat behind me, and I pulled back from Merrick reluctantly, turning to the other man who held my heart in the palm of his hand. Merrick let loose a disgruntled huff but didn't say anything as he pressed his bare chest against me, his skin rubbing against my shoulders. My fingers itched to explore his pecs, abs, and biceps now that this final barrier had been shattered around us.

Their hands shifted on me but refused to let go, as though any loss of contact may break the spell around us, and I was grateful for it. I never wanted them to let go, not now, not ever.

"You have no idea how long I've waited for those words to come from those luscious lips," he groaned, wasting no time as his mouth found mine, the kiss tender, soft, and seductive, a subtle burning heat compared to Merrick's all-consuming one.

I moaned into Kellan's mouth, my lips parting under his as Merrick kissed up the curve of my neck and sucked on the sensitive flesh. Kellan's tongue delved in to stroke against mine, and a languid heat rolled over me as the two of them built that flame higher and higher.

Kellan and Merrick. My two best friends—and the men I'd been in love with for as long as I could remember—took control of my body, and I lost myself in the bliss of us coming together, now and forever. Because this was a love that could never be broken. We couldn't ever be torn apart. Our souls would be tied for eternity, coming back together for lifetimes to come.

"Just drop me off here, the engine will wake—" A giggle slipped from my lips, cutting off my words as Kellan kissed up the curve of my neck, each caress light and sweet. I played with our fingers still twined together as we sat beside each other in the back seat, a goofy grin splitting my face. I swear I'd slept with it plastered there, and I'm sure it wouldn't fade for the rest of the day as I replayed everything that happened last night.

"I hate this. I wish we could see you before graduation," Kellan groaned, his fingers gently nudging my chin up so he could place a lingering kiss there. I sighed into him and he swallowed the sound, tugging me closer by the hand still tangled with his.

"This isn't fair," Merrick grumbled, the sound of him collapsing back in his seat making me reluctantly pull away from Kellan and end our sweet kiss much too soon.

I glanced at the time on his phone propped on the dash and grimaced. I only had a few more minutes to sneak in before Greg and Pam were up for the day.

"Come here, mister grumpy," I teased, and he huffed out an annoyed sigh but still turned in his seat to face me.

I grasped his face, the strong muscles jumping beneath the pads of my fingers as my lips met his. They were still for a moment until he cupped the back of my head, holding me close as his mouth hungrily devoured mine.

I lost myself for a moment until Kellan's light touch on my arm pulled me out of my trance, reminding me I was running out of time. I pulled away reluctantly and pressed a chaste kiss on his nose before bouncing away.

Begrudgingly, I opened the door and slipped out, grabbing my bag before either of them could pull me back, not wanting to stir up trouble with my parents, not when we were so close to leaving. I wasn't sure what I'd do if they held my job over my head and forbade me from seeing either of them for the rest of the summer.

"I'll see you in a few days," I murmured, keeping my voice low to not wake up the neighbors, and closed the door.

I blew them both a kiss as they drove off, careful not to press the gas too hard as they turned the corner. I waited until I saw the taillights disappear in the dawn light, the sun just beginning its ascent in the sky before I turned for my parents' house. I wouldn't think of it as my house, it hadn't been for years, and in two short months, I wouldn't have to come back.

Who knows, we could end up being friends once the weight of responsibility is lifted from their shoulders and I'm on my own, I thought hopefully. The events of last night brightened my mood as I walked up the narrow driveway, hoping for the best now that everything was looking up. A huge weight had been lifted off my shoulders, and I felt like I could finally breathe, could finally begin living life to its fullest in a few months.

We were really doing this and I didn't have to choose. The thought still sounded foreign to me, but it was slowly sinking in as I remembered last night and how natural it had felt to be with both of them.

"Ah, Giana," a tall man drawled with his back to me, facing toward my parents' front door.

My footsteps stilled and I sucked in a startled breath. I'd been so lost in my thoughts I hadn't noticed him standing there until he spoke. I attempted to place that voice I knew I'd heard before. He was dressed in a sleek, expensive suit despite it being five in the morning on a Saturday. "I've been waiting." His lips trembled, hands bunching into fists at his side as his mahogany eyes took me in—so cold and possessive.

My heart panged with the sudden earth-shattering loss that rocked through me. I clutched my chest, struggling to pull in a gasp of air past my trembling lips. Because I could see the future I had never dared to even dream of, the one that seemed too good to be true, silently slipping away as I stared back at Tommaso Barone.

CHAPTER TWENTY-TWO

MERRICK

NOW

I PAUSED ON THE stairs as the sounds of voices drifted down the hallway, her laughter ringing in my ears and piercing my chest. My hands gripped the railing tighter, nails digging into the already chipped white paint. Flakes floated to the ground but I didn't care.

It was a sound I hadn't heard in far too long, and even the times I'd seen her, there'd been nothing close to a smile on her face. Perhaps a sad one as a moment of nostalgia flitted past, but not the free sound that rang through the house now.

Despite how much I wanted to see her, to soak in the brightness of that smile, I couldn't move. I frowned as guilt twisted my stomach. It was all my fault. I was so headstrong, so cocky as a teenager, I never took a moment to think about the consequences of my actions. But she had. She'd been forced to live with them for the past six years while I hated her for doing it.

She'd been the first person I'd given my heart to—hell the only person I'd dared to give it to. I'd thought she'd trampled it for a life of the danger she'd craved and the wealth he could provide for her. But in reality, she'd done it to keep me from getting myself killed, or worse, getting us all killed.

I pulled in a deep breath and pushed back those thoughts. Regardless of her insistence that Tommaso would've found a way to get to her either way, I couldn't help but carry the burden of that guilt on my shoulders. That bruise on her cheeks was a glaring reflection of my faults, of what she'd had to endure to keep us alive. And every time I saw it, I had to remind myself I couldn't just go in and put a bullet between his eyes.

That was the old Merrick, the immature one who couldn't handle his emotions. But after being part of this life, I understood it wasn't just Tommaso or his father, there was a power structure we had to dismantle from the bottom up. We had to do it strategically, otherwise, I knew what the consequences would be ...

I glanced down the hallway, the sun beaming through the kitchen window, beckoning me forward, to where I knew I should be. So I pulled every ounce of strength I had and stepped off the last stair, not daring to stop until I made it there. I'd been avoiding her the past few days, as much for her sake as for mine, while battling the guilt coiling around my stomach for ever having doubted her in the first place.

But when Kellan told me about her coming to find him, the tattoo, and Spade taking her out last night, I knew I needed to face my fears. Not that I was scared of her—I could never be. I was scared of allowing her close to me, of giving her that power to utterly destroy me again. I barely survived it before, and I had no doubt if it happened again, I would dive off the deep end and into the abyss of darkness that had threatened to suck me in before.

I paused at the doorway and gazed in, focusing on her immediately. The sun beamed down on her from the kitchen window from her place at the table, a coffee cup poised in her hand as though she was about to take a sip but forgot.

Spade was speaking animatedly across from her about some sort of encounter at the bar, a run-in with some asshole that had decided to pick a fight with him. Kellan leaned against the kitchen counter, his eyes focused on her just as mine had been, a mix of awe and wonder in them as though he too couldn't believe this was real. I hadn't had this feeling since her eighteenth birthday when I thought it would be the beginning of the rest of our lives. She'd said she loved us too. I pictured the rest of my life as she'd said those three words, but that perfect picture had gone up in flames just a few days later.

"And then she tased him," Spade choked out on a laugh, glancing back at Kellan. He seemed to remember himself then, that trance of happiness and disbelief fading as he turned back into the conversation. "You should've seen her, it was glorious. She stole my heart, then and there."

He looked back at Giana, the same expression Kellan had just moments before washing over his features. Spade had already made it clear when he found out who Giana was, that he was interested—well, interested was an understatement. I swear he'd told that story hundreds of times already, and he'd been determined to find the wicked woman with the face of an angel as he'd described her. But when he found out that our Giana was one and the same, he added himself to the mix.

And judging by the smile that had spread across her face as she gazed back at him, her coffee completely forgotten at this point, she felt the same way. Although I wasn't thrilled at having to share her with another man, I'd known Spade for the past four years, and over that time the three of us had grown as close as I was with Kellan. And I knew by the way he was around her that he was serious about her. And who was I to stand in the way of someone that made my devil happy?

"Merrick watched it on the cameras afterward, didn't you, Mer?" Spade asked, a sly grin splitting his face. The question jolted me from my thoughts, my lips curling into a sneer at him for calling me out like that.

"You did?" Kellan asked, apparently hearing this part of the story for the first time.

But I didn't bother looking at him, only at Giana as her gaze flicked to me. I wasn't sure what I expected to see there, but it wasn't the wicked delight that gleamed there or the smile that curved those delicious lips.

"He sure did," Spade continued, but I didn't bother to spare him a glance. The rest of the room seemed to fade away and it was only her there and that smile I'd missed so much, the one I never thought I'd see again. "I caught him watching it over and over again."

I didn't care if she knew it, not when she was looking at me like that, not when an ember of hope still flickered in my chest that I might still have a chance to rebuild what I'd thought I'd lost forever. Hell, I didn't even care if she was with Spade too, because she fucking completed me, and I'd do anything to make it so that smile never left her face again.

"You should've kicked his ass, instead of using that taser," I grumbled, leaning back against the door frame. She cocked a brow in question, but her smile didn't falter as she waited for me to continue.

It was true, I had watched that clip countless times. And despite not knowing the truth yet, I'd hated myself for letting her walk out that door, and I'd despised myself even more for the danger she'd been put in just outside while I threw a tantrum like a teenager with a broken heart.

I was beyond thankful Spade had been there and that she hadn't been alone facing the creep. And more so that Spade had killed the fucker afterward. But I noticed how she'd relied on that taser. Yes, the satisfaction and pleasure she'd taken in bringing the piece of shit to his knees was fucking hot. But I'd taught her how to fight. Had she really fallen that out of practice that she hadn't been able to do that on her own?

"I did watch the tape, little devil," I internally cursed myself at the familiar nickname, unsure how she'd react to it now, but her grin only seemed to grow. "But what I didn't see was the moves I taught you."

I gritted my teeth as her smile faltered, hating myself for reminding her of what happened to make her fall out of practice, to lose that confidence to bring the man down with her own two hands.

"Kellan told me you want to be a part of this," I said calmly, and her lips parted in response, brows creasing with an argument clearly poised on the tip of her tongue. "I agree, this is as much your fight as it is ours. But if you're going to be in this I have to make sure you can still defend yourself."

"I can," she protested, slamming her coffee cup down on the table, the dark liquid spilling over the side and onto the light wooden table. The same one that had been in the firehouse, the furniture I'd stolen just because it had reminded me of her and that first day we discovered our home away from home.

"Then I have no intention of keeping you from this, but I have to be sure," I growled, my lips pressing into a hard line as I stubbornly dug my feet in. But that look—the still healing bruise caused me to pause, and I pushed down the small part of me that was still hesitant to put myself out there again, knowing she deserved to hear the reason why. "I couldn't live with myself if you got hurt or worse and I could've done something to stop it."

The anger fled her expression at that, her face softening as she scanned me over, taking in the loose shirt and sweatpants that barely clung to my hips. I couldn't have her looking at me like that, not yet, not when I needed to ensure her safety first—not when I still hated myself for believing her lie.

So I turned away from her, my fists clenching at my sides as I fought back the urge to pull her to me, to see if those sensuous lips still tasted the same.

"The basement in twenty minutes," I called back over my shoulder as I strode for the stairs already, needing to work off some steam on my punching bag before our training. Because right now I was about ready to hop in the car and drive straight to Tommaso's place and put him in an early grave for stealing the last six years from me and the woman I never stopped lov-ing.

CHAPTER TWENTY-THREE

GIANA

NOW

"YOU KICK HIS ASS, sugar," Spade murmured, his lips so close to mine I could smell the bitter coffee from earlier still lingering on his breath.

"Oh, I will." I grinned conspiratorially, unable to keep the smile from my face after last night.

Spade's own grin widened to match mine, his arm circling around my waist to pull me against him where we stood next to the basement door. A shiver of desire ran over my body as his mouth closed on mine, devouring me just as he'd done last night. Anticipation hummed through me, my body remembering the pleasure he'd wrung from it, already craving a replay despite how many times he'd taken me around that department store. One of my favorites was up against the glass display cases housing jewelry with tens of thousands of dollars. He'd thrust into me from behind, my breasts pressed against the cool glass as he'd bent me over it, our bodies rocking together as one.

"So fucking sweet," he murmured, pulling away reluctantly. He stared down at me, his eyes far off and distant as though this kiss had been a drug fogging his mind.

But awareness sharpened his gaze at the sound of fists slapping the punching bag just below us. Spade huffed out a breath of amusement and leaned against the open basement door, lazily perusing every inch of my body in the black skin-tight leggings and bright neon-pink crop top I'd hurriedly changed into after eating breakfast—not wanting Merrick to add any extra exercises to my warm up as punishment for being late.

"Come find me after." He winked, his hand sliding down to squeeze my ass. He jumped away as my hand raised to smack him, my palm swiping through the air as he was already striding back down the hall to the kitchen, whistling to an upbeat tune.

"Yeah, I'll find you," I grumbled, turning back toward the stairs and ignoring his amused chuckle that echoed down the hall.

I pulled in a deep breath, gathering my strength. My thoughts went back to the comment Merrick made in the kitchen. It was easy to be around Spade, there wasn't a lifetime's worth of history between us. But with Kellan and Merrick, they knew more, like how he'd noticed I hadn't been comfortable defending myself without the taser.

My running shoes slapped against the wooden stairs as I made my way down, the smack of Merrick's fists against the bag echoing around the wide-open space. But my steps slowed as I took in his massive form working the punching bag. He must've come straight down here since a thin sheen of sweat coated his muscles as they bunched, readying for his next strike.

I couldn't help but be drawn to him, my mind working to reconcile his body compared to when I'd last seen it. He was muscular and defined; his strength honed from the years of training he'd had.

He still moved the same though, his jabs and strikes silent and deadly despite the brute force he was unleashing.

I took another step, watching him intently, but the stair squeaked beneath my foot. His eyes widened as he took me in, his gaze catching on the tight sports bra that stretched across my breasts.

"Grab some gloves," he said, clearing his throat before he strolled over to a cart. There were supplies lined up on it including bottles of water, some tape, and a few pairs of gloves.

My eyes lit up when I spotted a pair that looked to be my size, in almost the same neon pink as my top.

"You got me my own pair already?" I asked, my smile beaming as I plucked them from the top of the pile.

"How do you know they're for you?" he muttered, swiping a bottle of water off the cart and cracking it open, attempting to act blasé, like he hadn't gone out of his way.

"I know you just as well as you know me," I reminded him, my look sobering a touch as I let him see how much I appreciated it.

Because that was what Merrick did, those small acts of service some may not even notice. But he remembered every detail like how I'd always wanted a set like this but had never had the spare cash to buy some.

He muttered something unintelligible under his breath in response and stalked over to the opposite side of the mats and over to a control panel on the wall. He pressed a few buttons and electronic music blared over the speakers I hadn't even noticed were mounted on the ceiling.

"How are you going to instruct me over this?" I shouted and strapped the Velcro tightly around my wrists.

"I'm not." He smirked, tilting his head back as he downed the rest of the bottle. I couldn't help but stand there mesmerized by the sight of his throat working as he swallowed the water. A few droplets rolled over his chin and followed their trail as they traveled straight down, between his pecs and over his abs.

My mouth dried, and I only realized my lips had parted in awe as he crunched the bottle in his fist and gave me a smug grin.

"You're doing jumping jacks."

I huffed out a breath of annoyance, but I was sure he couldn't hear it over the music blaring around us. Biting back my groan of displeasure, I began my warm-up, knowing from when he'd trained me before there was no getting out of this.

I let my body move to the beat of the music, the upbeat sounds driving me on. My ponytail bobbed with each move, the end brushing against my skin. I didn't bother to keep count, knowing Merrick would let me know when to stop. He'd always been like that, and if I complained he'd add at least twenty more reps.

"Push-ups," he barked, striding back toward the cart. I pulled in ragged pants, my pulse thumping in my ears almost as loud as the bass.

"Yes, sir," I drawled when I finally caught my breath enough to speak. I grinned at the tightening of his jaw, his muscles working as he clearly held himself back.

I'd always noticed the jolt of excitement he got when I called him sir. I could only hope there'd be a chance to explore that soon, because just the idea of him using that domineering tone on me in the bedroom made tendrils of desire lick up my spine.

They'd rescued me, heard my truth, and they were willing to let me be part of taking down the Barones, but I still didn't know where I stood with Merrick. Six years was long enough to fall out of love with someone, even if they were one of your best friends. I hadn't, not for a second, but he spent years hating me for leaving ... could I really blame him if he had?

I planted my hand on the mat, taking a moment to figure out a position comfortable with the padding over my knuckles. My body lowered and I lifted myself back up, my muscles burning with each rep. I was used to working out, it was one of the only times I was able to get a moment of peace away from Tommaso. It was one of the few places I was able to go alone, that was until he found me chatting with Ryan, the fitness instructor. I pushed away those vile memories, not wanting the guilt to cling to me anymore. I might like the violence, but not against someone innocent, who didn't have a chance to fight back ...

The music that had become a constant steady beat in my ears cut off abruptly. "That's enough."

I pulled myself up, sweat already coating myself from the strain. He tossed me a bottle of water, and I fumbled, trying to catch it with the gloves on my hands, and somehow, I miraculously managed not to drop it.

Cracking it open, I threw my head back and let the liquid glide down my throat, the water helping to ease some of the fatigue I was already feeling. I felt the weight of his hazel gaze on me before I even brought the bottle down. His jaw worked as he held himself back, hunger darkening his look for a moment. Relief flooded me at the lust in his eyes, some of my worries waning with the reassurance there was still a spark that lingered between us.

"Now, show me what you remember," he barked.

He picked up a pair of pads and slipped them onto his hands while he strode toward me. Throwing the bottle to the ground, I joined him in the center of the blue mat and bent my knees, preparing for the grueling session I knew was awaiting me.

To say I was out of practice was an understatement. But the movements came back after a few rounds, my jabs more lethal, my ability to sense when he was about to swing out, sharpening as I fell back into the rhythm. I'd tried to sneak off to a few kickboxing classes at the gym, but the lack of consistency had made my movements clumsy. But after a few hours in the gym with Merrick, that muscle memory snapped back, and I was going after him, my arms and legs burning with the effort, but I couldn't help the smile that stretched across my face as adrenaline coursed through my veins.

Merrick grinned back at me, even dropping the pads at the end to get a pair of his own gloves. Of course, we held our strikes back, not looking to injure the other, but excitement hummed through me as I rediscovered a part of myself I'd thought was lost long ago. My body flowed through the motions, and I pushed past the screaming in my muscles, never wanting to forget again how much power I had, or what my body, my mind could truly do. I wasn't a victim; I wasn't a trophy meant to make someone else look better while collecting dust on the shelf.

"I think that's enough for today," Merrick panted, his arms dropping to his sides. He tore off his gloves as he strode over to the cart to get some more water, passing me one as I approached.

"So, how did I do?" I asked, a wry grin curling on my lips as I peeled the gloves off my hands, knowing I'd proved him wrong eventually. I could take some asshole out; I had that power. But as Merrick's eyes met mine, they didn't hold the same excitement.

"Why didn't you smash your fist into that asshole's face when he grabbed you?" Merrick demanded, prowling closer to me.

"Because I—" I trailed off, the smile falling from my face. I knew what he wanted me to admit but thinking something in your head and saying it out loud were two different things. I'd kept everything in for so long, needing to protect others with secrets and lies. But I couldn't do that anymore, not when I had my guys back—and now Spade. I had no reason to keep everything bottled up inside any longer.

"Because you forgot," Merrick finished for me, stepping closer to me. "You forgot how strong you are, you forgot who you are."

"I did," I breathed, letting those words fully sink in. I'd lost so much of myself that even in a situation where I knew I had the ability to fight, I'd still relied on that weapon to make me feel powerful. No, not lost—forgotten. I'd been conditioned through the constant threats to anyone close to me to not fight back. But I was slowly regaining those pieces one by one.

"But you're not alone, not anymore, Gi." His throat bobbed and he took another step closer, his calloused finger sweeping back a stray strand of hair that had fallen out of my ponytail. "I'll remind you just how strong you are and cheer you on as you gut the fucker next time."

I stepped closer to him, just the idea of him watching me take an attacker down, watching the blood seep out of him sent a wave of desire over me.

"I know that now, Merrick," I whispered. "Thank you."

"For?"

"For never letting me get away with my shit, for making me face the hard stuff, no matter how much I wanted to turn the other way and pretend it didn't exist," I whispered, taking another step closer. I trailed my finger gently over his bicep feeling the hard muscle beneath. A groan slipped from his lips, as though that small touch would be enough to send him over the edge.

He closed the distance between us, and I tipped my chin up to look at him. He didn't bother leaning down and softly closing his lips over mine. No, his hands cupped either side of my ass and lifted me against him. My legs automatically wrapped around his waist, as though that was where they were simply meant to be, just as his mouth closed over mine.

The kiss was hard, hot, and demanding, his tongue wasting no time as my lips eagerly parted for him, his tongue delving in and stroking mine. I moaned into him and he swallowed the sound, my hips moving with a mind of their own and grinding against him.

Before I could even register the movement, he pressed me up against the gym wall, my back cushioned by the thick padding. He drove his hips against mine, his cock already hard and ready for me and showed me just how strong he was as he held me with them alone. He gripped my wrists and peeled my hands from where they clung to his shoulders, dragging them up and over my head, and pinning them with one of his.

He pulled his mouth away from mine for a moment and a whimper of protest left my lips at the loss, but the sound cut off as I saw the look in his eyes. They took in every inch of my body, devouring me greedily as though he might combust if he looked away. My chest heaved as I caught my breath, my body on display for him, and only him, in this moment. His free hand ran over my curves, pausing to run his thumb over my already hardened nipple, peaking through the thin material of the sports bra.

"So fucking perfect," he growled, before his lips found mine again, starving and desperate. I met them with just as much fervor, tasting them like they were the only thing I needed to live.

"Get ready you two, we're going out tonight," Spade shouted from the top of the stairs, apparently unaware of what he'd just interrupted. My heart jolted at the sound, our lips parting in shock, Merrick muscles tensing and poised to attack until he registered the voice.

I dragged in a deep breath through my swollen lips, our chests brushing against each other with how close we still were. I couldn't help the smile that stretched across my face as I gazed into Merrick's eyes. A missing piece of my heart seemed to fuse itself back together with the realization we would be alright. We had a second chance, and I sure as hell wasn't going to waste it.

I was strong. I had the power to bring anyone who came after me to their knees by my hands alone. And with these three men by my side, I knew we could take on the world.

CHAPTER TWENTY-FOUR

GIANA

NOW

"YOU STILL HAVE THE old piece of junk?" I quipped, patting the restored 1962 Chevy Impala on the hood. "Hey, the red paint doesn't even chip off anymore." I grinned at Merrick who was already glowering back at me.

"You and your smart mouth are going to get you in trouble one of these days, little devil," he growled, stalking over to me like a predator stalking his prey. His eyes hungrily devoured me as he approached, and I shivered in anticipation, craving his body close to mine.

A giggle slipped from my lips as he pressed up against me, his hips pinning mine against the side of his car like he'd done in the gym a few hours before. His wide palms circled around my wrists just over my leather jacket and lightly held them against the car, my body shuddering as desire sparked within me.

"Do you need me to take you back downstairs?" he asked, unable to keep the husky sound of lust out of his tone.

"Yes please," I purred, rubbing my body up against him.

He stiffened as I rubbed up against his cock, his length already hardening for me. I smirked up at him, my brow raising in a mischievous look. I bit my lip as my gaze roved over him, my mind wandering to our interrupted moment earlier, wondering if he'd taken matters into his own hands during his shower afterward ... because I certainly had.

"This is fucking hot," Spade groaned as he watched us intently.

"I'm going to stab you," Merrick grunted, narrowing a glare on Spade.

Kellan huffed out a breath of amusement as he opened the driver's side door, and one of Merrick's hands slipped from my wrist to toss him the keys.

"Sugar, can you sit between us in the back?" Spade asked, prowling closer to us, a devious smirk curling on his lips.

My mouth parted about to answer him, but Merrick cut me off. "Why?"

"Because I want to make our girl squirm between us. It is a ten-minute drive after all, I wonder how many times we can make her come." His smile stretched even farther as Merrick cursed under his breath, but I felt his cock press harder against me, clearly turned on by the thought.

"I vote no to that," Kellan choked out, his leg poised halfway into the car.

"Why is that?" I asked, turning my head to face him since Merrick still pressed his hips against me. Personally, I really liked the way Spade's mind was heading. After last night, I was ready to reclaim my body and relish every moment I could with these three men.

"Because if I need to listen to that while I'm driving, there won't be a chance in hell that we're making it to the bar," Kellan assured me, his sable eyes roving over me, pausing at my exposed cleavage in the sequin crop top to punctuate his words.

Heat erupted over my skin everywhere he looked, everywhere Merrick touched, the combination lighting me up. I could've sworn I was about to combust—that or usher them all back inside to take turns acting out the promises their words and bodies made.

"Don't worry, sugar, if you're a good girl there's always the ride back." Spade grinned before climbing into the passenger seat and closing the door behind him.

"I guess it's just you and me in the back seat then," Merrick drawled.

"I guess so," I breathed, his hazel eyes capturing mine like a fly caught in a spider's web.

He shifted his hips so his leg slipped between mine and the short pink skirt lifted slightly with the movement, allowing me to grind my already wet pussy against him. I bit my bottom lip as the delicious friction sent waves of pleasure crashing through me. My body was so fucking ready for him.

"Fucking hell, little devil. You're going to be the death of me," he groaned.

His lips closed over mine, the kiss hard, hot, and demanding—promising what he would do with me if I kept pushing him. And honestly, I wasn't that interested in going to the bar after the sensuous way his lips caressed mine.

He pulled away reluctantly, snaring me with a look that promised he'd give me everything I wanted and more.

"If you're quiet I'll give you something to think about for the rest of the night," he whispered in my ear, his warm breath teasing over the shell of my ear.

He did not have to tell me twice.

As soon as he eased away from me, I flung the door open, slid into the back seat, and eagerly clicked in my seatbelt. Merrick's chuckle echoed behind me as he slipped in, immediately angling us so that my back was pressed against his chest. Kellan put the car in reverse as soon as Merrick closed the door and the gate rolled open behind him. He pulled out onto the road, leaving the safety of the house behind us.

"Whose idea was it to go to the bar tonight?" Merrick asked, his thick fingers trailing a teasing path up the curve of my inner thigh. A shiver ran over me in response, my legs parting for him like they had a mind of their own. He lightly nipped the shell of my ear in approval as his hand went higher.

"It was mine," Spade proudly announced, the light of his phone glowing against his face, and I bit back my sigh of relief, glad he wouldn't be watching us back here. Well maybe glad was the wrong word, but Kellan already made it clear that he would pull the car over ... which I wouldn't be upset at either.

"And why did you come up with it?" Merrick asked.

I pressed my lips together to stifle my laugh, knowing that Merrick was trying to keep the conversation flowing so they didn't catch on to what we were up to.

"Because," Spade said, exasperation tingeing his tone. "My delicious sugar needs to get some time out of this stuffy old house, and since it's only the Devil's Demons in the bar tonight, it's the perfect time for her to unwind."

Merrick's thick fingers found the fabric of my lace thong and he let out a muffled groan as he felt how wet I already was for him.

"Besides, it will be good for all of us to have a night out, somewhere safe," Kellan said, turning up the radio and humming along to a familiar song.

Merrick used the opportunity to slip two fingers under the thin material, my arousal coating his fingers immediately.

"So fucking wet," he groaned in my ear, my excitement ratcheting up at the fact that he was circling my clit right behind my two other guys who sat there completely unaware.

He slipped into me, the delicious friction sending waves of pleasure over my body as he stroked me. I clenched one of my hands into a fist while the other rested on his thigh. My nails pressed into my palm so hard I was sure they left small crescent-shaped marks in their wake as I held back a moan of pleasure.

"I can't wait until I get to taste you again," he whispered, his tongue flicking out to lick the side of my earlobe, and I shuddered as I imagined him doing that on my clit while his fingers drove into me.

"I can't wait to feel your pussy around me." His voice was almost inaudible, and I had no idea how he managed it. "You have no idea how hard it is not to tell Kellan to pull over right now so I can fuck you properly."

He switched between his fingers curling inside me, and swirling on my clit, and I could feel myself getting closer and closer to that cliff. My bottom lip trembled from the effort of holding in my sounds of pleasure. So I just soaked in the things he was saying to me, letting them add to my pleasure. Because I know I would let something slip if I dared speak right now, with the pleasure he was coaxing from my body.

"I need to feel you come around my fingers, little devil," he growled, the lust thick in his tone. He was so close behind me I could make out the sound of him swallowing and his deep breaths as he fought to keep his own composure.

And with that I shattered, my pussy pulsing around his fingers as waves of pleasure washed over me. My hips pressed up into him as I clamped my lips together, willing myself to be silent. His fingers moved in me still, extending my orgasm and wringing out every last throb of my core.

It wasn't enough though, my body still craved more, needing to be filled completely by his thick—

Merrick's hand withdrew from me, shaking me from my thoughts. My legs closed feeling bereft without the fullness of his fingers inside me anymore. That was until he lifted them to his lips and sucked them into his mouth, groaning as he licked them clean.

My heart jolted as I realized how loud he'd been ... and how the music had turned off at some point.

"Sweet, isn't she?" Spade grinned. My eyes widened in shock at the sudden words echoing through the now silent car.

Kellan was fisting the steering wheel as he pulled in the parking lot of The Inferno, his eyes meeting mine in the rearview mirror, full of hunger and longing.

Swallowing thickly, I held his eyes, quirking my brow in a suggestive look. "I thought you said you'd pull over," I purred, spreading my legs again. I didn't fucking care about going out, not anymore, not after what Spade had said. I wanted all three of them, their bodies on mine, in mine—I wanted it all.

"We were too close to the bar already," he said, swallowing thickly. "Besides, there's always tonight."

"There is," I breathed, my throat bobbing as electricity hummed through me.

I almost wanted to say fuck it and drive back now, but we needed this, to unwind, to have some fun, before the fun we'd have tonight.

As WE STRODE IN, the bar seemed a little less crowded than it had the other night, Spade's arm casually slung around my shoulders. We paused by the bar, and I scanned the tables.

Some of the tension in my chest eased as I remembered that these were their men, only the people they trusted. I still couldn't shake the thought niggling in the back of my mind that someone would tell Tommaso I was here. But all these people were part of the force that attacked the engagement party—if they hadn't ratted the guys out then they surely wouldn't now.

"I have to go to my office for a second, but I'll be right back," Merrick murmured, his fingers threading through my hair. He drew me closer without pulling me away from Spade, and my lips tilted up to meet his in a searing kiss. His tongue trailed over the seam of my lips, before he pulled back and grumbled something under his breath.

"Don't worry I'll take good care of her."

"That's what I'm afraid of," Merrick groaned, and scrubbed a hand over his face.

"An adult is here to watch over them, don't worry." Kellan chuckled, sidling up to my other side and nudging Merrick out of the way.

"Where?" Merrick huffed out on a breath of annoyance, shaking his head before he went behind the bar and to the backroom he'd come out of the last time I was here.

"You know he's staking his claim, right?" Spade whispered conspiratorially like he was telling me something I didn't already know. I looked up and a few of the guys at a table closest to us ducked their heads as though they could somehow hide the fact that they'd been staring.

"I know," I whispered back, and a mischievous grin stretched across his face. "Just like you've been doing since the moment we walked in here."

He sucked in a sharp gasp in mock offense to the truth. "Me? Never," he said with faux innocence, clasping his other hand over his chest.

"Don't play dumb." I chuckled. "Kellan is the only one who's behaved since we walked in."

"Will I get rewarded for that later?" He smirked, wrapping a hand around my waist and pulling me closer to his side.

"I take it back," I groaned, feigning annoyance.

"Well this looks fun." My eyes flew toward the feminine voice that came from behind the bar. "I didn't mean to interrupt, that was entertaining."

I couldn't help the smile that stretched across my lips as I saw the bartender, Evelyn, from the first time I was here. The petite woman slung a cloth over her shoulder and propped her hands on her hips as she watched the three of us.

"It is fun," Spade exclaimed beside me, and placed a kiss on my cheek. I couldn't help the heat that bloomed there from the sweet gesture.

"I'm glad it looks like everything's worked out for you," she said, holding my gaze. The words were light yet there was real concern in the look she gave me. I wouldn't forget how she stood close that night we met, uncertain whether she should leave me alone with Merrick with the rage that rolled off him.

"Everything worked out better than I ever could've imagined." I beamed back.

"Well then, what can I get for you?" she asked, her answering smile just as bright as mine.

"I'm scared," Spade said in a half-assed attempt at a whisper.

My gaze flashed to him, and my senses went on high alert.

Kellan seemed to sense my unease as he rubbed his hand over the curve of my hip, helping to soothe me.

"I've never seen Eve smile before. I'm not sure whether she's having a stroke or you're some sort of witch," Spade responded, cringing as Eve bared her teeth at him, the look much more sinister than the smile that stretched across her face just moments before. He shuddered in response, letting out a dramatic small oomph as I tapped his stomach.

"You have guts girl, I've never seen someone hit Spade before and live to tell the tale," Eve huffed out on a breath of amusement, but nodded slightly in respect. "Some say he's a psycho."

A rumble left Spade's chest and he sucked in a breath, about to slam her with his retort, but I cut him off. "He might be a psycho, but he's my psycho."

"Fuck," Spade groaned, before his hand gently tugged my chin toward him and his lips devoured mine. His gratitude for my claiming words was evident with each stroke of his tongue as he delved between my lips.

"Don't mind me then," Kellan murmured, his hand slipping from my waist.

My throat bobbed as I pulled away from Spade, needing to look at Kellan and make sure he was okay. I was so drawn in by Spade and the feel of his lips on mine, I hadn't even considered how Kellan would feel. But as I turned to him there wasn't a look of dismay creasing his face, no there was a smile, bright and beaming, just happy to see me happy.

"I'll get a beer, and she'll get a sex on the beach," Kellan drawled, but he didn't look at Eve, his eyes glued to me as he gave the same order he gave on my eighteenth birthday. I hadn't dared have one since then, knowing the memories that would accompany it.

"You know just what I like," I purred, reaching out for him. He took my hand without hesitation, his fingers twining with mine perfectly, like that was where they were always meant to be.

"Okay then," Eve murmured, glasses clinking as she went to go make the drinks.

"What about me?" Spade asked, his hand reluctantly slipping from my shoulders as he went around the bar to tell Eve his order.

Kellan chuckled and shook his head as his friend traipsed off, taking the opportunity to wrap his arm around me and pull me into his side again.

"If this is weird—"

"No," he cut me off. "I'm just happy that you're happy, I know there's a lot we still need to go through and discuss, but seeing that smile on your face brings me more joy than you know."

I sighed a breath of relief, not even sure how I was about to continue. I already told myself I wouldn't give any of them up for as long as they wanted to be with me, but I could hold off on the PDA ... maybe.

"Here you are, one beer and one sex on the beach," Eve announced, winking at me and sliding the drinks over to us. Kellan placed a bill on the bar as Spade trudged back over to us, apparently having been told to wait for his drink.

"And a whiskey for the psycho." She grinned, sliding a glass of amber liquid over to him.

"Some people wouldn't call someone they consider a psycho that to their face," Spade said with lethal calm. "Some might be worried they'll get stabbed."

Eve's face blanched, her throat bobbing as she looked back at him nervously.

"She doesn't need to though, does she?" I asked, giving him a pointed look. I knew he wouldn't do anything, but after how Eve was ready to put her job at jeopardy to make sure I was safe, I already knew I wanted to be her friend.

"No," he grumbled, and placed a kiss on the top of my head. "You're lucky I like you; you're ruining my reputation."

"You're lucky I like you," I quipped back as Merrick strode back from the backroom and poured himself a beer.

"Don't I know it, sugar." Spade chuckled, giving me a sly smirk.

"What did I miss?" Merrick asked, his lips pursed as he looked between us and Eve.

"I honestly couldn't even tell you," Eve huffed on an amused breath. Giving me a parting smile, she moved to the other side of the bar to give us some privacy.

"What she said," Kellan added and guided me over to a booth by the front door.

Merrick and Spade followed after us, the latter grasping my other hand and attempting to tug me away from Kellan.

"Nope, she's sitting with me. You two assholes took up enough of her time tonight," Kellan said, cutting off whatever Spade was about to say and pulled me onto his lap. "As long as that's okay with you, little devil."

"It's perfect," I breathed, my lips closing on his in a tender caress.

"Fine," Spade groaned, but slipped into the booth on Kellan's other side and drew my legs over his lap.

Merrick grumbled something unintelligible under his breath, and took the seat opposite us, pulling my hand across the table to twine with his. I sighed in contentment and relaxed against Kellan's chest, enjoying the feel of all three of them touching me in some way. It was just like how it had always been, except it was more, with Spade now added in the mix.

It felt like he'd always been there, I noticed as they shifted into easy conversation, their friendship having deepened over the years. It was almost as if they knew we were all supposed to be tied together in some way and they drifted together, just waiting for the fates to align and bring us all together.

A LINE FORMED AT the bar, patrons crowding around the counter as they waited for Eve to grab their drinks. Merrick strode back over with our drinks in hand, well everyone except for Kellan who had decided to be our designated driver for the night and was still sipping on the first one.

"So are you hiring?" I asked Merrick as he sat down across from me where I was still perched on Kellan's lap.

Merrick chuckled in response, sliding our drinks over to us. His fingers found mine, immediately slipping back through them, fitting perfectly like they were just meant to belong together.

"I'm not joking," I said evenly before taking a sip of the fruity drink. "These are seriously like juice; I'll have to learn how to make them like Eve if I'm going to work here."

“You don’t have to work here; you know that right?” Merrick said, his brows furrowing as he held my gaze. Kellan pushed a stray strand of hair back behind my ear, the soft caress sending a hum of electricity over my skin.

“I know that.” I smiled back, rubbing my thumb over the top of his hand. “I want to though; besides it looks like you could use the help.”

I tipped my head up, gesturing to Eve hurriedly pouring drinks behind the bar.

“I can help out in other places too,” I continued. “I do have a business degree so I can help you both with any of your accounting or marketing.”

“Now that I could use your help with,” Merrick groaned, scrubbing a hand over his face. “You have no idea how much I despise all that paperwork.” He squeezed my hand appreciatively. I could tell he was much more comfortable with the idea of me in the back office, despite knowing I could handle myself. No matter what I knew, they’d always be concerned for my safety, just as I would be about theirs.

“I can only imagine.” I chuckled, squeezing his hand back in a sign of gratitude. I knew they didn’t save me to put my business degree to work, but I wanted to do this for them. I wanted to help out however I could because I cared for them, not out of some sense of obligation.

“We don’t have to talk about it right now if you don’t want to,” Kellan murmured low enough for only the three of us to hear. “But if you’re comfortable, I’d like to hear more about your life, aside from you know who, there’s so much more we don’t know.”

I looked at Kellan as an uneasy silence settled over the table. We'd skated around anything to do with the past the entire night, but it had to come out at some point. And there were some bright spots I could tell them about, some parts of my old life that didn't revolve around the Barones that kept me from falling into the deep end.

I placed a tender kiss on his cheek, grateful for his willingness to bring it up, to broach this topic no matter how difficult it might be to hear. Because if we ever planned to move past everything, there couldn't be six years of distance between us. I might not want to talk about all the details with Tommaso, past what I'd already told them, just yet. But I knew I would eventually, when the wounds weren't so fresh on both sides.

So I told them about my job, about my group of friends, and about Sophia, my friend that, despite the danger, was willing to risk it all to get me to safety. Even without knowing the whole story.

"Actually, would you mind if I used your phone to call her," I asked, chewing my bottom lip nervously as I calculated just how many days I hadn't been able to call her. "She must be worried."

"Of course," Merrick said, squeezing my hand in support. I didn't want to interrupt the conversation we were having, but I knew I couldn't put this call off any longer or else she might just wind up in the middle of this mess and that was the last thing I wanted. "You can use the phone in my office, it's patched into a line that's untraceable, just in case he has her phone tapped."

My lips pursed and I nodded tightly, internally scolding myself for not thinking about that.

"Do you want me to come with you?" Spade asked mischievously, waggling his eyebrows at me as he trailed his fingers up my calf.

"No," Merrick growled.

At the same time, I chuckled. "Not this time."

Spade shifted his hand from my leg, begrudgingly letting me swing them over to sit up. And Kellan placed a swift kiss on the curve of my neck, his hands slipping from my waist so I could stand.

"Besides, how would I be able to have any sort of girl talk if one of you is there with me?" I teased, my hand trailing seductively against Merrick's collarbone as I glided past him. A groan slipped past his lips, causing my lips to curl in a smug grin.

I strode around the tables with an extra sway to my hips for my guys, knowing their eyes would be on my tight pink skirt. My heels clicked on the varnished bar floor, and I was about to turn to go behind the bar, when a sharp cat-calling whistle pierced my ears, stopping me in my tracks.

That smile slipped off my face instantly, my brows lowering into a glower as I turned to the idiot grinning at a table a few feet away. Apparently he was brave enough to try hitting on me in such a disgusting, demeaning way. As if women were there for his entertainment, for him to harass as he pleased. But I could bet he wouldn't be such a tough guy once I got my hands on him.

"Whistle at me again, and I'll break your fucking jaw," I purred with a saccharine smile plastered on my face, letting the violence and delight I'd get from doing just that shine through.

I brought my hands up and cracked my knuckles one by one just to punctuate my words.

His throat bobbed and he hurriedly glanced down at the wooden table, silence washing over the surrounding tables. The only sound was Spade's raucous laughter echoing through the bar. The scrape of a chair pushing back was the last thing I heard before I turned on my heel, knowing I wouldn't be able to call Soph, let alone stay at the bar if I watched Merrick pound that asshole's face in. Nope, because, I would definitely join in, and then drag Merrick to the back seat where he could fulfill the promises he'd made earlier.

I continued to the backroom, biting my bottom lip as I heard the shouts out in the bar and the telltale scuff of chair legs, meaning Merrick had already pulled him from his seat. I sigh in disappointment, but despite how much I wanted to be out there and join in the violence, I also wanted to call Sophia to make sure she was okay.

There wasn't much back here except a few offices and a stock room a bit farther down the hall. Merrick's office was of course the closest to the bar and the action. Huffing out a breath of amusement, I paused to take in the mess of a room. Papers were strewn everywhere, laid haphazardly it seemed, with a L shaped desk along the far wall with a computer atop it. I pulled out the fabric swivel chair and grimaced as the itchy material brushed against my thighs. *That is definitely one of the first things on my to do list, redecorating and organizing this office.*

"I'm glad that asshole is going to get some sense knocked into him," a deep masculine voice rumbled from the doorway, catching me off guard.

My heart jolted, but I didn't let him see the surprise, and instead turned to face him slowly as though my senses weren't on high alert. The hulking form of the bouncer I'd aptly named Mountain Mike last week loomed in the doorway.

"Spade asked me to bring you this—said you wouldn't want him coming in here," Mike grumbled, placing the glass down onto the desk.

"Thanks." I grinned, knowing Merrick and Kellan had probably deterred him from coming back here like he wanted to.

"Let me know if you need anything," he muttered, backing out of the office and closing the door behind him.

I turned in the chair so I could keep the closed black door in sight. I couldn't let someone sneak up on me like that again. Sure this may be Merrick's bar and his people, but who knew what could happen.

Dialing Sophia's number, I leaned back in the chair, attempting to have the least amount of exposed skin touching the chair as possible. This was definitely the first thing that would need to go. The ringer buzzed in my ear, and I grasped the cool glass, water beading on the outside from how long it had been sitting there untouched while I relayed what I could about New York, and I brought it to my lips, letting the sweet alcohol wash over my tongue. I seriously had to learn how Eve made these things so fucking delicious.

My job and my friends had been two things that had kept me going. I'd gone into it looking for a future that would keep me from being dependent on anyone and I'd found that, if it hadn't been for Tommaso. Of course it was in the corporate world so I'd always answer to someone, but it was a good job and would've afforded me a good normal life if that had been what the fates had planned for me. But in reality, I wasn't normal. I'd always craved danger, violence, and bloodshed, so maybe I never would've been happy with a run-of-the-mill job and life.

"Hello?" Sophia answered hesitantly after a few rings, clearly not recognizing the number.

"Hey, Soph," I breathed, a relieved smile curling on my lips at the sound of her voice. Just a week before I'd called her, letting her know how my plans had been turned upside down and Tommaso had moved us out of the city. But now it was like that life was a distant memory, my life night and day compared to the last phone call, just before the first time I came to this bar and saw Merrick after six years.

"Holy shit, Giana," she gasped, sucking in a sharp breath. "Do you have any idea how worried I've been?"

"I know, this is the first chance I've had to call you," I said, properly chagrined after hearing the concern in her tone.

"What the hell happened? I was about to rent a car and drive down there." Her voice was muffled as I vaguely heard her canceling a taxi.

I grimaced at the thought, grateful I called her just in time. I could just imagine her storming into town and demanding to see me. That would've been really bad ... especially when Tommaso wouldn't hesitate to use her against me, even if her father was a senator.

I pulled in a deep breath and debated what I should say. I didn't want to put her in danger, but I knew how horrible of a friend I'd been. I barely told her anything about my past, or about the guys who'd been the most important people in my life, since just the thought of them before had made guilt twist my stomach and the pang of loss slice through my chest.

"A lot," I sighed and took another long swig of my drink before launching into our story, the one of a girl and her two best friends and the obsessive man that threatened their lives.

"Holy shit," she breathed, the sound of her collapsing back onto her leather couch echoing through the phone. "So that's who you're with now? And what about that Spade guy,? He sounds delectable."

"Yeah, I'm safe with them," I breathed, blinking as I attempted to clear the fog that had just clouded my vision.

"I—I think I have to go," I interrupted abruptly, the sound of her voice echoed in my ears, but I couldn't make out what she was saying.

The phone clattered from my hand, bouncing on the hard desk as I gripped the edge of it, needing something to steady me as I tried to stand. Sweat beaded on my brow, my heart seeming to slow despite the horror gripping me. My pulse should be pounding in my head, I vaguely realized, as my clammy palms slipped against the wood.

My eyes blinked closed as I fought to hold on to consciousness, the faint glow of the fluorescent light fading in and out as my body slid from the swivel chair, unable to hold itself up anymore without anything to support it and I tumbled to the floor, landing in a heap.

I willed my muscles to move as I crawled to the door, needing to open it, for someone to see and call my guys. But my movements were too slow, my body already slipping under the heavy weight of whatever this was pulling me down into its dark abyss. I fought against the urge to let my eyes slip closed as the door swung open, the bright lights from the hallway filtering in. A massive form took up the doorway and thick mitts slipped around my body to pull me up as the last shred of strength I had faded away into nothing.

CHAPTER TWENTY-FIVE

GIANA

SIX YEARS AGO ...

"WHAT ARE YOU DOING here Tommaso," I asked hesitantly, planting my feet firmly on the asphalt. I glanced around him at the large bay window at the front of the house, attempting to see if Greg and Pam were up yet. "Our date isn't until tonight."

"I didn't want to wait," Tommaso drawled, stalking closer to me, each step vibrating through me like a blow to the chest. "Now the better question is, where were you?"

I swallowed thickly as he approached, like a lion stalking its prey, it was animalistic the way he viewed me as a victim, as a commodity he could just order around.

"I just went out for breakfast," I lied, inching my bag behind me knowing it was already too late, but I couldn't let him guess where I'd actually been.

"Lie," Tommaso breathed, closing the distance between us. He stroked the side of my face and cupped my cheek in his hand, tsking in disappointment. "You were with them, weren't you?"

My chest tightened as I readied another lie on the tip of my tongue. "No, I was—"

"Lie," he whispered again, leaning so close I could smell the thick scent of his cologne. "That was your second strike, lie again and I can guarantee you won't like the consequence."

His finger trailed along my jaw to tilt my chin up, forcing me to meet his mahogany eyes. My throat bobbed as I took in the predatory gleam in them, like a dragon hoarding his treasure—except it wasn't gold and jewels he was guarding—it was me.

"You look delicious, Giana," he trailed off, his lips mere inches from mine. "I always like how my women look freshly fucked. I just prefer to be the one doing said fucking."

My lips parted, a protest poised on them, but it was pointless. I couldn't take the risk of seeing what that third strike would entail.

"Good girl," he murmured, easing away slightly, his eyes roving over me. I'd thrown on just a crop top and a pair of yoga pants to sneak back in and his eyes scoured every inch of bare skin as though it was meant for him and only him.

"I only agreed to a date, Tommaso. That's it," I said hoarsely, trying to inject as much conviction as I could into my voice, but it was no use. Both he and I knew it was pointless for me to protest—he was a Barone and they always got what they wanted. And if they didn't, they left bodies in their wake as an example to the next person.

"You and I both knew it was so much more than one date. Stop being so naïve, it isn't a good look on you," he scolded, shaking his head in disappointment. "A man doesn't wait two years for one date."

I bit back the sob that threatened to rack my chest, knowing it would only bring him some sort of sadistic enjoyment. This had been two years in the making. It didn't matter what any of us did, he was always going to find some way to make me his. I knew that before the fight two years ago, and Merrick had known it too. It was why he fought him that day, to teach him a lesson—but no one taught the Barones anything.

"Ah, you're finally understanding." He grinned, realization clearly evident in my features. "But just in case you don't understand just how serious I am—"

His words cut off and he took a step back, pulling a phone from his pocket. He tapped it a few times before turning the screen to face me. It was a live feed of both Merrick's and Kellan's houses, their parents' cars parked in the driveways. The Chevy Impala cut through the shot and pulled into Merrick's driveway where the two men climbed from the front and back seats.

"Stop." The unbidden word slipped from my lips before I could clamp down on it. He turned off the screen much to my surprise and slipped the phone back into his pocket, his eyes brimming with triumph.

"In case you didn't catch the clear threat there, I'll kill them both, their families, and yours if you don't come with me."

"I know," I grumbled, anger boiling in my veins.

"Now, now, it doesn't have to be this way," he cooed, stroking my cheek lightly. "I know you, Giana, we spent enough time together before I graduated. I know what you want, what you crave, and I can give it all to you."

My throat bobbed as I looked back at him. It wouldn't be the same as a new start with my guys, but this was my life now. The one I'd only ever dreamed of had been dashed away the instant I'd spotted Tommaso on my porch. I'd hoped it would be as simple as making sure the date went poorly, trying to convince myself everything would work out in the end ... but it wouldn't. In this world the villains always got what they wanted, no matter the cost.

Resigned, I nodded, not wanting anyone else to get killed for my mistakes. Because I knew even if I ran, if I resisted in this moment, he'd kill them and take me against my will. And not just my guys, Merrick's mom, who was too sick to leave her house most days, Kellan's parents, struggling to keep their bookstore afloat to keep their house. My own parents ... who although we didn't have the best relationship, didn't deserve to die. And it would all be because of me.

Pain sliced through my chest as I remembered last night, at what the three of us almost had. That morsel of everything I'd ever wanted with them. It was so close it was almost in my grasp. But my own mistakes as a sixteen-year-old girl with a crush on the eighteen-year-old crime heir was the undoing of us all.

I'd always liked Merrick and Kellan, but at that point I was convinced they'd never see me as more than a friend. So when Tommaso and I had been paired together on an assignment in one of my advanced classes, I'd flirted, attracted to the darkness that surrounded him and his family, not thinking about the consequences. I'd quickly shut it down, but it had sparked an obsession in Tommaso, one he'd never gotten over apparently. And when Merrick caught wind of it, he'd taken matters into his own hands, and almost got killed because of it.

All because of me. My jealousy, my naïve belief I could just walk away from a man like Tommaso. At the end of the day, it was all my fault. And this was what I deserved for it. At least I'd gotten a taste of how things could be before it was snatched away from me, the cold weight of reality settling on my shoulders in its place.

"Good." He grinned, his eyes sparkling with delight at the defeat that slumped my shoulders, sensing he'd won, that I'd lost my will to fight and was at his mercy. "Now go pack whatever things you need. You'll be staying at my parents' house until graduation, and right after we'll be leaving for New York."

My brows creased and a flicker of fight lit within me, but I pushed it down, knowing it would do no good to argue with him over this. There was a reason he was standing outside my house all night, and this was it. This would be the last time I saw Merrick and Kellan, that brief kiss goodbye wasn't nearly enough, but graduation ... What the hell would I do when I saw them there? Panic bubbled up in me, but I refused to let it show.

"Fine," I grumbled and went to stomp past him, but his hand clasped around my wrist and pulled me to a stop.

"I could do without the attitude, mi amore," he purred, his hand tightening uncomfortably around my wrist. "We're going to spend our lives together; we should at least make it enjoyable."

My breaths came in ragged pants as I pushed down the flames of anger burning brightly inside me. It wouldn't do any good to piss him off, not now, not when the phrase "rest of our lives" echoed in my mind. So I looked back at him and pulled a mask over my face, nodding as though I was perfectly fine leaving with him, perfectly fine with living the rest of my life by his rules and at his side.

"Good," he sighed, his fingers slowly uncurling from my wrist. I turned back to the house, willing my steps to be calm and steady, grateful he didn't follow me inside. There may still be some way I could leave without my parents noticing me if too much time hadn't passed yet. I could just leave them a note explaining as much as I could. Because I guaranteed with one mention of the Barones they wouldn't argue, they wouldn't call, wanting to get as far away from any tie to that family that they could ... unless it benefited them of course.

I pulled the key from my pocket and unlocked the door slowly, attempting to be as silent as possible. But when the door creaked open, light filtered out from the kitchen, hushed voices audible even from the doorway.

I pulled in a deep breath and stepped inside, letting the door close behind me. I winced at the click in the latch knowing that the nearly silent sound would draw their attention. And sure enough, just as I'd predicted, the two of them came storming out already dressed in their usual black slacks and button downs they wore to work.

"Why the fuck is a Barone outside our door?" my mother screeched, storming over to me. My hands fisted at my side, nails biting painfully into my palm as I tempered my own rage. No concern at all for their daughter—no, only fear for themselves, that's how it had always been.

"You don't need to worry about it," I huffed, dropping my bag by the door as I strode passed them to the stairs.

"What do you mean we don't need to worry about it? He's outside *our* house. He woke *us* up in the middle of the night looking for *you*," Greg ground out, wrapping a meaty palm around my bicep and pulling me to a stop. "Where the hell were you anyway?"

"Get your hand off of me," I seethed, glancing back over my shoulder to pin him with a glare. My life had been completely shattered already. Tommaso had already grasped me like I was a possession, rather than a person, and I couldn't handle it if someone else did it too.

"You're still our child. We'll tell you what to do," he grumbled, but his hand let go, apparently satisfied that I would stand there and endure them berating me for something I had no fucking control over.

My actions may have caused this shitstorm, and I held myself partially responsible, but no one should obsess over someone for this long—no one should force someone else to be with them when they so clearly didn't want anything to do with them, when they, as he'd put it, came back "freshly fucked" by two men who were not him.

"Oh, so you did completely forget it was my eighteenth birthday yesterday," I huffed out in disbelief. I'd thought they just hadn't bothered to mention it, not that they'd completely forgotten what yesterday was.

"Nobody cares that it was your birthday, you little bitch," Pam seethed, stepping closer to me. My hands shook at my sides with the effort it took not to do something to keep her away with the vindictive glint shining in her eyes. "I care that you brought trouble to our doorstep."

And with that her fist came hurtling toward my jaw, and pain bloomed where she made contact, my face throbbing as she pulled back. She didn't even have the decency to look shocked, she just stared back at me with a hint of satisfaction as though she'd been waiting to do that for a very long time.

"Do you feel big and strong, Pam?" I asked, my voice thick with hatred. "Does hitting your daughter make you feel like you're actually worth something?"

Silence rang through the entryway, her face falling slightly as I stared back at her, unflinchingly. Her body trembled slightly, not from remorse, but fear. She hadn't expected me to take the hit like that, she had wanted me to fall at her feet and beg for forgiveness. But that wasn't the person I was. I wouldn't let her see the pain her strike had caused, nor would I let her see the betrayal that pierced through my heart like the final nail in her coffin.

"If you touch me again, I'll slit your fucking throat," I hissed, raising my chin in defiance, letting that mark she'd undoubtedly left shine like a mark from battle, something I would wear with pride as a symbol of this split from these two vile excuses for humans.

"Giana," Greg chastised, but I sneered at him, my eyes begging him to try something. Because I wouldn't falter. She got one hit, but that was it. The next time either of them tried anything, they were dead. He fell silent though, his throat bobbing as I glared back at him, showing the promise that laid there. It wasn't an empty threat, far from it.

I stomped up the stairs and into my small room, my brain already making a list of what I had to take. I wouldn't let them have anything I worked for, any money I'd earned. No, that would be stored away for a rainy day, whatever I earned after college would go to that, for the chance to leave, to escape. I moved about the space methodically searching in every single hiding place I'd stashed my valuables, never trusting my parents wouldn't come in while I was out and take what they wanted for smokes and alcohol.

Fuck them, I fumed, gritting my teeth and swallowing back the bile that rose in my throat as pain radiated through my jaw. They'd been verbally abusive to me for many years but hadn't done more than a shove or a push or grabbed my arm hard enough for their fingers to leave a bruise. But for Pam to strike me, to deal that final blow ... they were lucky to walk away alive. They had no idea how strong I was after my lessons with the guys, the training I'd done to prepare myself if this ever happened.

I held myself back only because I was gone. They had no more control over me, couldn't beat me down with their words or their fists. I was free from them, just to be locked up in another cage. I guessed that was all I was meant for, to be locked away at someone else's mercy, destined to keep that part of myself caged too, the one that wanted to bring all of them to their knees and watch them cower for once. But Greg and Pam sure as hell weren't worth it, they were scum, not worth the bruises they'd leave on my knuckles. And Tommaso, well that would never happen—could never happen as long as he held the lives of my friends and their families over my head.

I shoved everything I needed into the small suitcase and pulled it behind me as I trudged down the stairs, grateful they'd gone into the kitchen so I wouldn't have to see their faces again. Hatred for them burned in my chest as I vowed never to see or speak to them again. There was no coming back from this, no chance at perhaps understanding each other with distance. They showed no remorse, no care for me past what this would all mean for them. They could rot in hell for all I cared.

I grabbed my bag by the front door and pulled it open, the fresh morning air hitting my face in a welcoming embrace, strengthening me for this new beginning. I wouldn't allow myself to break with this new set of chains clanking around my ankles, just like I hadn't before. I let the thought of someday escaping push me forward and give me the drive to fight. I slammed the door closed behind me just like the life I was effectively leaving behind.

"What is that?" Tommaso barked, his fingers tentatively reaching out toward the bruise blossoming on my jaw.

"It's nothing," I sighed, moving out of his reach, about to stride past him.

"I'll kill them." His jaw worked as he stepped forward, and I knew he would. He'd kill anyone that even looked at me wrong.

"They're not worth it," I breathed, my hand taking his, my stomach twisting at the contact. "Let's just go." It would be so easy to just let him march in there to take them out with two shots from the telltale bulge of the pistol under his jacket. This was my final act of mercy for them, for the man and woman who should've never had a child they weren't prepared for, who were kept down by their circumstances. But there would never be another.

His mahogany eyes glanced down at where my fingers twined with his, a delighted grin stretching across his lip. "Let's go home."

CHAPTER TWENTY-SIX

GIANA

NOW

"SHE'S HOME?" THAT ALL too familiar voice asked. He sounded distant though, like he wasn't entirely in the same room.

An ache radiated through my neck as the blackness faded, a faint light trickling in through my closed eyelids. I peeled them open slowly but didn't dare move a muscle, not wanting to give away the fact that consciousness was gradually seeping back in. Sleep coated them, gritting against the inner corner of my eye, and I pushed back the urge to wipe it away. My mind quickly pieced together that I wouldn't be able to anyway, since my arms were tied behind my back, my body slumped uncomfortably on a chair. I wiggled my fingers, tentatively grasping at the back of the slightly familiar wooden slats.

My head pounded but I pushed the pain aside as my adrenaline kicked in, my memory sparking with recognition as I looked at the familiar furniture and marble floor of the entryway. I was back in Tommaso's house. My memory filled in the rest of the pieces at that realization. The chair I'd been placed on as one of the new ones that had been delivered for Tommaso when we made the move.

My head was lolled to the side, and I absently wondered just how long I'd been out for as daylight trickled in through the windows. No wonder my neck ached and my muscles barked in protest.

"Yes, sir. I took her back to your house like you asked me to," a deep masculine voice rumbled in the distance. Relief washed over me as I realized Tommaso wasn't here, his voice had just echoed over the speaker of my captor's phone.

There was still a chance to get away, or to prepare myself for when he came, because there was no way I'd let myself be tied to a chair when he arrived. I pushed down the rage that simmered in my veins I wanted to slice him and whoever took me to shreds, but I couldn't do that—not yet.

"Is she awake?" Tommaso asked brightly, his tone brimming with triumph. I fought against the scowl that curled on my lips, needing to pretend I was still unconscious. That would be the only way to escape.

Footsteps pounded in my direction, echoing off the hardwood floor from where my kidnapper must've been standing in the kitchen. I let my face relax and my breathing calm, not letting any sign past my façade. The steps stilled before me and

I waited for him to answer Tommaso, to tell him I was still out and for him to walk away so I could formulate my next move.

But instead, a cool wave smacked against me, and I sputtered as water splashed against my face. I spat out anything that had made its way between my slightly parted lips, fearing what may be in it.

The liquid ran down my chest in rivulets and soaked into my clothes, leaving me completely drenched as I blinked against the moisture, my eyes flickering open to the sight of the massive form of Mike, the bouncer, poised before me. His lips curled in a sneer as I pulled in a ragged breath now that my mouth was clear of the liquid. I bared my teeth right back at him, my fingers curling, ready to claw at the restraints so I could tear that look straight off his face.

"Watch it," Tommaso growled possessively, the smack of his hand pounding against something. "I told you she wasn't to be harmed."

"It was just a splash of water," Mike groaned.

"I'll deal with you when I get there," Tommaso ground out.

I pursed my lips at how familiar that sound was as he attempted to regain a level head, turning that burst of anger into a lethal rage.

"Giana," he breathed. I swallowed thickly, almost choking on the air with how dry my mouth was. Of course the fucker had to throw the water at me rather than giving it to me ... not that I would trust anything he gave me to ingest again. "I'm so glad you're finally home safe."

I ignored the cheerful way he delivered those words, as if he'd saved me. But we both knew the truth. If he'd been rescuing me, there would've been no need to drug me, let alone have me tied up.

"This isn't my home," I wheezed, using what little moisture I had in my mouth to wet my lips, hating how weak I sounded.

"Shh, mi amore. You've been through a traumatic experience," Tommaso soothed, and I bit back the derisive snort that begged to slip from my lips. "I'm flying back from New York. I will admit though, they did do a great job at covering their tracks."

My throat bobbed as I held back the question I knew he was dying for me to ask. He wanted to cause a rift between us, to make it seem like I couldn't trust the guys, that they'd lied to me. But none of them had told me about the rest of the plan, no one told me they'd led him to New York. Frustration mounted in me at being left out, especially since they had no idea how dangerous that plan had been. Tommaso very well could've gone after Soph as a way to lure me out and none of us would've had any clue until it was too late. This had to end, the secrets and the lies, on both sides.

So I stayed silent, letting him stew in the silence, because I knew one way or another he'd let the information slip.

He sighed ruefully but continued, "They made it seem as if they'd taken you back to New York, so I've been scouring the city looking for you. But little did I know you were still in town, just under my nose."

I glanced at Mike in confusion. I hadn't seen anyone's faces the night the guys had descended upon the engagement party, and they'd shuffled me into the house. But I'd figured since he worked at the bar he would've known before tonight. Mike's jaw worked at the pointed look, but I didn't dare look away. I wouldn't let this mountain of a man intimidate me, and even if he did swing at me, I knew I could take it. I was strong, and I'd been through a hell of a lot worse.

"Unfortunately, I hadn't thought to pay off anyone at the bar until they took you, and it seems I chose the wrong person," Tommaso grumbled, clearly sensing where my thoughts had gone. "He hadn't known where you were until today."

And judging by the exasperation in his tone, I knew there'd be consequences for the man towering before me. But if I had anything to say about it, he'd be on the floor bleeding out by the time Tommaso even stepped foot into this house.

"You have no idea how much I missed you," he soothed, and bile rose in my throat just at the thought of Tommaso putting his hands on me again.

"I didn't miss you," I purred back, glad my voice wasn't as raspy anymore. I needed some water but at least some of the moisture was returning to my throat. "So why don't you do us both a favor and tell this meathead to let me go?"

A rumble shook from Mike's chest and his face contorted in rage. Stepping closer, his hand lowered slightly, about to chuck the phone away—

"Don't let her rile you, Mike," Tommaso cut in, his tone light, yet there was a real warning to his words. "She's only trying to get you to do something you'll regret."

Mike stilled at that lethal tone, seeming to realize that only death would await him if he took another step. Some of the anger fled his expression as he retreated slightly.

"Now, what did I say would happen if I saw you around them again, mi amore?" he asked, his tone wicked and bloodthirsty. I had no doubt he'd just been waiting patiently for this opportunity, for the chance to fulfill his promise of killing the two of them for stepping foot near me again, and now he had it.

"Don't you fucking touch them," I seethed, ready to break through these bonds and break Mike's neck just to get to them.

"Oh I wouldn't dream of it," Tommaso jeered, my chest turning to ice at his tone. "At least not until I can make you watch me put a bullet between their eyes."

Mike chuckled in response, apparently attempting to save his ass by sucking up to Tommaso.

"Now be a good little wife-to-be and wait for me to get home," he huffed out on a breath of amusement. "If you behave, I won't even draw out their deaths, I'll make it swift and almost painless. My wedding present to you."

"You're sick," I seethed, refusing to let his words take hold. I would get out before he came, and I'd make sure the guys were safe.

"I thought that's what you liked," he taunted smugly, and I bit back the scream that vibrated through my throat. I hated that he knew anything about me.

I'd been scared of him before, held fear for the darkness that shrouded his soul. But I realized it wasn't the darkness I was scared of. No, the dark called to me, singing sweet lullabies coaxing me into the abyss. Tommaso was a monster because he wanted to own me, control me like I was his property. He could as easily turn on me as his enemy. But not my demons, they were just as dark—hell, maybe even more so—but I was one of them, my own person with my own thoughts and feelings, my own free will. I wasn't a trophy to keep locked away, suffocating in a musty bookcase. I was a part of them, I was their devil and they were my demons. And I would gladly burn in hell with them by my side.

"You're nothing compared to them," I sneered, vitriol leaking from my every word. "You're just a jealous little boy who hates being told no and likes to order people around to do your dirty work."

"Oh, mi amore, I can't wait to prove you wrong," he growled, the line disconnecting cutting through the silent room like the crack of a whip.

I let that scream out then, the sound rasping in my throat, still parched and aching, but I didn't care. The sound echoed off the walls and Mike took a step back, his hands clasping over his ears. I screamed for the girl who would've cowered to Tommaso just a few weeks ago, the one who had forgotten her strength, had pushed aside that dark side he'd alluded to. I'd pushed away that attraction to the violence and bloodshed out of fear I would become sucked into that life, that I would forget the people I'd left behind.

But I could see the difference now. The Barones did everything they did for money and power, killing people without any purpose other than serving their own means. But the Devil's Demons were meant to combat that force. Neither was good or right, but I knew they wouldn't kill someone innocent or cripple an entire town's ability to live just to gain a few extra dollars—truly chump change in the grand scheme of their investments for the Barones. But it was a power move to keep everyone subservient to them.

“You’re lucky he said I can’t touch you,” Mike growled, before stalking back off to the kitchen, muttering something under his breath.

My scream tapered off and I sucked in a deep breath, filling my greedy lungs. I had to compose myself, to make a plan to get the fuck out of here. Because I wasn’t the same woman who was stuck by that door merely a few feet from where I now sat. That woman had been a shadow of who I truly was, a mask meant to keep me safe until I could get away. And this would be my last escape, because after this it was my turn to stack the deck, my turn to make the rules of the game.

I took inventory of anything I could use that was around me. But of course the living room was still spotless, completely devoid of the knick-knacks that would betray that someone actually lived here and it wasn’t just straight from a magazine.

I tugged on the ropes binding me, attempting to work out how exactly they’d been bound. Each wrist was tied meticulously to the two wooden posts, and the rope stretched between them joining them together. The back of the chair was mounted into the seat by those two wooden posts that my hands were tied to and smaller wooden slats ran between them.

What Mike didn’t know when he chose this chair, is that I had to put it together. Tommaso had ordered everything to be delivered to the new house and once he’d seen that some parts needed to be assembled, he left it for the workers to do, saying he had a business call and took off upstairs so he wouldn’t have to do anything—but I did. The workers already had enough to do with moving everything in so I offered to help. Really it wasn't hard, the back had to be inserted into the seat, there was supposed to be glue that went around it too, but I'd been so pissed off I just shoved them in there, hoping that one day someone would lean back and they'd fall, ruining the perfect image that Tommaso tried to portray. But now it looked like that simple act of petty revenge was working in my favor.

My fingers wrapped around the wooden anchors and slowly began wiggling them, careful not to make too much noise. The pieces started to loosen, groaning as they eased out of the setting. They were in there pretty securely, but not putting that glue had saved me, otherwise there wouldn't be any way I'd be getting untied without drawing his attention.

With one final tug the back popped out, and I tightened my grip, not wanting it to fall backward onto the hardwood floor. I lowered it gently until it slid the final few inches. I held my breath, keeping my body completely still as I glanced over to the kitchen. Mike hadn't noticed a thing, clearly too engrossed in the contents of the commercial-sized stainless-steel fridge to hear the quiet sound.

Confident he wasn't about to catch me, I tested my weight on my feet, not wanting to tumble sideways when I actually stood up. I only had one chance at this, so I had to make it count. Thankfully it seemed like the effects of whatever he'd given me had worn off completely since my bare feet held firm, apparently having lost my heels at some point along the way.

I lifted onto my feet a bit more, making sure to keep my head tucked low, and slid the rope under me and behind my knees. Using the seat, I pulled my legs through the loop the rope created with my arms, one at a time, until my hands were able to rest in my lap.

Sighing in relief, I tested my hands and mobility, needing to know exactly what I could manage. With my hands around the front, I could do a lot more but I was still restrained. My eyes lit up as I looked at the rope, knowing exactly what I could do with it.

I took one last look at the door, making sure no one else was about to come, before I made my move. This would only work if I could move silently, and someone coming in behind me and giving me away would not turn out well.

Sliding silently from the chair, I tested my full weight on my feet, grateful when my footsteps were silent on the marble floor. I moved stealthily down the hall, only stilling as the fridge door closed. Stepping back behind the wall, I waited as his footsteps echoed on the marble floor to see if he would return, but the clatter of utensils sounded a moment later, signaling he wasn't done yet. I peeked around the wall tentatively as he pulled a loaf of bread from the drawer and went about slathering on a heap of mayo.

Taking that as a sign to continue, I glided toward him, my breaths stilling as I got closer. Three—two—one, I counted in my head as I closed the distance, my hands raising in preparation. I was tall, but he still had almost a foot on me—I could make it, but I only had one chance. So I made sure I struck fast and true, my knee striking the back of his leg swiftly, and he buckled just enough for me to bring my arms up and around his neck. He let out a startled yelp as I pulled my arms back, the metallic clang of the knife he'd held clattering to the granite countertop. Not hesitating, I jammed my knee into the center of his back to add tension as I used all my strength to cut off his airway.

Redness bloomed in his face as I pressed harder, his lips parting in a sputtered gasp as his hand scrabbled for purchase on the thick rope—the one he had tied around my wrists just hours before. He'd signed his own death warrant as soon as he'd given me that drink. He'd given up whatever life he had when he attempted to take mine away from me, depositing me back into Tommaso's clutches.

One of his hands dropped away from his throat, while the other clawed against his skin, raking desperately and drawing blood with each scratch of his nails. My eyes focused on that blood beading there, nearly missing the sunlight glinting off the steel of the counter.

A muttered curse slipped from my lips as his other hand closed around the knife handle, needing to make a split-second decision. My stomach dropped as he used his last ounce of strength to jab the point back at me—but I was already gone.

I leapt out of the way, begrudgingly lifting the rope away from his neck in an effort to put space between us. I was so close, I could see the life draining from him, but, I'd barely gotten out of the way in time.

He pulled in a long wheezing breath and swung the knife back wildly behind him, ensuring I didn't move back in.

"You—fucking—bitch," he seethed between frantic gasps of air. "I'm going to slit that pretty little throat of yours."

"I'd like to see you try," I said on a derisive snort, my mind flying through what move to make next. Anger was the best fuse I had to throw him off his game. I had to make him attack before he fully recovered.

"What sort of muscle are you? You let a woman half your size sneak up on you while you were stuffing your face," I huffed out on a mocking laugh.

"You little bitch," he growled, stumbling toward me. But my eyes were trained on the knife he still held clutched in his meaty palm. I pulled in a sharp breath and waited as he stormed toward me, his steps seemingly progressing in slow motion.

His hand came up to his shoulder, a sickening laugh booming from his wide chest, but I didn't dare take my eyes off the chef's knife plunging toward me. My hands snapped out as soon as he got close enough, a hand on either side of his wrist and I snapped them inward, watching the blade clattering to the marble floor and sliding under the kitchen table.

A roar of outrage bellowed from his mouth, and I darted to the side before he had a chance to regain his composure.

"Sorry, who's the little bitch?" I asked coyly, my foot connecting with the side of his knee. His leg buckled beneath him as a cry of pain pierced through the room, my teeth gritting against the sharp scream. I chanced a glance toward the front door, not wanting anyone else to hear him. I'd be stupid to think he was the only one here and there weren't guards stationed along the outside. But I didn't let the tendrils of fear creep in over how I'd eventually get past them, not yet.

But just as I looked, gunfire erupted beyond the front door. I cursed and leapt under the table, the muttered words barely audible over Mike screeching in agony. I held my breath for a moment as the pops of crossfire sounded outside—outside, but they weren't directed inward ...

Hope flared in my chest. The guys must be here, they came to help me escape again, but that also put them in danger. They didn't have the added security of the bombs that had been planted at the party—this time it was one on one, and that scared the shit out of me.

I had to get out of here, I had to get past this idiot and get to my guys. I wasn't some damsel in distress, I could fight this asshole, and I'd watch his blood spill onto my hands. I glanced down at the floor about to crawl back out when the gleaming metal caught my eye about a foot away. Leaning forward, my finger clasped the edge of the handle, but before I could grasp it completely a massive hand clamped around my ankle.

Desperately I lunged forward, needing to catch more of the handle. My fingers just closed around it, securing it in my grip when he tugged. I jolted backward, and kicked out with my free leg, frantically trying to find purchase as I turned the knife toward me and sawed at the rope.

Thank fuck we never cooked, I thought to myself as the knife cut through the braided rope easily, but it was slow, too slow as he yanked me out from beneath the table. I kicked out at him again, my foot finally finding purchase.

A rumbled curse burst from him as I made contact with his knee again, his hold on my ankle slipping slightly. I used that moment to make one final slash with the knife, cutting completely through the binds.

I slashed out with the blade, the edge slicing along the hand that still clung to my ankle. He stumbled back clutching his hand to his chest as blood welled on the long cut. I used his distraction to spring to my feet, readying for his next attack.

"I'm going to gut you," he seethed, baring his teeth at me before barreling straight for me. I waited for him to approach and dodged out of the way, aiming a slice at his side as he stumbled past where I was just a second before.

His eyes widened in shock, the pain finally registering as crimson bloomed through the side of his white shirt. I watched each movement as he turned to me, his anger evident on his bright red face. But that rage made him sloppy, and in his attempt to take control with his brute force, he left his torso wide open.

I didn't miss a beat, feigning to strike him in the knee again, but he was ready for that. He reached down aiming to grab my leg and send me toppling over. But instead of striking him, I planted my foot and drove the knife straight into the center of his chest.

He stumbled a step back, but I pushed forward as blood seeped from the gash in his chest, spreading around it as quickly as the thin material could absorb it.

He grasped for the knife, attempting to pull it out, but I pushed it in farther, coaxing a sharp gasp from him. I relished the feeling of his life blood flowing from him down onto my skin, grateful that his death would be by my hand. How many other women had he done this to, for men just as wretched as the Barones? How many hadn't been as lucky as me?

This was no innocent man, and I could tell by the cold fear gleaming in his eyes that he knew that. He'd be finding out any second now if there truly was a hell.

"I didn't know you were a demon," he wheezed, before pulling in a ragged breath and confirming my thoughts. He'd believed I was weak, someone he could easily overpower, a victim for Barones to do with as they pleased, as long as he got paid.

"Oh I'm not a demon," I drawled, twisting the knife in his chest.

His face contorted as an agonized cry split from his lips. He tried to pull in a breath but his lungs refused to fill, and instead he coughed against the blood bubbling up his throat. It poured from between his lips, coating his chin and spraying over my chest. The blood ran in thick rivulets over my hand and dripped down onto my feet, slapping against the hard marble floor. I yanked the knife out, not wanting to take any chances as his knees gave out.

"*I'm* the fucking devil," I whispered.

He weakly reached for his chest, attempting to press his hand against the gaping wound there. The blood now soaked his white shirt, drawing me to the crimson shade. The last flicker of life faded from his eyes as he stared back at me, his lips parting in one final attempt at a gasp before he stilled, his body frozen forever as death collected his shards of soul that remained.

My head snapped toward the door as the hinges creaked, my legs bunching, already poised to leap away. I knew that none of Tommaso's other guards would attempt to kill me, but I had to find another way out, I couldn't stay here—

"Giana," Kellan breathed and rushed forward, his steps slowing as he scanned me, worry clouding his sable eyes as he searched for any signs of injuries as Merrick and Spade followed behind him.

I let the knife clatter to the ground, satisfied that not an ounce of Mike's damned soul remained in that body, and stepped closer to the guys—my demons. I scanned them each head to toe, searching for any signs of injuries, my shoulders slumping in relief as it finally registered they were all unharmed. Each of us were coated in someone else's blood. It stuck to our skin, drenched our clothes.

Kellan closed the remaining few steps and pulled me into his warm embrace. Sagging against him, I soaked in his comforting strength and pulled in a ragged breath, fighting back the onslaught of tears that pricked at my eyes.

I hadn't let myself feel the icy tendrils of fear that skittered up my spine, at the thoughts I might be taken again, that I might never see the guys again, that I might die. My mind was too focused on trying to survive—the adrenaline masking it all, until this moment when it all slammed into me.

Merrick turned me from Kellan and pulled me in against his hard chest, heedless of the thick spray of blood that coated me as it mixed with splotches covering his own shirt. I let the steady beat of his heart against my skin wash away that prolonged fear trickling in and reassure me that we were all here together as one.

There was a long game to be played here, and I now knew I needed to switch to the mastermind, to the puppet master pulling all the strings because I wouldn't allow this to happen again. I would never allow Tommaso the opportunity to take me again, to make me feel like the victim. I was the predator and he was the prey this time around. And I wouldn't stop until my hands were drenched in their blood, the sticky mess clinging to my skin in a constant reminder of who I was, and what I'd done.

I glanced over Merrick's shoulder as thick boots thudded closer. Spade paused by Mike's lifeless body, a mix of rage and delight mixing in those wicked violet eyes, and he brought his foot back, swiftly kicking the corpse in the face, once, twice, three times before turning to face me.

"We have to go, sugar," Spade said sweetly, tugging me from Merrick and into his arms. A wide grin split across his face before I rested my head against his shoulder and relaxed into him. That look promised death and pain to anyone who crossed us, seemingly already knowing the direction of my thoughts. "I love you," he whispered in my ear, his warm breath caressing the shell of it. My chest warmed as I clutched him closer.

It was our turn to play, and the four of us—oh we would paint this town red with the blood of the Barones' when we were finished.

"No more lies," I said, just realizing how raspy my voice was, my throat still parched. I pushed back from Spade to look back at all three of them, the sound of gunfire cracking in the distance. "I know you sent a fake trail to New York without telling me. No more lies, no more keeping things from each other."

"I guess this would probably be the best time to admit I put a tracker in that leather jacket, right?" Spade asked, completely unrepentant. I wanted to be angry at that invasion of privacy, but I couldn't—not when it could very well be the reason I got out of here tonight.

"Yes, it would." I huffed out an incredulous sigh, and he beamed back at me, his chest puffing out with pride and completely oblivious of my tone.

"We're a team," Merrick agreed, flashing a look of disbelief toward Spade before focusing back on me. He pushed back a strand of my hair, sticky and coated in blood.

"No more lies," Kellan echoed, his thumb swiping tenderly over my cheek as he took Merrick's place, his eyes searching, questioning, seemingly asking the same as me.

"No more secrets." Because I too wasn't innocent in all of this, I'd kept things from them countless times, but the only way we'd be able to move forward and take the Barones down was if we all worked together, their knowledge of organizing attacks, coupled with all the dirt I had on them, all the secrets I'd been privy to.

In this world, villains always won ... so I guess I'd become one.

To be continued in Devil's Game.

Other Titles

Fated Pack Series

Bonded and Betrothed

Bonded and Betrayed

The Ethereal Gods Series

Ascension

Deception

Revelation

Redemption

Endcliffe Academy: Monster Hunters

Stalked by Monsters

Hunted by Monsters

The Devil's Demons

Devil's Escape

Devil's Game

About the Author

Rachel lives in Toronto, Canada with her husband and her pup Callie. When she isn't writing, or reading, she can be found on a patio or at a farmers' market. She loves traveling and hitting up her favorite wineries.

Follow Rachel's Author Page for updates and news

https://www.facebook.com/rachelcallahanauthor
Join Rachel's reader group for all the latest updates

https://www.facebook.com/groups/2923804647855064
Join Rachel's newsletter for exclusive scenes and previews

http://eepurl.com/hAvBWr

ACKNOWLEDGMENTS

To my husband, whether it's pushing me towards my dreams or supporting me when I need to take a break, thank you for always being there and being my number one supporter.

Thank you to my family, who I know one day will sleuth their way into finding my books (most likely, my husband will sneakily tell them). I'm so grateful for all of your support.

Thank you to my wonderful friends for your kind words and support.

Thank you to my amazing alpha readers and friends, Samatha, Ari, and Amy. You girls have helped me more than you'll ever know. Love you girls, and can't wait to have more amazing convos and hopefully meet in person soon!

Thank you to my exceptional beta readers: Gemma, Camilla, Mhairi, Kassandra, Brenda, Jennifer, and Michelle! You girls are the best, and I am beyond grateful for all of your help and comments.

Thank you to my incredible developmental editor Cassie, you're truly amazing at catching the small details.

Thank you to my awesome editor Dee, thank you for working with me on this book!

Thank you to my PA Shayna, you're incredible and I swear I don't know where I'd be without you!

Printed in Great Britain
by Amazon

25502153R00239